DIPLOMATIC RESURGENCE

DIPLOMATIC RESURGENCE

THE EMPRESS' SPY™ BOOK THREE

S.E. WEIR

MICHAEL ANDERLE

DISRUPTIVE IMAGINATION

Copyright © 2021 LMBPN Publishing
Cover by Mihaela Voicu http://www.mihaelavoicu.com/
Cover copyright © LMBPN Publishing
This book is a Michael Anderle Production

LMBPN Publishing
PMB 196, 2540 South Maryland Pkwy
Las Vegas, NV 89109

Version 1.00, July, 2021
eBook ISBN: 978-1-64971-916-4
Print ISBN: 978-1-64971-917-1

THE DIPLOMATIC RESURGENCE TEAM

Thanks to our Beta Readers:
Larry Omans, Jim Caplan, John Ashmore, Kelly O'Donnell,
Mary Heise, Rachel Heise

Thanks to the JIT Readers

Diane L. Smith
Jackey Hankard-Brodie
Dorothy Lloyd
Deb Mader
Zacc Pelter
Wendy L Bonell
Daryl McDaniel
Peter Manis
Dave Hicks
Misty Roa
Larry Omans
Jim Caplan

If we've missed anyone, please let us know!

Editor
Lynne Stiegler

DEDICATION

To all those who have supported and encouraged me every step of the way. This is as much your book as mine.

- S.E. Weir

To Family, Friends and
Those Who Love
To Read.
May We All Enjoy Grace
To Live The Life We Are
Called.

—Michael

CHAPTER ONE

QBBS *Meredith Reynolds*

(After the establishment of the Etheric Empire and twelve years before the battle of Karillia.)

The couple waiting within the room looked up when Link walked through the door. "Ah. Chris and Zoe. Thank you for being prompt."

Chris nodded, his thick, dark hair hardly moving. Zoe shifted, her gaze intent on Link. "Your summons proved mysterious enough."

The man grinned as he turned toward his wife, his eyes warm. "That's all you need to do to get Zoe's attention. Be mysterious enough."

Zoe rolled her eyes and gave him a brief look of skepticism before smiling in amusement. "It worked for you, anyway."

"Yes, yes…" Link waved away the lovey-dovey stuff. He'd heard it from them before. Not to mention that it made him wistfully jealous. "You can do that on your own time. Let's get to why you're here, shall we?"

Zoe nodded solemnly. "Yes, please tell us."

Chris turned his focus to Link. Excellent. Their ability to relax around others as well as come to rapt attention when needed were a couple of the many reasons why they were two of his top people.

"You have both been instrumental in gathering information and giving us a leg up in negotiations as we establish the Empire in these systems over the last five years." He looked at the woman in front of him. She was a skilled negotiator who used those skills to establish connections and gain information. "You have proven that you are committed to the Empire and are with us to the end. The Empress has authorized me to offer you both a procedure to increase your longevity, so you are with us no matter how long this war with the Kurtherians takes."

The two gave him identical stares, then looked at each other as if they could speak mentally; the idea was crazy, of course. No one could do that except for Bethany Anne and Barnabas, although that ability was under tight wraps.

The two spies turned to Link, their faces hopeful but wary of being disappointed. They both nodded at the same time, and Chris spoke. "We appreciate the offer and the Empress' trust in us. We want the Empress to win, and we will do everything we can to help her. But what we want more than anything is a baby."

Zoe added hopefully. "Could you give that longevity to our baby?"

Link stared thoughtfully at them for a moment. "Let me get this straight. You two provide services to the Empire and could have your lives extended for a long time, but instead, you want to have a baby?"

The two nodded again. Zoe threaded her fingers together, her expression closed. "You know I can't carry a baby on my own without help. All the doctors I went to on Earth agreed that my body could not carry one to full term. We are hoping the Pod-doc or the doctors here could help?"

Link examined the people in front of him, not certain what he was looking for. Chris' usual charismatic face had almost shut down. He reached over and captured his wife's hand, betraying his concern. Zoe's face appeared impassive, but her eyes pleaded. It proved too much for Link to resist.

"ADAM? You following?"

The spies didn't react, given their training, although they looked hopeful.

ADAM's voice came over the speaker. "Yes, DS."

"What do you think?"

"I have reviewed the health records of Zoe Waters and conferred with TOM and Bethany Anne. We can do it."

The two spies' eyes grew wide at the mention of the Empress. Zoe straightened, her free hand coming up to her heart. "Bethany Anne agreed?"

Chris gripped his wife's hand tightly and swallowed. His eyes developed a slight sheen. "We can have a baby?"

Link nodded with his best Greyson Wells smirk. "Yes. Congratulations! You're going to have a baby. I imagine you will need to get into the Pod-doc for a physical to see what needs to happen."

Chris and Zoe Waters sat in the hard plastic chairs of the med unit, holding hands. Their expressions held shock, which warred with joy.

"I am already pregnant?" Zoe gasped in disbelief.

ADAM and TOM had asked the technician to leave before speaking to the couple.

TOM spoke earnestly and tried to reassure them. "Yes. That is the good news. There is, however, bad news."

"I'm losing her, aren't I?" Zoe couldn't hold back her tears and Chris tightened his grip on her hand, his eyes filled with pain. This was Zoe's fifth pregnancy, and the grief had taken a toll on them both.

"Yes," TOM responded uncomfortably.

"But there is good news," ADAM broke in.

"Yes," TOM agreed cautiously.

"There is?" Chris asked in relief as Zoe urgently pleaded, "You can save her?"

"Yes," TOM repeated. "However, to do so, we will need to adjust her DNA to account for the chromosome issues we found. She will appear normal and develop on schedule physically, but aside from that, I can't state for sure what might be altered. There could be side effects that some consider are for the better, and others might call them a burden. She will be different from other children, which might become more obvious as time goes on and will need to be monitored by us. Some possibilities are that she will have an increased IQ, super sensory perception, maximized memory recall, enhanced pattern recognition—"

"I don't care about any of that." Zoe broke in fiercely. "She's our daughter, and all that matters is if she will be healthy."

"Oh, yes," TOM assured her. "Optimized health and growth. I doubt she will even get normal colds and illnesses that others on the station catch before getting the treatment."

Chris sagged in relief and embraced his wife as tears of happiness fell down Zoe's face. "Will I be able to carry her to full term myself?"

"We will do what we can to keep her in the womb as long as possible, and I don't think it will be a problem," TOM assured her. "Even if she needs to be born within two months of your due date, she will be fine."

The couple held each other and sighed in relief. "Thank you. Thank you so much!"

"You are very welcome," TOM answered. He paused before continuing anxiously, "You must realize we can't do this procedure for everyone. You need to keep this information to yourself. If you tell anyone about being able to carry your baby where you previously could not, please only mention that the Pod-doc was able to fix the problem. You are welcome to tell her when she is old enough to make decisions on her own, perhaps at fifteen, or better, twenty-one?"

Chris and Zoe solemnly agreed, and Chris added, "Of course. We understand and very much appreciate your willingness to help us."

"Zoe, I am curious about something. You are certain your baby is a girl, and while you are correct, we hadn't yet told you that. May I ask why you are so certain?" ADAM asked matter-of-factly.

"Because..." Zoe straightened and wiped her tears with the back of her hand. "Determined women who fight through adversity to become stronger run in my family. I have no doubt our baby will be the same." She reached down to gently touch her belly with a smile. Her baby would be gifted in more ways than one.

Chris smiled at his wife with love in his eyes as he squeezed her other hand. "We will name her Seraphina, our fiery angel."

Zoe's eyes lit up. "Oh, Chris, that's perfect. Seraphina Grace. The Empire will have a guardian angel watching out for her even after we are gone."

Chris nodded slowly as he touched his wife's hand where she held it over her belly. "Agreed. Perfect."

Unknown Location (current time)

Phina floated. In the air? In water? She didn't care. She felt at peace, young and happy, sensations that felt oddly incongruent with her normal state. She blinked in confusion and looked around, but every view was a grayish-white landscape. Lightning briefly brightened everything.

The plane in front of her stretched endlessly, empty of everything except a slight buzz in the air.

The buzz wasn't noticeable to her ears, but she felt it in her brain. It was distinctly odd. A stray memory came to her of her mother telling Phina about dancing in the rain as a little girl back on Earth and how excited her mother had been when she felt electricity in the air, as if it were charging or priming itself for the storm. This buzzing sensation felt exactly like that but bumped up several notches.

Where was she, and how had she gotten here? And now

that she was here, how could she leave? While this floaty, happy feeling felt good, it wasn't *normal*. Right now, Phina wanted to feel normal more than anything in the universe...until that desire slowly drifted away from her, leaving her at peace again.

Sometimes she heard conversations between two or three people that intruded her into awareness, but they didn't last.

For hours, perhaps days, she existed in that gray plane. She felt like she might have moved as she focused on certain spots in the distance, but she couldn't be sure. Though she felt at peace, Phina couldn't help certain thoughts surfacing, such as wondering about her friends and the people she cared about. Was she cut off from them entirely? What was the state of the Aurian planet?

As quickly as the thoughts and questions surfaced, they drifted away until all that existed was the gray-white plane, the charging energy, and her sense of peace. It could have been days or weeks, or years; to Phina, it felt like both an eternity and the blink of an eye. For a while, she was content to stay in this state and place, with this sense of peace.

After some time, she heard beautiful, harmonic music. It made her feel better than she had felt for some time. She became more aware and less hazy. Her mind reached for the music. She could almost understand it, but the meaning slipped away from her, leaving only hope. As she listened to the music, she longed for her friends. Before coming to this gray-white place, Phina had felt like she belonged somewhere, which was a rare sensation.

At the moment, she wanted to know what had caused

the changes. ADAM hadn't told her who or what he thought had done it before she had collapsed. Phina had her suspicions, and time would tell if they were correct. Right now, she had to find her way back to normal in a place that felt anything but.

As she struggled to look for a way out, Phina finally felt a tug on one side and turned her body to face that direction. Her feet wouldn't move, though. She frowned and tried again, but her body wouldn't turn any more. The landscape around her was still gray-white. Finally, she closed her eyes and focused on moving toward the tug she felt. She almost cried out in relief when she felt a sense of movement, although she couldn't open her eyes.

When Phina focused on her body, she felt an increasing sense of weight and physical presence. The more she thought about her body, the more real it became. The sensations were overwhelming after the empty nothingness of the gray world...dream... Whatever it had been.

Her muscles felt like they were healthy but recovering. Her strength returned with every moment that passed. Gradually, she began to surface and was able to utilize her senses. Her hearing was muffled until her ears popped with a painful crack. Her body felt like one big bruise that had been left alone for far too long, although that sensation was fading as well. Her mental faculties seemed to be fine, though unless she suddenly couldn't remember or do something like normal, how would she know the difference? Emotionally, she felt...calm and better than she remembered, since the last thing she'd known before the gray world was agony and pain.

Familiar voices spoke in her hearing. Though muffled, she could hear the words without issue.

"…vitals are stronger. It appears she's bringing herself out and should be waking up any time now." Doctor April Keelson, her brain supplied. The doctor sounded as if she were moving away from Phina. "I'll let you see her, but I'll be in to look her over before too long."

"Yes, I see. Thank you." Phina heard the faint sound of a door opening and closing. "ADAM, you ready to share your findings now?" Link's voice sounded weary.

"When Phina is awake. I told you before that TOM and Bethany Anne knew and had taken action."

"Don't you think Phina should have had some say in that decision?" Link sounded annoyed. Why did that make her want to smile?

"DS, you know the Empress couldn't and wouldn't wait to act. It might be Phina's life, but it's the Empress' Empire, and she takes her responsibility to her people very seriously."

"I know that, but…" Link sighed from nearby, then grumbled, "That damned woman needs to look at the person whose life she almost snuffed out due to her misguided notion."

"Agreed. She almost lost Phina due to her blindness, regardless of her intentions. She was so focused on her own agenda that she missed being thorough in her research."

"Oh?" She heard Link's voice move as if he were facing away from her. "What do you know, ADAM?"

After a brief pause during which Phina stirred, trying to hear better, ADAM's replied, "That is information Phina should hear firsthand and when she isn't waking from her self-induced coma."

Self-*what*? Before she could process ADAM's comment, she heard a flurry of movement by her side, then a whoosh of air as the Pod-doc opened. Of course, she was in the Pod-doc. Where else would she be to heal from this crazy reaction to an unknown source?

Phina's eyes fluttered open. She winced at the bright light overhead, then blinked and squinted to adjust to the light. After the soothing gray nothing plane, the light seemed harsh, let alone everything else in the room that assaulted her senses. Part of her wanted to go back to the calm numbness, but she shook it off.

>>**Phina, you have clothes you can put on next to you. Welcome back.**<< Her friend spoke through her implant, so the conversation was private.

"Thanks, ADAM," she whispered, not certain if she'd spoken out loud or in her head. She sat up carefully and saw a privacy screen with a shelf extended that held basic clothing.

Feeling restless, she sat up, narrowly missing bumping Link's head as he leaned back. She turned to drop her legs over the side of the Pod-doc and realized that aside from feeling physically and emotionally overwhelmed, she felt… pretty good. Not weak like she was expecting from having been lying down so long.

However long she'd been here.

She reached with trembling hands for the clothes and slowly put them on. She didn't feel weak so much as… foreign in her own body. That was strange.

After dressing, she pressed a button that removed the

privacy screen, then turned her attention to the person on the other side.

"Link?" Her voice was scratchy and thick from disuse. How long had she been lying here? Her thoughts were scattered as she looked around the room.

"Phina..."

Her thoughts focused at once, her gaze moving to the man sitting next to her. The hesitation in his voice was not normal. Neither was Link's use of her name. Come to think of it, Link appeared wearier and somewhat ragged. He looked close to his age, and he hardly ever did. His eyes gave her the most pause, showing such a mix of emotions that they overwhelmed her.

"Link, what happened? How long has it been?"

He swallowed, his eyes flashing bleak weariness that faded quickly into relief with a hint of unease. "It's been a while."

Phina stilled. "How long?" she whispered.

Link took a ragged breath and nodded, letting out the words in a rush. "Twenty months, one week, three days, and nine hours."

CHAPTER TWO

Phina's eyes widened in shock. "Twenty months?" she whispered. "That's... That's..."

"A hell of a long time, my dear," Link finished, his eyes watching her with concern.

She nodded weakly. "Why?"

His eyes rose in surprise. "Why has it been so long, or why were you in a self-induced coma to begin with?"

Phina raised her free hand to rub her face. Her skin was far more sensitive than she remembered. She shook her head in disbelief. "Both?"

Link looked at her, his eyes frustrated, sparking life into his weary features. "Those are two questions I've been waiting quite a while to ask you."

She dropped her hand to look at him with a frown. "To ask *me*?"

He leaned forward. "You are telling me you don't have any idea why you put yourself in a coma for over a year and a half?"

Phina frowned. "Well, I have ideas, but I don't know for

certain. All I remember is pain, both in my mind and my body."

Link sighed and sagged, his shoulders slumping. He looked so tired and concerned that she wanted to reach out to him. Just like that, her mind slid into his, and she knew exactly how he felt and what was on his mind at that moment. He wanted to believe her, but he couldn't quite bring himself to do so.

Phina stilled, and her eyes unfocused. Her mind froze; all she could focus on was Link's lack of belief that she would tell him the truth. Were these his normal suspicious thoughts talking, or had something happened while she was in the coma to cause him to doubt her?

When Phina had stirred and opened her eyes, Link had felt like gathering her up and yelling, "Hallelujah!" He was so relieved that she was finally awake. He hadn't, of course. It wouldn't have been seemly. He kept his stoic expression on his face. Still, he thought his emotions must have been visible, given how strong they were.

Link had been very eager to hear why Phina had slept for so long, as well as to have her be present to question her aunt. The desire to bring justice and punishment to the woman who had harmed Phina was burning him up.

Hearing that Phina had no idea why she had been in a coma had brought him up short, his mind spinning. How the hell could she not know what was going on? It was called a self-induced coma for a reason. She had to have known something. It was the only thing that made sense, based on what everyone had told him about her condition.

So, why did she feel the need to hide what had happened? Did she not trust him?

"Phina?" Link sounded concerned, but she couldn't bring herself to verify that. It didn't seem to matter. She knew his concern for her was genuine, even if he didn't believe her.

She looked at Link as she sighed. "What?"

Link hesitated as if he were about to say something, then shook his head. "What do you want to know first?"

Phina's thoughts were all over the place, but one stood out. "Alina?"

He smiled faintly. "She's been here every day to talk to you."

She blinked back tears at the rush of longing inside her. She needed to see her best friend, so much so that her mind surprised her by reaching out to connect with Alina's. What astounded her wasn't that she could connect to her friend's mind, but that Alina was occupied with…well…

Phina shook her head, disconnecting before she got stuck in something she wasn't ready to experience.

Foremost in her mind was that mentally reaching out seemed easy. Almost *too* easy. Far easier than before she had fallen into her apparently self-inflicted coma. What had happened to her to cause these changes while she had been unconscious? The questions swirled in her head, overwhelming her. She closed her eyes.

Everything from the air draft blowing on her arms to the floor under her bare feet felt weird. Phina didn't need weird right now. She needed *normal*.

She steadied herself. Link reached for her but dropped his hand when he caught her look.

He hadn't believed her.

She closed her eyes again to mask the sensations and emotions flying through her. Too much sensory and mental input.

Just as she was about ready to pick up her pillow and scream into it to relieve the pressure, she heard footsteps in the other room. The door snicked open, revealing Doctor Keelson.

April entered with a huge smile, her comfortable white clothing accentuating her form. "Phina! It's so good to see you awake again. How are you feeling?"

Phina shook her head. "I can't answer that in a meaningful way. My mind is getting used to my body and the sensations, which are far more enhanced than I remember them being. Then there are my emotions, which are all over the place. I am still not sure what is going on. Has it really been over a year and a half since we left the Aurians' planet?"

Doctor Keelson's smile dimmed and she nodded. "Yes, it's been quite some time. Braeden said your conscious mind was absent the times he checked for activity. He did say that your cognitive functions were still present, but that was all he could tell us. Do you have any idea what happened or why you were in a coma for so long?"

Phina shook her head, frowning. "The Pod-doc couldn't

do anything either? I've heard it could heal just about anything."

April sighed. "We had you placed into the Empress' personal Pod-doc, the one all the others are patterned after. It stabilized you, then we did everything we could to isolate the problem coding in your nanocytes. Your body wasn't adjusting properly to the nanos in the serum your aunt gave you. Eventually, ADAM and TOM rewrote your nanocyte code to bypass the previous programming so your body could properly function." She frowned, then nodded. "At least, that's my understanding of it." The doctor narrowed her eyes. "What's wrong?"

Phina had frozen. "My aunt…gave me a serum?"

Holy hell in a handbasket.

Doctor Keelson turned to look at Link with a scowl. "You didn't tell her?"

Link rubbed his head in frustration as he sagged into his chair. So much for his original plan. "I was waiting until she had adjusted to being awake." His eyes hardened at the look of admonishment he received from the doctor. "Believe me, April. Phina deserves to know, but she's just woken up. I was giving her time."

Phina raised her hand to pause the conversation, took a deep breath with her eyes closed, and she straightened her shoulders. "All right. Please explain why you believe my aunt did this."

April shook her head, lips pressing together. "I don't know for sure, but that is what I was told."

Link glowered at the woman. Why did people insist on interfering with his plans? He knew he should have whisked Phina away to recover by herself. She needed to have information given to her gradually. "We know. ADAM has been very thorough."

"ADAM?" Phina's voice practically melted.

Hang it all, she sounded like a love-sick puppy. Such things did not improve his mood. Of course, he had to wait for her to finish her welcome home conversation with the AI before he explained about her aunt.

Link stewed as he waited for Phina to finish. This homecoming was not what he had thought it would be after waiting so long for her to wake up. Why couldn't she focus on the important things? Had she always been this distractable? Perhaps it was an effect of her months in a coma.

ADAM. Phina's heart warmed when she thought about her friend, but she found herself almost scared to ask him now. Once he told her what evidence they had to convict her aunt, she would have no choice but to believe it. Even though Phina had suspected Aunt Faith, part of her—the part that had known the softer side of her aunt as a child— had hoped she was wrong.

Damn it. Phina refused to be a coward.

"ADAM?" she whispered.

"Hi, Phina," ADAM replied through the speaker.

Her shoulders relaxed when she heard the AI's voice. "Tell me, ADAM."

Her implant sparked to life, turning their conversation private. >>**I'm happy you are all right, Phina. We were...concerned.**<<

Phina squinted in confusion. She sat against the platform. *We?*

ADAM's confident tones showed no hesitation. >>**Stark and I.**<<

Really? Her interest sparked for the first time since she woke up. *Stark was concerned?*

>>**Yes. He made the transition to AI on the trip you fought the Skaines on Lyriasha, the Aurians' planet. The decision to risk his engines and the integrity of the hull of his ship to get you here was the tipping point that pushed him to ascend.**<<

Phina's eyes brightened. *That's amazing, ADAM. I remember we talked about the possibility not long before that trip. Can you tell him thank you for risking himself for me? I hope that rush didn't cause him too many problems.* Remembering that the trip had been quite some time ago caused her smile to dim.

Doctor Keelson eyed her in concern and stepped forward. "Are you all right?"

Phina nodded, then sighed and spoke out loud. "Okay, ADAM. Just tell me. How do you know it's Aunt Faith?"

April and Link looked at her in concern but she ignored them and listened to ADAM. It didn't matter what they thought. She needed to know from the AI.

"Do you remember the day she came to visit, and you ate with her, then fell asleep?" ADAM asked, using the speaker.

Phina frowned, her mind bringing it up. She had

arrived to find her Aunt Faith acting oddly. They'd had a pleasant enough lunch, then she had felt overwhelming fatigue. Aunt Faith had said it was dehydration and she was not taking care of herself properly. "Yes?"

ADAM continued, "When your aunt arrived on the *Meredith Reynolds*, she carried the serum onto the station and gave it to you with your lunch. I suspect it also had a sedative in it to make your body stay calm while the nanocytes began the transition."

Her thoughts reeling, Phina shook her head. "But how? Station security checks for suspicious things like that."

"She brought groceries with her," ADAM explained. "The serum was mixed into the container of orange juice, and she'd programmed the nanocytes to remain inert until the serum hit your digestive system. Security checks things thoroughly, but not at the microscopic level."

Phina brought her hands up to her face, her thoughts spinning. She shook her head, uncertain what to think or feel. What was there to say when the person who had taken care of you for years betrayed you in such a big way? She brought her hands down and looked at Link and April, tears shimmering, though she focused and contained her emotions before they could fall. "Did she admit to doing it? Did she say anything about why?"

Doctor Keelson nodded, her expression compassionate. "She admitted to it."

Link leaned in, his eyes glinting. "She won't say why, though. She says only you get to hear that."

Phina eased herself onto the pad of the Pod-doc. It was too much. "I... I don't think I can see her. Not now."

Link's face was unreadable. Phina couldn't help wishing

she knew what was going through his mind. In another breath, she did know, and she stilled as Link's eyes flashed with anger. She withdrew her mind so fast she almost gave herself mental whiplash.

"Phina Waters, you are being a coward!" Link's words pierced the mental noise, causing her to stiffen and making her wish she had found a reason to leave. As she got up to do that, she got angry. A coward, was she? Nice to know what he thought.

Phina turned her icy expression on Link, her eyes blazing like fire. "I'm a coward?" she asked softly as she stepped into his personal space to glare at him. "Really? Because I don't wish to speak to the woman who raised me for half my life and who I just found out gave me an unknown serum that caused weird abilities and ended with me screaming in torment? Because I'm overwhelmed to learn that I just woke up from a year and a half in a coma that I apparently put myself into and don't even know why?"

Link's face had lost any hint of anger, and his skin had paled. She was close enough to see the weariness that had been eating away at him, but the distress she felt at his lack of belief in her, combined with his accusation, caused her to ignore it.

She stopped inches away and stared at him. His eyes had darkened with an emotion she didn't recognize, but she didn't feel like trying to find out what it was. "If that's what you really think of me, then screw you. I'm not dealing with this crap right now."

Phina straightened and strode toward the door.

"Phina, wait!"

She ignored Doctor Keelson's call as she opened the door and sped into the next room, flying past the people milling around without noticing who they were.

Several people turned and shouted her name as she headed through the next door and into the hallway. She thought she heard someone running after her, but she quickly left them behind. At the next intersection, she hit a crowd and slipped through as fast as her feet could take her.

She needed time alone so she could process everything that was happening to her.

———

Seeing Phina freeze was too much. Seeing her face turn to stone when he knew she was suppressing emotion was too much. Never mind that Link had refined her natural talent to hide her emotions. There was a difference between showing no emotion and feeling no emotion, and it was a different thing altogether to suppress that emotion to avoid feeling it.

Link's words about Phina being a coward had burst out of him unbidden, which rarely happened. At least not before this last year-plus of almost no sleep and little break from worry. He struggled to provide a reason for his outburst. He had meant what he said, but only in connection to her suppression of feelings. Nothing else. He couldn't pinpoint when that had begun to grate on him. Perhaps it hadn't before now. There were too many unresolved issues and things going on, and nothing had gone right since Phina woke up.

But her face told him it was too late. The damage was done.

Phina's blazing eyes had punched him in the chest and left him searching for breath. "I'm a coward?" she'd asked softly as she stepped into his personal space to glare at him. "Really?"

Link could only sit there, his energy draining while Phina gave him a much-deserved dressing down. He had said the wrong thing. The least he could do was let her speak.

Before he could respond, Phina was gone, leaving him feeling he had allowed his inner turmoil to make a mistake he wasn't certain he could fix with practically the only family he had left.

CHAPTER THREE

ADAM and TOM had been monitoring Phina as she woke up to make sure everything was fine. ADAM kept track of the conversation in the room with one part of his AI brain, answering when needed. With another part, he focused on the readouts they were getting from Phina and the room.

The results were what they'd expected, with some differences they would have to figure out. As Phina's emotions became intensified and she ran out of the room, one set of readings shot up.

>>TOM, you are seeing this?<<

Yes.

>>Well, now we know.<<

Yes.

>>You thought it might be possible.<<

Yes.

>>She will need help assimilating this.<<

Yes.

>>Are you finally going to talk to her?<<

Yes.

>>TOM?<<

Yes?

>>Stop saying yes.<<

Yes. Right. Oh, no.

>>What?<<

We need to tell Bethany Anne.

>>Dammit. She's going to curse again.<<

Yes.

QBBS *Meredith Reynolds*, Training Facility

Phina flew through the corridors, easily dodging everyone, though her passage caused quite a stir behind her. She entered the hallways leading to the exercise rooms where she had been training. She quickly approached the entrance of the APA. It wasn't until she saw a weapon pointed at her that she stopped feet away from the guard she didn't recognize, her hands up and eyes wide as she panted lightly.

"I apologize, but I am not here to attack you. I merely meant to come in and use the facilities."

The sandy-haired Marine slowly lowered his weapon. The burly male had a firm jaw and wary eyes, appearing to be in his thirties. "If you wanted to work out, you could have approached at a normal speed, lady. I don't know how fast you were going, but that wasn't normal." He squinted apprehensively at her, glancing at her bare feet. "Not for a human, at least. Are you a Wechselbalg?"

Phina lowered her hands, keeping her eyes on the man in front of her. His comments arrowed into her, causing her to flinch internally. No, she wasn't normal. Phina hadn't realized how much she wanted to be until she had traveled so far past the definition that it didn't appear to be in her dictionary anymore. "I was upset and trying to find a place to get it out. I think better when I'm moving."

He nodded, relaxing. "I can relate to that. A good workout can help clear the mind."

She smiled tentatively, nodding. "Yes." She paused, glancing at the door. "Could I go in now?"

The Marine didn't smile, but he did seem easier. "Sure. Just need to see your ID."

Phina's smile faltered, then she looked down, absently patting herself. She was wearing tight, stretchy clothing similar to her workout clothing but in a thick white fabric instead of her normal black. However, unlike her normal blacks, there were no pockets. As comfortable as it felt, it proved to be lacking as she had nothing to show her identity.

She sighed and looked up after plastering an apologetic look on her face to find him standing rigidly.

Phina was becoming concerned when her implant activated.

>>**I am telling him he can let you through.**<<

Her shoulders dropped in relief as she responded the same way. *Thank you, ADAM.*

>>**Phina...**<<

She frowned at the hesitancy in his voice. *What, ADAM?*

He responded slowly with a tone to his voice she didn't recognize. >>**They should be good to go now.**<<

ADAM? Why do you sound weird? What aren't you telling me?"

>>**I understand why you are upset. But at the same**

time, I understand why Link got upset and said what he did. It feels very...disconcerting.<<

Phina frowned as she listened but pushed away her irritation that ADAM understood why Link had been upset. She didn't want to hear it since she still felt kicked in the gut that Link didn't believe her or thought she was lying to him.

Still, ADAM was her friend...

What feels disconcerting?

>>**Being in the middle. I don't like this feeling.**<< ADAM's voice still sounded unsettled.

Phina sighed, more mentally than physically. *No one likes being in the middle, ADAM. Sometimes we end up there, anyway.*

Hearing a cough, Phina focused on the beefy Marine in front of her. He was standing with an eyebrow raised and the barrier open, waiting for her. She nodded and stepped forward. As she did so, she noticed an odd expression on his face. Again she wondered what he was thinking about, and her mind automatically reached out to his.

Halfway through the barrier and right next to the man, Phina paused, her gaze slowly moving up to meet his.

Keeping her expression the same, Phina nodded before heading inside, her heart racing. She hadn't heard all of the thought. It was just one phrase. A name that sparked a memory of the fateful day she and Alina had snuck into the Marines' workout area.

Todd Jenkins.

Phina entered the corridor of the active participation area, her mind whirling so much she only paid partial attention to the people she passed. Link would have scolded her for not having situational awareness. Phina pushed the thought away with a scowl.

She arrived at the out-of-the-way room she had used for training before her coma. Upon entering, her eyes widened in shock, then her head and shoulders slumped in defeat. Phina hadn't thought about what it would mean to be gone for so long, but the evidence lay right in front of her.

Her weary eyes took in her precious gymnastics equipment, dismantled and set against the wall. The objects that had been used to build her obstacle courses were either removed or also set to the side. The only equipment of hers still set up in place was her larger tumbling mat and the pole in one corner of the room.

Her equipment had been replaced with random strength and exercise equipment. The sight left her feeling displaced and depressed. The scent of sweaty men and testosterone in the air made that feeling worse.

Phina remained so preoccupied with the visual representation of her involuntary convalescence that she didn't hear the door open or steps walking toward her. When soft, kind words from a deeper baritone voice came from behind and to her left, she jerked her head around in surprise.

"They waited a long time for you, you know." Todd Jenkins' gaze was welcoming, though his face held a somber look.

Phina mentally scolded herself for forgetting situational awareness because Link would have done so before remembering that her current opinion of Link wasn't favorable. Then again, it wasn't the first time she had practically run into the man next to her.

Todd gave her a small smile before turning toward the room and continuing, "It took six months before anyone would admit that you might not wake up and they couldn't understand why. TOM and ADAM took a long time to accept that it was down to you. Even for them, as quick and smart as they are, and knowing it likely wouldn't work, they still tried to figure out options for waking you up for quite some time."

Phina felt her stomach drop. Ever since she had woken up, she had thought only about how *she* felt about being in a coma. She hadn't let herself think about how everyone else would have reacted to it or how long they may have tried to do something about it.

Todd leaned forward, snapping her out of her horror at realizing that she had been so selfish. "Phina, you are all right. It's normal to be more concerned about yourself when you are in pain or recovering from a trauma."

Her startled eyes rose to his. "How did you know?"

Todd gave her a small smile. "I've been injured and recovered. It tends to change you, either for better because you develop more compassion, or worse because you become less caring about the needs of others."

Phina blinked, then frowned thoughtfully. "That's a wide dichotomy. I suppose it makes sense. I didn't mean to not think about what other people went through. I've been overwhelmed ever since I woke up. My senses are still feeling overloaded, though it's gotten better."

The big man nodded, his eyes both sharp and intelligent. "And when you are overwhelmed, you run?"

She stared at him in surprise. How did he know? "Yes... in both senses of the word. I need space to figure things out. Do you read minds?"

He grinned and shook his head. "No, but I was in the outer room of the medical center and saw your mad dash to escape. You might have set a record there with the fastest outtake. I also lead many men and women, and they have often had similar questions and responses."

She reddened at realizing he had seen her mad dash. A tense knot inside Phina relaxed, and her eyes widened. "Wow. That's amazing."

Todd tilted his head questioningly. "What is?"

Phina put her hands on her chest where the knot had been. "How much better I feel knowing that how I'm reacting is normal. You have no idea how much I needed to feel normal in some way when nothing in my life feels like it's normal."

Todd leaned against the wall. He crossed his arms, a look of concern on his face. "This sounds like more than the effects of a long-term coma."

Phina nodded and opened her mouth to speak before she paused, questioning herself. She wanted to tell Todd everything when normally she would keep her mouth shut and not say a word. She rubbed a finger on her jaw as she thought about it, then realized his concern was part of the pull to say something. She eyed him as she thought this over. She'd seen hints of it before in their previous conversations, but there was something solid and reassuring about Todd that made her think things would be all right.

He made her feel normal, like a person instead of a freak, or a prodigy, or mind or body to be trained. It felt...restful.

Phina blinked as she came to this conclusion with a slight frown.

"Is something wrong? You don't need to tell me anything."

She looked up and realized he had been standing there watching her stare into space for who knew how long. The thought gave her a funny feeling. She mentally slapped herself and shook her head. "It's not that. I had a strange thought and needed to mull it over." She shifted her weight as she focused. "Are you certain you want to hear this? It may take some time."

His expression didn't change much, except for a warmer look in his eyes as he nodded. "I have time, and ADAM will make sure we are not disturbed."

Her eyes widened at that reminder. She activated her implant to speak privately with her friend. *ADAM, is it okay to tell Todd everything that's happened? Is he in the know?*

>>**Is he in the circle of trust, do you mean?**<< He paused. >>**He doesn't know everything that's happened, but you can share what you know with him.**<<

Phina frowned at that. *You are talking like there's more going on that I don't know about.*

>>**Yes.**<<

She sighed, her shoulders drooping. *One of these days, you need to tell me everything you know about me, ADAM. It's not fair to keep it from me.*

ADAM remained silent long enough that Phina thought he wasn't going to respond. Then he spoke in a resigned tone. >>**Agreed.**<<

Phina frowned, feeling frustrated. *You don't think I should be given information that concerns me?*

>>**No, I agree you should know. I merely find myself concerned that you may be angry with us when you find out. I don't want you to be angry. Or hurt.**<< He finished in a thoughtful tone.

Wow. This must be big information. But I agree. Later. She paused, then spoke more quietly. *ADAM?*

>>***Yes, Phina?***<<

Thank you for everything you've done to help me.

His tone warmed. >>**You're welcome, Phina.**<<

Phina looked up to find Todd waiting with a patient smile on his face. She grimaced in apology. "Sorry about that."

He lifted a shoulder. "I can tell when people are talking to ADAM."

Phina nodded as she took a breath and let it out. Normally she would feel nervous sharing something this big. She looked at Todd with a slight frown as she realized she didn't feel nervous. Perhaps another change from being in a coma for over a year.

"Do you remember when we had that semblance of a fight last…I mean, about two years ago? A little over?" She frowned and shook her head. "I don't even know what day it is."

He nodded, but the wry amusement in his eyes told her he remembered more than the basics of the event in question. Remembering why she had been there—for Alina to ogle the men working out—caused her cheeks to flush, and she looked away. "Yes, well, that incident had unexpected consequences."

Phina related to Todd the circumstances of how she had joined the diplomatic institute, her uncertainty that she wanted to live as a diplomat, and her desire to be a spy like in her favorite stories her dad had told her when she was younger.

Todd nodded in satisfaction. "I can see that. Diplomacy takes someone cool under pressure, with quick reactions and the ability to work independently with an overarching directive from their boss. That seems like the life that would suit you."

Phina gave him a large smile of appreciation. "That's very insightful."

The bigger man grinned ruefully. "I know people tend to overlook me because I don't have any of the super-charged abilities, even though I'm in a prominent position. I'm basically human, though I'm faster and stronger than normal. However, I still have a brain in my head and what I do well is notice patterns and connections with people. I read subtext and make inferences. What that tells me is that you, Phina, would never be happy with just diplomatic duties. There's too much fight and brain in you to be satisfied with those as your only tasks."

Phina couldn't help it as her mouth dropped open and her eyes widened. She sputtered for a moment. Then she stopped and collected herself, watching the silent, observant man with a speculative eye. Todd had hidden depths, and it sounded like he noticed as much as she did. They just focused on different things, Phina on facts and information and Todd on people. Still... "What makes you think you know me well enough to say that?"

Todd shrugged, his blue eyes intent. "Am I wrong?"

She slowly shook her head. "No, you're right. And it isn't all I do. I'm mentoring under the person they call the Diplomatic Spy. I've been doing a lot of training for both."

Todd whistled silently. "Greyson Wells is the Diplomatic Spy?" He shook his head. "Pieces are falling into place, and everything is making so much more sense."

Phina winced internally. Right. She hadn't meant to reveal him, but if anyone knew Greyson Wells, or Link as Phina called him, was her mentor, then sharing her secrets meant sharing his. Fudging crumbs. She sat down on a seat attached to an exercise machine behind her and leaned to one side on the padding, trying not to show how flustered she felt. "Oh? He wasn't making sense?"

Todd raised an eyebrow and smiled. "No, he often broke the patterns and connections I saw. This fills in a lot of those gaps." His smile turned amused. "You know, I often compared him to Puck in my mind, the legendary creature described in Shakespeare's *As You Like It*. Popping in unexpectedly, being a nosy busybody listening to gossip, starting gossip, causing trouble, thinking he knows what's best, solving problems, and leaving people wondering what the hell just happened. You see it, right?"

Phina forgot her uneasiness and laughed, her head thrown back and eyes sparkling with amusement to match. "Yes! Now that you mention it, yes! That fits him perfectly."

After watching her laughing for a moment, his warm and friendly gaze became concerned again. "So, I'm guessing something happened to change things sometime between when you began learning to become a diplomatic spy, which sounds fun, by the way, and when you ended up in a coma?"

Phina's amusement died. "Yeah. You could say that." She took a deep breath and let it out in a sigh. "Okay, so here's what happened..."

She explained about training with Maxim and finding out that her aunt blamed Wechselbalgs for the deaths in their family and how Faith had taken steps that she had called consequences. She described her meal with her aunt and how she felt afterward.

"So, it turned out that my aunt drugged me with this nanocyte serum that made me change..."

CHAPTER FOUR

QBBS *Meredith Reynolds*, Training Room

Phina hesitated in relating her story and looked down, unsure what Todd would think about her freaky abilities. However, from what Doctor Keelson had said, her abilities —however they turned out to have changed since she'd woken up—were locked in, and nothing would change it now.

She shook her head, frowning. She wouldn't be shouting about them in the bars and restaurants, but some people would have to know. Anyone who interacted with her for longer lengths of time would notice unless she kept it strictly hidden, and she felt exhausted just *thinking* about that life.

No, there would be a circle of people in the know, and Todd seemed to want to be one of those people. Better for him to hear it from the source. Or so Phina tried to convince herself.

Todd's voice turned gentler. "You changed? How?"

Phina looked up to see that same gentleness in his eyes,

which contrasted with the harder planes of his face and body. In talking to him, she had forgotten Todd made his living as a warrior.

She finally nodded and continued. "I was able to move faster, hit harder and stronger, my thinking process sped up, and I developed the ability to sense...things." She swallowed, feeling uncomfortable. No one wanted to know that she could read their mind. Phina didn't feel comfortable with it, and she was the one who could do it. She had been all right with what she could sense before the coma, for the most part, but after her incidents with Link and Alina earlier, it felt like a huge invasion of privacy.

Phina explained how her abilities developed and described how her body drew in excess energy and needed to be dispersed through activity. "After that, we had another training mission but with much higher stakes." She paused, then frowned as she realized how much time had passed since then. "Have you heard of the Aurians? Did they get their planet terraformed yet?"

Todd straightened in surprise. "That's right. You were on the team that went to rescue them? The planet was terraformed earlier this year. The Aurians left a couple of weeks ago to see the planet's revitalization. The Gleek representative named Braeden as well as Drk-vaen, Sis'tael, and Ryan Wagner went with them. I believe they were on your original trip."

Phina sagged in both relief and disappointment. She hadn't realized how much weight the Aurians' needs were on her mind until the concern was gone. She would have liked to see the small, deep blue beings again, but she felt happy they were now in their reformed home. Although she appreciated that her friends were taking care of the Aurians since she couldn't be there, she couldn't deny a desire to see them again with her own eyes. Especially Braeden. She longed to hear his gentle wisdom and correction.

Although, Todd hadn't been doing too badly. She eyed the man as she nodded in confirmation, then explained what happened leading up to the trip and the revelations about her body breaking down.

Phina wouldn't have noticed Todd's shock if she hadn't been trained to see it.

"You mean you went to a dying planet while you were dying to save a dying people?"

Phina grinned humorlessly. "Yeah, there was a lot of dying happening. It wasn't fun."

He shook his dark-haired head. "I'll say. So, what happened when you got there?"

She blew air out in a puff, then chuckled before continuing to tell Todd about disobeying Link's orders and everything that happened in the fight with the Skaines. She described what had happened with the energy drain on Braeden and their journey to the cave on the other side of the world. As she talked, she began moving her feet around. She should do some exercise after this. Though, it was nice to not feel driven to move constantly like she had been before her coma.

Phina paused in her story, remembering the difficult journey through the cave and reaching the bubble that contained the life energy of the planet. She suppressed a shudder and finished relaying what they'd found with the machine and He-Who-Thinks. Phina looked down as she finished, bringing her knees up and wrapping her arms around them. "Unfortunately, before we got onboard our ship again, the yo-yo effect of going from space to planet to forcefield and back proved too much for my body to withstand. All I remember is collapsing in agony and wishing desperately for anything to make it stop."

She closed her eyes as her body shook with remembering. She had fallen unconscious into a coma in part to escape from the pain.

Phina was certain of it.

Todd listened intently to a story that he would have found fanciful if he hadn't been committed to following Bethany Anne over the last thirty years. His Empress was a woman who had been called a vampire queen by some on Earth even though she didn't need to drink blood. During his time in the Empress' inner circle, he had seen some crazy things and heard of many more.

While Phina had been sharing her story, he had been interested in the matter-of-fact way she spoke. He was intrigued by the way she held herself back from sharing the more emotional aspects of the story, unlike most people did when engaging people. The only way to glimpse a hint of it was to pay close attention to her eyes. He was also impressed with how she downplayed her role in events to make it sound like it was the team doing the work as a whole, although he suspected she played a much more prominent role. All in all, she was a complex, complicated woman who'd found herself in a twenty-year-old body when she still thought of herself as eighteen, and she had the mature attitude of an adult of many years due to her experiences.

Even now, as she remembered the pain that had precipitated her coma, he found himself admiring the way she struggled to shake it off and return to her more unaffected stance. He shifted, contemplating hugging her, but didn't think they knew each other well enough for her to accept that. He settled on crouching and putting his hand on hers briefly.

When she looked up, surprised, he smiled reassuringly. "I won't pretend to understand how bad it was or how you felt, but remember that it's done and gone. It's just a memory now. You are the one to decide how much power it has over you."

Phina nodded, her eyes still wide. Still, the note of panic and fear he could see lessened. She gave him a shy shaky smile. "I'm sorry for freaking out on you."

Todd gave her an easy smile. "Only natural with everything you just told me. I would have been more concerned if you didn't have any reaction."

She frowned as if that concept was strange. "Wouldn't having less of a reaction mean that you are stronger and better able to handle it?"

He shook his head, struggling to keep his surprise and dismay from showing. What had everyone been teaching Phina that she would think a nonreaction was better? Or would this be an idea she had despite teaching? After observing Phina for a moment, he decided it was some of both, which concerned him.

"Not really. Think about it. Someone close to you dies.

Is it better to show you are affected or unaffected? If you cared about that person, then whether you show everyone, or a few close people, or just yourself, you will have some aspect of being affected. Feeling grief, perhaps anger they are gone, shows you cared about that person and will miss them. That person touched your life, gave you something no one else did, and altered your life in a way it wouldn't have been if you had never met them. Feeling and showing emotion lets you know how you are responding to life, which is valuable for yourself, as well as for those around you."

Todd looked at her closely as he continued, "I'm guessing part of your training is to show you are untouched by the events around you, which can also be valuable when you are in the work you are part of. However, just because you can hide your emotion, even from yourself, doesn't mean the emotion isn't there. No matter how you mask or suppress it, that emotion is present inside you, waiting to be acknowledged. Some-times ignoring that emotion can make a person sick, and sometimes it can cause problems with those you care about because they won't understand."

He tilted his head as he remained crouched next to her, his hands balanced on his knees. "Do you ever feel a weight inside or a knot of pressure?"

Phina had been still and quiet as she listened with her knees up and her arms wrapped around them, her green eyes watching him curiously and steadily. At his question, her eyes grew wider in surprise and alarm.

He saw the question in her eyes, how did he know? "This weight or pressure, I believe, is the emotion you suppress and try not to feel. It causes stress on a person's mind and body. It can also cause you to feel depressed when you have nothing to be depressed about."

He paused for a moment, then decided to share something more personal. "There was a time when I felt I shouldn't show my emotions. I was married to my high school sweetheart. I thought we were in love and committed to each other, but when we were separated due to my life in the Marines, she cheated on me and eventually left. I thought I had to be strong, show that I could do it all and not reveal that I was confused, sad, angry, and in pain. To show those things was a weakness, I thought."

"What changed?" She spoke quietly.

"I had a leader who pushed me and pushed me until all of that emotion came pouring out in the form of aggression. It drove me to become harder and faster than I had ever been before, but it also blinded me to the circumstances, and I nearly killed him." He looked down at his hands, which he had used to pummel the man over and over. They had fisted tightly, so he consciously relaxed them before looking up into her eyes that had grown stark with understanding and compassion. "I thought I would get court-martialed, but he merely gave me a look and told me never to let my emotions control me like that again."

Phina had a crease of puzzlement in her forehead, so he explained his leader's reasoning. "What I had been doing by suppressing the emotion wasn't me controlling my emotions, but allowing them to get so large that they were controlling *me*. It felt like control, but it was a false control, and they took over when I was pushed too hard."

Understanding, concern, and frustration moved

through her eyes, but he felt heartened to see Phina was thinking through the implications and what it meant for her.

"What did you do to change it so you were in control of your emotions?" she asked, an intensity shining from her that gave him an idea as to the inner strength she possessed.

Todd took a deep breath. "I let myself feel even when it was overwhelming. I identified my emotions and verbalized what they were and why I felt them. I made myself talk about them with a couple of close friends and people I cared about. That helped me to understand what decisions I needed to make. Not that I made decisions solely based on my emotions, but I was better able to identify the options that were distasteful and why, or why the ones that meant something to me were important." He shrugged. "That's why we have them, to show how we are responding to the life we are living and what's around us, so why not use them for what they are made for?"

"Sounds easy when you put it that way."

"No," he answered dryly. "It wasn't that simple or easy. Those are the cliff notes version."

Phina had focused her gaze on a point somewhere in between them and looked up briefly with a small smile. He realized Phina was becoming overwhelmed again. Better to change the pace and let her process differently.

"So, what do you say we spar again now that you know what you are doing?" He gave her a small smile to let her know he was joking.

Todd was not prepared for the way her face lit up in a blinding grin.

CHAPTER FIVE

QBBS *Meredith Reynolds*, **Training Room**

Phina had never felt more alive. Her body could have been practically emaciated after a year and a half in a coma. On Earth, before Bethany Anne changed the world, her body would have been. Yet, between the Pod-doc, the serum, and ADAM's and the doctor's fixes, her body was in the best shape it had ever been. She shied away from the oblique reminder that she needed to address her aunt and focused on sparring.

Todd and Phina had moved the exercise equipment off to the side and cleared the mat before getting ready to spar. Oddly, as she faced Todd to begin their session, she had a sense of familiarity. It added elements of both comfort and uneasiness to the mess of emotions inside her that Todd had rightly pointed out she had been suppressing.

At the moment, she couldn't help it. She had spent too many years learning to suppress her emotions so they didn't affect her. That part of her mind mulled it over and dissected the possibilities while they sparred went without saying.

No sooner had Phina begun to think Todd was waiting for something, he moved, She responded, slowly getting a measure of both his movements and abilities and her own. She didn't let him get a punch, kick, or throw in, countering his movements with defensive measures. Occasionally, she returned with a punch, kick or throw of her own, which he blocked about as easily as she had.

Just as Phina was getting comfortable in the rhythm of the movement, it changed. Todd pushed harder, his kicks and punches more sudden and difficult to block, his throws becoming trickier to anticipate. However, she adjusted and set herself into the new rhythm, working to anticipate his next move.

"Phina, stop playing defense and come at me." Todd grunted as he continued his attacks, aiming for her stomach, which she redirected. She shook her head as she stepped to the side and raised a leg to block a kick to her knee. She could see that her refusal sparked something inside the man, but she couldn't observe closely enough to tell if it was anger, determination, or something else in her focus on countering his movements. "Phina, what happened to the acrobatics, the playfulness, the fire?"

"I don't want to hurt you!"

At Phina's admission, Todd stopped moving and remained motionless during one of the few times she had thrown a punch at him, this time in the throat. Her mind froze, her eyes flying open as she realized she may not be able to stop in time. Her reflexes kicked in, and she stopped with her fist less than an inch from his throat.

She stood staring at him with shock, her breathing heavy. Her brain caught up. "What the fudging hell was that? I could have killed you!"

Todd smiled, his gaze unwavering. "I trust you, Phina."

Phina blinked, and an odd sensation moved through her before he continued.

"Do you see that you don't need to worry about hurting me? I will tell you if something you do is too much, but I trust you to stop before there's a serious concern."

She continued to stare at him for a moment before dropping her hand and stepping back. "What if you're wrong and I do hurt you?"

He grinned, which eased his strong features and gave him a light in his eyes that proved to be rather endearing. "That's what the Pod-doc is for, right?"

Phina didn't smile, but her mouth twitched in amusement. Finally, she nodded and settled into her ready stance. "Let's hope you are right."

She closed her eyes briefly and took a deep breath to calm herself and quiet the fears. Todd was right. These emotions weren't going to go away.

When Phina opened her eyes, she had seconds before Todd came at her with a combination of attacks faster than before. She had no time to think, no time to plan; she had to sink into her awareness, trust her training and her body, and *move*.

Left fist, right fist, jump his leg sweep, block, strike, reach for a grab, block his kick, push him back with her feet as she sprang into a flip, then a leg sweep of her own before pushing off into a kick with a turn, and she was standing again. It took several more movements for her to realize she had a grin on her face and almost certainly a light in her eyes that showed she was loving it.

For the first time since Phina had developed her powers, she felt free.

Todd settled himself in for a fight after provoking Phina into realizing she was afraid to trust herself because she didn't want to hurt him. She had fought well before, but her movements had been so controlled they were rigid and lacking the fire and passion he had seen in her when they had sparred two and a half years ago.

Untrained, unfamiliar with combat, and afraid of... something he had later deduced was fear of getting caught, Phina had displayed intelligence, passion, and the ability to think outside the box as she kept out of his reach and used her skills and strength to surprise him.

Seeing her movements so rigid and controlled had practically hurt.

Now that Phina had awakened to her abilities, he had hoped she would show him more of the skills and passion he knew she possessed. She did all that and more.

Phina blazed.

Todd often sparred with his best friend and counterpart, Guardian Commander Peter Silvers. Peter's hits were methodical, carefully placed, and powerful.

Most people didn't fight him often enough to understand how controlled the man fought. Rarely did he let himself off the leash he placed on himself. The two friends challenged each other and made each other better fighters.

Fighting the Bitches, Bethany Anne's elite bodyguards and super soldiers, often felt like fighting a waterfall. Todd could gain some ground if he was at his best, but eventually, he had to concede defeat. John Grimes and Gabrielle, their leader when Bethany Anne wasn't around, even more so. He felt swept away and couldn't recover.

Sparring with Bethany Anne, the Queen Bitch and Empress of the Etheric Empire was comparable to being hit by a hurricane. If she thought someone needed to die, likely because of disrespect or attempting to kill her people, she would destroy them completely.

Thankfully, Bethany Anne liked him and wanted to help him get better. It still felt like being destroyed, but then she helped him rebuild stronger and better than before. In the meantime, he felt pain. *Lots* of pain.

Fighting Phina proved to be like none of these. Instead of the more methodical straightforward method of Peter, she kept him off balance with the opposite, often anticipating his moves. Rather than being swept away like with the Bitches, she danced and included him in the steps but came from random directions and used various fighting styles. Instead of destroying him like Bethany Anne usually did, she dismantled him, piece by piece, figuring out his fighting style and what made him tick before using that knowledge against him.

She glowed as her knowledge and practice, combined with her abilities and skills came together in perfect unison. The grin on Phina's face as she fought completed the picture.

He dodged, blocked, then failed to block the next attack, taking a bruise, but he didn't stop. Phina hadn't hit him with anything harder than a bruising force, which had everything to do with Phina's control over her own body and energy and not a lack of ability.

Phina feinted, struck, caught him in a throw which he barely slipped out of, blocked, another feint...nope, that was an attack. As he responded, she slid underneath his reach and popped up on his side, where she hit him with an open palm to throw him off balance before sweeping his leg. Only his training kept him in the game when his brain struggled to keep up. He pushed himself up in time to see Phina launch herself at him. Her legs locked around his neck, and she pulled him back.

The momentum flipped him over her body, but rather than letting go, she flipped with him and landed sitting on his chest, pinning his arms with her forearm at his neck. Her bright grin matched his own as she laughed. It took him a moment to realize that although he had difficulty keeping up once she got going, that was the most fun he had sparring in quite a while.

Todd had just gotten over the surprise of Phina landing on his chest and begun to realize how close she was to him when a loud female voice sounded from the doorway.

"Phina!"

———

Phina's head jerked up from where she had Todd pinned. Her happiness at being able to feel like her body and mind were working perfectly together dissipated like the air in a popped balloon. Alina and Maxim stood in the doorway, looking at her with mixed expressions of relief and hurt.

Guilt at the realization that she hadn't sent Alina a message letting her know she was okay caused her to scramble off Todd. A flush rose on her neck and cheeks as she realized how close they had been.

"Alina! Maxim!"

Alina rushed over to throw her arms around Phina, with Maxim a beat behind. She felt enclosed and crowded but mostly warmed that they cared about her. "Why didn't you come to me first to tell me you were okay?"

"I…"

Phina felt a large hand briefly touch her back. Todd had gotten off the floor and was headed for the door. Remembering how happy she felt to mesh her mind and body while fighting and how Todd had helped her and listened to her earlier caused her to reach out to him mentally without thinking. *Thank you.*

Feeling Todd's surprise as well as her own that she could connect to him that way, she shut her mental senses down hard, cursing herself internally. Great, now he would look at her like she was a freak the next time she saw him. Which could be another two years from now. Her frustration caused her to be incautious as she burst out to Alina as she pulled from them both. "I tried! Alina, you were one of the first thoughts I had, but when I reached out to you, you were…"

Phina belatedly realized what she was saying and clamped her mouth shut. She turned away to calm down. Alina and Maxim turned to look at each other with confused but wondering expressions. She crossed her arms and closed her eyes, wondering why life couldn't come with do-overs.

"Phina…" Alina sounded both curious and cautious. "How did you reach out to me? There wasn't a message or anything from you. I checked."

Phina shook her head, not wanting to admit to her best friend how different she was now. After the incidents with Alina and Link, reading minds felt like a breach of privacy, and she didn't want her friends to feel afraid that she would intrude whenever she felt like it.

She felt a hand touching her arm and turned her head to see Alina looking at her with concern. "Phina, it's us. We haven't been able to talk to you for over a year and a half." Her eyes began tearing as she bit her lip. "Please, Phina."

Phina turned and wrapped her arms around Alina, who clung to her and cried. Phina's eyes teared up too, and she focused on holding her best friend and reassuring her that she was here with her.

After a few minutes, Alina lifted her head and began wiping the tears away. "I look a mess."

Phina shook her head and wiped her own eyes with the backs of her hands. "Shush, you. You look beautiful." She looked closer at Alina and took in her appearance, smiling. "Yup, like a damp squib, but totally and completely gorgeous. Even more so than the last time I saw you."

Alina squawked as she pulled away and smacked Phina in the arm, which curiously, she barely felt. Phina saw Maxim was hiding chuckles.

Thankfully, Alina had missed it. "What! I am not a damp squib!"

Phina grinned. "Trust you to focus on that part rather than being completely gorgeous."

Alina smiled briefly before looking at Phina in

concern. "You're okay? I can't believe you're walking around! Were you *sparring* before we came in?" She looked at Phina accusingly. "You couldn't have waited one day?"

Phina sighed and rubbed her neck. "I needed to do something while I sorted things in my head. You know it's easier for me to do that when I'm moving and doing something. It's been... There's..." She remembered what Todd had told her about keeping her emotions in and that it was better to share her pain with friends.

She shook her head and took a breath before looking at Alina with her unguarded pain and heartbreak shown clearly. "It's been a year and a half for you, Alina. But for me, it's been a muddy mix of blankness with snatches of semi-awareness. While you guys lost me for a year and a half, I lost everything for a year and a half. Completely, suddenly, with no warning and no time to adjust. I don't know what I'm doing yet. I'm just reacting and trying to process everything."

Alina reached out and hugged Phina again. "I'm so sorry, Phina. I shouldn't have jumped all over you."

Phina pulled her arm out from where it was stuck between them and carefully squeezed Alina. "It's okay, Alina. I should have asked ADAM to let you know since I didn't have my tablet."

Her friend pulled back and smiled, her eyes determined. She stood a half-inch taller than Phina, which meant for once she hadn't bothered to put on her crazy high heels. "Phina, please tell me what you meant about trying to reach out to me."

Phina slumped, a strand of hair falling out of her braid.

She leaned her head on Alina's shoulder. "I don't want you to hate me or be scared of me."

Alina gently pushed Phina away so she could see her face. "Hey. That would never happen. I wouldn't and couldn't hate you. I'm scared *for* you, not *of* you. Whatever it is, you can tell me."

Phina glanced at Maxim, feeling awkward. He stood a few feet away, looking tall, masculine, and concerned. Phina could see why he appealed to Alina. She cared about him being her friend, although Alina's friendship trumped everyone else's. "If you're certain."

Her friend frowned. "*Phina.*"

Raising her hands, Phina nodded. "Sorry, just…making sure. You can't unknow once you know, you know?"

Alina nodded solemnly, her eyes twinkling in amusement. "I know."

Phina sighed and looked away. "Since I woke up, it's been relatively easy to slip into other people's minds. When I wanted to know where you were, my mind reached out to you."

Alina looked surprised but not shocked or disgusted, which relieved Phina. "Well, why didn't you say something?" She grinned, though she also looked concerned. "It might have startled me, but it would have been a relief to hear you!"

Phina's cheeks grew warm. "Well, you were busy at the time." She glanced at Maxim. Alina's mouth opened and closed like a fish as she tried to recover from her surprise. Finally, Alina looked at Maxim and burst out laughing. He gave her a shrug but grinned.

"Well… That must have been awkward." Alina laughed

another full minute, holding a hand to her chest to contain her laughter. "Phina, it's fine. I don't think we would want it to happen all the time." She snorted another chuckle. "I'm not going to be mad if you slip up accidentally."

She nudged Phina. "It would probably bother you more than it would me, honestly." Alina sighed and wrapped her arms around Phina, giving her another big hug. "I missed you so much, Phina. It was like my arm was cut off and a piece of my heart missing."

Phina relaxed against Alina, hugging her tightly. "I'm here now. I'm sorry it took so long."

Alina hugged her for another minute, then pulled back and smiled brightly. "Phina, we've been waiting, hoping you would wake up soon. I'm so happy you are! I've got something super exciting to share with you and ask you."

Phina tilted her head to see Maxim's fond smile as he watched Alina. His eyes shone with something that took Phina a minute or two to recognize as she hadn't seen it since her parents died—love. What would it be like to love someone that much? Her musing was interrupted as she jolted at Alina's excitement.

"Phina, would you be my maid of honor?" Alina's smile glowed with happiness as she turned toward Maxim with a blinding grin. "We're getting married!"

CHAPTER SIX

QBBS *Meredith Reynolds*, Holding Area

Phina cautiously stepped up to the guarded doors and showed her ID. "I should be on the list to see Faith Rochelle."

The serious guard took her ID and placed it on his tablet. He scanned the screen for a moment before nodding and looking up, his eyes solemn as he handed the ID back to her.

"Head to the right. A guard will escort you."

She thanked him and put her ID away as she stepped into the hall. A second guard opened the door for her with a nod. "This way, ma'am."

Phina blinked at the address and glanced down at her black pants and t-shirt to make sure she wasn't having an out-of-body experience. Sadly, her jacket didn't quite fit right anymore given the changes in her body, so Alina was making a new one for her with some additional spy-approved features.

As the guard escorted her, Phina decided to face facts. She was nervous and trying to find things to distract herself. She had no idea what state she would find her aunt in. Enraged? Bitter? Remorseful?

She sighed as the guard opened another door for her. Maybe she should have waited another few days before seeing her aunt. Phina wanted to do this and get it done so she could move on. Maybe with some semblance of closure, though she wasn't counting on it.

After stepping through the door, Phina paused at seeing her aunt sitting on the other side of a table with her head down. She wore simple, plain clothing that she wouldn't have been caught dead in before, and while her hair was neatly combed, it wasn't styled or shaped.

Phina walked over to sit in the chair that had been placed there for her. Once she had settled in her seat, her aunt looked up with a resigned expression.

Faith did a surprise double-take at seeing her there. "Phina!"

She attempted to remain impassive. "Hello, Aunt Faith. Are you surprised to see me alive?"

Faith's brow furrowed in confusion, revealing deeper lines on her face that hadn't been there before. "What? Why would I be surprised about anything except that you are here? They wouldn't tell me what was going on, and they have refused all my requests to see you!"

Phina's eyebrows rose at the news that everyone had kept her aunt ignorant. She felt comforted knowing they were protecting her. "Yeah. Surprise. Being in a coma for a year and a half will do that."

Her aunt's eyes widened in disbelief. "A coma? For a year and a half?" She frowned. "What doctors were in charge that it took that long? And what have you gotten yourself into that you've been in a coma? Were you doing something dangerous?"

Phina clenched her jaw and slammed her hand on the table, which caused her aunt to jump. "Stop! Just...*stop*! I can't believe you are acting like nothing is wrong and things are the same as they've always been!"

She leaned toward her aunt, who felt more like a stranger, both hurt and anger rising. "Did you or did you not give me a serum with altered nanocytes?"

Faith looked like she didn't know how to take Phina's outburst, whether to be confused or offended or upset. "Well, yes. I told them this months ago when they brought me here. Haven't they told you anything?"

Phina's shoulders sagged as the emotion drained out of her, leaving her feeling weary and sad. She shook her head. "Of course they did. I wanted to hear it from your mouth. What I need to know is why. They said you would only tell me about it, though I'm sure the Empress knows anyway."

"The Empress is why!" Faith burst out. "She's got super-advanced nanocytes that we aren't allowed to work with, but I know about them. There's no way she got the abilities she has from the nanocytes they gave us. It doesn't work that way. I tried every test I could think of, and those nanocytes aren't the same."

Phina frowned and shook her head in confusion. "What does the Empress have to do with giving me nanocytes?"

Faith leaned forward, her eyes not quite focusing as she waved her hands in the air. "Because she can do all those things to protect herself, and she's survived things no one else could! Have you seen the history of everything that happened on Earth? That happened since? Do you not understand that living here is dangerous? That following her to hell and back will get people killed? People like my brother and my Simon and your mom?"

Her eyes turned both angry and shattered. "Why shouldn't we have the same protection the Empress has? You weren't being careful with yourself, and I had to do something to make sure you would live! So, I adjusted the nanocytes to make you powerful like the Empress is, so you would be able to protect yourself and not die like our family. They were everything to me, and then they were gone! I couldn't stand it if I lost you too, Phina. I couldn't stand anything else!"

Phina closed her eyes against her aunt's tear-stricken face and leaned her head in her hand, attempting to push through the swirling thoughts. She shook her head and wiped her hand down her face. She looked down at the table. "You wanting to protect me is interesting because I haven't felt protected by you for a long time now. In fact, I felt like I had to protect myself, and I was doing that just fine before you stuck your serum in me."

Phina glanced at her aunt, who looked at her like she didn't understand. "What in heaven's name do you mean by that?"

Phina sighed and stood up, pushing the chair in like her aunt had taught her to do. She crossed her arms and stared at Faith, who looked at her anxiously between darting glances at the door.

She didn't want to, but Phina felt like she needed to

know if her aunt was telling the truth. She cautiously and reluctantly opened her shields.

She immediately knew the guard's thoughts, which alternated between pity and lasciviousness; the thoughts of the guards, administrators, and prisoners in the surrounding area. Her senses extended beyond that and she pulled them in, using her will and determination to focus on her aunt.

Moments later, she slammed the shields shut, her breathing quickening with the effort to shut out the overwhelming amount of information. She shook her head, her lips pressed tight in her effort to refrain from saying anything she would regret as she processed it all.

Finally, Phina quietly responded. "I mean that I would have died from the serum you used. I was in a coma because you messed up the coding. The nanocytes you gave me were faulty and my body couldn't cope with the changes you decided I should have, and it shut down. You wanted me to be able to protect myself and live? Congratulations. I will. But it wasn't because of your actions. It was Bethany Anne and my friends, even Maxim, who you dislike so much, who did everything they could to save me from the situation you put me in."

Faith's eyes widened in shock as she sputtered. "But...but...I.."

Phina lifted her hand as she swallowed the emotion that was beginning to surge again. "I don't need you to respond. Thank you for taking care of me when I was younger and the times you actually tried when I was older. I don't expect to see you again and wanted to make sure you knew that."

She turned and walked to the door. The guard standing next to it looked like he had decided pity won out.

"Phina!" her aunt burst out in anger. Her tone turned to a plea when she kept walking. "I did it for you, Phina! I did it for you!"

Phina stopped in the doorway and turned to look at her aunt, who was broken inside mentally and slowly dying physically. She had taken an earlier serum that was less powerful so the burnout rate was slower and could still be months away, but that didn't change that without intervention, Aunt Faith would soon be gone.

Phina shook her head, "No. I know you believe that, Aunt Faith, but you're wrong. You did it for *you*."

She continued out, absently nodding to the guards when she passed by. Her thoughts turned to the people who had acted on her behalf because they were afraid she would die. She realized that there was a fundamental difference in her friends and chosen family's response as opposed to Aunt Faith.

Her friends shared their concerns with her and tried to convince and even control her to a degree, such as Link had before her coma. However, in the end, they accepted Phina's choices even when it was difficult. Link had admitted that he had been wrong.

Her aunt had taken the decision away from Phina by giving her the serum without involving her in the process. Aunt Faith had not admitted she had been wrong, a behavior that had always driven Phina crazy in the past. It still bothered her, but she realized that the hold her aunt had on her was greatly lessened. She didn't feel hung up.

Hmm... Maturity due to age, though she didn't

remember the last couple of years? Or was it due to the processing she had done the last couple of days?

Shaking her head, Phina pulled out her tablet and tapped out a message.

A— I wanted to tell you that I'm always in your corner and love that you guys are getting married. Seriously. You two are so great together. Let me know anything I need to do as your maid of honor. — P

QBBS *Meredith Reynolds*, Diplomatic Institute, Anna Elizabeth's Office

"Welcome back, Phina!"

Phina blinked, her eyes growing misty at seeing the same elegant and warm smile from Anna Elizabeth that she had remembered from before her coma. Since she had awakened, she had been astounded to realize how much things had changed, both in the lives of her friends and on the station. Seeing things that remained the same gave her reassurance and comfort. Especially after the visit with her aunt.

Anna glided across the room with her hands outstretched and a glowing smile. She clasped Phina's hands then pulled her into a hug before pulling back, her eyes bright. "I'm so happy to see you out of that awful coma. We all rushed to see you when we heard you were coming out of it and were surprised to see you leaving so quickly. How are you doing, Phina? Are you well?"

Phina found holding Anna's gaze difficult. She hesitated

and let her gaze drift, her eyes catching on the other occupant of the room who smiled in welcome. Returning Jace's smile, Phina nodded, then looked at her boss and teacher. "I'm doing well enough. It still feels unreal. I keep expecting things to be the same, and when they aren't, it's a jolt."

Anna nodded in understanding, her expression compassionate and reassuring. "It's all right, Phina. Shocks take time to work through. Braeden and Sis'tael, as well as Drk-vaen and Ryan, will be back within the next two weeks so you will see them soon." She gently squeezed Phina's hand one more time, then withdrew to walk around her desk. She sat down, steepling her fingers. "Now, what are your thoughts and plans for the future? Do you still want to continue through the program here?"

Alarm shot through her, though she did her best to suppress it. "Is… Is that okay? Was I kicked out of the Institute?" A thought drifted through her mind and she quietly ventured, "Did Greyson take someone else to mentor?"

Surprise drifted across Anna's face. "As far as I know, Greyson still considers you his trainee. Didn't you speak to him about this ?"

Phina shifted her weight uneasily, her favorite boots reassuring her even though they were only footwear. Anything familiar was a comfort. "I haven't spoken to him since shortly after I woke up."

Shock caused Anna's eyes to widen as her lips moved soundlessly. After a moment, she recovered with a small frown of concern. "I'm surprised to hear that. Greyson was quite distraught about your condition. He requested to take fewer duties so he would be available for you when you came around."

Phina's eyebrows drew in with confusion. Link had asked for fewer duties so he could be there when she came out of the coma, yet the first thing he did was to accuse her of lying and not believe her? Something didn't add up. She was speculating on the possibilities when she realized someone was speaking to her.

"I'm sorry, could you say that again?"

Anna Elizabeth gave her a patient but admonishing look. "I am wondering if you are still interested in completing your studies."

Phina's thoughts scattered and came together several times. She finally realized that this was an opportunity to freely choose rather than be reactive to circumstances. She opened her mouth to respond, then hesitated. What *did* she want?

She thought about everything she had learned about being a diplomat and what she had learned about being a spy. She examined how she felt when she used her body to fight and when she used her brain to solve problems. Finally, she replayed her interactions with the Gleeks, the Baldere, and the Aurians, how she'd felt about learning more about them and their interactions while she was helping them with their respective issues.

Phina realized there could only be one choice. She lifted her head and nodded, her green eyes meeting Anna Elizabeth's kind but firm blue ones. "Yes. I would like to complete my studies."

Anna nodded briefly, looking pleased as she smiled. "Wonderful. Now, I do need to explain some changes we had to make a year ago. After resolving the issues with having a rogue diplomat, we realized the diplomats are too isolated. Your suggestion of the appreciation event for the Senior Diplomats proved inspired and greatly increased our diplomats' satisfaction in their job. Several people started families. Several others decided to retire to pursue a quieter lifestyle with their families, old and new. So, that part was a complete success."

She smiled warmly and Phina returned it, reassured about her contribution even if she hadn't been there to see it.

Anna Elizabeth continued, "In addition, one of the complaints we received after opening up lines of communication with everyone, again per your suggestion, was that I had too much power over determining when a student was able to graduate."

Anna's expression was sour, although she didn't appear too troubled about it. Perhaps time had lessened the aggravation. "To minimize this issue, all students now need to have each teacher's approval to pass their class. Do you understand what that means?"

Phina frowned and shifted her weight. "It means that although I know the material given out for each class, I still need to attend each class or get the teacher to sign off on their area?"

Anna Elizabeth nodded, her hands clasped together on the desk. "Yes, that's exactly what it means. It will be up to you to prove your knowledge to each teacher, whether that be attending class or testing out. Once I receive approval from them, you can graduate from the program."

Phina sighed and nodded. She could already feel the

boredom of learning nothing new while she strove to prove herself to her teachers. "If that's what I need to do."

Anna Elizabeth smiled as she leaned forward. "Cheer up, Phina. It won't be as bad as you think. In the meantime, there is always something new to learn. You taught me that before rather effectively."

Phina nodded, then gestured at the door questioningly. Anna tilted her head curiously and looked at Phina for a moment before holding her hand out toward the door. "Of course. You should have your schedule now. It will be adjusted when you pass a class. Do you have any questions before you go?"

"Not at the moment, no."

Anna turned to the silent observer. "Jace, if you want to take some time with Phina, go right ahead. You've been working hard. I'll be fine for a couple of hours." She smiled gently and waved her fingers toward Phina and the door.

Jace had matured in the last year and a half. His eyes were more serious than playful now, his hair no longer flopped and spiked but lay neatly on his head, his jaw had squared out more, and his clothing showed more masculine elegance than she remembered. He was a good-looking man, but one she had difficulty reconciling with the almost-friend she remembered.

He nodded solemnly before standing and following Phina to the door. Phina hesitated and looked at Anna Elizabeth, realizing then that her hair no longer had gray streaks and that her wrinkles weren't as pronounced as they had been before her coma. She looked to be in her early thirties instead of her early fifties. Slumping in disappointment, Phina turned to walk out.

Apparently, everyone and everything was different now, even if some of those things were for the better.

———

Jace followed Phina out the door and tapped her on the shoulder before gesturing for her to follow him. He led her farther into the Institute and into a small room with a desk and a couple of chairs. On the desk lay his tablet and a few other things scattered on the top.

As soon as she stepped in behind him, Jace closed the door then wrapped Phina in his arms, hugging her tightly. "Phina! You don't know how happy I am to see you."

"I'm getting an inkling." Phina's voice was muffled as her face was pressed against his chest. "I know I've been gone a while, but I don't remember us being the hugging kind of friends."

"Oh, right." Jace released Phina and took a step back, feeling relieved and nervous. Phina also took a step back and looked at him warily, almost as she had when they first met. Jace sighed and ran a hand through his hair, feeling deflated. At thirty years old, he didn't think he should feel nervous about talking to a woman a decade younger, but he couldn't help it. "I know we got off to a rocky start before, but weren't we becoming friends when everything happened?" He waved his hand, flashing her a wounded smile.

Phina considered Jace for a moment before smiling more easily. "Well, it's good to know that something is the same." Her smile drooped as she shook her head. "So much has changed in a year and a half."

He tilted his head as he dropped his hand. "You've changed too, Phina. You look great but still different."

She froze, her eyes watching him with something akin to dread or horror. Jace turned to lean against his desk and crossed his ankles. He put his hands down on the edge of the desk and leaned forward. He shook his head as he watched her with concern. Well, he considered her a friend even if she didn't feel the same. "You didn't know that you've changed?"

Phina swallowed, looking younger for a moment, her more confident and challenging behavior gone. "Jace, you know I'm not interested in you, right? At least, not as anything more than friends."

Jace grinned and straightened. "So, that's what you are worried about? I know that, Phina. I've been dating someone for almost six months, and it's pretty serious. I wasn't trying to make a move on you, just pointing out how much you've changed and how great you look now."

Relief mixed with confusion warred on her face in subtle ways. "Like, healthy? I knew I had changed in other ways, but I didn't realize I had changed so much physically."

Jace chuckled. "So in the week since you woke up, you haven't looked in a mirror yet?"

She shrugged as she turned to lean against the wall in front of him, regaining her normal attitude and lack of emotion. "I don't look in a mirror every day. Or at all, if I can avoid it."

Jace's mouth dropped open, and his eyes widened. He searched for words before finally closing his mouth and swallowing. "Wow, you really don't know how beautiful you are, do you? I thought that was you…I don't know, being humble or something."

Phina appeared puzzled. "Thank you, Jace, but you don't have to flatter me. Alina and Bethany Anne and Anna Elizabeth are beautiful. I'm just me."

Jace laughed humorlessly before rubbing his face. "Yeah. Okay. Well, you're beautiful, but you've been beautiful. That's not how you've changed. You're more…" He frowned as he waved his hand. "More…muscular? No. Well, yeah, but it's more than that."

She raised her eyebrows skeptically. He looked at her closely from where he sat, finally nodding. "It's like you were distilled down or something. You're more beautiful. More muscular, and it shows. More…vibrant, maybe?" He shrugged. "Who you are is more visible, I think."

Phina blinked, appearing stunned. He smiled reassuringly. "Hey, it's a good thing."

She gave him a pointed look. "Except for when part of your job is to spy on people and be invisible."

Jace stopped for a second, then nodded. "Right. Yeah."

He sighed. Jace was smart, at the top of his class all his life, and he still felt like an idiot sometimes with Phina. He didn't know if it was that she was that much smarter than he was or that she off-balanced him that much. Probably both. He looked up to take her in again. Yeah, both.

"So… You haven't talked to Greyson since you woke up?"

Phina's eyes rose to meet his, giving him nothing, the emotion gone. "No. You have a problem?"

Jace shook his head slowly before letting out his breath. Dang, this woman could do scary better than anyone but the Empress and her Bitches. Her eyes cut right into him. "No. But *you* might."

She tensed, but her arms remained by her sides. She watched him for a moment before responding. "I'm not sure what you mean."

He winced, then nodded. "It's not easy for me to talk about so, bear with me, please."

Phina frowned, tilting her head forward. "Jace, why would something between Greyson and me be difficult for you to talk about?"

"Because I'm not talking about you and Greyson. I'm talking about me and Greyson." He glanced away for a moment before meeting her eyes again. She still appeared confused, so he clarified.

"He's my guardian."

Phina's eyes widened as her mouth dropped open. She couldn't have concealed her response if her life depended on it. Link was Jace's guardian? Images of the past when Jace had looked to Link for approval but never seemed to get it suddenly made sense.

For some reason, Phina thought she should have known something like that, but when it came down to it, she didn't know much about Link's background. She thought she was the only one he had given the name Link to, which she suspected was real. However, it seemed more like a nickname than his whole name, and he had never mentioned his last name.

Of course, when you live with a name like Greyson

Wells, it becomes your own. He had lived with that arrogant, demanding persona for so long that it pretty much became who he was…a good bit of the time, anyway.

Phina's mouth finally closed with a click, halting her rambling thoughts. Jace had been watching her with wary dark eyes. His half Earth Asian looks made his appearance tilt on the pretty side, though still masculine.

"What's the look for?" she asked.

"Why?" He watched her for a moment before answering the question she was really asking. "My parents worked for him before they died. After they were gone, there wasn't anyone else to take care of me, and he felt he had a responsibility to do something about it."

She frowned. "Was he a good guardian? You two hardly talk."

Jace shrugged, hunching his shoulders. "Yes and no. He made sure I had everything I needed, but he was working so much that I didn't see him very often. Maybe twice a week. Sometimes longer, and sometimes it would be a week or more in between."

Phina's eyes widened. "How could he get away with that? Leaving a child alone that much would be awful."

He blinked in surprise before he understood what she meant. "Oh! No, I was sixteen when they died, so I was pretty self-sufficient."

Her shoulders dropped in relief. "Well, that's better than younger, but it still sounds lonely."

"Yes." Jace nodded and seemed to pull himself in. "I was mostly used to it. My parents had been gone a lot before then anyway. They didn't have any family here. They paid for babysitters and nannies and such to take care of me for a while when they were going to be gone."

She watched him as she assimilated it then nodded. "So, why would Greyson being your guardian cause me trouble?"

Jace sighed. "Because I think he feels like he let me down, and now that you've had problems, I think he's feeling like he let you down, too. So, all of that together could cause him to have problems in your interactions. He doesn't handle his reaction to strong emotions very well."

Phina's head whirled. No wonder Link had reacted so strongly when he thought she would die on the Aurians' planet.

"What are you thinking, Phina?"

She shook her head. "That I should have seen something like this coming. That I grew up much the same as you, except my aunt watched me. Also that I should have overruled my scruples and read both of your files."

Jace grinned then raised his eyebrows. "You mean you didn't read our files? Hang on. You have scruples about hacking?"

Phina gave him a flat look. "Of course I do. Everyone has lines about what they find morally or ethically objectionable. One of mine is that I don't hack my friend's files unless it's an emergency."

He nudged her foot with his as his grin widened. "I knew you were warming up to me and we were friends."

She sighed. "Yeah, yeah. Don't make me regret it, Mister Mouth."

"Mister Mouth, huh?"

"Would you prefer Mouth Boy?"

"Err, I guess Mister Mouth, then. How did I deserve this charming epithet?"

Phina raised her eyebrows. "Because you think by running your mouth, of course."

His laughter was the best thing Phina had heard in days.

CHAPTER SEVEN

QBBS *Meredith Reynolds*, Diplomatic Institute

Four days later, Phina was wondering if she should have said no to resuming her studies. Here she was in class again, learning the same things she had learned two years ago. These students were all new. The classmates she had been familiar with were gone, most of them into their apprenticeships, the rest dropping or failing out.

She sighed and leaned on her elbows, trying to pay attention in her Current Events class, but what had interested her before had descended to boring since she had learned it all already. Only references to the last year and a half perked her interest.

She had been able to get signatures for two of her classes so far, Languages and Ethics. Languages were easy for Phina. She had a fifteen to twenty-minute conversation in each language to demonstrate her fluency with the teacher who facilitated the class. If it was possible to over-pass the class, then Phina did since she was fluent in five languages and passable in the three others she had started learning before her coma. Having to exhaust herself before sleeping had led to her learning several new languages and subjects. Ethics had been passed after a three-hour conversation with her Ethics teacher, Mister Prez, who had some interesting thoughts on the ethics of mind-reading that Phina was still mulling over. She had used the rumors surrounding Bethany Anne as her example for the question.

Phina's eyes drooped and she yawned, sagging in her seat. Ever since she had woken up from the coma, being unable to sleep hadn't been a problem. If anything, Phina felt fatigued often. Her mind drifting, she realized she was aware of the minds of the students around her. They each felt different and as she sleepily focused on what she was picking up, Phina realized that she could identify each mind by the feel of it. Curiously, she wasn't overwhelmed like she had been when scanning her Aunt Faith. She frowned as she focused on the difference. She glanced around the room at each person her mind had touched before looking curiously at the teacher.

She had kept her mental senses mostly clamped shut since she woke up from the coma because she didn't want to intrude on people's privacy, and she hadn't yet figured out her code for when it was okay. Her conversation with Mr. Prez had helped, but she was still working through the issue.

However, what intrigued Phina was the realization that she could hear her teacher's real thoughts and knowledge about what had happened, not just the socially acceptable ones he filtered through his words.

"The Gleek Accord has been an asset to the Empire

over the past year. Who can tell me what benefits we have gained from our alliance with them?" *And what a narrow thing that was. I still can't believe how close they came to declaring war on us. Hmm... That Waters girl supposedly helped make it possible, but I'm not sure how much I believe that. Anna Elizabeth is being so closed-mouthed about it.* "Yes, Liane?"

As she listened to the new student proudly describe the knowledge and nature-based technological advantages the Empire had gained, Phina stared at her teacher. The short man occasionally glanced at her. His dark hair thinned at the top in a circle, giving him the appearance of a reverse Jewish yarmulka. Professor Emerson had come on board recently, formerly a diplomat in the field. So far, Phina did not feel impressed.

However, from what she sensed mentally, he had a strange fixation on her role in what had happened with the Gleeks. Phina frowned at her discovery since she hadn't wanted to use her mind-reading abilities. She didn't want to know what people were thinking and feeling. It was frustrating enough trying to navigate her own life, let alone witness everyone else's lives up front and personal.

Yet... If she could figure out a way to do it that didn't feel intrusive to her, it would be an undeniable advantage.

She tentatively reached out mentally to her teacher and listened to his surface thoughts rather than going deeper. It was more akin to hearing what his mind shouted and didn't take much effort on her part.

Ah, this student shows promise... So eager to learn... If all students showed such eagerness, it would make teaching less tedious. "Yes, thank you, Liane. Anyone else?" *Shame that the*

Waters girl seems so dull... I heard she was bright, but I don't see anything to indicate that's true.

Ugh. Perhaps she didn't want to do this after all. She rubbed her hand over her face before realizing that she didn't feel as tired as she had earlier. Strangely, the sleepiness had all but disappeared. That realization caused her to miss the next few moments.

"Would that be correct, Seraphina?"

Phina's eyes jerked up to meet her teacher's face. She saw a gleam of satisfaction in his dark eyes. Hmm...

Just as I thought. She wasn't paying attention. I bet she doesn't even know what turned the Gleeks' minds from war to working with us. Genius protégé, my ass. She seems like a stupid bint.

Irritation at the man's attitude welled up, and an edgy smile formed on her face. Clamping a hold on her temper, she quickly and lightly scanned the minds around her until she found the statement he wanted her to confirm or deny. The result confused her. What could be the teacher's goal here? Though she loathed the idea, Phina felt dipping into the teacher's head was worth it to find the answer.

That answer infuriated her, causing the edge of her smile to turn harsh. Most of the students in front of her jerked in surprise or looked shocked. Alarms went off in her head as she felt her blood pressure rising in response to her anger. She closed her eyes briefly and calmed herself as the teacher sneered in response to her lack of an answer.

"Well, since Seraphina has no answers, perhaps someone else does."

Barely, Phina remembered that she needed this teacher's approval to pass her class. That didn't seem important at the moment. That passed as a blip of relevance. Only her natural mask and her training as a spy allowed her any shred of ability to hide her anger.

"Professor Emerson," she began with feigned sweetness, "I'm afraid I need further context for your question before I answer."

He frowned, his brown eyes looking like a beetle's as he eyed her with indifference and disdain. "We have been discussing context. What further context do you need to know to answer whether the Gleeks chose to go to war over insults?"

Phina allowed a tiny smile. The student in front of her, a young man about her age or a little younger, frowned from his turned position as he watched her in concern. "Well, Professor, this is not a yes or no question. It is a very complex one requiring various factors to be considered. However, two very basic requirements must be met for the Gleeks to consider stepping on the path leading to war, and yes, they are insults of a kind."

"Oh?" He leaned forward eagerly with a greedy expression on his face. "Enlighten me as to what those requirements would be."

"The murder of one of their own, combined with intense disrespect to their people as a whole. Which was the case in the events being examined." His surprised expression would have given his thoughts away even if she hadn't had a way to see his mind. He hadn't expected her to know anything, believing her answer to be evasiveness, and had asked the question to trip her up.

She kept a tight lid on her emotions. "I believe you are imagining the Gleeks to have a vendetta like a criminal mob or the warriors of the religious crusades that occurred on Earth. That is not the case here."

His face turned blank, but she had been monitoring his mind and knew that her words were accurate.

"In reality, the Gleeks are a mostly peaceful race, concerned more about knowledge and furthering their own goals than warring with other species. Think of them as a mix of Earth's Tibetan monks and Japanese ninjas. They seek peace but have a deep sense of honor and justice. When someone acts against them in such a manner as I described, they will retaliate in kind."

Professor Emerson's face twitched in displeasure. She could feel it radiating from him.

"How is it you know this, Seraphina? Have you been poking in places you shouldn't?"

Her monitor on his mind told her he had heard rumors about her forays into reading textbooks before they were assigned. Ah, one of his good friends was a teacher she'd had issues with her first year. Phina merely smiled while keeping her expression as bland as possible. A chuckle from the young man in front of her drew both Phina's and the professor's attention.

"What is so amusing, William?" the professor demanded.

"You, Professor Emerson." The young man grinned. "You don't seem to realize who she is."

"I fail to see why one student is more important than another."

Phina's mouth twitched. If it hadn't been said with such disdain and condescension, the statement would have redeemed him somewhat. Sadly, she could see he only used the question as an excuse to try to put her down. Still, she turned to look at William, wondering what it was he seemed to know about her. Having strangers aware of her felt disconcerting.

The young man coughed—to cover a laugh from the sound of it. The professor's beady eyes narrowed. Speaking quickly, William explained, "She's one of the authors of the text we were assigned to read for class, *History and Sociology of Gleek Culture.*"

Their professor raised his bushy eyebrows. The other students murmured in the background while they checked their tablets to see if he was correct. Phina carefully smothered her surprise. After Link had dropped the bomb on the way to the Aurian planet that she would die faster the more she moved, Braeden had distracted her with documenting the history and culture of his people for the Empire between meditation sessions. Heavily edited documenting, of course. Some things, the general population of the Empire didn't need to know. A separate document had been prepared for Bethany Anne containing more information for her eyes only. They hadn't quite finished by the time the team had reached the planet, but someone must have completed it during her coma.

Professor Emerson gave William a scalding glance. "That document was written by the Gleek representative."

"Yes," William agreed. "Representative Braeden wrote it, but Seraphina Waters is listed as the co-author."

If she hadn't been expecting it, she would have flinched at the force of the professor's glare.

"I'm sorry you got roped into this with me."

Will shrugged at the quiet words of the young woman walking down the corridor next to him as they followed the professor. She stood a few inches shorter than he did so he didn't have to bend down to hear. In contrast to his slacks and buttoned shirt, Phina wore a t-shirt and dark pants. Her face appeared impassive, with only the slight tightening of her jaw and regretful look in her eye showing any hint of emotion.

His mother had always told him that secrets bound a person up and weighed on their soul. If Will was any judge, Phina had many secrets weighing on her soul.

He grinned as he shook his head and whispered to her, "Don't be. I knew what I was doing and relished every second of it."

Phina turned her head with a look of surprise that she quickly suppressed. "You planned that confrontation?"

Will pursed his lips before shaking his head. "Planning implies intention. No, I didn't plan it, but I knew what I was walking into with my eyes wide open. When I saw you come into class the other day, I knew right away we would be good friends. So far looks like I was right." He winked playfully.

She blinked in surprise before nodding, and that was all the conversation they had time for as they stopped behind a glowering Professor Emerson. He knocked on the dean's office door after giving them a look of pure spite.

The door opened, although no one stood behind it. Will suspected Meredith. As the three of them filed in, Will took a gander at the office area, noting its fairly large size and the desk where the dean sat looking like butter wouldn't melt in her mouth as she watched them step forward.

After an assessing glance, in which he felt certain she saw more than Will wanted her to, the dean turned her cool stare on the professor. "What was so urgent that you interrupted your class to bring you three here, Walt?"

Though her tone sounded stiffly sweet, her words made it clear she had not been pleased with the professor's decision. Will struggled not to grin. Perhaps he wouldn't get in trouble after all, which would be a handy thing.

Professor Emerson put his hands behind his back before he began speaking in a pompous tone. "Dean Hauser, surely you know the nature of the students you have allowed into the Institute. This girl has already been in trouble before about a conflict with a teacher. She is a troublemaker. That this boy worked with her to make me look foolish should be a mark against him as well."

The dean sat calmly at her desk, watching the man twist events to suit his agenda. Great. Did she believe this guy? Will almost spoke up, but a flicker in her eye made him hesitate and then decide to wait and see what happened.

When the professor finished, the dean raised an eyebrow delicately. "Yes? Anything else you have on your mind while you attempt to do my job for me?"

The professor drew himself up before his tone turned frosty. "I have no idea what you mean. I am merely attempting to convey a problem that needs to be resolved."

Dean Hauser nodded in understanding. Will got the sense she was struggling not to give him a verbal lashing. He hid his grin at the thought that the dean didn't like the professor any more than Will did.

"Of course. I will handle it from here. You may return to your classroom." Her tone dripped dismissal, as did her casual hand wave.

Professor Emerson's face turned red as he sputtered, then nodded and turned toward the door after giving the two of them one last poisonous glare. Will felt himself relax in relief once the door had shut behind the other man.

The dean watched him leave and nodded in satisfaction before turning to the two of them with a more expressive gaze of expectation.

"So, what actually happened?" She glanced between the two of them before looking at Phina with raised eyebrows. Phina explained the confrontation in the classroom while Will watched the women with considering eyes. Phina seemed to know the dean far better than most students would. Even for someone who was back in class after being gone for a while.

He had heard rumors floating around about Phina before the information had been posted that she would join classes several days ago. Since then, the stories had stepped up.

Speculation had run rampant as to what she had been doing for the last year and a half, from secret missions to running away, a disagreement with Anna Elizabeth, breaking off her internship with Greyson Wells and leaving to become a dancer, to a whirlwind marriage that she had since come to her senses about and sent the bastard packing. Will didn't know what the real story was, but he felt dead certain it wasn't the last one. She was too levelheaded to marry on a whim. A secret mission seemed much more likely considering the secrets he had sensed earlier.

Will looked up and realized the dean had been looking at him speculatively. He tilted his head as he watched her in return. The dean gave Phina a pointed look. He felt a slight pressure on his mind and a sense of warmth. What the hell? He eyed the unfocused glaze in Phina's eyes, wondering if that sensation had come from something she had done.

Her gaze slowly refocused, and she gave him a searching look before turning to the dean and nodding. "He's okay."

The dean's face showed shock. Whatever Phina had just done was new to her, too. Interesting. Will mentally rubbed his hands together with glee.

Oh, yes. He and Phina would be great friends.

CHAPTER EIGHT

QBBS *Meredith Reynolds*, Diplomatic Institute, Anna Elizabeth's Office

Phina watched Anna Elizabeth's face drop in shock as she realized that Phina had read William's mind. She didn't think it would have been that shocking, given that Phina had been feeling people's intentions before she had her coma, but perhaps Anna Elizabeth had forgotten about that.

William's eyes flicked between the two of them, a mixture of nervous excitement emanating from him. Phina relaxed in her chair, working to convey that things were normal. Nope, nothing to see here. Everything is fine.

Finally, Anna collected her thoughts and continued, filling Phina with relief. "So, to sum up, Walt believes that Phina is an attention seeker and a disruptive influence." She assessed William with curious eyes and raised eyebrows. "William Wallace Turner Sawyer Jameson. He believes you are..."

William grinned, shrugging unapologetically about his behavior. "Likely the same, just with a different cause."

Anna Elizabeth nodded, looking like she had bitten into something sour for a moment, before taking a deep breath and sighing. "And here I thought things had been exciting and stressful before. I had no idea." She shook her head ruefully. "You would think my staff are prideful, egotistical, elitist agitators the way you seem to find them, Phina. I promise not all of them are bad apples."

ADAM broke in from the speakers in the room, "Phina is a catalyst."

Anna Elizabeth looked up with a surprised and considering expression. "ADAM? Could you explain what you mean?"

Phina heard Will whisper excitedly. "That's ADAM? So cool!"

"A catalyst is someone or thing that precipitates change or causes a reaction by their presence without being affected themselves," ADAM explained. "I have been analyzing her interactions, and I believe that Phina is a natural catalyst. Just by being present or interacting as normal, she will bring out conditions or qualities that may not have been apparent in people before."

Will looked intrigued by that, while Anna Elizabeth appeared thoughtful. Phina felt uneasy and concerned. What exactly did that mean to be a catalyst beyond the definition? Should she be less active in things? More? Something to discuss with ADAM later.

Anna Elizabeth thanked ADAM before turning her attention to Phina. "Tell me."

Phina nodded, knowing the dean was asking what she

had sensed wrong about the teacher. "He purposely pushed me about what I knew. He had heard rumors about me and disbelieved them, thinking they were fictitious." She glanced between the dean and her classmate. "I don't know what everyone is saying, but what I've heard is nuts." Phina shook her head. "Who in their right mind believes that stuff?"

At the dean's look of amusement and William's grin, Phina shrugged and continued, "However, what concerns me is the reason why he wanted to show me up."

Anna Elizabeth focused on her, her amusement gone. "What do you mean?"

Phina clarified, "He wanted to discredit the Gleeks and show them to be warmongering troublemaking delinquents." When Anna Elizabeth raised an eyebrow, Phina shrugged. "His words."

Anna sat back with a frown, her arms dropping from her desk to rest on the arms of her chair. "I see."

As Anna Elizabeth contemplated, Phina eyed William, wondering what his thoughts were about this. Did he know she had read his mind to determine his trustworthiness or that it was why she had spoken in front of him so candidly? Or that her abilities were how she knew this information about the professor? William peered at her with a knowing assurance in his blue eyes.

Hmm. Maybe he didn't realize. She would have thought if he knew then he would be looking at her with wariness, perhaps anger or disgust.

When Anna Elizabeth leaned forward again, Phina jerked her attention to the dean. "All right. Thank you for bringing this to my attention. I will handle Walt. In the meantime, while I don't believe what either of you did warrants disciplinary action, I can't help taking advantage of the opportunity you both present." She looked at them both searchingly before nodding. "Yes, I believe you will do very well."

"With what, Dean Hauser?" William leaned forward and placed his arms on her desk briefly before she gave him a scathing look. He quickly removed them.

"With a diplomatic situation that needs resolving." Anna Elizabeth waved a hand vaguely in the direction of the upper deck before continuing. Phina thought through the station schematics and realized that would be the direction of the receiving halls where many of the diplomatic issues were ironed out. "Greyson is in charge of resolving this matter. I wasn't sure if he would need assistance, but I think it would be beneficial for both of you to participate in the situation."

Phina felt surprised, pleased, and concerned. She'd hoped Anna Elizabeth would still trust her, but she hadn't felt certain of it since she didn't trust herself. Thinking about Greyson, or Link, being in charge gave her cause for concern. If he didn't believe her, then perhaps he didn't trust her anymore. She didn't know how well she could work with him knowing that. She stuffed the sadness that thought caused down the internal well where she stuffed the rest of her emotions.

William nodded and gave the dean a grin. "Of course. Whatever I can do to help and learn."

Anna Elizabeth eyed him thoughtfully. "Thank you, William. I will keep that in mind."

"Just Will. William is my great uncle," he quipped with a smile.

Anna Elizabeth returned the smile and nodded. "Of course. You will need to arrange a time to meet Greyson to get caught up on everything involved with the Qendrok situation. It should be soon, so don't wait."

They both agreed, and Anna Elizabeth gave them a nod of dismissal. After filing out, the two students realized they only had a few minutes until class ended for the day. Phina pulled out her tablet to send a message to Link, letting him know they had been assigned to help him and asking where to meet him for a briefing.

As she tapped out her message, Will watched her fingers fly over her tablet with interest. "So, is it true that you're a hacker?"

Phina glanced up in surprise before looking down at her task. Not knowing whether he approved or not, she kept silent, wondering if he would say more. Sure enough, he obliged her.

"I'm curious. It seemed both fitting and random if it was true." He sounded sheepish yet intrigued. She found herself unwilling to shut him down as she had done to Jace two years ago. Look how that interaction had ended up, anyway. Better to get ahead of the curve.

"Perhaps once we know each other better, I will share what I can do and what I cannot." She tempered her answer, wondering if Will would ever be someone she could confide in. She completed her task and opened up another app.

Phina felt a small sense of relief when he nodded. "Fair

enough." He grinned. "I know you and I will be great friends."

Although warmed by his assertion, for some reason she felt compelled to ask, "Oh? How do you know?"

He watched her finish and grinned when she looked up, wondering why he hadn't continued. "Have you ever met someone or gone somewhere and had a sense of importance? That the place or person would become someone close or valuable or priceless? Just a sense of knowing?"

Phina frowned and thought about it before shaking her head. "I don't think so."

Will nodded, seeming to expect her answer. "Well, that's how I know. Mom says that Gran was a psychic, and that's where I get it from. It's possible. This sense hasn't been wrong yet."

Phina frowned, ready to dismiss the idea of psychics before remembering that she read minds. It would be hypocritical not to at least be open to the idea. As she came to this conclusion, a message came through from Link. However, Will distracted her by his next words.

"So, is it true that you ran naked down to the Open Courtyard one night?"

Shocked, Phina looked up and blurted, "What? I was *not* naked!"

He grinned and put his hands in his pockets. "Well, that's disappointing." When her eyes widened, he winked. "Don't worry, Seraphina Waters. That's not the kind of relationship we're gonna have."

Feeling bewildered and wondering how she had entered into an alternate dimension, Phina shook her head. "Let's go. Greyson is waiting for us."

He turned immediately for the exit and began walking. "All right. I hear destiny and a beautiful friendship calling."

Phina sighed as she followed him. "That's your stomach."

Will turned in a circle and grinned at her, pointing. "Yes! See.., *that's* the kind of relationship we're gonna have."

Phina couldn't help but think her life had taken a weird turn, but strangely she felt a whole lot better than she had this morning. Her tiredness and fatigue were gone.

QBBS *Meredith Reynolds*, Secret Bar

Will entered the room with his eyes wide. Holy hell in a handbasket, as his mom would say. What was a bar doing here, up a hidden staircase, behind a secret door, in an ordinary office complex? The mind boggled. He loved it.

He followed Phina past the half-full tables in the bar, and they entered the short corridor in the back. She knocked on the last door on the right before opening it. Though the corridor light was dim, the flash of the light inside the room illuminated Phina's face briefly as she entered. The flash of uncertainty on her face brought out his protective instincts. Will cautiously entered behind her.

The room inside was divided into three parts: A bar, a lounge, and a conference/dining table. All were done in high-end materials with a focus on comfort. In front of one of the chairs in the lounge stood a nondescript man in his fifties with sandy brown hair and brown eyes. His posture indicated the man was conflicted about something.

Noting the stiff way the man appeared to be avoiding Phina's gaze, all the while being aware of every small movement, it didn't take a genius to figure out that there was an issue between them. Will magnanimously decided he would be a buffer for them and stepped forward to introduce himself.

"Will Jameson." He stretched his hand out to the man who stared at Will's hand before finally stirring himself to accept the handshake.

The man's absent gaze was penetrating and searching. "Greyson Wells."

Will nodded, watching Greyson every bit as much as the older man watched him. Finally, Will grinned as he stepped back and took a seat next to Phina, who had taken the chair farthest from Greyson. He crossed his ankles and splayed his hands out.

"I've heard a lot about you, Mister Wells. How much of it is true?"

Greyson smiled as he sat in the chair across from him, his darkened eyes lightening. "I would venture to say most of it."

Will examined the man's mannerisms and found the similarities and contrasts between Greyson and Phina enlightening. "So, what brings us here?"

Greyson glanced at Phina, who studiously avoided his attention. If Will hadn't been watching him carefully, he would have missed the slight flinch before the man looked away and nodded as he turned his mind to business.

"Right. There's a species of alien called the Qendrok. They are green, four-armed humanoids. Have you ever heard of trolls in fantasy literature? That's the closest I can give you as to what they resemble, although their build is more slight than traditional depictions." He tilted his head in thought. "However, their second set of arms usually remain close to their body, and that gives them more of a bulky appearance, so I suppose it's an accurate enough portrayal."

Greyson cleared his throat, glancing at Phina again. "The Qendrok have a religious ruling authority who can be recognized by a red amulet with a seal they wear. A shadow arm of this group are assassins who wear an amulet with a black ring around this seal."

Will's attention was drawn to Phina, who had straightened and was giving Greyson her full attention. He wondered if Phina had run into this group at some point in the past. It seemed likely given both their responses. He listened as Greyson continued.

"A couple of years ago, the Empire helped them resolve an issue regarding some of their people impersonating members of their ruling authority. After some messages back and forth, they have indicated a desire to join the Empire or become allies. Our job is to meet with them and facilitate this discussion, including creating a treaty if one is needed. Any questions?"

Will nodded and leaned forward, his eyes intent on Greyson. "Two of them. First, what time is the meeting?"

Greyson nodded from where he had slouched, his fingers tapping together where his hands were steepled in front of him. "Tomorrow at two station standard time in the secondary receiving hall. And the second question?"

Will glanced between the other two people in the room, realizing they were too much alike not to need a push in the right direction. He hoped this move didn't kill his new friendship with Phina. He wasn't playing around when he said he knew they would be good friends. Will hoped that would be sooner rather than later as he had waited long enough.

"How long has Phina been able to read minds?"

"What?"

Will's question hit like a bombshell. Link half stood up from his chair, face pale and eyes a strange mix of anger, fear, and confusion. After an initial flinch, Phina sat as still as a statue.

Will looked at her apologetically. When she looked at him with puzzled eyes, he subtly tapped his head.

Oh. Phina reached out mentally just in time to hear Will's apology.

So sorry I threw you in the deep end. I thought he knew.

"What do you mean?" Link demanded. "What is he talking about, kid?"

Phina's eyes drifted to the unhappy spy. Link looked more flustered than she had ever seen him. His normally cool, calm, and collected exterior was replaced with a frazzled and anxious demeanor.

She had been avoiding his gaze since she walked in the room and wondered how much of what she was seeing was the result of Will's question and how much had been there to begin with.

"I'm gonna wait outside." Will's whispered words barely penetrated her thoughts as she stared at Link, wondering if he had been miserable like she was. She certainly didn't want to use her abilities to find out.

Thankfully, she had gained control since she woke up from her coma.

After the door snicked shut, Link turned from staring at her to pacing the room. He began waving his arms, his voice a mix of frustration and curiosity. "Do you want to explain?"

"No."

Link frowned at her answer. "Is what he said correct?"

"Yes."

His brow furrowed deeper as he continued to pace. "Is that why you ran away and have been ignoring me? Because you read something in my mind?"

"Yes, and no."

He stopped pacing and glowered at her. "Well? Is it yes, or is it no?"

Phina's gaze frosted over. "Yes, it was why I was upset. No, I haven't been ignoring you."

Link huffed and thrust his arms in the air. "Then why haven't you spoken to me since you woke up?"

She stared at him for a good long moment before raising her eyebrows. "Communication goes both ways. I haven't been ignoring you. I've been avoiding you. There is a difference. Ignoring implies you have tried to get in touch with me. That isn't the case."

He wrinkled his brow in disbelief. "*The hell I haven't*! I've sent you several messages. Once I messaged twice in a day."

Phina knew without checking that he wasn't lying. She looked down in confusion and pulled out her tablet. She brought her messages up and checked for any communication from him. Nope. Still nothing. She turned her tablet around and showed Link her inbox. His eyes reflected her confusion once he understood the messages were not there.

Link swallowed, looking uncomfortable, before asking, "And you haven't deleted any of them?"

She looked up, not understanding his tone until it hit her. The only ones who could have interfered with her messages in that way were Reynolds, Meredith, and.....ADAM. Her friends.

The ones who had listened to her muttering to herself in the time since she had woken up and run out of the medical room.

The ones who taught her everything she knew about hacking.

The ones who watched her every step and movement from waking to sleeping—and she wouldn't bet against the sleeping, either. They were the most dangerous beings in the Empire, except for the Empress.

Fudge in a bucket.

CHAPTER NINE

QBBS *Meredith Reynolds*, Secret Bar

"ADAM?" Phina whispered. "Was it you?"

"Yes." The AI spoke the word simply through the speakers within the room.

Phina shook her head with a frown. "Why did you do that, ADAM?"

"Because he hurt you, and you needed time to heal from that."

Floored that ADAM had taken it in his mind to protect her without asking, Phina felt conflicting emotions running through her. She didn't like that ADAM had taken it upon himself to make this decision without her, but she knew the AI well enough to know that he'd considered the people involved when making his calculations.

As she came to terms with her thoughts, Link began a blistering tirade.

"I hurt *her*? What did I ever do? I stayed by her side, talking to her half the time she was in her coma. I was there for *months*, waiting for her to wake up. But sure, yeah, *I* hurt her."

Phina shook her head, avoiding his gaze. She spoke over her implant to ADAM. *Thank you for protecting me, ADAM. If there is a next time, would you please ask me first?*

>>**Of course. Are you...upset with me?**<<

I was upset, but I was more surprised. You haven't intercepted any other messages, have you?

>>**No, but I did consider it. I didn't like how long you were in that coma. You looked like you needed time to deal with the changes without more emotional pressure.**<<

Phina felt warm inside her heart. *I appreciate your concern and protection. Thank you for being my friend, ADAM. I am sorry I worried you.*

>>**It was difficult waiting for you. Unknowns are uncomfortable, particularly related to my friends. I decided I didn't like them and want to avoid them as much as possible.**<<

You and every other control freak, my friend.

Phina realized silence had permeated the room. She turned curiously to see Link watching her with an unreadable expression on his face. Oops.

"Is it true?"

Can I read minds is what he really wants to know. Phina sighed, then nodded.

"And this has something to do with why you aren't looking at me or talking to me?"

Phina flinched and looked away. From his sigh, she felt certain he knew the answer. Link stepped forward and crouched in front of Phina's chair, waiting until she finally turned toward him.

His brown eyes were steady but had several emotions showing through. Curiosity, amazement, pride, and pain. He nodded and spoke quietly. "So, what did you read in my mind that hurt you?"

Phina took a deep breath and realized that if she didn't take this step now and speak the truth that something would break between them. Since the pain of that thought hurt more than talking about it, she answered just as quietly, "When I said I didn't know why I was in a coma for so long you didn't believe me."

Link took a deep breath and nodded. "I wondered why you had started acting funny after that. And later?"

Phina frowned at the man, her eyes narrowing. "You called me a coward."

Link sighed and sat back on his haunches. "Right." He rubbed his eyes with the heels of his hands then dropped them. His eyes blinked, then firmly focused on her. "Okay, let's clear the air about this. When you listen to people's thoughts, you are going to need to learn to not just dip in and out. When a person thinks one thing about something, that's usually not all they are thinking. Take a minute to consider your thoughts. Do you ever argue with yourself? Try to convince yourself about something? Are you ever uncertain about a thing that happened or what you want to do?"

Phina nodded as he continued while making hand gestures and running his fingers through his hair. The man was going to go bald. "This is what most other people do as well. So while you may hear one part of those thoughts, you won't hear all of them or their conclusions until you listen long enough to know it."

He stopped and looked at her more closely. "Does that make sense? You are correct that I didn't believe you." He held up his finger as she opened her mouth to respond. "At first. I didn't want to believe you didn't know because I wanted it to be a simple answer to a question I've waited months to ask you. Then what I know about you kicked in, and I concluded that it had to be true because you aren't in the habit of lying. Does that coincide with what you know of me, and do you believe me?"

Phina thought it over, then nodded. It made sense. Link often reacted before his thoughts caught up, at least when it came to relationships. "And the other one?"

He raised his eyebrows. "Calling you a coward?" She nodded and he sighed. "That was both an overreaction and a miscalculation. You were shutting down because you were overwhelmed. Hearing your aunt had irrevocably changed you was the last thing you needed to know when you were still coming to terms with being in a coma for so long. I could see it in your eyes, and I panicked and channeled my anger and frustration at the situation you were in."

Link shook his head. "It wasn't fair to you, but I hoped what I said would prod your anger and pride so that you would fight instead of shutting down from being overwhelmed. It worked." He shrugged and pushed himself up so that he stood looking down at her, quietly holding his hand out. "I'm sorry, Phina. Can you forgive me for speaking rashly?"

Phina looked up at Link, searching his face intently.

Finding what she was looking for, she grabbed his hand and pulled herself up with it, then wrapped her arms around him. "Missed you."

He wrapped his arms around her, leaning his head against hers. "Me too." His voice sounded gruff.

"Ready to do this meeting now?"

"Oh, good. This hugging thing is still weird for me."

Phina rolled her eyes and slapped his arm as she stepped back. "Come on, old man. Let's get to what you do best."

"Hey, there's no old men here!"

"Nope, but only because I'm not a man or old."

Link gave her a sour look, then shook his head and gestured at the door. "Get Billy the Kid in here so we can get moving on this."

Phina turned toward the door and smiled to herself. It always felt better when she and Link were getting along than when they were fighting.

QBBS *Meredith Reynolds*, Secondary Receiving Hall

"This is unacceptable!"

Xoruk stood in the posture of acceptance and devotion, with his four arms wrapped around himself and his head bowed. His red clothing wrap covered his hips and thighs, extending up over one shoulder to tuck into the back. Xoruk stood beside Jokin, who was clothed similarly. Both remained two steps behind their very visible leader, Qartan. Their red amulets were visible on each of their chests.

It was Qartan who blustered in Yollin to the delegates

of the Empire, vile language though he viewed it. Never mind that the Qendrok and the Yollins had once been valued allies and friends. No. Qartan would never admit that and go against the teachings he had been spouting for the past twenty-four years.

Xoruk surreptitiously angled his head to see behind him. Sure enough, the two guards, Gunit and Zudin, still stood there, the twitches on their faces showing they found the situation amusing.

Xoruk did not feel amused.

Carefully, Xoruk moved his head to see the delegation of the Empire in front of him. Three people were standing in front of Qartan, as well as another four standing guard near the entrances of the room. Those four seemed to be typical of the soldiers the Empire employed; one two-legged Yollin, one more big, burly human, and two smaller but still capable-looking humans.

The three who made up the delegation of the Empire were human; one elder male, one young male, and one young female. At a glance, the presence of the young female proved to be the source of Qartan's current tirade.

Not because she was female, though Qartan would like that fact little enough. Not because she was young, though Qartan would like that little better. No. The tirade stemmed from one reason. The female glowed with power, and Qartan hated anyone more powerful than he was. Not that he would admit to that being the reason for his anger. The Qendrok didn't advertise their ability to see masses of energy as it gave them a small advantage.

Personally, Xoruk merely felt relief that the young female had been present and not the Empress herself.

Seeing how this young female glowed, and if the stories were true, Xoruk felt certain that the Empress would blaze with power. Qartan could get away with insulting this female, though it may cause an issue between the Qendrok and the Empire. Xoruk felt certain that insulting the Empress would have been deadly.

Xoruk would like to live, thank you very much.

Qartan's life? Well, that was optional, in Xoruk's opinion. Life would be very much easier without the insufferable male mucking things up. Of course, Qartan was so consumed with his power grasping that he might not remember that as part of the Empire's delegation, insulting the young woman meant he insulted the Empress. If only Xoruk could be so lucky.

"I will not stand for a female barely out of childhood to be a driving part of this treaty!"

The older male's face turned cold and unreadable, his tone short. "Then you will sit for it because Delegate Waters is staying."

A grimace crossed the young woman's face as she leaned closer to the older male and whispered. The younger male leaned closer as well and looked like he wanted to object but remained silent. The older man shook his head, but the female looked determined. Finally, she turned to the Qendrok contingent and stepped forward, her eyes intent.

"If I prove to your whole delegation my qualifications and ability to give value to the discussions, will you withdraw your objection?"

Qartan's smile bore malice. Xoruk could hear it in his voice. "No."

The female merely nodded as if expecting the response. However, she did not seem discouraged or affronted. Xoruk found himself staring at the strong, pulsating glow of power around her that seemed to condense around her head.

He had never seen such a display when viewing power surrounding a person. Normally in those with power, the glow remained a light constant emanation throughout the whole body, with a slight focus within the person's core. He closed his eyes for a moment then checked again. Still the same. If Xoruk hadn't needed to remain motionless to maintain his posture of acceptance and devotion, he would have scratched his head. This female was anomalous.

Unless this configuration was typical of the humans from the Empire? He scanned the males from the corners of his eye but didn't see any sign of a glow beyond a normal life force, let alone the same glow of power the female possessed. Perhaps this phenomenon occurred only in the females?

Xoruk resolved to find out. He was startled from his thoughts by the female's firm response as she scanned the Qendrok with an assessing gaze.

"Then I'm afraid your prejudice and bigotry have caused your request to be denied until such a time as your leader is willing to speak with me. *Gerden duv prakken.*"

To Xoruk's surprise, she bowed with her hands together in the correct Qendrok form to address the highest present leader of their people, then straightened and walked toward the door. The other delegates from the Empire turned and walked behind her.

Xoruk thought she had to be bluffing, hoping to give

Qartan reason to change his mind. Any second, one of them would come back to negotiate.

Any second.

The three of them filed out the door and did not return. As it sank in that the three delegates were not coming back, Qartan began cursing and throwing a fit. Xoruk let the familiar sound wash over him as he stared at the door the humans had left through, his thoughts speeding through his head.

Just who was this female?

QBBS *Meredith Reynolds*, Secret Bar

Will followed Greyson Wells and Phina from the reception hall to the meeting room behind the bar. Once the door was closed, he looked at them both with raised eyebrows. "Well, that sure was different."

Phina grimaced and fidgeted with the top of her tablet peeking out from her pocket as she moved over to a chair. "It was different, yes. Not fun, though. That alien does not like me."

Will frowned as he took a seat next to her. "Yeah. What was up with him? Is that kind of word vomit common in diplomatic discussions? It seemed excessive."

Greyson Wells smirked from his chair opposite of the two students and twiddled his thumbs as he spoke. "Absolutely not. What are both of your observations from the meeting? Kid, you go first."

"Well, I—" Phina stopped as Greyson held up a hand.

"Sorry, I meant the other kid." Greyson laughed lightly. "That's what I get for using generic nicknames."

Phina shrugged, then gestured at Will, whose eyes darted between them. "Gee, thanks. Throw me in the deep end, why don't ya?"

The older man grinned and spread his hands out. "I think I just did. Go on, then."

Will sobered as he put his thoughts together. "Let me see. It was obvious that the head guy didn't like Phina. I don't think it's for the reason he said, but that's a gut feeling. I couldn't tell you why. Some of the other ones in the delegation were watching us while trying to look like they weren't. I got the feeling at least one of them doesn't like the head delegate but, again, couldn't tell you why. Umm..." Will thought for a moment, then shrugged. "Can't think of anything else."

Greyson steepled his fingertips as he gave Will an approving nod. "Not bad, kid. Phina?"

Will's self-appointed new friend opened her mouth once, then paused, appearing startled. She finally began speaking slowly. "That's interesting."

Greyson's eyebrow rose. "What is?"

Phina glanced at Will before addressing Greyson. "My memory recall is a lot better since my coma."

Will's eyes widened. "Coma? Is that where you were the last year and a half? That's crazy." He paused, then added, "Though I like it better than the elopement story."

Grimacing, Phina shook her head. "That one was ludicrous. But yeah, I was in a coma. Long story, and I can tell you later if you want to hear it."

Will waved her on as his mind reeled at the information. He had so many questions. He decided to kidnap her later so she could answer them. Then he'd give her some of his mom's cookies. Everyone loved his mom's cookies. Will nodded at the plan then focused on Phina.

"I can remember a lot more details now. Whole conversations and accents and everything. Weird." She shook her head quickly and moved on. "Anyway, I think Will is right about both things. I couldn't get much of anything regarding thoughts since they had mental shielding. That makes me think they have experience with mental abilities."

Greyson nodded his agreement. "A reasonable assumption. Go on."

Phina nodded as she leaned forward. "However, what I did get was a mix of emotions and a hint of their direction. One of the guys standing behind Qartan felt disgust and disagreement when he was spouting that at me. I don't know if it was toward Qartan in general or because of the way he spoke, but it felt like both. Qartan himself has a fanatical feel to him. I don't think he will be willing to work with us if he remains in charge."

The other man frowned and nodded thoughtfully. "Which begs the question, of course."

"Why is he part of the delegation if he's so closed-minded?" Will hazarded a guess.

Greyson lifted a finger from their steepled form. "Bingo."

Phina frowned in thought. "I felt surprise from all of them at first, and intense focus from a couple of them at the same time as Qartan was feeling outraged. So, whatever Qartan finds objectionable about me, it seems as if most of the others can sense or see it as well."

Greyson nodded as he twiddled his fingers. "That lines

up with my observations. Too many of them were focused on you for a normal interaction."

Will had a thought but hesitated to bring it up. Phina glanced at him and nodded before asking matter-of-factly, "Would it be better for me to abstain from the diplomatic talks with them? It might go over better."

Oh, good. Will didn't want his new friend to be upset with him, but she seemed to understand.

Greyson shook his head at the question. "If this delegate has an issue with you, he's likely going to have an issue with any other female we bring in. Or any he interacts with while he's here. Not to mention if he ever met Bethany Anne or Gabrielle, or any of the other women we have in authority—*if* it's women in authority positions that he has a problem with."

He raised another finger at that, then with elbows on the rails, he tapped his chin as he thought. "If it's somehow connected to your abilities, then it's likely he would have a problem with Bethany Anne as well. His life expectancy would be cut radically short if he disrespected her or her people in her presence. So, no, I don't think it would help to have you absent yourself from the discussions if they do occur. Your presence may serve to stir up things that we need to be aware of when he's less than watchful about his words, as those with strong emotions tend to do."

Phina nodded her head, appearing somewhat relieved.

After a short period of silence, Will queried, "So, what's the next step? Do we wait for them to come to us, or do we approach them?"

Greyson shook his head at Will. "We wait. Phina told them to let us know when they are willing to work with her. If we approach them first, that implies that we need their alliance when the truth is that we don't. It's convenient but not a necessity as their star system is out of the way of higher traffic between other systems. So, approaching them first puts them in an advantageous position. It will be better for them to come to us. I'll bet my best hat that they are having internal differences and this blow-up was a symptom of it."

Phina scrunched her nose at her mentor. "You don't wear hats."

Greyson grinned at them both. "No, but if I did, I'd bet one."

As Phina shook her head and rolled her eyes, Will felt a sense of camaraderie and belonging that he hadn't felt with anyone outside of his family. He glanced at Phina with a smile. Yeah, he knew they would be friends.

But now he had the feeling they would become more like family.

CHAPTER TEN

QBBS *Meredith Reynolds*, Training Room

Phina pulled herself up on the bar, rotated around it, and released her grip. She flew up, wincing as her head came far too close to the ceiling, and focused on grabbing the bar again as she twisted and came plummeting down.

After she stretched out her fingers and grabbed the bar, Phina swung her body around for the dismount, her muscles bunched to get her over the bar, then let go. Rather than her normal flip in the air and landing on two feet some distance away, she shot across the room.

Gritted teeth and focus allowed her to twist so she could see in front of her, then grab the vertical pole that stood near the corner instead of hitting the wall. Her arms jerked and her palms burned briefly as she landed and spun around the pole, slowing herself down. She bent one leg to wrap around the pole closer to her hips and pressed the other foot down lower to take a breather. She spent a minute doing strength and stretch positions, then flipped to land on the floor.

Frustrated, Phina wiped the sweat off her face with her shirt. She caught a glimpse of movement by the door and froze. Todd stood leaning his tall, muscular body against the wall, his arms crossed as he watched her. She noticed he was dressed for working out or sparring, with similar clothes to her formfitting black shorts, shirt, and exercise bra. Well, Todd skipped the bra.

Which reminded her that she was currently maybe flashing him her bra, but certainly revealing her stomach, as she still stood with her shirt pulled up in her hands. Phina dropped the edge of her shirt in an instant and tugged down on the bottom to make certain it lay as normal. She shifted uncomfortably until she realized that Todd was walking toward her.

"May I make a suggestion?" he asked.

Phina nodded and hid her uncertainty about what he was going to suggest under her normal impassive lack of expression. "Of course."

Her mind raced. Did he have tips about her positioning as she set up her flips or a different way to land? Would he tell her she should try a different type of exercise? She knew other fighters didn't do part of their workout on gymnastics equipment or as close as she could get to it this side of the galaxy. Perhaps he thought she should work on new weapons. That might be fun. Phina began speculating on which weapon she might like to try next and almost missed his response.

"I think you are trying too hard."

Phina blinked and frowned as she focused on Todd's face, which held a slight smile as if he knew what she had been thinking. "Excuse me?"

He stopped and stood a couple of feet in front of her, his feet and body position relaxed but ready for anything. "I think you are focusing and trying to control yourself so much that you are overdoing it. You need to relax your brain and let your body take over."

Phina mulled that over for a minute before slowly nodding. "I think I see what you mean. However, doing what you suggest is difficult because I'm thinking and focusing all the time."

Todd raised an eyebrow as he smiled. "All the time?"

She crossed her arms and nodded. "Pretty much, yes."

He narrowed his eyes but continued. "You don't take time to yourself to relax?"

Phina blinked, confused. "Of course I do, but that doesn't mean my brain stops working."

Something Phina couldn't identify moved through Todd's eyes before he leaned forward to clarify. "So your brain is working all the time? Your brain doesn't take breaks or let you rest?"

She frowned and realized that Todd sounded bothered by that fact, but she didn't understand why. "Yes, that's what I said."

He tilted his head in consideration. "What about sleeping?"

Phina raised her eyebrows and inclined her head forward in confusion. "What about it?"

"From what you said, you wouldn't be sleeping well."

She stared at him for a moment, then answered. "No, I don't sleep well, except occasionally in the last couple of weeks since I woke up. It seems to come and go."

He nodded, appearing lost in thought for a moment before his gaze sharpened on her. "Would you like to spar?"

"Yes. Thank you. That would be great."

Todd watched Phina's face brighten as she stepped over across from him on the mat, then she paused and frowned.

"Something wrong?" Todd stepped forward. "Did you decide not to spar after all?"

"No." Phina shook her head and turned to him, both determined and regretful. "I need to apologize for speaking into your mind last week without permission. I didn't realize I was doing it until I saw you were startled."

Todd gave her a reassuring smile and relaxed his position. He had thought about it a lot since the last time he saw her and knew his answer. "Don't worry about it, Phina. Feel free to speak as you did any time you like or need to. However, I am less comfortable about you reading my mind, but that isn't because I don't trust you. I know a lot of confidential information. My bosses, as well as the people I'm responsible for, share things with me in confidence."

Nodding, Phina relaxed. "That makes sense."

He had a thought and added, "I will say that if there's an emergency, especially if someone's life is on the line, then you do whatever you have to do. Saving lives trumps anything else. I believe that's what Bethany Anne would say as well, though you should ask her about it to be sure."

Phina nodded more slowly and murmured, "I'm sure that will happen at some point and sooner than I'd like."

"Oh? What makes you say that?" Todd felt puzzled as he hadn't previously gotten the sense that Phina had a problem with Bethany Anne, although Phina had layers she didn't let many people see.

She waved a hand and shook her head dismissively. "I'm not used to talking to her casually yet. I have a difficult time talking to those in positions of authority over me, likely because of the issues I've had with my aunt. I'm working on it." She glumly sighed. "It takes time."

"Anything worthwhile does." Todd gave her an encouraging smile as his mind raced. He hadn't poked into the situation with her aunt thus far though he had been curious. Perhaps he should pay the woman a visit.

Todd stood with his arms crossed as they talked about the Empress. Phina felt surprised by how easy it was to talk to him. Not quite the same as Alina or ADAM, but similar.

"You ready to spar now?" Todd asked.

Phina nodded and shook herself out one more time before taking her ready stance. It was the perfect way to work out her frustrations, both with her earlier difficulties and waiting to hear from the Qendrok delegation.

Todd settled into a fighting stance again, watching her with an assessing gaze before springing into motion.

He moved fast for an enhanced human. The skill, strength, and stamina Todd displayed proved to be impressive. Forward kick, block a punch, punch, backhand, block a kick to the groin, roundhouse kick, block and hold her arm as he kicked, then a flurry of punches. Phina blocked most things well enough, but once he got hold of her, she found it difficult to break his grip. It took her whole body strength to get enough leverage to get her the position she wanted.

Hmm. Perhaps she needed to switch up how she did things. She usually sparred with Maxim or Link, and they often had gotten into certain patterns of doing things without realizing it. Todd seemed to flow and read what she would do almost before she did it, which amazed her given that they had only sparred once recently, and he had none of the mental abilities she did.

Phina threw herself into the fight, deflecting punches, blocking kicks, moving out of the way of attacks, and responding with attacks in between. The next time Todd gripped her wrist in a hold, she twisted her hand and grabbed his wrist, then ran up his body using his arm as support and leverage and jumped off his chest.

As the force of the jump pushed them apart, Phina let go of his wrist and found his slipping off hers. She twisted in the air and landed on the ground in a roll before popping up and readying herself for a follow-up attack.

Todd lay on the mat some distance away, looking dazed. He shook his head and lifted it to look at her with his hand rubbing his chest and an amused smile on his face. "Damn, girl. Maybe we should call you Wonder Woman."

Phina's tension flowed away and she relaxed, smiling. "I like Black Widow. She's pretty badass and doesn't need any special powers."

Todd rose, then stood with his feet apart and his head tilted as he considered her. "Beautiful, intelligent, super-spy, martial artist, technical whizz, and all-around badass?" His smile widened into a grin. "Yeah, I can see it."

Phina's chest heaved as she laughed silently, then finally laughed out loud. She hadn't ever considered herself beautiful as she usually reserved that for Alina, but to hear Todd describe her as such, among the other great epithets, gave her a warm feeling.

Todd remained silent, watching her. When her laughter subsided, she looked up to see his assessing gaze on her and looked at him questioningly. He nodded and began speaking thoughtfully. "That gives me an idea. You are pretty strong and fast now, but you will still be smaller than many of the opponents you will have. Your daggers are useful, but they require you to get within arm's length of your opponent, which would give them an advantage. What do you think about adding a different weapon to your practice? One that would give you a longer reach?"

Phina brightened, feeling excited for the first time since Alina told her she and Maxim were getting married. That made Phina feel down again because she hadn't seen Alina much since then. Their schedules had been busy, and Alina spent much of her free time with Maxim. Phina had been practicing on her own since she didn't think she had anyone assigned to her now. She looked up and realized Todd was waiting for a response.

"I think that sounds logical and practical. It's a good idea."

He nodded in acknowledgment before asking, "Do you have anyone training you right now?"

She shook her head simply. A pang hit her, and she realized she tried to appear as if she hadn't been shunted to the side by other people. Or so it felt like lately. Everyone showed her they were happy to have her back, but they seemed to forget that since she had been gone, many things had fallen to the side, and they hadn't been picked up again once she had returned.

"I'll do it," he offered.

Phina looked up, startled. "You will?" She squinted her eyes and looked at him in confusion. "Why would you do that? You must be busy as the leader of the Marine Corps."

He nodded but grinned at her and gestured for her to take a seat. As there was a lack of chairs in the room, they ended up next to each other on her balance beam, which wasn't a bad perch for Phina.

Todd looked somewhat uncomfortable with his seat as he continued, "Yes, but not so busy that I can't take time to train you for a while. If I'm deployed, I'll arrange for someone else to take over. For now, I will train you."

Phina slowly nodded but remained hesitant. "You are certain my...changes don't bother you?" She gestured toward herself.

His eyebrows rose in surprise. "You mean that you are faster than me, stronger, more flexible, and can do amazing things like reading minds?"

At her wordless nod, he smiled. "No, they don't bother me. I'm used to hanging around with people exactly like that."

Ah... right. Empress Bethany Anne, her inner circle fondly called the Empress' Bitches, and his best friend Peter, an Alpha Wechselbalg who turned into a wolfman. Her body relaxed, releasing tension she hadn't realized she was holding.

Todd shifted, then straddled the beam and leaned forward. "I'll tell you a secret that I've learned while observing them over the last three decades." Phina's interest was piqued, and she leaned forward as well without realizing. "It's not what powers you have, but what you can do with them and for what reason that makes the difference. There have been many enemies we have fought, some of which had greater powers or numbers, but while we have lost some battles over the years, we have won every war."

His eyes warmed as he continued speaking, becoming more animated. "We fight for Justice and the right to live. We fight so that those who are weaker have protection against those stronger who would take advantage. We fight not just for the Empire as a whole but for every individual person. They all matter. Most of all, we fight so that those Kurtherian bastards from the seven clans the Empress has been chasing won't continue to use the universe as their socio-science experiment!"

Todd shook his head, with his lip curled up in disgust. "You should see the things they've done to some of the worlds the Marines have been sent to. It's a sad display of what happens when a race develops a god complex. It would probably sicken you as it does myself. Some are relatively harmless, with minimal adjustments of DNA and core attributes." He paused and pressed his lips together. "Some are so far gone there is little trace of their previous existence. They have erased entire cultures and species. It's…"

"Barbaric and arrogant." Phina finished quietly. Todd

glanced up upon hearing her. He swallowed and nodded, his expression stark.

She hesitantly gave his arm a gentle squeeze. "I'm sorry for what you've lost in protecting us, but I thank you as well. You and your Marines hold the line and keep us safe. It's easy to lose sight of that when flashier things are happening, but that doesn't make your actions less worthy."

"Thank you." His eyes warmed as he smiled and squeezed her hand before releasing it and swinging his leg over the beam to stand. "Ready to go again?"

Phina jumped up and nodded, a small smirk growing on her face. "Yup, I'm ready to kick your ass."

"Oh." He grinned and set himself in a ready position. "The student thinks she's overtaken the master already?"

"I guess we'll see," Phina lightly replied as she stepped into her position. She ran a couple of steps, jumping up into a flying takedown that mostly succeeded. Todd managed to turn it into a deflection that almost took her down at the same time. She twisted and broke the hold he had on her before whirling to meet the next attack.

When she saw his grin, she paused and laughed. To think, almost two and a half years ago when she first started, she hadn't wanted to learn to fight, and she had badly but surprisingly defended herself in a fight with this same man. She shook her head.

Life had taken a strange turn, but she had begun to realize just how much she enjoyed it.

CHAPTER ELEVEN

QBBS *Meredith Reynolds,* **Docking Area**

Phina entered the docks to wait for the ship bringing Braeden, Sis'tael, Drk-vaen, and Ryan Wagner home. ADAM had contacted her and relayed that the ship would be docking within the hour. She had been excited to hear the news and hurried so she would be here before the ship arrived.

When she walked farther inside, she heard loud yowls and meows mixed with words in her head.

Get your paws off me, you mangy mutt! I'm here looking for my human! I'm sure you fall far short in comparison with your stuffy shirt and scratchy vest. A cage!? You dare to put me, Sundancer of the 9th Preeminent Family of Previdia in a cage?! I've never been more insulted in all my 127 years of life! You have never been paired with a Previdian, you rabid beast! When my human gets here, she will tear you new holes to breathe from!

As Phina moved closer out of curiosity, she could see a poor immigration employee struggling to close a latch to a cage. The employee finally got it shut, then straightened and sighed in relief. Her shirt and vest had been shredded around the arms and chest, although no blood was visible. A definite relief.

She turned to see Phina watching her curiously and blinked before stammering. "Ca-can I h-help you?"

Phina walked over to the desk and eyed the cage before turning to the beleaguered woman. "I wondered what was going on. He's telling you he's looking for a human, so why is he in a cage?"

My human! You're my human! It's about time you showed up.

The woman opened her mouth as she glanced at the cage. Phina heard the words in her head from the creature, her eyebrows rising in surprise as she turned to look as well. She responded in her head before the woman spoke. *Wait, you say I'm your human? I don't think I know you.*

"Is th-that what he's b-been s-saying? I n-never g-got the implant update for animals."

Of course you are my human, you silly girl! Why would I have traveled almost a whole solar year to find you if you weren't my reason for being here?

Two conversations at once. Again. If she didn't have this cocktail of nanocytes in her body, she would be developing a headache.

I see... Well, you could have been traveling for fun. How would I know the difference? How do you know I'm your human and not someone else? Are you sure you aren't just trying to get out of your jail sentence in there?

Affronted silence permeated her thoughts.

She responded to the woman quickly. "Well, that's what

I'm hearing. He says *I'm* his human. I've never seen him before, so it's something of a surprise to hear."

I'm greatly disappointed you haven't gotten me out of here yet, or torn her new breathing holes as I told her you would, so we all have our burdens to bear.

Phina ignored the caustic comment to focus on the woman who was looking at the cage in dread as she asked her next question. "Is there a problem with him being here? I can translate if you need."

Priscilla, Phina had belatedly noticed the name tag, sighed, and glanced at the cage glumly but voiced no objections.

"I need his p-papers t-t-to travel. The c-captain of the sh-ship who b-brought him s-said he was a st-stowaway."

A stowaway! The rotten liar! I paid that dirty captain two good rats for passage. I laid them on his desk neatly and everything. The creature sniffed in her head.

Trying not to smile or laugh, Phina relayed the information to Priscilla who blinked and queried, "And th-the p-papers?"

Silence greeted the question.

>>**Phina?**<<

Her AI friend's voice greeting her through her implant was a relief. *ADAM?*

>>**I am seeing what's happening. This creature is saying he belongs with you?**<<

Are you always watching the docking platforms? Yes, that's what he says.

>>**Reynolds and I get pinged whenever there's an altercation of any kind so we know how to respond if we are needed. We can waive the lack of papers if you**

take over supervision and responsibility for him and fill new ones out now. What species is he? He was squirming too much to tell.<<

I don't know, ADAM. I haven't seen him yet.

She reached out to speak to the creature who had claimed her. *Could you step forward so we can see you better?*

I am always happy to show myself to be admired.

The small being stepped forward to the door of the cage, revealing the body of a hairless cat with wrinkled pink skin and overly large eyes and ears. He seemed both adorable and somewhat vain.

>>**Phina, this creature matches the entries I have for the Sphinx cat on Earth.**<<

That's why he looks familiar. I've seen a picture before. I did have the thought that they looked like little aliens.

A tutting sound filled her head. *Please, I am Sundancer, a magnificent specimen of Previdia. You are my human, and you are failing to do your duties to worship me.*

Phina froze, her eyes moving as she blinked in disbelief. *Are you serious?*

He looked affronted. *I am always serious about worship! Where is my food? Where is my soft, comfortable bed near your head so I can give you advice and tell you when your life is going wrong? You are my human, and you have duties you are failing at! Such as,* why am I still in this cage?

Phina was too stunned to speak for a moment, her mouth flapping open as she tried to respond.

"Are y-you okay?"

Phina blinked and turned to stare at Priscilla, who gave her a sympathetic glance. "He's y-yowling. He must b-be saying something b-bad."

"He wants to be let out of the cage."

Priscilla's shoulders dropped as she turned to glance at the cage before looking down at her shredded clothing. "Oh, damn."

―――――

Phina found herself holding the pink hairless creature in her arms as she continued to where the ship was docking. She had used up her extra time handling the cat's paperwork.

I have a name, you numpty.

"I'm still not sure I'm not dreaming this up in my head."

I'm still not sure you're my human. Surely my human would treat me better by giving me a pillow to travel on and tasty nibbles of fish.

"All right, I'll put you down and let you go on your way."

No, the hairless cat yowled as Phina bent over to carry through on her words. His claws held onto her sleeves so she couldn't put him down. *Previdians are honor-bound to stay with their charges. If you put me down, I'll just follow you. I'll make your life miserable until you take me with you.*

Phina raised an eyebrow as she stared down at him. "Seriously? You have no idea what I've been through in the past couple of years. This is nothing."

He looked up at her gravely and nodded with seriousness. *I do know, actually. Well, parts of it. That is why I am here.*

Both eyebrows rose in surprise. "Say that again?"

The cat frowned at her repressively but looked

adorable. *You are not growing hard of hearing. You know perfectly well what I am saying.*

"I'm not growing hard of hearing," Phina responded impatiently as she resumed walking, the creature still in her arms. Passersby gave her odd looks and hurried past her. She ignored them. "I don't understand what you mean by 'that's why I'm here.'"

I heard your call into the universe almost a galactic year ago. Are you saying you have no idea what I'm talking about? He sounded personally affronted as he squirmed around in her arms so he could see ahead. *A Previdian who is paired hears the call and answers by traveling to find their charge and make certain they succeed in their endeavors, including their connection to the Etheric. I have traveled in two small ships, a cruiser, a merchant vessel, two military vessels, and a shuttle to get here. I endured aliens with tentacles, inadequate food supplies, dozens of rough soldiers, hyper-controlling captains, a steward with garlic breath, and an abominable female who shrieked and clutched me to her chest while speaking to me as if I were a simpleton. I knew my charge was human, but I don't hold that against you. I knew my charge was youngish, but I don't hold that against you either. It's the lack of fish and other tasty nibbles and comforts I find disturbing.*

She stopped and looked down as the bright blue eyes of the Previdian turned up in question. "Wow...okay. First, taking galactic and solar years into account, that would have been around the time I had an increase in my abilities. I had issues on a dying planet and then went into a coma. I can't think of anything else relevant that happened around that time. But I certainly didn't purposely put out a call for someone. I don't know the first thing about Previdians, lovely though you sound," Phina added hastily when he looked at her indignantly. She looked around for the correct dock as she continued walking.

Phina frowned as she recalled the time in the cave that she had woken up in pain after passing through the barrier and had thoughts of a cat in her head. Could that be when Sundancer had heard the call? It was odd but too coincidental to dismiss. "Who paired you with me? How did you know I was human and young? And lastly, I just found you. Give me some time here. I need to meet my friends off their ship before we can do anything about food. I'm hungry too."

Sundancer looked mollified at the information. *Yes, it was when your connection to the Etheric grew stronger. As I said, I heard your call. It flared suddenly, and I knew you were in desperate need of my advice, so I graciously decided to come immediately. After I caught enough victuals for the journey, of course*, he added stiffly, as if he thought she might disapprove.

She frowned as she processed that.

Previdians are only connected to those who have strong minds and can connect to the Etheric realm, Sundancer continued. *That makes the pairing possible. The universe, fate, higher power, or whatever else you want to call it, paired you with me. Previdians say the ancestors. It is your privilege to have my advice and instruction on connecting to the Etheric.* He regarded her gravely. *I wouldn't have heard you on Previdia if we hadn't been paired. That's how it works. I heard the call and got a sense of who and where you were so I could find you. It has worked that way for generations of Previdians.*

Phina stopped in shock and surprise and held

Sundancer up so his eyes were level with hers. "Hang on. You are saying that not only do I have to deal with losing a year and a half of my life and all the emotions and issues that brings, and learning or proving I know everything I need to pass the Diplomatic Institute, and help with Alina and Maxim's wedding, and all the super-secret things I can't talk about in front of other people like the ones currently staring at me like I'm crazy, but now I also have to train to use energy from the Etheric realm?"

I'm not certain yet if you are bright or slow. I'm leaning toward slow.

Phina shot him a look. "Sundancer."

He waved a paw. *Yes, yes, that's what it means. I train you to use the energy from the Etheric. You could drop some of those other things if you want less to do. You need more time for training.*

Lost in thought, Phina tried to wrap her head around this new reality. "So, if Previdians come to those who have strong minds that are connected to the Etheric, how come I haven't heard of your species before? We have several people who fit that description here, including the Empress."

Sundancer gave an imperious glare. *Do those persons already have mentally connected companions of their own?*

Phina squinted, then remembered that Ashur, a dog who had been enhanced to the size of a small pony, had become Bethany Anne's companion long before they had entered space. She listed others that might qualify in her head and realized that those people either had companions in the form of one of Ashur's children or had been established adults by the time they had reached space, having long come into their abilities. "Huh."

The cat sniffed disparagingly. *Precisely. Those overgrown mutts had connections with those persons. The ancestors don't send us where we aren't needed.*

Phina wanted to scratch her head, but her hands were full. "So, saying all those who have Previdian companions are connected to the Etheric is like saying all Previdians are like cats, but not all cats are like Previdians?"

Sundancer's eyes narrowed dangerously. *I. Am. Not. A. Cat.*

She scowled at him. "Well, I'll tell you one thing. I'm not going to drop everything in my life for this training."

Yes, you are, he immediately responded.

Shaking her head, tempted to find a wall to bang it against, Phina gave Sundancer a wary look before she turned into the dock she was looking for. She lowered her arms and tucked him in the crook of one arm like those American footballs she saw in the old movies. "Not happening, cat."

I am not a cat! He yowled in her head. *I am of the ninth family of Previdia! Give me some respect, human.*

Phina walked toward the occupied dock as she replied, "Respect goes both ways. If you want me to respect you, show some respect to me. How much respect are you used to if you are in the ninth family, anyway? That doesn't sound very high."

He sniffed, not wanting to admit she had a point, and replied stiffly. *It is plenty high when there are thirty-seven families in total.*

She wanted to respond, but she saw a familiar figure coming out of the cargo hold of the ship in front of her.

"Braeden!"

"Braeden!"

The tall, slender Gleek looked at the sound of the familiar voice, but he wasn't able to see much of his friend before she hurtled into him and threw an arm around him. He didn't get a chance to hug Phina before he heard yowls of protest and felt tiny sharp daggers in his belly.

Stop squashing me! Honestly, how will you be able to train if you can't properly take care of me?

Phina quickly stepped back and put down the small creature that had gotten smooshed between them. "Oh, sorry, Sundancer. I forgot. I was so excited to see Braeden."

The creature gave her a look of disdain and began washing his paws. *Clearly.*

Braeden blinked at the creature with a perplexed expression before remembering that he had knowledge about this type of creature stored in the brothers' collective knowledge. He would need quiet to retrieve them.

He turned to Phina, realizing that she stood in front of him. When last he had seen her she had been deep in a self-induced coma. He had caught enough from her across the systems that he knew she was awake, but he didn't realize until now that he had to see her before his mind eased.

He looked at his young friend and felt pleased with what he saw. She looked much healthier than the last time she was awake. She looked ten times better since the last time he saw her in a coma.

"Phina, you are well?"

Phina's face twitched as if she couldn't decide the answer, but she nodded with a small smile. "I'm so happy to see you, Braeden. So much has happened in the short time I've been awake, and a lot happened to everyone else in the year and a half I've been in a coma. Everything feels strange and normal at the same time. It's been something of a struggle," she admitted as she stepped forward to hug him again.

Braeden wrapped his long, gangly arms around Phina's shoulders and gave a gentle squeeze. His young friend, who was more like a sister, was the only being in the universe who thought to hug him. It gave him an odd but welcome sensation in his core where his two hearts resided.

Phina stepped back and grinned at Braeden. "So, how's my favorite alien?"

A hacking cough sounded behind her. *What am I, chopped liver?* Phina looked down to see a trance-like expression on Sundancer's feline face as he licked his mouth with his long pink tongue. *Mmm...liver.*

Phina smothered a laugh as she replied. "I've known Braeden for years at this point. I haven't known you for an hour."

The cat sniffed reproachfully. *That should make no differ-*

ence whatsoever. We are paired, human. Paired. I don't think you understand the gravity of the situation.

Looking serious, Phina nodded slowly. "Likely not. I'm sure you will explain it to me in great detail. Later."

"Phina!"

She turned to see Drk-vaen, Sis'tael, and Ryan Wagner running down from the cargo hold with grins on their faces. They converged on her at the same time, Yollin and human arms flying everywhere as they hugged her.

"Oof! Hi, guys." She closed her eyes as she attempted to hug them all back. She had missed them since she woke up, but it had been much longer for them. She felt warm inside and sighed. The rest of her chosen family was home.

When they didn't let go, she wiggled her fingers. "Uh, guys? I'm not disappearing."

They withdrew with smiles on their faces and relief in their eyes. Phina kept her mental shields tight so she didn't get any stray thoughts.

"So, what's been going on with you guys?" Phina smiled and put her hands on her hips, feeling awkward. Alina and Maxim had just started dating before the coma, and now they were getting ready to marry. How much had changed with these friends since she had been absent?

"What's been going on with us? What about you, Phina?" Sis'tael looked like she wanted to jump on Phina to hug her again. "When did you wake up?"

"A couple of weeks ago." Phina shrugged. She knew she would need to share what had changed with her but wanted to delay that as long as possible.

Drk-vaen appeared thoughtful and looked at Braeden.

"Wasn't that around the same time we had that celebration for the Aurians' new planet?"

Braeden nodded, his long face and body posture engaged and interested. "Yes, I believe it was that day."

Phina told them the exact day and time, and they exchanged glances. She looked at them warily. "What?"

"That's the exact day and time of the celebration, Phina." Ryan appeared excited. "Is there a connection? That can't be a coincidence."

Braeden stirred and nodded. "I did reach out to Phina at that time and tried to share the songs the Aurians sang for their lament that has turned to hope for the planet. I thought I felt Phina wake up."

The others appear surprised.

"What?"

"You did?"

"You didn't tell us that!"

They looked from Braeden to Phina, who was also surprised but tilted her head in thought as she took her mind back to being in the gray nothing place. "I do recall hearing music. I knew there were words, but they weren't quite registering. It was what pulled my attention and started waking me from where my mind was."

Ryan's eyes widened. "I recorded it. Let me pull it up." He reached into the bag that he had dropped before hugging Phina and pulled out his tablet. After a few taps of his fingers, beautiful music streamed out and began filling the air around them.

Phina concentrated and was about to tell them that it was the same music, but she stopped and listened as she heard the words.

"Our old world is gone, but we have hope. Our people are lost, but we have hope. Our life is changed, but we have hope. We are still here; we are still alive. We have each other, we have new friends. We have a new world to enjoy, a world to explore. Life will be different, and everything has changed. Life will be good, and life can be better. We have each other, and we have hope."

The melody and the words filled her mind and began edging out the despairing and depression-tinged thoughts she had been struggling with since she had woken up. Her emotions had been in turmoil over the changes, but the music turned them to a more positive outlook—one of hope. Phina shook her head to blink the tears away and saw the others doing much the same.

"Damn, their voices are potent without the damper but so beautiful." Ryan wiped his eyes as he put his tablet away.

Nodding, Phina gave a wobbly smile. "That was just what I needed to hear. And yes, that's the music I heard."

"I'm so happy you are awake, Phina!" Sis'tael lunged in for another hug and they all piled on again, laughing.

"Ouch!" Phina felt a sharp pain as a claw pierced her leg through her pants and looked down around human and Yollin arms to see Sundancer's wrinkly pink face and bright blue eyes looking up at her with a grave expression.

We need to talk. Now.

CHAPTER TWELVE

QBBS *Meredith Reynolds*, Phinalina Residence

Phina walked into the apartment suite and shut the door after Braeden and Sundancer followed her in. When Phina had asked Sundancer what he wanted to discuss, he had told her it was about her abilities, so she had invited Braeden as well. She had said her goodbyes to the others along with promises to meet up with them soon before they came back to her apartment suite.

Phina gestured for Braeden to take a seat on the couch, then entered the kitchen to get drinks for the three of them. After returning, passing out the drinks, and sitting in her favorite chair, Phina gestured to Sundancer to begin.

"Go on, Sundancer. What did you need to talk about?"

Braeden sat in an introspective position, acknowledging that she had given him his favorite drink with a nod.

Sundancer looked up and licked the milk off his whiskers with his long tongue before he spoke. *Very well.*

Have you been feeling very tired and run down, like your energy is depleted?

Phina sat up straight in her chair. "Yes, often. Does it have to do with my abilities? Should I not use them?"

Sundancer shook his head emphatically. *Absolutely not. It's quite the opposite. Have you not felt a positive difference in your energy levels when you begin using your abilities?*

Phina froze and thought back to when she was sitting in class and feeling tired. After she had used her abilities to figure out what the professor was up to, she had felt much better. Had that continued the rest of the time? She recalled times she'd felt more exhausted and realized she had been clamping down tight on her shields during those times.

"I see the correlation now that I'm thinking on it, yes. But the times I've been completely open, I start feeling overwhelmed by all the information that hits me. Is there an in-between?"

Sundancer tilted his head toward Braeden. *Yes, but tell me. Why is the overgrown human here again?*

Braeden stirred from his introspective position and reached for his glass of Coke. "I am not human. I am Gleek. The lack of hair and differences in cranial structure and appendages should make that clear." He stretched out his free hand, gesturing to his shoeless feet, each showing four fingers or toes. His hairless elongated skull was apparent.

Sundancer immediately turned to gape at the Gleek, his sharp teeth and pink tongue flashing out of his open mouth. *Ancestors above. You are? And you understand me the same as my human does? Extraordinary. My people have heard of you.*

Braeden nodded once after taking another sip. He had told Phina before that he enjoyed both the bubbles and the effect that the sweetness of the Coke had on his physiology. From his description, it had the same effect as that of a beer for a human.

"We have heard of your people as well. I was reviewing the information. There seems to be a conflict, however. We have met your species you call Previdians. Yet, there was also a similar species we have encountered in Estaria that called themselves Sphinx."

Sundancer waved a paw and gave Braeden a sour expression. *Yes, yes. Those miscreants were Previdians at one time. A long time ago, a great, great uncle of mine visited the planet humans call Earth. He stayed there for some time and even had children there. The humans who called themselves Egyptians couldn't understand his words, but they revered him and called him a Sphinx cat. They made statues in his honor, although he lamented that they didn't display his beautiful wrinkles.*

He narrowed his eyes at Phina. *We are not cats. That uncle eventually returned to Previdia and shared his stories with the rest of the Previdians. The story caused unforeseen issues with one family that had a more purple hue of skin instead of my family's lovely pink. They liked the idea of being revered, and the stories my uncle told of the Egyptian's afterlife and decided that meant the Egyptians were able to ascend to a different realm.*

Sundancer sighed in a long-suffering manner. *They liked it so much they thought this idea of ascension was the most important thing they could pursue, even above our vows. Since our elders disagreed and told them to cast aside their pursuit of ascension, this family changed their designation to call them-*

selves Sphinx and left Previdia. *Last we heard, they had settled on Estaria. Good riddance to them.* Sundancer sniffed then examined a paw to wash.

Phina frowned. "Why was it such a big deal for them to pursue this idea of ascension? Why did they need to leave?"

Sundancer finished a lick of his paw and looked up with a grave expression. *Because they had cast aside their vows in pursuit of it. Our vows are sacred to us. If they had kept it as a hobby, it would have been a mere curiosity that other Previdians found strange.*

Braeden inclined his head. "Thank you for explaining."

"You are welcome." Sundancer looked up at Braeden with a fierce expression. *Now, what have you done to my human that has made her so sensitive to the Etheric fluctuations?*

Phina's eyes widened while Braeden leaned forward with interest. "What is it you know, little one? I have done nothing but try to help her. If there is something wrong, it is not my doing."

Sundancer scowled. *Well, someone did something. This sensitivity is not natural.* He paused then added with a small sniff, *And don't call me little.*

Phina pinged ADAM through her implant, and he responded immediately. *ADAM, have you been listening?*

>>**Yes.**<<

Sundancer says someone did something to me that has made me much more sensitive to the Etheric than normal. Is this what you haven't talked to me about yet?

>>**It is in part. Let me see if TOM is available. He has things he needs to explain as well**<<

All right.

Phina was curious as to who TOM might be and what

he had to do with her life as she relayed the information to Braeden and Sundancer, who sat up at alert, his whiskers twitching. By the time she finished explaining, ADAM and TOM greeted them through the speakers in the room.

"Hello, Braeden and Sundancer." ADAM's voice came out in clear, crisp male tones.

TOM's voice sounded more fluid but still male. "Greetings to you all."

Sundancer nodded gravely then asked out loud, rather than in his mental voice, in an aggressive tone. "So, what have you done to my human?"

TOM answered immediately. "What we needed to so that she would live."

Phina's head jerked up in surprise. "What do you mean, TOM?"

"To explain the full story, not just the changes that have been made, we need someone else to join us. I believe they are here now."

While they waited, Phina stared at Sundancer. "You can talk out loud too?"

Sundancer sniffed. *When I choose.*

The door buzzed. Shaking her head, Phina absently told Meredith she could open the door to let the person in. As the door opened, Phina took a deep breath then turned to see who stepped inside.

Link entered the room with a grave and wary expression on his face.

Her breath caught at the realization that Link had yet more secrets and ones that pertained to her. Shaking her head again, she introduced Sundancer to everyone then spoke in a sharp tone. "Anyone else joining us?"

Link shook his head at the same time as ADAM and TOM answered. "No."

Phina pulled her legs up to cross them under her then rested her hands on her thighs. "All right. Who is going first in this convoluted story which involves me but no one seemed to think I needed to know?"

Link winced, then nodded. "I will start. This story begins with your parents."

Phina tightened her hands into fists to stop them from trembling. Her parents? She didn't think she could speak, so she swallowed roughly and gestured for Link to continue.

"During the first five or so years after we came through the Gate...." He paused, then shook his head. "No, I need to back up further and tell you the entire story, or some things later won't make sense."

He looked around the room with a fierce expression. "I will be sharing things that could compromise the safety of myself or Phina should word get out to certain people, so I ask you to keep what I will share with you a secret. Everything I am about to say is not to be mentioned at any time or place in the future. Will you make this promise?"

Braeden and Sundancer agreed, although the hairless cat huffed at the thought that he might compromise his human's safety.

ADAM hesitated. "DS, I would like to agree, but I can't promise I won't share this with Bethany Anne."

TOM agreed, adding. "She would be the only one I would ever think to share it with."

Link waved his hand. "That's fine. She's probably read most of it from my mind, anyway."

ADAM and TOM agreed.

After giving Phina a half-hearted smile of reassurance, he rubbed his hands on his thighs nervously. "My name is not Greyson Wells. Or any of the other names I've used. I was born Lincoln Sherwood Grimes. John Grimes is a cousin, though we had never met before I joined TQB— Bethany Anne's company on Earth before we came to space that later became the Etheric Empire. I mention it because it will be relevant later."

He let out a sigh and continued in a rough tone, "My parents were not the most involved people. My mom took care of me as best she could, but she was more interested in her hobbies. My father hated me and took it out on both of us."

Phina's eyes widened. So that's why he got so worked up about any slight mistreatment by her aunt. She leaned forward and listened intently.

"When I was nine, my mother died, likely of a broken heart. She just faded away. My father got worse in his treatment of me after her death, so I spent less time at home. I still went to school, but I found myself wandering the streets more." His lips pulled into a smirk as he grew lost in his recounting.

"I learned how to get what I needed. How to speak Arabic, Hebrew, and Spanish—the main three languages on the streets where I lived—and how to blend in wherever I went to look like I belonged. I didn't have a lot of money, but what I did get I saved for school. I knew as a young kid that college would help me get a leg up so I could get out of the house and leave my father behind for good."

He shrugged. "College and I didn't get along, mostly

because I had trouble with the rules. Then I became friends with a really smart guy who made me feel like I belonged somewhere for the first time since my mother died." Link looked up at Phina, his brown eyes the most emotional she had ever seen them. "It was Chris, your dad. His ethnicity was mixed and he had experienced what it was like to be on the outside much of the time. He saw I didn't fit in with the others and told me to come sit with him, that we would be friends from now on."

That sounded so like her dad. Phina couldn't help the tears that welled up but she remained silent, nodding that he should continue.

"One afternoon, Chris met with someone who had contacted him about a possible job. The offer sounded strange to me, so I tagged along. I used the skills I had acquired to blend in and make it seem like Chris was alone. The guy he met was a headhunter looking to recruit him for the CIA, an agency in the United States that spied on other countries to make sure they weren't trying to attack us or screw us over."

"A human hunted his own kind for their heads?" Sundancer yowled scandalously. "You humans are barbaric!"

Link chuckled and explained. "No, it's a term that means he looked for people to hire for his company. He wanted them alive."

Slightly mollified, Sundancer murmured a few imperceptible words and bent down to lap up some more milk while Link continued.

"This agent made the job sound very attractive to both of us and almost tailor-made to both our interests. I revealed myself, causing the guy to lose a few months of his life." Link chuckled. "After his initial surprise, he grew very excited to have us both in the agency after we graduated."

"Fast forward a couple of years, the two of us graduated and had started training at The Farm. We both took to the training like we were born for it. It was there that your dad met your mom."

He looked at Phina with a small smile on his face and it made her realize how alone Link had been since her parents had died. Her heart pinched in sympathy. She wasn't the only one who had felt devastated by their deaths. Phina gave him a reassuring smile in return. He nodded his understanding and continued his story.

"She was also of mixed ethnicity, partly Japanese. Your parents were drawn to each other immediately. They had to be careful, and it took time for their relationship to develop. Everyone was suspicious of each other in the training camp since we were often pitted against the others. However, Chris and I were solid and inseparable, and we included Zoe more as time went on."

Mixed emotions flicked across Link's face, but he continued. "Fast forward another six years. Zoe, Chris, and I, along with another agent named Brian Anderson, were at the top of our field in the agency. There had been talk of moving a couple of us into the fast track to the top of the company. However, several things happened within a couple of months of each other. Chris and Zoe were growing anxious to get married and start a life together, something that was not likely to happen with their current careers as spies."

A quick intake of breath was all Phina showed on the outside, but on the inside, her heart thumped loudly.

Her parents were spies?

She almost couldn't believe it since they had always said they were soldiers. Marines. Yet, given her father's spy stories and the way they had taught her to be independent, constantly curious, and questioning everything... It made too much sense. Phina had to rein in her thoughts so she could hear the rest as Link continued.

"Brian had begun a relationship with a Japanese agent named Chuya Fumiko and had taken a lot of heat from our superiors for it. They knew it was only a matter of time before they were killed or forced apart for endangering their respective agencies. Zoe's cover as a political negotiator had also been targeted by an extremist group who hated women being outside of their narrow-minded box and had to be careful about being seen publicly.

"Not long after, I heard from my family's lawyers that my father had died and I needed to take care of the estate, whatever there was of it." His tone changed at the mention of his father's death. "Around the same time, we had grown extremely uncomfortable with our orders to infiltrate and investigate this secretive company that had come out of nowhere. They were building technology that was far beyond anything the rest of Earth possessed. Our objective was to steal as much of the proprietary tech as we could."

Phina spoke as she realized. "TQB. Bethany Anne's company."

"Right." Link nodded, his eyes approving. "We didn't agree with the orders, but disobeying orders is not healthy in any of the agencies. So, the others investigated the company to see what they were up to and if there was a way to fulfill our orders without compromising our integrity—such as it was for those who spy on others." Link shrugged. "Meanwhile, I returned to my father's house to take care of things. While there, I found in the paperwork a letter from my grandfather written years before that mentioned a rift between my father and the rest of his family. There was an old picture of my father and his brother holding an infant boy the picture labeled John."

Link's face turned focused and intense. "When I received an encrypted report from the others, there was a document listing the CEO of the targeted company and her closest associates. A man named John Grimes was on the list. There could have been two different men with the same name, but I had been taught to rule out coincidences. I investigated and learned they were the same man. I concluded that while my father wasn't worth the space he took up, John was a good man who had his people's backs and wouldn't support someone shady."

Phina nodded and sat back. That matched with what she knew of the big man. Link glanced around the room. Phina's eyes followed and saw that while Braeden was quiet, he was intent on the story. Sundancer had laid down and had his eyes closed, but a twitch of his ears told her he was still awake and likely listening.

"This is longer than I meant it to be, but it helps you understand what happened later and why." He cleared his throat and looked around for something to drink. Phina got up and got him some water. He drank half in one gulp as she settled herself down again before he continued.

"To make a long story shorter, we contacted the company and were transferred to a man named Frank Kurns, who we learned was head of intelligence. We offered him five highly trained spies and our help in keeping the agencies from finding out the information they needed if TQB took us with them when they left. After some negotiations, he agreed, and we used the remaining time we had to disseminate information through various channels that included false trails, leads, and disinformation.

"Within several months, none of the agencies had any idea what was real and what was fabricated." He grinned in satisfaction. "Of course, we had no idea at the time that ADAM was helping with that behind the scenes. Between us, we had established relationships with many groups and agencies around the world, and we used them to disperse our false information. By the time they realized we had played them all—and by all, I mean everyone we had contact with in the United States and out—we were gone into space with the rest of TQB."

CHAPTER THIRTEEN

Braeden stirred for the first time in a while, leaning forward. "That was a large risk for you. You used your sources to help a company you weren't familiar with. You were very trusting."

Link nodded, his eyes very solemn despite his smile. "We call that putting all our eggs in one basket. We had checked TQB out thoroughly, and everyone we talked to, including those who didn't like them, said that they kept their word. So, being desperate and looking for a way to have a life on our terms, we took the chance. And it worked."

He grinned for a moment, then dropped his eyes as his smile died. "I'm certain that joining the Empire was the best and only real decision we could have made. However, it wasn't without cost. The first few years, we struggled to battle the rebel Yollins specifically and anyone else who seemed to get a hair on to attack the Empire. One of the biggest areas we expanded immediately was intelligence. The five of us were always busy and much happier since we didn't feel like we were compromising ourselves to do our job. Brian and Chuya were married and almost immediately had a boy they named Jason, who they called Jace."

Link looked up to meet Phina's gaze. She nodded to acknowledge that she knew. "He told me a little about your connection on the first day I saw him again."

"He told you about the guardianship?" Link asked in surprise. At her nod, he looked thoughtful then let out a deep breath. "Well, that's coming, but not yet. Chris and Zoe had been trying on and off for years to have a baby and never managed it. Maternal leave was one of the few acceptable reasons for a woman to not be required to be in the field while we were at the agency, so by this time they knew Zoe had a condition that prevented her from having children, although they still tried."

Phina frowned at that new information. Obviously, something had happened to change that, or she wouldn't be here.

"Chris and Zoe threw themselves into their work after we came to Yollin space, doing everything they could to be assets to the Empire. Even though we worked in the background, their efforts and dedication were noticed by the Empress. They got an offer to have their bodies upgraded with nanocytes that would allow them to remain younger for a long time, until the end of the fight with the Kurtherians."

Phina leaned forward eagerly. Her parents hadn't shared much information about the past, and this was new and fascinating to her.

Link looked straight ahead as he continued. "The Empress calls it *Ad Aeternitatem*, words from an old Earth language that means 'for eternity.' Only a small percentage of the Empire will ever get this offer because it means you have proven your dedication, Something that takes full focus and heart, backed up with actions. When I gave them the offer, I asked them if they would accept. Your parents told me that what they wanted most in the universe was a baby."

He gave Phina a small smile, and her vision misted again. Phina knew her parents loved her, but she had no idea they had given up so much for her.

"What they didn't know at the time was that Zoe was already pregnant. However, the pregnancy was in danger of miscarriage due to her condition. That brings us to ADAM and TOM's part in this story."

He looked up with a gesture, then surreptitiously wiped his eyes before picking up his glass to finish the water.

TOM began speaking matter-of-factly, which was a welcome relief for Phina from the charged emotions. "Hello, Phina. I have spoken *about* you often to ADAM and Bethany Anne, but I believe this is the first time we have spoken."

Phina smiled and wondered if TOM saw through the camera the same way as ADAM did. "Hello, TOM. Are you an AI like ADAM?"

TOM chuckled. "No, I am not an AI. It is a badly kept secret, but not for public consumption." Phina nodded and shifted to one side to prop her chin on her hand. "I am a Kurtherian."

Phina straightened in shock. "What? But aren't we fighting the Kurtherians?"

"Yes. You see, our people lived in clans a long time ago.

They split into two factions—one side believing that they were superior to all other beings and had the right to use and alter others as they saw fit. The other side believed that Kurtherians were no more deserving to be elevated than any other species. The first group consisted of seven clans, so we often refer to them as the Seven. Our clan was one of the five who opposed them."

At this, TOM's voice hardened. "The Seven separated themselves from the Five and focused on taking over the universe one species at a time, either through subjugation or genetic altering, or both. Over a thousand years ago, I left my clan to recruit others to fight them. I had a light crash into Earth which I was lucky to survive with my ship mostly intact. However, I realized the damage was enough that I wouldn't be able to leave for quite some time, if ever."

TOM's tone was very much that of someone relating facts and not the events of his life.

"After a time, I inadvertently created what humans called vampires when a human male stumbled into my ship near death. I hadn't encountered humans before and didn't have their genetics mapped in the Pod-doc. The encounter was very painful for him, and although he was healed, he left right after. Fast forward a very boring thousand years for me, and that same man brought Bethany Anne to be adjusted with nanocytes so that she could live and take over as head of his family. Well, I won't share more of her story, but let's say Bethany Anne and I have been friends ever since, and that put into motion the events that brought us into space to fight the Kurtherians, those of the Seven."

"I see," Phina responded slowly. "So, the Pod-doc is Kurtherian technology. As are the nanocytes."

"Yes," TOM answered simply. "Which brings us full circle to you. Phina, as you may have surmised, you were the baby Zoe was pregnant with during the conversation with Greyson... Pardon, but would you prefer me to refer to you in close company as Greyson or Lincoln?"

Link looked up with a frown, his eyebrows furrowed. "I've gotten used to Greyson, but if you call me Link privately, I'm not going to quibble."

"Understood, thank you. Phina, there was an issue with your genetics."

Phina sat back and tried to think this through. She had a basic understanding of genetics, but it wasn't something she had ever explored. "Do you mean something was wrong with my chromosomes?"

"Yes. There are several conditions that can cause miscarriage in humans. Several of these conditions are caused by a fetus carrying extra chromosomes. Yours in particular was a condition doctors call triploidy. Normally a human would carry twenty-three chromosomes from their father and twenty-three from their mother. However, you had an extra set of chromosomes from your mother, totaling sixty-nine. This condition is usually fatal in the womb, and those babies who do survive don't tend to live very long."

Phina listened intently, her eyes widening. "Since I'm still here, I'm assuming you did something to change that?"

"Yes. Zoe had a Pod-doc treatment to stabilize the pregnancy and infuse you with nanocytes. However, because your fetal body couldn't handle the fluctuations of the Etheric, Zoe was still close to miscarrying you."

Phina's mind raced in putting together the implications of the information TOM had relayed. "Does that mean you used Kurtherian DNA to adjust mine?"

"Yes. While it is uncommon for humans to carry sixty-nine chromosomes and survive, it is very common for Kurtherians. It is part of what gives us higher intelligence and the ability to use the Etheric in small ways. We informed your parents of the potential consequences, but their only concern was to have a happy, healthy baby."

"How does that work? Why do I still look human, then?" Phina's mind raced, thinking about the ramifications of this one little piece of knowledge. No wonder she had always felt different! Phina couldn't sit still anymore and got up to pace behind her chair.

"Because ADAM and I were very careful. We were in territory we hadn't encountered before. We carefully spliced your DNA with Kurtherian to make you stronger and better able to handle the nanocytes. Once that happened, the nanocytes optimized your DNA, which made your body able to accept the rest of the adjustments. Your mother was very patient with us and knew we were trying our best to give you as normal a life as possible.

"You did come to have increased mental capacity and desire for logic, finding complex mathematics much easier. That is a part of the Kurtherian makeup. You had inherited a fluid understanding of languages and patterns from your mother and an intuitive nature from your father. Your sensitivity to the Etheric is also in part from your mother. Each of these traits was expanded by the genetic changes and later became enhanced by the nanocytes from the serum."

Phina had stopped pacing and stood half-stunned after hearing ADAM's explanation. She finally shook her head. "Wow. I don't know what to say."

Link appeared surprised as well. "I hadn't heard any of this before, TOM. Why wasn't I told?"

"Because you didn't need to know. Up until now, only ADAM, Bethany Anne, I, and Phina's parents had any knowledge of this. We told them not to share it with anyone but Phina when she was old enough. That didn't happen because Zoe and Chris were killed while on assignment. We are trusting you, Braeden, and Sundancer to have Phina's best interest at heart. We didn't want people to look at her any differently, nor did we want others to ask us to do the same for them.

"We gave assurances to Phina's parents that she would be all right. However, we were aware there could be factors we hadn't accounted for and couldn't determine until she reached the peak of her growth formation. This would have happened around the age of twenty-five. Now, with the interference from Faith Rochelle, we still won't know for certain if she would have needed an intervention from the genetic changes." He had a note of disappointment in his voice but continued, "All I can tell you is that as of now, everything in Phina's body is stabilized, her nanocytes are optimized, and genetically there shouldn't be any issues from now on."

"I understand," Link murmured, lost in thought.

Phina gathered her thoughts then turned with an earnest expression to Link, Braeden, and Sundancer, who had his eyes open and was watching her intently. "Thank you, TOM, ADAM, and Link for your parts in helping me, both in being born healthy and more recently with what landed me in the coma."

Link looked up and gave her a rare full smile. "My pleasure, kid."

TOM responded, "Of course. You're very welcome."

ADAM replied over her implant, >>**You are welcome, Phina. Do you want to hear the rest now or later?**<<

Phina's eyebrows rose in surprise and she spoke out loud. "There's more? How much more?"

"Ah," TOM answered. "Yes, there is more related to the circumstances that led to your coma, but it is less involved."

"Go on." Phina sighed as she began pacing again. "I'm going to need some major processing time after this."

The Kurtherian paused, then spoke again. "ADAM, would you care to explain since you brought it up?"

"Phina, the changes TOM and I made before you were born allowed your sensitivity to the Etheric to come to a sense of balance, where you were not closed off to it entirely, but neither were you able to use it. This was a delicate process and a large part of what allowed you to live a mostly normal human childhood. However, when your aunt gave you the serum, it caused your system to be massively overbalanced. Those of us who are connected to the Etheric have an energy transfer system that acts much like a two-way street. When the serum, with what we will colloquially call altered vampire nanocytes, was introduced to your system, it created a traffic jam with your connection."

She frowned as she turned on a heel in the other direction. "Do you mean like with cars?"

"Yes," ADAM confirmed. "Remember when we watched *Independence Day* and there were so many cars on the road after the aliens showed up that they got stuck? How in some cities the throughway was blocked with traffic, so others decided to take the road going the wrong way and caused accidents? Your connection is behaving very similarly. The path between you and the Etheric was opened, but it's messed up. Your body knew you needed more energy, so it caused you to consume massive amounts of food to make up for it while still intaking Etheric energy at an irregular rate. Then the excess energy was trapped, which caused you to need to increase your energy output."

"Wow, okay. That explains a lot." She frowned in concentration as she thought through the process. "So, because the connection was fluctuating and not flowing properly, it was overwhelming my body and causing it to begin breaking down. At the same time, it greatly increased my ability to mentally connect to and use Etheric energy, which allowed me to sense other people's minds. Do I have that right?"

"Yes."

"And this connection is stabilized now?"

ADAM paused a beat then answered. "Yes, after we inserted code that instructed the nanocytes to ignore part of the changes your aunt had made. However, one of the changes that your body needed to make, which I had recently suspected due to the readings we had taken and has now been proven, is that your brain has changed. It needs an input of Etheric energy to be able to process properly with enough space for all your functions."

Phina stopped pacing and sat in her chair again, stunned. "So, this is why Sundancer told me earlier that I couldn't keep my mental shields completely closed all the time. Because it cuts me off from part of my brain functions? That's why I've been feeling more tired and sleepy since my coma? Because I've kept my mental shields shut tight?"

"Yes."

"Okay." Phina tapped her fingers on the arm of her chair as she thought. "Then this need to stabilize the Etheric connection between both parts of my brain is likely why I went into a self-induced coma." She looked up sharply. "TOM and ADAM, what does the Etheric look like? Is it a gray space that stretches forever?"

TOM answered, "Yes," at the same time as ADAM responded, "That is correct."

She sat up straight, looking at those present in the room. "Then that is definitely what happened. I was aware and partially in the Etheric. I could sometimes hear conversations that weren't quite discernible, as well as sense shifting energy. I could see the Etheric, but I wasn't physically present. I could move, but only with my mind."

Her thoughts flowed in several different directions until TOM broke in. "That confirms what we know and some of what we have suspected."

Phina looked up, startled, then took a deep breath. "Thank you all for taking the time to share this with me and listen, but that's it. My capacity to handle new revelations is overfull. I need to go do something and process."

She paused and looked around the room. "You've told me all the secrets you've been keeping about me, right? There's not something else major you need to share or haven't told me yet?"

"No," ADAM answered. "That is everything I am aware of."

The others agreed, except for Link. He stood up and walked over, reaching into his pocket to pull out an old-fashioned letter in an envelope. He held it out with a grave expression but a warmth that he didn't always allow to show. "This is the last one that I know about. It's a letter from your mom. She wrote one before every mission and gave it to me for safekeeping, then took it back when she came home. This was the letter she gave me before they left on their last mission."

Phina's hand trembled as she reached out to take the envelope then stared at it, her fingers smoothing out the rough and yellowed paper. "So, they weren't regular Marines? They were spies, and the way they died in their file isn't the truth?"

Link crouched down in front of her and touched her hand briefly, causing her to look up. He shook his head slowly, eyes dark with regret. "No. I told you everyone in Spy Corps has a cover. That was theirs. They did die heroes, working to gain information from the Leath. We had sent in an unmanned EI pilot into the Leath system. They volunteered for the follow-up, and after the battle on Karillia ended, we sent your parent's ship in. They were there for almost a week, gathering information. We lost contact just after they sent a message that they had been spotted by another ship."

Phina's breath stuttered. "Could... Is there any chance they are still alive?"

At Link's head shake, tears began welling up again, and she roughly wiped them away. "No, my dear. The Leath don't take prisoners. If they had been able to get back, they would have by now. They wouldn't have left you. They loved you more than anything."

Looking up, Phina saw her sorrow reflected in his eyes. "You loved them too."

He nodded, blinking more quickly than normal. "I still do. They were my family, and so are you."

Phina threw herself forward and wrapped her arms tightly around him, the letter still in one hand. After a minute, her voice sounded muffled against his shirt. "And Jace?"

He sighed, then chuckled, the rumble next to her ear. "Yes, and that scamp too."

She pulled back to look him in the eye. "How come I don't remember you? Wouldn't you have visited us?"

Link shook his head regretfully. "I was the most visible out of all the spies because of my diplomatic role. I had acquired enemies. I didn't want them touching you. I made a vow to your parents that if anything happened to them I would watch out for you and keep you safe. When your parents died, I thought about raising you, but you had your aunt. I had learned with Jace after his parents died years before that parenting is not a skill that I have." He rolled his eyes and shrugged.

Phina raised an eyebrow and teased him. "What? There's something Greyson Wells isn't good at?"

The corner of his mouth turned up and his eyes lightened. "Yeah, yeah. Yuck it up, kid."

She flashed a grin before asking, "So, why did you choose me to recruit and train as your replacement instead of Jace? You know he wanted it."

Instead of answering right away, Link thought for a moment. He finally answered as honestly and thoughtfully as she had ever heard him speak. "Because you were family. I trusted you. Even though we hadn't met officially yet, I had kept tabs on you to make sure you were all right and that I knew what you were up to. You had already taken steps to become a spy, and I figured training you would keep you safer in the long run.

"Being a spy ran in the family, so to speak, so that was another reason, but if you hadn't had the skills, that wouldn't have meant much. We are a lot alike, more so than you maybe realize." He gave her a crooked grin that morphed into a look of pride. "But also, I wanted the best. I knew that whatever you chose to do, you would be brilliant at it, and I wanted that brilliance to shine in a direction that could use that light, even if you had to keep it hidden from most.

"Jace wanted the job, but he wouldn't have been the right person, and we both knew it." He shook his head with regret in his eyes. "He was stubborn about it because he wanted to prove himself, which caused me to lose patience with him. It eventually caused a rift between us. I think he's happier now. Maybe we can bridge that rift in time."

Nodding slowly, Phina gave Link a small smile. "Thank you for choosing me, Link." After he gave her a brief smile and nod, looking uncomfortable, she raised an eyebrow at him. "You done with all the mushy stuff now?"

He sagged in relief. "Hell, yes!"

"Good, because now I have even more to process. I need to move and do something."

Link gave her a knowing smirk. "Have fun flipping and whacking things."

Phina rolled her eyes as she turned away, then paused. "You said you don't want anyone to know about this. Does that mean I can't tell anyone about it?"

Face growing serious, Link frowned in thought before sighing. "I know you are going to want to at least tell Alina. That's fine. Just make sure anyone you tell is trustworthy and won't share it around. The last thing we want is old enemies coming at you."

Phina nodded in understanding, then thanked TOM and ADAM again, gave each of the males present hugs, earning brief smiles from Link and Braeden and a scandalous howl from Sundancer that it was undignified. From there she went into her bedroom to change and put her mother's letter somewhere safe. Phina carefully placed the envelope in a treasure box of her important things. It lay next to her mother's silver pendant. She lingered for a moment, fingering the paper. She finally shook her head and closed the lid.

Later. When she wasn't overwhelmed. Phina changed, then left and decided to go for a run.

CHAPTER FOURTEEN

Etheric Empire, QBBS *Meredith Reynolds*

Phina raced out of the door and threaded her way through the people on the walkways. She headed for her workout gym, feet flying as she navigated the lesser trafficked corridors. When she reached hallways that were filled with more people, her brain calculated the speed, angles, and path to avoid everyone. As she sped past, she saw startled faces, curious ones who craned their head after her, and oblivious ones who were too intent on their conversations or destinations to notice her.

When she reached the corridor where the Marines guarded the entrance, she slowed down and finally came to a halt. She reached into her pocket and showed her pass to the guards who were often at the entrance and were becoming familiar with her.

After putting the pass away the guard on her left looked down and pointed. "Is that a new friend?"

Phina glanced down and saw the pink Previdian sitting

behind her, his chest puffed out more than normal. "Sundancer? How did you follow me here?"

He gave her an imperious look. *I am a noble and fierce predator, swift and sleek like the wind.*

Frowning, Phina nodded to the guard that Sundancer was with her before responding. "But I was running fast. I didn't think cats could run that fast."

Sundancer gave her a quelling look before following her into the restricted area. *I am not a cat! I'm beginning to think your brain has a malfunction.*

Phina persisted while she led the way past the Marines moving in and out of the other training rooms to her smaller one. "But you have similar physiology. It shouldn't be biologically possible for you to run as quickly as I did."

Grumbling, Sundancer finally looked up after padding into the training room behind her. *All right, fine. I used the Etheric to keep up.*

"Ah, that makes sense." Phina moved toward the mat to stretch. "At some point, we should talk about the connection between us. What you can do, and what you believe I can do."

Must we? Sundancer settled himself at the edge of the mat, where he could lie down and watch her at the same time. He rested his chin on his paws and closed his eyes to a slit. *I suppose we must. That would be the logical thing to do.*

Phina began stretching her body, gradually lengthening the contortions as she grew more limber. She straightened and walked toward the bars, then paused and turned her head when she heard the door open.

Todd stepped into the room, the perspiration on his

forehead showing he had been working out for a while already. He gave her a small smile in greeting. "Hey, Phina."

"Hi. Did the guard tell you I was here?"

"I asked Meredith to tell me when you came to work out so I could join you when I'm free." He stopped when he noticed Sundancer, who eyed the man suspiciously. Todd walked over to the Previdian and crouched and petted him, offering his hand to smell. "Who's this little guy?"

"That's Sundancer." Phina stepped closer as she watched the hairless pink creature rise and sniff Todd's hand delicately, then twitch his nose. "He tells me he's a Previdian with a connection to me through the Etheric."

Sundancer replied mentally. *Because we are connected.* He yawned, flashing his sharp teeth, then leaned forward to allow himself to be petted. *I am also beginning to question your intelligence with how difficult you seem to find this concept.*

"Well, with those teeth, he's no doubt a small but fierce warrior, just like you." Todd flashed her a grin.

Sundancer uttered pleased meows. "This one is a wise and discerning individual." He stretched so Todd could scratch under his chin after he recovered from his surprise. "You can keep him."

Todd startled at the verbal response then chuckled. Phina sighed and rolled her eyes. "Thanks, Sundancer."

"This isn't your usual time to train. Did you need to get some energy out?" Todd gave Sundancer a few more scratches and pets, then rose to listen to the answer, leaving a grumbling Sundancer to lick his paws.

"Sort of." Phina shrugged and began stretching again since she had been standing still for a few minutes.

"There's been a lot of revelatory information over the past few hours and I needed to process."

"Anything you want to talk about?" Todd inclined his head toward the mat. "Or would you like to spar? I have some time. Meredith will let me know when I need to leave."

Phina thought about Todd's offer while she assessed him. He appeared sincere and not asking just to do so. She didn't want to breach his trust by checking mentally. She was still trying to find a balance between being mentally open to the Etheric but not so open that she was overwhelmed by what she sensed from everyone.

I'll show you some exercises for that later.

Phina glanced over in surprise at Sundancer, who had laid down again to watch them. *Deal.* She moved to the middle of the mat and fell into a stance. Should she share? Link said to make sure anyone she told was trustworthy. Phina eyed Todd again briefly before nodding. "Could we do both at the same time?"

"Sure, we can try that." Todd appeared good-humored until he settled into a sparring position. Everything else fell away into a gaze of clear focus and awareness. When he saw she was ready, he sprang forward. In between blocks, kicks, holds, and handsprings, Phina told him what had happened that morning, beginning with meeting Sundancer and seeing her friends again and ending with the revelations from Link, TOM, and ADAM. She left out Link's real name. She figured that was private and for him to decide who should know.

Todd huffed his words as he slid to the side of an attack

from her then moved forward to kick the back of her knee. "Wow. So... How are you feeling about it?"

Phina blocked the kick then raised her elbow to block a punch. She sprang to the side and swept his leg, causing him to fall to one knee. "I don't know. It's all mixed up."

She stepped back and blocked his rush as he surged up from his knee, then slipped around him and jumped up to put her arm around Todd's neck in a move that should have rendered him unconscious within ten seconds.

"Maybe satisfaction that I finally know what happened." She ground out as she continued to press his neck.

He bent over and pulled her off so that her back would have slammed onto the mat if she hadn't kept rolling. She stood up and turned to face Todd, who paused to catch his breath as he listened. She was also winded. She thought seriously about the question.

"I'm proud that my parents were so highly respected, grateful that they loved me that much, and really, really wishing that I could talk to them right now."

"You have the letter," Todd pointed out quietly. "It's not the same, but it's still their words."

Phina blinked back tears as she nodded, determined not to cry. "True. I'll probably read it soon. I wanted to get used to everything I learned first. There's only so much change I can handle at one time, and I've had a lifetime's worth of change already." The side of her mouth curved up as she tried to smile but didn't quite make it.

Todd shook his head thoughtfully. "I think you sell yourself short. You can handle a lot more than you think you can. You haven't needed to, so you haven't discovered the depths of your capacity yet."

"Oh?" Phina's smile worked better. "Think you know me already, huh?"

He flashed a small grin. "I'm beginning to. Want to continue?"

Phina thought back to Link's response earlier to being done with the mushy stuff and realized that maybe Link was right, and she had a lot more in common with him than she thought. She had no trouble returning Todd's grin. "Hell, yes."

Etheric Empire, QBBS *Meredith Reynolds*

Sundancer followed his human to her residence after she had gotten her mind and body aligned again. There had been a lot of information, but the male human who was interested in his charge was correct that she could handle more than she thought she could.

You do realize why you feel the need to start moving, right?

Phina stopped outside her door and looked down with a puzzled frown on her face. "No? There's a reason beyond being overwhelmed?"

He shook his head sourly. *Do I need to spell out every-thing? You humans are a lot of trouble. I'm sure my cousin's Torcellan isn't this high maintenance.*

"From what I hear, no Torcellan is low maintenance." His human snorted and shook her head as she began moving again. He followed after her, taking his time. "Am I supposed to figure it out on my own, or ask a passing mystic, or guess a magic word, or something?"

As entertaining as those might be, you can just ask.

She opened the door to her residence and waited for

him to enter before closing it. "I can, huh? Because that's worked out great for me so far."

The nerve! he yowled as his human went into the bedroom to change. *Hey, I offered to help you earlier without being asked. Because I'm a magnificent and magnanimous being.*

He waited for an answer but got only silence. He quickly trotted after her, passing a dark room with old heavy floral and fruit scents. His human always got in trouble when she was by herself. And silent. He didn't have to know her better to know that. He found her in her room, holding her tablet. She glanced over as he changed his gait to slow and sleek. The ultimate predator on the prowl. Not in a hurry in the slightest.

"Well, training or tips or help is going to need to happen later. My best friend Alina wants me to come see her at work."

She began pulling off her shirt and he hastily turned around then nonchalantly sat to groom himself. Nobody needed to see that. He shuddered. Human biology and habits were so strange. Then again, a trip out to see his human's friends might be what he needed to understand her better. *Where does your friend work?*

"A boutique clothing store. She's an assistant designer there."

Sundancer shuddered again and shook his head. *I'll let you go on your own, then. I'm sure I will find something much more interesting to do.*

Phina chuckled, then walked over and picked him up from behind. He let out a surprised yowl, then subsided and rubbed his head on her newly clothed chest. "A typical manly male, huh?"

He looked up at her with long-suffering eyes. *If manly males think clothing is strange and unnecessary, I'll gladly be one of those. You bipedal creatures have an unnatural obsession with clothing.* He paused, then continued thoughtfully. *Then again, perhaps you need all that clothing to cover your hideously deformed bodies.*

His human rolled her eyes and chuckled as she put him down. He mewed in protest. He had rights, and one of those was to be carried and snuggled!

Phina quirked an eyebrow at him. "Did you change your mind about coming with me?"

Sundancer immediately stopped and looked up at her innocently. *Hurry back with fish or liver. Or both. Now, liver, that's an obsession worth having.*

His human grinned and walked out, calling over her shoulder, "Don't get lost or into trouble."

He snorted delicately. Him? Into trouble? He was a Previdian, not a Sphinx.

A Previdian never got into trouble without being able to get out of it on his own.

QBBS *Meredith Reynolds*, White House Fashions

"You want me to do *what?*" Phina stared at her best friend in shock. She certainly hadn't seen this coming, but knowing Alina, she should have.

"Oh, come on, Phina, it will look adorable on you! It's the perfect dress!" Alina bounced and danced around her new backroom office as she spoke, her fingernails twinkling pink sparkles under the lights above when she moved the dress she held in her hands. The sparkles went along with the pink accents of the sharp accessories that gave some color to her black and white outfit.

Alina displayed one of her newer designs, an asymmetrical white skirt with a black top displaying an off-the-shoulder neckline and elbow-length sleeves. Black knee boots that came to just below the lower hem of the skirt completed the outfit. Mal, Alina's boss, had recently promoted Alina to assistant designer, in part because of her new ideas to brand and advertise their clothing. If one were to examine Alina's outfit closely, a pattern of tiny faint WH marks would be visible and embossed into the fabric of the clothing, a new White House Fashions exclusive trademark.

Not that Phina wanted to get that close to Alina at the moment. Especially since she bore a monstrosity of the highest order in her arms. Phina leaned back and tucked her hands behind her, not wanting to display any eagerness since she had zero available. She shook her head and widened her green eyes. "Adorable is not the word that comes to mind for that."

"Oh?" Alina stopped and blinked at Phina, her face brightening even more if that was possible. "What word were you thinking of?"

"Hideous."

Alina's face and arms dropped, losing all animation for almost five seconds.

Phina blanched. Holy fudging crumbs. She should have known better.

Alina finally sucked in a breath before her eyes began bugging out of her face as she screeched, "Seraphina Grace Waters, you take that back *right* now! You know my clothes aren't hideous so why would you say such a terrible thing?"

As Phina began opening her mouth to reply, ill-advised though it would have been, Alina's tone changed to worry. "Unless it *is* hideous... It needs to be perfect." She looked at the dress she had begun bunching in her hand and relaxed her hands to smooth it out.

Phina sighed and shook her head. "No, it's not hideous. It's just...not to my taste."

Alina turned toward Phina with a flat look and a raised eyebrow. "Stylish and sexy?"

Phina nodded. "Exactly."

Alina rolled her eyes and shook her head before holding out her dress-laden arms. "I'm putting my foot down. You can't say anything else about it until you try it on."

Phina sighed again and took the dress. "All right. That's fair."

Alina made a face as she put her hands on her hips. "Forget what's fair. It's what's going to happen."

Phina smiled weakly and nodded. "Of course."

She went into the changing room in the corner of Alina's office and put the dress on, moving slowly. Her fingers lingered on the fabric and she reluctantly admitted that it felt nice against her skin. It wasn't silk, but it was as close as a synthetic fiber could get. She should have trusted Alina and tried it on in the first place, even if she didn't feel comfortable with it.

The waistline was high with layers of skirt pieces attached like petals of a flower landing just below mid-thigh, along with a leotard insert. Butterfly sleeves draped from the shoulder. The outside layers of both sleeves and the skirt were varying shades of violet, while the inside layers were a golden-yellow. Alina had made a beautiful dress.

She pushed back out of the changing room to show Alina. "All right, fine. It's not as bad as I thought it would be."

Alina grinned and waggled her fingers for Phina to come closer and turn around. "You should have learned by now to always trust me when it comes to clothes."

Phina obliged and turned her head as she twirled to smile ruefully. "I know. I should have."

When Phina turned around again, Alina stood looking at her sharply. "Phina, what's wrong?"

Her shoulders sagged. She could never hide anything from Alina for long. Phina had only managed this long because her friend had been preoccupied with her wedding preparations. After glancing at the door to make sure it was shut so they had privacy, she told Alina everything that had happened as her friend fussed with the fit of the dress, adding a pin here and there.

By the time Phina had finished, the dress had been taken off, she had dressed again in her own clothes, and Alina had most of the alterations done.

Her best friend looked up and asked with concern, "Phina, are you doing okay with this? It's a lot to take in. At least now you know why you had all those quirks that no one else had."

Phina nodded, took a deep breath as she thought then nodded again. "I am. It helped to talk to Todd earlier and now you. For some reason talking it out a couple of times has helped me to put it into better perspective."

Alina smiled slyly as she waggled her eyebrows. "Todd, huh?"

Phina rolled her eyes and shook her head. "Stop. We're just friends."

"Mmhmm," Alina murmured as she finished the alterations. "He listens to you, spends time with you, and volunteered to help you out of his massively busy schedule. But sure... You're just friends."

"Well, we are," Phina insisted. "There's nothing else happening."

Alina paused and looked up to study Phina briefly before she resumed her sewing. "I see."

"You see what?" Phina asked warily.

"You're scared because you don't know how to handle a relationship." Her friend nodded knowingly.

"I know how to handle a relationship." Phina insisted, purposely misinterpreting Alina's comment. "We've been friends since before we could walk."

Alina gave her a flat stare. "That's not the same thing, and you know it."

Phina shrugged halfheartedly but belligerently. "So?"

Returning her focus to her task, Alina shook her head. "One of these days, you won't be able to ignore it. Or Todd will bring it up himself."

"Until that day," Phina insisted firmly, "I will keep my mouth shut and ignore it. I would hate to ruin our growing friendship if he doesn't think about me that way."

"Oh, he does," Alina responded airily as she knotted the

last thread. "He's got that look in his eyes when he's watching you."

"Well, then he can eventually tell me himself, and if that day comes, maybe I'll be able to think up an answer."

Alina shook her head sadly. "When it comes to dating, you're hopeless."

Phina's face brightened. "Just the way I like it."

CHAPTER FIFTEEN

Etheric Empire, QBBS *Meredith Reynolds*, Open Court

Phina exited White House Fashions and joined the foot traffic heading to the inner station, which housed the resident apartment suites. As she walked through the crowds, Phina had to constantly remind herself not to stare at people as she passed, although she could hear most of the conversations in a wide radius around her.

Once she focused on her hearing, the conversations grew louder. She kept shaking her head and trying to adjust the volume. It moderately helped. Just before the turnoff, she heard cries in the distance from the direction of the shops.

"Has anyone seen my daughter? SofRey? SofRey, where are you?"

Frowning in concern, Phina pinged ADAM as she turned to the Open Court.

>>**Yes, Phina?**<<

ADAM, do you or Meredith know what's happening in the Open Court Area with a lost child?

>>Yes. We're backtracking the woman to see what happened to the Torcellan child.<<

Torcellan? Phina asked as she jogged around shoppers and visitors of varying species.

>>Yes. She's somewhere in the vicinity of Kolen Clothing.<< ADAM replied, naming one of Mal's competitors.

Phina scanned the crowd as she approached the area. She saw the frantic mother with alabaster skin, long white hair, and deep purple eyes talking with the security guards. Phina continued to scan as ADAM confirmed, >>The girl is not outside the clothing store. Cameras see her ducking into the store, then they lose her. She is short enough that she can sometimes disappear from view. She never reached the back of the store, so she must still be there.<<

ADAM, do you have a way to handle this?

>>Yes, Meredith has protocols, but whatever your way is would probably have a higher likelihood of success without upsetting the child further.<<

Leaving the mother to the guards, Phina entered Kolen Clothing. The employees and customers were either craning their necks to see what was happening or going about their business. At a glance, Kolen Clothing was shooting for a colored contrast to the white and black clothes that were core in the White House Fashions brand.

Phina set that tidbit aside for the moment, focusing on looking between the rows. Having failed to find the girl that way, Phina looked out to see the mom still calling out and the guards searching the area.

Sighing, Phina closed her eyes and attempted to open

the shields on her mind just a little. An influx of information shot into her brain, and Phina slammed the shields shut. However, as she processed the thoughts and sensations, Phina knew the girl was close.

Focusing on that mind, she cracked the shields open a sliver. Phina turned in that direction and opened her eyes. Two large racks of floor-length dresses stood in front of her. Phina slid by a customer asking about alterations and quietly stepped in between the racks. She inclined her head, listening, and heard a light scuffle to her right.

Phina thought about the best way to get the girl to come out when she didn't know why the Torcellan child was there. She thought back to her own childhood and considered the little she'd gotten from the child's mind. Finally, she crouched down as if about to sit. After waving off a concerned saleswoman, Phina began talking in Torcellan as if to herself.

"I was thinking about ice cream. Maybe that could be the next stop, to get a bowl of vanilla ice cream, or maybe a nice cone with chocolate. Or maybe that one with the cookie pieces. What was that called again? Cookies and something." She watched the clothing rack carefully from the corner of her eye. "But, you know... It's too bad I don't have anyone to go get ice cream with. It's much more fun that way. My friend Alina and I used to go every week to get ice cream from the shop."

A deep purple eye peeked out from between two dresses. A small hesitant voice spoke, muffled by the clothing. "I like ice cream."

"You do?" Phina turned with a smile, hoping it looked encouraging.

The little girl nodded solemnly and crawled out. "I like the cake one."

Phina exaggerated her surprise. "They have *cake* ice cream? I don't know about that. Maybe it doesn't taste as good as the cookie kind."

"No," SofRey protested, popping her whole head out. "It's the best one!"

Phina slowly nodded as she looked at the disheveled girl about the size of a human four-year-old. She looked like a mini version of her mother. "I see. Well, if it's the best one, I'll have to get a big bowl of it. Would you want to help me eat it?"

Purple eyes widened in excitement. "Yes! I love ice cream." Her face fell a moment later. "I need to find Momma. She will be looking for me. I've been hiding a long time."

Phina nodded. "We should talk to your mom first. What made you decide to hide?"

Her face grew concerned, purple eyes wide as she looked toward the entrance. "I saw a scary man. Momma told me to hide if I see scary ones. Is he still there?"

Phina thought through her scan of the mall outside and didn't see anyone who looked scary to her. But, she also wasn't a small Torcellan child. She didn't know what SofRey may have been taught aside from the Torcellan custom of abstaining from violence. She cracked open her shields again and searched for anyone with bad intentions, but she couldn't sense anything.

"I didn't see him, but you can help me look when you leave." Phina leaned forward with a small smile. "Do you want to know a secret?"

SofRey quickly nodded her head.

"I have friends who watch everyone in the station here all the time to make sure that the only scary guys here are the ones who chase the bad guys away. When people come to the station, they are watched all the time to make sure they behave. The bad ones are taken away where they can't scare anyone anymore. What do you think?"

SofRey glanced outside, biting her lip. "There are lots of people. What if they miss a scary bad guy?"

Phina smiled reassuringly. "It doesn't happen very often. But if it does, my friends shut the doors down so the bad ones can't leave the area and immediately tell the security team so the guards can take care of them. It's pretty quick."

"Does anyone get hurt?" the child asked anxiously as she clutched the clothes she hid behind.

"You know, that's a good question," Phina said approvingly. "Let me ask my friend."

She spoke over the implant. *ADAM? Any injuries that would concern our friend here?*

>>I checked as soon as I heard you ask. There were small injuries to bystanders or security, but the only major injuries happen to the people they've subdued.<<

I'm assuming you scanned for her scary man?

>>Of course. She saw a large Marine out of uniform meeting his girlfriend a few stores down. He would look intimidating to a small girl.<<

Ah. Thank you, ADAM.

>>You're welcome, Phina.<<

Phina nodded and relayed the information to SofRey. The little girl looked relieved, then her mouth formed a small pout. "I didn't see you talking. You made that up. I'm not a baby. Mommy says to tell the truth."

Holding up a hand, Phina told the girl somberly, "I solemnly swear I won't ever lie to you, SofRey. You just couldn't hear him."

From her pocket, ADAM's voice came out of her tablet. "Hello, SofRey."

SofRey's purple eyes grew wide.

SofRey dashed over to her mother while holding Phina's hand and pulling her behind. "Momma, Momma!"

"SofRey!" The woman gathered up her daughter and hugged her tightly, glancing at Phina questioningly. She was visibly relieved. Light applause broke out among those watching before they moved on. "Where were you?"

SofRey pulled back and looked up at her mom. "I saw a scary man, so I went to hide. 'member, you said to hide when scary men come? Phina found me and told me the scary guy was gone and we could go get ice cream. Please, please, please, can we have ice cream? Phina said we would get a big bowl of the cake one."

As Phina watched SofRey negotiate with her mother, she realized that as much as she struggled with her new abilities at times, they weren't all bad. In fact, they could be pretty useful. She just needed to get training so that she wasn't overwhelmed so much of the time, and training meant more time with Sundancer. Time to find out the kitty-cat's story.

As they walked up to the ice cream shop, Phina snickered to herself as she imagined hearing Sundancer yowl at her again that he wasn't a cat.

Hmm... Maybe Link's penchant for poking buttons was rubbing off.

After waving goodbye to SofRey and promising another ice cream outing when she could manage it, Phina headed home again.

She looked forward to relaxing in her apartment while talking to Sundancer. This day had gotten pretty long, and it wasn't close to dinner time yet.

Phina turned off into the corridor that connected the outer ring of the public station with the inner station that only citizens of the Etheric Empire who resided there and their guests could access. She hoped she would make it home and have time to consider dinner options.

Those hopes were dashed when she approached a cross corridor and felt a fluctuation in her mental shields. Immediately alert, Phina looked around and saw a hooded figure a short distance down the side hallway. Her gaze sharpened on a hand with skin in a shade of green that beckoned her to follow.

Phina had a fairly good idea as to who the hand belonged to. Curious but exercising caution, Phina made her way down the corridor after the alien while she pinged ADAM.

ADAM, are you seeing this?

>>Yes. I've tasked part of my processing power to always keep track of you and what you are doing. I don't

want any more surprises for you without us knowing about it.<<

Phina's heart was warmed. *Aww, I love you too, ADAM.*

He gave the digital equivalent of an embarrassed cough, then simply answered, >>**Yes. Do you have an idea as to where he is leading you, or his intentions?<<**

She watched the alien's back as he turned a corner to head down a different hallway. He apparently had a particular place and purpose for their interaction.

Well, Phina responded slowly. *Either he intends to lead me meekly to my death, or he wants a private conversation without his compatriots knowing about it. I'm leaning toward the latter.*

Phina frowned as she stopped behind the alien as he paused to open a door. *There is also the possibility that he wanted to speak to me without Link or Will there.* She paused as she stepped in, her mind whirling before responding, *Or both, without either side. I think that's the most likely possibility.*

Once the door was shut, the alien gestured to seats that were arranged for conversation but more for business than recreation.

ADAM, where are we?

>>**You are in a private reception room. I told Meredith to let him in.<<**

I see. Thank you.

Phina took a chair and folded her legs up to cross under her. She folded her hands together and looked at the alien who sat on the edge of his seat and pulled back the hood. The Qendrok attendant, who had seemed far too interested in their group and particularly her, stared at her with curious and assessing black eyes.

He spoke earnestly, and the translation chip picked it

up for her. She had read up on the thin collection of documents the Empire had on the Qendrok culture and language. She hadn't yet had time to become fluent. She could pick words out here and there as she listened carefully.

"I beg your pardon, Delegate Waters, for the manner in which I gained your attention."

He drew the hands from his top set of arms forward to bow over them while his second set of hands were held out to her.

Phina nodded and gestured for him to continue. "Of course. For what reason did you use this method to speak to me?"

He straightened, bringing his second set of arms in close to his body, and gazed directly at her face, occasionally glancing at her forehead as he spoke. "Several reasons, Delegate Waters. The first reason is to warn you."

Eyebrows raised in surprise, Phina leaned forward. "Warn me?"

The Qendrok nodded stiffly. "Yes. Qartan has fixed his malevolent gaze on you. He is part of a faction of our people that values those with power over all else. However, they believe only certain beings should have that power, mainly themselves, I'm sorry to say."

Phina watched the alien's stiff movements, wondering if these mannerisms were normal for him or if he felt uncomfortable with speaking with her. "Why are you sorry? Do you not agree with him? You wear the same medallion." She gestured at the object lying visibly on his chest.

"No, I do not." He stated firmly. "Our people are divided

into two factions. One is more religious, and the other is not. The religious faction has suborned the symbol of our historic ruling government for their own, believing it gives them legitimacy." He lifted the medallion and briefly placed it on his bowed forehead, then kissed the symbol in the center and released it. "It is a symbol of our great history, and that is why I wear it. Qartan belongs to this religious faction which has gained popularity in the higher reaches of our people. Because his faction controls the government of our people, Qartan has the power to send our assassins after you." His alien face was longer and broader than a human's, with wide-set black eyes that looked at her with speculative interest. "He has been ranting for days about you and your unlawful nature."

He paused, his gaze searching before slowly admitting. "He has named you an abomination."

Phina's heart lurched. That was her worst fear. She steadied herself by taking deep, even breaths. None of her friends and chosen family had ever had the slightest thought that the term was true about her. She'd be damned if she'd believe a bigoted alien over her family who loved her.

After a few moments passed, she asked flatly, "Why does he believe this?"

The green alien shifted uncomfortably. "What I am telling you is in part from what rumors have come to me and partly what Qartan has verbalized in his rants. They are very secretive about their practices." He continued speaking slowly to make sure he was understood. "They have a goddess who has promised them power. Qartan is adamant that only his goddess should have this power available to her. It is why he refused to speak with you before. You are young, human, and a female with power."

Phina frowned and began processing this while she clarified. "You said he revered a goddess. He has no issue with this female?"

The Qendrok nodded agreeably while changing his arm positions. Interesting. Perhaps their body language meant something in particular. She almost missed his next words in her distraction. "No, Delegate Waters. However, she is not young, she is not human, and she has promised him power. These factors overwrote his particular prejudice about females."

She couldn't help asking, "Does he consider your own females to be less?"

He shifted again, appearing uncomfortable. "Yes, but they are traditionally not given positions of power. They are nurturers rather than rulers or protectors. Qartan views that as the rightful order, rather than a personal preference due to nature."

The doors behind the alien silently opened, revealing Sundancer quietly padding in. *I knew you were getting into trouble.*

Shh. Quiet, Sundancer. This nice alien is telling me all about what's wrong with me.

The pink cat sniffed as he settled down on the side of the room where he could see the Qendrok but remain out of the alien's line of sight. *There's nothing wrong with you aside from a distinct lack of worship in the tune of livers for me.*

Sorry, humans don't do worship of any form well.

Believe me, that fact has not escaped my notice.

"I see." Phina considered the alien as she gathered her

thoughts again, then frowned. "I'm sorry, I never caught your name."

"Xoruk, Delegate Waters." He bowed his head in the Qendrok greeting to an equal. "Your pardon for the oversight."

"No problem, Delegate Xoruk." Phina thought through everything he'd told her before Sundancer walked in. "So, you said there were several reasons, and the first is that you came to warn me that Qartan will send assassins after me. What are the other reasons?"

Xoruk nodded and straightened as he continued, his black eyes earnest. "I wished to tell you the nature of Qartan's distaste for you, yes. I also wish to request that your delegation meet with a smaller portion of ours. Just myself and one other."

He glanced at her forehead again, and she couldn't help calling him on it. "Delegate Xoruk, is there something on my head that's distracting you?"

His eyes widened, body posture conveying embarrassment. "I beg your pardon for my rudeness, Delegate Waters. Your power is visible to us Qendrok, but it is not the same as it is with others, and so it is distracting."

Phina straightened. "You can see it?"

"Yes," Xoruk mirrored her movements. "All Qendrok can. Most have a small amount of power themselves, enough to give them the sight to see. The Qendrok who have more power tend to be those who rise higher in our government. Most power we see in others is amassed in a person's core." He gestured at his thoracic region where his heart and lungs resided. "However, your power is anomalous in that it centers on your brain instead. It is something that hadn't been seen before to my knowledge, and so it draws my attention. I certainly didn't mean to be rude in my distraction."

He means your ability to connect to the Etheric is centered in your brain, Sundancer told her. *It is why most, if not all, of your abilities will be of the mental kind. I have seen in your thoughts that your Empress can move through the Etheric. This would be a physical manifestation of Etheric use rather than a mental one, which means you will not be able to do the same on your own.*

Phina shook her head. *Later, Sundancer. I have many questions, but I need to finish this conversation first. Thank you for the information.*

Sundancer mentally sighed at the delay but finally simply responded, *You are my human.*

Phina waved a hand dismissively at the Qendrok. "I appreciate the apology, Delegate Xoruk, but I'm fine. I wondered why you kept giving me the looks you do. Now I know. We can set up a meeting. Perhaps tomorrow, around this time in this room?" She figured the later hour would give her and Will time to finish class and other things for the day before the meeting.

Xoruk inclined his head and moved his arms into another position. Her mind kept poking at the possibilities as there had to be meaning there. "The time is agreeable, Delegate Waters."

"All right. Were those all the reasons for this discussion?" Phina hoped the answer was yes as her belly began rumbling.

After hesitating for a moment, Xoruk inclined his head again. "To meet and speak with you myself, Delegate

Waters. The last topic might be better left until we meet tomorrow."

Phina nodded, then unfolded and stood, giving the appropriate Qendrok greeting for an equal. "In that case, I will see you tomorrow, Delegate Xoruk."

Xoruk stood as well and returned the greeting looking pleased. "And you, Delegate Waters."

He turned and caught sight of Sundancer, his eyes widening the furthest Phina had seen yet. "You are bonded to a Previdian!"

Sundancer looked up with interest. *Finally, someone who understands my magnificence. You should take notes.*

Phina's eyes darted between the two aliens wishing she was alone with Sundancer so she could speak her mind. She settled for a brief quelling glare. "Yes. That's what he tells me."

Xoruk appeared not to know which body position he wanted and ended up twitching several times before finally bowing his head with his palms up. "I see. I thought perhaps human females were the ones with power, but I didn't see many females with power as I walked through your station. Being paired with a Previdian changes things. You are one to watch, Delegate Waters."

She frowned. That statement could be taken in many contexts. "As someone who causes trouble?"

He raised his head and looked at her as if she were something wondrous. It made her shift uncomfortably. "No. Previdians are mentioned deeply in our lore and accessed by very few. But those records are clear. You are one to watch because those paired with Previdians do great things that often change the course of their people."

CHAPTER SIXTEEN

Etheric Empire, QBBS *Meredith Reynolds*

"Phina, wait up!"

Recognizing Will's voice, Phina stopped walking down the hall toward the exit of the Diplomatic Institute and turned to wait.

Phina felt pretty good. She had shuffled Xoruk's revelations to the side and spent the last evening talking to Sundancer and training her mental abilities after dinner.

He'd had her lie on the floor—so she didn't fall asleep on the bed, Sundancer had told her—and he had settled himself just above her head. First, he'd shown her the best way to shield her mind while still allowing the Etheric energy to flow. Then for the next few hours, he'd taught her different ways of shield filtering: to keep her thoughts in, to keep other thoughts out entirely, to filter other's thoughts so she heard only what she wanted to hear, to be able to skim surface thoughts over a large area while blocking the deeper thoughts in case she needed to find someone such as the scary guy SofRey had mentioned, and finally how to block everything else but one person so she could go deeper.

I don't want to do that. I don't need to see or hear that stuff. It should be private, Phina had protested when they got to the last one.

Sundancer had been quiet for a moment then asked, *What if you could save a planet by searching one man's inner thoughts? Your Empire? The Empress? Your friends?*

Phina hadn't protested after that and renewed her focus to learn as quickly as possible. She did end up giving him the small amount of liver she had found and let him sleep on the bed. He hadn't believed her in the morning when she told him he snored and refused to speak to her further before she left for class.

Class this morning had been much easier without having to worry as much about keeping her shields shut tight. Her filters hadn't been perfect, but the difference gave her hope that they would be soon, and she felt much more confident and less frazzled.

After lunch, she had gotten another three classes checked off that tested rather than requiring discussion: History of the Empire and two sections of Law and Politics, one from each year. She hadn't gotten the scoring back yet, but she knew how many answers she'd gotten right, and it was more than enough to pass. There were a few questions in the Law and Politics exams that she'd had to make educated guesses for since they could be solved with several different approaches.

Students passed with questioning glances as Will drew closer with an open smile and worried eyes. "Hey, I got your message about the meeting tonight. Anything we should worry about?"

Phina shrugged and tried to look unconcerned and not like she was under condemnation by a whole group of people. "I don't know. It probably will be a worry to someone, but I don't know which person it will be."

He gave her a quick grin and looked at the time. "We have a couple of hours until then. Are you doing anything?"

"Nothing in particular. Why?" Phina asked, wary.

He flashed her grin. "Ease up there, sister. I wasn't going to ask you for a date. I already told you that's not the kind of relationship we're gonna have."

Her shoulders eased the tension she had begun to feel. "Okay, good. Just wanted to make sure. Some guys say one thing, but they are just waiting to pounce on you when you aren't looking."

He chuckled. "That's exactly what guys say about women."

Phina smiled at the quip then took a breath. "All right. So, what did you have in mind?"

Will grinned and tugged her toward the door where other students were leaving. "I'm going to take you to meet my mom."

She groaned as the tension returned. "Oh yeah, that's *much* better."

Will led her back to the inner station. For time's sake, they took the tram. On the way, Will asked her about her experiences growing up on the station and shared some of his own.

"Wait, which school did you go to?" Phina frowned after he shared a story from his school years.

He flashed her a smile as they exited the tram. "I went to the same one you did until I went to the Etheric Academy. I applied because I heard you and your friend Alina talking about it one day."

She stopped, causing a small pile-up of people before he grabbed her arm and escorted her out of the way with a chuckle. "You tend to do that."

"Do what?" Her thoughts were still on his earlier comment.

He grinned at her and guided her out of the way of other passersby. "Get stuck in your head and not be aware of what's going on around you."

Phina grimaced and tugged her arm free as she followed. "I've gotten better about it, but surprising revelations tend to shock me out of it." She turned narrowed eyes toward Will. "If you were there with us in school, how come you didn't talk to us? Did you want to be a creeper?"

Will laughed, then grinned. "I suppose it would look like that. I did try, but as I've just pointed out, you tend to be in your head and don't notice other people unless they warrant your interest. I complained to my mom that I knew we would be friends, but you weren't cooperating. She told me that meant it must not be time yet and I had to be patient."

"Huh." Phina blinked and tried to be more aware of her surroundings as she looked around. "That must have been frustrating. I'm sorry. Your mom sounds great."

Will gave her an appreciative smile. "Yeah, she always gives me the best advice. Just wait until you meet her."

Will led her to a corridor of apartment suites that looked like any other. The smells that wafted toward them were fantastic.

As they stepped inside the apartment suite where the delicious aromas originated, Phina heard a pleasant female voice call out from the kitchen, "Will, is that you, love? Just a second while I take these out of the oven and put dinner on simmer."

"Yeah, Mom. I'm here, and guess who I brought with me?" He flashed Phina a mischievous grin.

She narrowed her eyes and whispered, "You were trouble as a kid; I can see it."

His grin widened, but his reply got lost as a tall woman who had Will's eyes and mouth, or the other way around, stepped through the doorway. "Who did you..." Her eyes widened, and she gasped. "Seraphina! It's really you!"

She stepped forward with a wobbly smile. "Can I hug you?" Phina barely got a nod in before the woman's arms folded around her and held her tight. Rather than feeling uncomfortable, it was nice. Almost like she remembered her mom's hugs.

Phina's eyes watered but she blinked the tears back. Finally, the woman stepped back with a watery smile and led her to the couch then grabbed a tissue.

"I'm sorry for the waterworks." She wiped the tears away and blew her nose as she walked to the kitchen.

Phina glanced over to Will, who sat down next to her as she heard the sink run, but she wasn't able to do more than open her mouth before his mom was back and settling into the chair across from them.

"Sorry about that." She gave Will a smile filled with love before turning to Phina. "So, you're finally here with us."

Phina tried not to fidget as she looked at the woman, confused. "I'm sorry, Will didn't tell me your name."

"Oh, my gracious. Will!" The woman shook her head at her sheepish son before responding. "I'm Fiona Jameson. I'm married to Paul Jameson. Will and Rayna are my recalcitrant children, and I knew your mother."

Phina straightened in shock. "You what?"

Fiona sighed. "I should have handled that more delicately, sweetheart. I apologize. Yes. Your mother and I were friends and talked a lot when you both were younger. We met when she was pregnant with you and I was pregnant with Will. We kept in touch and found we had a lot in common." She looked at Phina anxiously. "You've read your parents' letter, right?"

Phina glanced away. "Not yet. I just got it yesterday."

"Well, then I won't go into that." Fiona shook her head with a frown. "I don't know what Greyson was thinking by waiting so long. Done is done, and we can't change that. We can only move forward."

Phina saw Fiona's kind smile, and a memory clicked. "You're Mrs. Jameson. You taught English when I was nine."

Fiona smiled and leaned forward. "Yes, that's right. English, History, and Art. I moved around different grades as needed, but I loved high school as we could talk literature and history a lot more, along with so many great art projects. Sadly, I wasn't there when you were in high school."

Will rolled his eyes in mock exasperation. "Where do you think I got so many names from?"

Fiona narrowed her eyes at her son though she also wore a small smile. "And aptly named you were for a historical freedom fighter, an expressive revolutionary painter, a brilliant, eccentric inventor, and an honorable federal judge."

Phina smiled as Will gave his mom a look of exaggerated long-suffering. "I know, Mom. I'll do something brilliant at some point. Aside from Great Uncle Judge Jameson, those guys didn't get acknowledged until they were dead, so I've got time."

His mom laughed and gave them both a grin that Phina returned with a smile. Fiona was easy to talk to and reminded her of her mom in a way.

"Can I ask why we never met before now aside from English class if you knew my mom?"

Fiona's smile turned lopsided as she slowly shook her head. "It isn't my story to tell, sweetheart. Read the letter first, then you are welcome to ask me any questions you like."

Phina couldn't help using one of her new filters, the one that would allow her to sense the mood and intention of the people around her. Will was happy about her and his mom getting along yet anxious about the meeting later. And Fiona... Phina had a hard time not reacting. She had the intention of welcoming Phina and regretted not being able to share. But it was the depth of love the woman felt that caused Phina's throat to tighten. She blinked back tears.

She nodded as Fiona stood and flashed a smile at them

both before she returned to the kitchen. "Would you like some fresh cookies? And Seraphina, please, won't you stay for dinner?"

Will called after her. "Only if we're okay to eat early, Mom. We've got an important meeting to go to later."

"Come in here and tell me about it," Fiona called.

Will glanced at Phina, and when she shook her head, responded, "Sorry, Mom. It's classified." He stood and walked into the kitchen.

Phina looked at the pictures of their family that were placed in open spaces on the walls and furniture as she followed Will. It was cozy and comfortable. A home more than a place to sleep. She glanced at a small desk over on the side and saw a picture collage, one of which showed a younger Fiona with Phina's mom. They both looked young and happy, each smiling down at their own baby bundle.

Phina swallowed and shut down her emotions to give herself a break. She joined Will in the kitchen as he continued, "This is the keep your mouth shut kind of meeting."

"Come talk to me about other things, then." She handed them each a warm cookie with chocolate bits, then drew them to the table for a chat while she finished preparing dinner.

Phina felt warm inside and realized that she had begun to add another part to her found family.

Etheric Empire, QBBS *Meredith Reynolds*, Private Receiving Room

"So, here we are at your request, Delegate Xoruk." Link sat back with steepled fingers as he scanned the two

Qendrok with a curious gaze. "Please expound on what you told Phina yesterday."

Although Link understood the reasons for the approach, he didn't like it one bit that Xoruk had approached Phina when she was alone. After getting Phina's message about the impromptu meeting and the topics of discussion, Link's protective instincts were pinging.

Xoruk blinked his black eyes and frowned. "Your pardon, but I am not understanding this word 'expound.'"

Phina leaned forward from her seat next to Link. "It means to expand on or explain further."

"I see." Xoruk moved his arm positions, but while Link was sure it meant something, he didn't have a damned clue what it meant and felt too irritated to try to figure it out. The delegate continued. "I can, as you say, expound. I assume Delegate Waters shared with you the contents of that meeting and that she is *vadrakken*?"

Link shook his head and glanced at Phina, who also looked puzzled. "She relayed the conversation, but this word '*vadrakken*' isn't translating."

"Hmm." Xoruk brought his fingers together much in the same way as Link's were. "One who brings change to events around her by her presence."

Surprised, Link leaned forward. "A catalyst. That's been suggested before."

Nodding, Xoruk continued. "Yes, and with the power she holds, the danger is very real. She is young, so the effect will grow stronger as time moves on and her strength of will increases. Some of those appearing in our history were assassinated before they could gain that strength. This is another reason why Qartan has targeted Delegate Waters."

Link glanced at Phina at the same time as Will, who also looked unhappy at the knowledge. Damn it. He knew there had to be a reason for his instincts to act up. Phina attempted to remain impassive but Link could see red creeping up her neck. So, she hadn't shared everything about the conversation. He would address that later. Link eyed Phina briefly before he turned his gaze to the silent Jokin. "Do you agree?"

The slighter Qendrok had been staring at Phina, which had made Link, and he was sure Phina, uncomfortable. He turned to Link at his question and gestured to Xoruk in small movements. "It is as Xoruk says. She is becoming a power, and that is a threat to Qartan and his faction. They hold their power tightly to themselves and are jealous of others who hold it. What they cannot possess, they do not allow to exist. It has become their way."

"I see. Are the assassins on the table?" Link had encountered them before and didn't want one after Phina, let alone a whole contingent of them. His fear and anger rolled together inside.

Xoruk moved his arm position again and bowed his head briefly. As he raised his head, his black eyes held regret. "I'm afraid that Qartan has put the process into motion. This will need to be stopped. This warning is part of why we requested to meet with you once we knew Delegate Waters existed, but we had already decided to seek a discourse before our arrival."

This sparked interest in Link. "Oh? For what reason?"

Jokin answered with a tinge of rebuke that set Link's

teeth on edge, but his words pulled the wind out of his sails entirely. "When you disrupted Gazaq's mission almost a solar year ago and rooted out his group, you set our faction back by ten years. This allowed Qartan to gain more power."

Link's heart sank. That mission had been wearying and difficult, but he had persisted because he had thought he was taking out a terrorist cell. To hear it was the other way around cut into him. He shook his head regretfully. "I'm sorry. I didn't know. I was acting on the information we had at the time, which was that a small group was using the station here to subvert their government." Which was true, he realized. He hadn't had the information to know they were justified in their rebellion. "The information came from a trusted source. It didn't occur to me that it might not be accurate."

Which brought up a whole other set of issues he couldn't think about yet.

Xoruk changed his position and spoke soothingly. "We know. Qartan and his group made sure that you wouldn't find out. However, we find ourselves without the resources to make the changes we need for our people."

Link met Phina's gaze, which showed sorrow for the loss of their people and his part in it, as well as determination to help. He nodded and turned to see that same determination in Will. Straightening, he nodded at Xoruk and Jokin. "What do you need?"

Xoruk's and Jokin's posture changed, but the intent was clear this time—supplication. Xoruk spoke quickly but clearly, his eyes beseeching. "We humbly and respectfully request the Empire's aid in overthrowing the faction that has ruled over and oppressed our people. Over the last two decades, Qartan's oversight has become untenable. We need change and cannot do it from within. The assassins follow the acknowledged leaders, and the rest of us cannot hope to defeat them. Once this is done, if you will have us, we will join your Empire. An agreement between us will not be reached with his faction in place. Their fear and hatred of Delegate Waters and your Empress will prevent it."

Link assessed them both for sincerity, then nodded. "We will take your request to the Empress."

Etheric Empire, QBBS *Meredith Reynolds*, Private Sparring Room

Phina was slammed to the ground, her whole body shocked from the impact. She scrambled to collect her thoughts.

After concluding their meeting with the Qendrok, Link had asked ADAM for the first available slot to speak with the Empress. The AI had responded that she was available now if they were willing to volunteer as sparring partners. Link had winced and appeared to shrink with dread but agreed.

Phina hadn't understood the response then, but she did now.

Clearly and with up close and personal experience.

As they'd entered the sparring room, Bethany Anne had pointed at Link and then at Phina. "You talk while we spar."

He had hesitated a glance of sympathy toward Phina.

Will had been starstruck and hadn't attempted to speak, only stared at the Empress as if not certain she were real.

Phina had frowned in confusion at Link's concern but had stepped forward as her Empress beckoned and settled herself into her ready stance. She had barely twitched when she had been hit by a speeding comet and slammed into the floor.

Or that was how it felt. Todd's fist to the stomach back when this began was nothing compared to this.

Phina stuttered to catch her breath as she stared up at the ceiling, wondering what had just happened. Her body had already begun healing; her mind was taking longer to catch up.

The beautiful black hair-framed face of her Empress leaned into view, shaking her head. "Now, that's sad. I know you can do better."

Phina wheezed, "Yes, Empress."

"I thought I was clear about the 'Empress' shit?" Bethany Anne held out her hand to help Phina to her feet. "We are not in a formal setting, so you don't need that stick in your ass. Call me by my name."

Phina nodded wordlessly. She pulled herself up and rubbed her chest, which was beginning to ease.

Bethany Anne withdrew a few paces and faced Phina with an expectant look. "Continue, Link."

Link continued to explain the situation with a somewhat anxious look in his eye. Phina had a feeling the Empress already knew everything he was telling her.

Shaking herself out, Phina's thoughts raced. She hadn't seen the Empress move and she hadn't had any time to respond. Which meant that as much as she had held back for Maxim and Todd, she didn't need to for the Empress.

Phina realized she wouldn't be able to match the Empress, but at least she didn't need to worry about keeping herself in check. A smile grew on her face.

Bethany Anne raised her eyebrow in interest. "Good. You're getting it. Now stop thinking and let's go ."

Phina settled and indicated she was ready.

Well, as ready as anyone could be when faced with Bethany Anne's particular method of teaching.

Phina let herself go. She got in a dodge and two strikes that were blocked before she was on the floor again. "Better," she heard through the ringing in her ears. She shook her head and got up.

The Empress paused the lesson to show her a different way to stand. "Here, brace yourself this way when you are fighting someone stronger or with more power. It's all in the hips."

Phina made painful contact with the floor twelve more times, gaining a few seconds more between impacts before the Empress stopped Link mid-sentence, her eyes flashing with anger.

"What's the bottom line here? I'd rather not kill half their people if we can help it, but I can't ignore oppression on their planet, and I sure as shit don't appreciate being manipulated." Bethany Anne bared her teeth and her eyes turned red. "That those fuck-knuckles used us to root out a justified rebellion has earned them an ass-kicking aside from the one I intend we give them for what they've done to their people."

"Well, I doubt it would take an entire half of their

people to make your point," Link ventured carefully. "We could give the faction an ultimatum and leave it up to them whether they wish to die or not."

Phina lay still, grateful for the distraction. She gathered the energy to stand, more filling her with every second that went by. She could feel the influx from the Etheric. However, since the connection went mainly to her mind instead of her body, the healing process was taking a few extra steps to facilitate.

"That works," Bethany Anne told Link. "Suggestions?"

Groaning, Phina finally pushed herself up. "Accept revolution or death?"

Bethany Anne grinned, her eyes fading to black as she let go of her rage. She shook her head ruefully. "I'm told I can't always go to the extreme measure first. They haven't acted against us yet, just used us for their ends, so we may need to moderate the verbiage."

The Empress paused, her eyes unfocusing. "The Qendrok are leaving right now. Either they caught the two you met with, or they realized they weren't going to get anywhere with their bullying tactics." She glanced at the three of them, her eyes flashing red again. "I fucking *hate* bullies. The faction will submit, or they will die. Their choice. I'm going to send a delegation to state our requirements for peace. You three will go to their planet and take a large contingent with you. You will need enough fire-power to show we are serious. Dan Bosse will work with you to organize. This situation may take some time to work through."

Phina felt a pang of guilt. Bethany Anne flashed Phina a knowing smile. "After Maxim and Alina's wedding next weekend should be soon enough and give you time to get things ready. We won't mess with their wedding. They have delayed their plans enough. Funnel any further updates or requests over the next few weeks through ADAM and I'll review them."

Link nodded with of hint of a bow. "Yes, Bethany Anne."

Will almost squeaked something but changed his mind when Link gave him a warning backhand to his chest. He nodded as Link did and gave her a shaky smile.

The Empress nodded at them in acknowledgment then waved her hand. "Now leave, please. Phina and I have things to discuss in private."

Will's and Link's gazes darted to Phina, whose eyes had widened, but she slowly nodded.

"Thank you, Bethany Anne," Link repeated, then turned to the door. Will copied the actions but mumbled the words "My Empress" with a wide-eyed glance at Phina.

Holy Shit! Can you believe we have been in a meeting with the Empress? She authorized a huge delegation for us? And you've been sparring with her? I could barely see you guys moving! Holy shit!

She caught the thoughts he practically yelled and smiled, raising an eyebrow. *You don't need to yell, and she can probably hear every word you are saying.*

Bethany Anne's mouth quirked to the left in amusement. She nodded, confirming Phina's supposition.

Will's mouth dropped open in shock. "Shit!" He paled and hurried out of the room as fast as he could move.

Phina smiled as the Empress chuckled.

"Let's chat." All traces of humor were gone from Bethany Anne's demeanor.

"All right," Phina replied cautiously. She could only think of one topic the Empress might bring up, and she wasn't in a hurry to discuss it.

Bethany Anne looked at her seriously, knowing what Phina was thinking. "I have to do something about your aunt. I heard you've visited her and I know what she told you. I also scanned her when we first brought her here after you went into your coma. The only reason she isn't dead is that her thoughts showed a desire to protect you. Her method was shabby, selfish, and ill-advised, but well-intentioned." Her voice was steel, but she gave Phina a look of compassion. "You have to know that she isn't well. She broke when the rest of your family died."

Phina felt her throat tighten, but she nodded, her movements stiff. "I know. I also know she loves me. I felt it when I read her mind, but I can't help being angry with her because she showed it very badly."

"Yes." The Empress sighed and shook her head. "I can leave the decision until after the wedding, but I won't delay much more than that. She's waited a year and a half."

"I'm sorry." Phina felt a pang that her aunt had been in limbo all that time. She was angry with her aunt, but she didn't hate her. That shocking thought distracted her until Bethany Anne's words broke through.

"It wasn't your fault."

Phina looked up to see the Empress giving her a kind smile. "We should have scanned her again after their deaths. She had been scanned when we gave her the job working with the nanocytes since it's a sensitive area, but she was healthy and stable then. That she fell through the cracks later was unfortunate. A lot happened around that time, and it happened quickly, although if she had exhibited any obvious concerning behavior, it would have come to our attention and it wouldn't have mattered how busy things were." She shook her head regretfully, her gaze piercing Phina. "None of that was your fault."

Taking a deep breath, Phina gave Bethany Anne a wobbly smile. "I'm trying my best to believe that. You know she is dying?"

The Empress nodded. "Yes, and that will be a factor in my decision." Phina nodded in understanding. "Talk to me about your training."

The more they chatted, the more relaxed Phina felt in Bethany Anne's presence. She found herself sharing some of the moves she had tried and finally shared the move that had flung Todd to the ground in a daze after she launched off of him.

Bethany Anne laughed, slapping her leg. "I bet he *loved* that."

Phina gave her a small grin and admitted, "He said we should call me Wonder Woman. I told him I prefer Black Widow."

Bethany Anne laughed harder. "Even better." She sobered and gave Phina a searching look so intense that she felt certain the Empress was also reading her mind for the answer. "Black Widow wasn't just a badass warrior. She was also the one who went to the wall, doing whatever it took to accomplish the mission without question. She did what no one else would do, which is why she was chosen for black ops over the other Avengers. She understood sacrifice. Are you prepared to do the same?"

Seeing how serious the question was, Phina took a moment to think about it. She finally nodded. "I've never been one to push to the front of a group. I don't need recognition, and I've always felt more comfortable behind the scenes. From experience and growing to know myself, I would do whatever it took to protect people, particularly those I care about."

Bethany Anne flashed a satisfied smile. "Good. Things aren't adding up, and I need to know that if I ask you to jump off a cliff, you'll do it."

Determination filled Phina. "If it's to protect the Empire, all you'll have to do is point."

CHAPTER SEVENTEEN

Etheric Empire, QBBS *Meredith Reynolds,* **Training Room**

Phina's eyes widened at the object in Todd's hand. She glanced between her new weapon and Todd's amused face with an expectant look.

"I'm assuming it does more than sit there since you said you wanted me to have something with reach?"

Todd grinned and held up the ten-inch-long metal rod. "This is pretty slick. Watch."

He pressed a button that Phina hadn't noticed since it sat flush with the rest of the rod. Immediately, the ends telescoped out to transform the rod into a four-foot-long staff.

Phina's eyes lit up. "That is so cool!"

Todd chuckled as he handed it to her. "It is. I asked R&D for something that would give you reach and be easy to carry but wouldn't immediately be obvious. This is what they came back with."

She twirled it around as she thought about how much

better and stronger she felt. The bout with the Empress the day before had taught her some things. Phina had been working on them when Todd had walked in earlier with her new weapon. Phina held it up closer to her face to search for the button.

"It's right..." Todd's voice trailed off when Phina found it and the staff retracted. She grinned and pushed it again to telescope out.

"This is awesome!" She looked at him, still grinning. "Thank you for getting it for me."

He gave her a pleased smile and nodded. "Of course. Are you ready to try it out? I can show you the basics, but I'm not an expert. I'll have to find one for you."

Phina let her fingers slide up the staff, feeling the smooth metallic surface and the tiny ridges that marked the edges of the cylinders that extended. She shook her head with a small smile. "Don't worry. I know a guy."

Etheric Empire, QBS *Emissary*

Zultav held the posture of attention and obedience as he stood guard, internally wincing at each lash of the whip he heard across the room. He wished he were almost anywhere else.

"Tell me!"

Qartan's voice grated as he leaned in closer to his victim's face, spittle flying. He straightened and gave the second victim another five lashes.

Xoruk jerked at every impact and shuddered when Qartan withdrew the whip, tearing small pieces of his flesh away at every strike. The floor behind him was striped and streaked with blood that had flown off the whip.

Zultav glanced away, his eyes meeting those of the first victim, Jokin. They had grown up together as boys but lost track of each other when Zultav had been selected to be trained as an assassin.

Jokin's face gave little away, but Zultav couldn't help reading condemnation into his old friend's face. Why not? He felt it himself. He couldn't help thinking he should do something, but every time he had that thought, he went back to the training they had been given as assassins.

Assassins were taught to obey and follow the word of the religious leader. The rule had been put into effect a couple of decades before when they'd realized that some younger assassins were swayed by others to act on their own for their own or another's gain. Once this was discovered, those assassins had been executed and the rule established.

It hadn't taken too many punishments of their peers for them to fall into line. Even now, it felt unthinkable to disobey. To go against his leader's wishes was treason and immediate death.

This was the only thing keeping him in his spot despite the shame and self-condemnation he felt at bearing witness to this erroneous travesty.

Qartan sauntered to the front of the two men and made a show of displaying the whip he had been using, its end dripping with their blood. "Well? Are you ready to tell me what I wish to know?"

Jokin answered from his position of openness and

acceptance, his eyes still watching Zultav. "We have not betrayed the Qendrok. We have done nothing wrong."

Qartan growled, his fingers clenching on the whip. "That is not what I asked."

"We have not spoken to an abomination." Xoruk rasped as he trembled, attempting to remain in his upright position. His back had to be in a lot of pain. Qartan had seemed particularly delighted to whip Xoruk, the scourge at the end digging deep. Zultav uncharacteristically wondered if the enthusiasm displayed by Qartan had been because Xoruk was quietly popular among their brethren and Qartan couldn't stand anyone being in higher regard than himself.

He almost shook his head at his wayward and traitorous thoughts before remembering he was still standing guard. Guards were to remain motionless unless given a task by the leader, he reminded himself. Guards were to obey the leader in mind and body.

The will of the leader is the will of the guard. This was the way of his people.

Qartan scowled and snarled in Xoruk's face. "That is not what I asked! You will answer my question, Xoruk, or you will be shown to be in contempt!" He turned to glare at Jokin, who had yet to move his gaze, still focusing on Zultav. "And you too, Jokin!"

Jokin finally turned his eyes toward Qartan, giving nothing of his thoughts or emotions away aside from a hint of disapproval. "This is not in accordance with the law."

Qartan backhanded him with a lower hand, a sign of

disrespect, as he scowled. "I *am* the law, you smarmy little maggot! You all answer to me!"

Zultav frowned at this blatant misinterpretation of the law of their people. That is not how the Qendrok ruled. The religious authority as a whole ruled, not one person. Qartan may have been the leader of the religious group, but that did not mean he was the law or that he was above it.

This did not sit well with him. The whole situation did not sit well with him. Yet, he was just an assassin and a guard. What could he do?

Qartan finally grew tired of the two Qendrok withstanding his questions and gestured to the guards to take the whipped Qendrok away.

Another guard reached for Xoruk, who had to be carried over a shoulder as he could barely move. As Zultav half-supported, half-carried Jokin out of the room, he heard Qartan call for a particularly proud and self-righteous but obedient assassin named Ventok to report for a special assignment.

Zultav attempted to support Jokin in a way that didn't cause the Qendrok more pain, but given the extensive wounds, he feared there was little hope of that. He remained silent although he felt Jokin's gaze on his face.

As they turned a corner to the room where the Qendrok were being held, Zultav heard Jokin whisper, "The humans have a saying. 'The only thing necessary for the triumph of evil is that good men do nothing.'"

Zultav frowned and slowed his pace behind the guard carrying Xoruk before speaking quietly. "You are calling Qartan evil?"

"After everything he has done to use and abuse our people over the last two decades for the sake of himself and the goddess, can you call him good?" Jokin asked.

They approached the room and were too close to the other guard for Zultav to reply, but he wasn't sure what he would have said, anyway. His thoughts whirled as he helped Jokin carefully lie on his belly on the mat and supplied them both with water and food.

His thoughts still were a mess of confusion as he walked back to his post.

Was Qartan evil?

To question was not the way of their people, particularly not the way of the assassins. Yet, all he had was questions.

The question Zultav most wanted an answer to was if he could be considered good.

Etheric Empire, QBBS Meredith Reynolds, Event Hall

Phina tugged her dress down and walked on her heels, feeling uncomfortable. It was the same violet and golden-yellow dress she had tried on in the boutique not that long ago.

Phina had thought for sure Alina had said it was her maid of honor dress. However, Alina had sent a message that morning saying there was a party tonight to celebrate Alina and Maxim's engagement, to be on time or be in a world of hurt, and to wear this dress or be in twice the pain. She had found the violet dress and matching heels in her closet not that long ago.

She had stared at the apparel and spoke louder than normal. "Meredith?"

"Yes, Phina?"

"Did you let Alina into the suite earlier?"

The EI spoke matter-of-factly. "Alina Burke is still listed as claiming this suite as her residence. Is this incorrect? Should I remove her access?"

Phina shook her head as she reached in to pull out the silky garment. "No. Could you please let me know any time someone enters when I don't personally let them in?"

"Of course."

"Thank you, Meredith."

Phina had dressed and got ready quickly, adding a few swipes of mascara so Alina wouldn't get on her case about not using makeup.

Now, she was feeling uncomfortable, naked and exposed although she was fully clothed. It took a few minutes as she walked down the corridor to realize the problem was a lack of weapons. She had gotten used to wearing at least her knives, but especially her tablet. She needed to ask Alina to help her design a long pocket for her pants that she could slide her collapsed staff into.

Not that it would help her with a dress.

Phina grimaced and continued to the event hall marked in the message. She frowned as she walked up to the entrance, hearing shushing sounds inside with her enhanced hearing. She lowered her shield filters enough so she could tell that there were many people inside and they were trying to be quiet.

Her curiosity getting the better of her, she opened the

door and stepped inside before continuing the scan further.

Immediately shouts of, "Surprise!" and "Happy Birthday!" rang out in the room, causing Phina's senses to briefly overload. She automatically hunched down and reached for her daggers but found nothing but fabric.

She blinked as her senses adjusted, then shook her head and smiled ruefully as she took in the crowd of curious, concerned, and questioning people in the room. She straightened, smoothing her dress down again. "Well, no wonder I was told to wear a dress! If I'd had my weapons, someone could have gotten hurt."

Chuckles sounded while Alina skipped up with a big grin. "Come on, birthday girl! Let's have some fun!"

Phina leaned over to whisper hurriedly, "Alina, it's not my birthday."

Her best friend leaned back, her smile playful but her eyes and tone serious. "I know that, silly," she whispered, "but we missed two of them because you were in the coma, and we wanted to make sure you knew we love you."

Stopping immediately, Phina turned and gave Alina a huge hug. "Thank you. Sometimes I get down, but you always know what to do to pick me up again."

Alina leaned back with unshed tears shimmering in her eyes that she blinked with a wobbly smile. "That's what I'm here for, bestie."

Purposely pushing back her tears, Phina gave Alina another quick hug before turning to view the crowd with a smile. Link was there, of course, and Braeden. She knew Sundancer was close by, although she couldn't see him. Drk-vaen, Sis'tael, Ryan, and a gorgeous red-headed woman Phina didn't know but was clearly attached to Ryan were over by the food. They looked up and gave her welcoming smiles, as did Anna Elizabeth and a man she didn't immediately recognize but later realized was Dan Bosse. They stood off to the side, relaxed as they quietly talked. They were too close for friends, which surprised Phina. Yet another change.

Jace stood near Anna and Dan, holding hands with another unknown woman, but since she smiled at Jace with affection, Phina figured this was the serious relationship he had mentioned. Will and his mother Fiona were there with a handsome gentleman and an older teen girl who must be Will's sister Rayna. Todd stood with Peter Silvers and Maxim in a little group by the bar. They gave her nods and smiles. Mister Prez and Mal were also there talking quietly together, but they paused to give her wide, welcoming smiles.

Phina smiled as she made a circuit of the room to greet everyone individually and thank them for coming. She felt extremely uncomfortable being the center of attention, but was able to think of everyone as being there individually, which helped her feel less overwhelmed in the crowd.

When she got to the group by the food, the tall, beautiful woman with Ryan clung to him and looked at Phina with jealousy, which didn't make much sense to her.

She pinged the guy who would probably know. *Hey, ADAM?*

>>**Happy birthday, Phina! Though I know it is not really your birthday, I understand why Alina wished to celebrate it.**<<

Thank you, ADAM. Do you know what is bothering the

woman with Ryan? Something seems wrong, but I don't know what it might be.

>>Ah.<< He paused. >>**Normally I would keep this in confidence, but since it does affect you, I will say that Ryan has been telling her a lot about you. Perhaps too much.**<<

Phina felt puzzled until she ran through the same scenario with Maxim and Alina and hazarded a guess. *She doesn't like him talking about another woman instead of her?*

>>**That is what I have surmised from their conversations, yes.**<<

Thank you, ADAM.

When Ryan introduced the woman as Celeste Rivers, Phina tried to relieve the woman's anxiety by smiling in welcome and relief and shaking her hand warmly.

"Hi, Celeste. Thank the stars Ryan finally found a woman who can handle his macho attitude and keep him out of trouble with the poor beleaguered women."

Celeste appeared puzzled but did relax some. Ryan, of course, protested. "What are you talking about? I never got into trouble!" He turned to Celeste anxiously. "I never got into trouble with other women, baby. I swear."

Phina raised her eyebrows then looked around playfully as she patted her dress. "Where's my tablet? I'm sure I've got evidence."

She smothered a grin as Ryan began tugging Celeste away, a small smile curving the woman's mouth, as Ryan called, "You're an evil woman, Phina!"

Celeste leaned into Ryan, who pulled her close as they walked away. However, Phina still heard her amused remark. "I like her."

Phina sighed in relief, then turned to meet Melia Banks, Jace's serious girlfriend, who gave Phina an amused smile and whispered, "Nice job. I wondered if she would start marking her territory."

Phina grinned and shrugged, not worried about keeping her voice low. "Ryan is all bluster and doesn't understand women as well as he thinks."

"Hey!" Ryan turned from halfway across the room. "I resemble that remark!"

They laughed and Phina was able to relax more and chat with Melia. She was friendly and seemed to fit well with Jace's newer mature attitude. When she teased him, Melia showed she could handle his mischievous side, too.

Phina clapped Jace on the shoulder and smiled. "I'm so happy for you, Jace. You guys seem good together."

He grinned and flashed a warm smile at Melia who moved closer to him with full intent to kiss him. Phina smirked and half-rolled her eyes as she turned away.

Then the activities started. After suffering, or rather playing games designed to simultaneously celebrate and humiliate Phina with baby pictures, sound bites, and stories that should have been banned from public consumption that Phina assumed she had Alina and Meredith to thank for, Phina finally sat down and took a breath.

Within a minute Todd quietly sat down beside her and lifted an eyebrow in amusement. "This isn't really your thing, is it?"

Phina shook her head emphatically. "Hell, no, but I needed it anyway."

Todd turned to face her. "Oh? How so?"

She opened her mouth, but he answered his own question. "Oh. To remind you not to take everything seriously and that you're loved and appreciated."

Phina nodded slowly. "Yes. And to remember the people I love. To remind myself I'm not alone, no matter how I feel sometimes."

Todd smiled warmly and was opening his mouth to respond when Will sat down on the other side next to her and leaned forward with a smile to Todd as he extended his hand. "Hi, I'm Will."

"Todd." He returned the smile with curious eyes as he shook Will's hand.

They chatted for a while before Will turned to Phina, his face worried and tone anxious. "Phina? I'm having one of my feelings, and it's a bad one."

Todd leaned forward to hear more. Phina frowned and put down her cup of sweet, frothy beverage. "I thought your feelings had more to do with who you might be friends with?"

He nodded with his eyebrows furrowed in concern and a hint of fear. "Normally, yes. The last time I had a bad one like this, my dad almost died."

Phina's eyes widened and glanced at his dad, who was speaking to Anna Elizabeth, then looked at Will in concern. "Wow, but he seems okay now?"

He gave her a lopsided smile though his eyes still showed concern. "Yeah, it was several years ago. He took a couple of months off to heal up and have a break. He's good now."

Todd leaned forward with a small smile. "I know your dad. He's a good guy."

Will nodded with a small smile of appreciation as he picked up Phina's cup and moved it around in his hands. "He is. We wish we could see him more, but Mom's been amazing at keeping everything steady. He makes up for it when he's home."

Phina frowned and shifted in her seat, feeling brushing sensations on her leg. She glanced down but didn't see anything. She shook her head, her thoughts processing Will's information. "So, you think someone here might be in danger?"

He nodded, though he looked hesitant. "The feelings I get about becoming friends with people vary in strength depending on how close the relationship will be. With you, it was strong, so I knew we would be close friends." He glanced at Todd and shook his head. "Not like that, more like family."

Phina looked between the two men warily as Todd nodded, scrutinizing Will. They seemed to understand each other. She mentally rolled her eyes and waved it away, moving on. "The bad feeling?"

Will lifted a shoulder and continued to look anxious. "It was only the one time, so I can't be sure, but this feeling is stronger than the one I had about my dad. Which probably means the danger is greater and to someone close to me. I can't see it happening to my family since there is no threat to them. My dad is currently stationed here, so it's not likely to be for him."

He put the cup down and turned to face her, his eyes and whole body expressing seriousness. It looked wrong for the usual playfulness in his eyes to be gone. "The only person I have a relationship with that has had a death threat is you, Phina."

Sundancer stalked around the room, listening to everyone at the party. They all chatted about one of three topics: Phina, speculation on how the Empress would handle the Leath, and the upcoming wedding.

No one could see him at the moment since he had combined his natural stealth with a mental "don't see me" projection. It had taken Sundancer almost a full hundred years to learn as it took a lot of control, particularly in rooms full of people. As he paused under a table to listen to Phina's conversation, he wondered how long it would take her to learn. She had learned the basics of shielding a lot faster than he thought she would. It had given him a lot to think about.

His attention was pulled to Will's concern as the conversation progressed. *Intriguing.* He absently swished his tail against Phina's leg as he considered the situation. His human was a trouble magnet. This was not something he had anticipated when he had first heard the call.

Before the call, he had expected his pair to be a lot more like himself, perhaps a scholar or a priest. Someone oratory and persuasive. Calm and collected. Dignified.

He snorted at that thought when Phina reached down to rub her bare leg. *Oops.* He turned so he could still be close to Phina but wouldn't be touching her with his tail and resumed his thoughts.

Phina was far younger than he had expected and not a

priest or an orator. She could be persuasive, though, and that would grow with time. She did project a calm and collected demeanor, but he had yet to see her be very dignified.

She also had the admirable and yet irritating trait of throwing herself between danger and those she considered friends and family. How was he going to be able to help her if he couldn't anticipate what she would need?

He stewed on that as Phina assured Will that she would be careful and the party continued.

It still permeated his thoughts as the party broke up and people began to leave.

Phina crouched to presumably check on her shoe and whispered, "Sundancer, I know you are here."

I should hope so since we are paired. Pairings always know where the other one is and can find each other even across long distances.

She frowned, then stood and continued the conversation mentally. *That's how you found me?*

If you continue to ask questions you already know the answer to, this teaching process will grow to become tedious.

His human sighed and said goodbye to the last few people before turning to walk out.

The big man who had an interest in his human stopped them.

"Phina, let me walk you home."

She frowned and protested. "Todd, I'm perfectly fine walking home on my own. ADAM will let me know if there's a problem."

Sundancer was miffed, sniffing as he responded. *Or I will. I'm not invisible here.*

Well, never mind. He was invisible. His human ignored him as she listened to Todd's response. Sundancer grumbled, *Well, I'm not chump change at any rate. I can warn you when there's a problem and help protect you.*

Phina finally agreed to the escort, which would have been fine with Sundancer if he wasn't being ignored. He sighed and followed his human as she left, his thoughts occupied with his earlier musings.

His understanding was beginning to take shape. He would have to train Phina as quickly as possible and teach her what he knew about the Etheric. In the meantime, he could warn her of dangers coming. *And better than that brain in a tin can*, he pouted in thought.

A moment later, he felt massive fluctuations in the Etheric.

Phina!

CHAPTER EIGHTEEN

QBBS *Meredith Reynolds*

"Phina, let me walk you home." Todd requested quietly but insistently.

Phina frowned and protested that she could protect herself, but Todd just looked at her and said, "Indulge me."

She finally agreed while Sundancer grumbled his complaints.

Todd seemed preoccupied as they walked, although he remained aware, his eyes scanning the corridors. After a few moments, he asked, "Why didn't you mention that you had been marked for death by assassins?"

She sighed and shook her head. She also scanned their route as they walked, but so far, nothing had popped out as a problem. "Part of me knew it was a legitimate threat, and the rest of me didn't want to treat it as such and make it real. If I talked to anyone further about it, that makes it serious. I didn't want to think about it."

He nodded and glanced at her. "I can understand that. At the same time, you can't be prepared for a problem if you aren't anticipating it, and you can't anticipate if you aren't aware of it."

Phina took a sharp intake of breath at the gentle admonishment but let it out with a nod. "That's fair. I shouldn't have stuck my head in the sand about it. I wanted some time to feel normal and not like the strange being I've become. That's what Qartan finds so objectionable about me."

Todd raised his eyebrows as they turned a corner, pausing briefly to make sure it was clear before proceeding. "Now, that's where I need to disagree with you. No, you aren't abnormal, but what you aren't seeing or realizing is that what isn't 'normal' about you is extraordinary. A normal life would be quieter and more peaceful, but from what I've observed that would bore you to no end."

"Huh." Phina thought that over and nodded. "You aren't wrong about that. I guess I still have a hard time accepting that what makes me different is a good thing. I was told for years that I should behave a certain way, or I was wrong in some way. I didn't realize how much it had affected me."

Todd gave her a sympathetic glance as they passed a small group of people. "Another issue affected by your aunt? Sounds like she has a lot to account for."

Phina pressed her lips together briefly as she remembered her visit to her aunt weeks before. "Yes."

Just as Todd opened his mouth to respond, Phina felt Etheric fluctuations coming toward her on a trajectory that would converge behind her.

Phina!

She ducked at Sundancer's warning and crouched as a

large Qendrok appeared, stabbing knives where her neck would have been if she hadn't moved.

Phina felt very aware of her lack of protective clothing and weapons. Since all she had was her hands, she punched the Qendrok in his nethers with as much force as she could muster.

Unfortunately, while it startled the assassin—Phina recognized the red medallion with a black band that was on his neck—the Qendrok didn't react as badly as a human male would have done. Grimacing, Phina slid back to get more space and stood up, her violet and yellow skirts swishing around her.

The dark eyes of the assassin met hers as he hissed in disgust and determination before he moved forward. "Death to the abomination!"

Phina didn't know whether to laugh or to make a sarcastic comment. She knew she wasn't normal, and so did they. Todd told her that what was abnormal about her made her extraordinary. She wasn't sure about that yet, but she did know that if she had been sent as an assassin, keeping her mouth shut would have been her choice.

Todd had brought weapons with him, including his knives. He pulled a black rod out of a side pocket and tossed it to her without looking as he moved in to use one to help fend off the assassin.

"Phina, catch!"

She grabbed it out of the air with her quick reflexes and was happily surprised to see that it was a duplicate of the rod that Todd had gotten her. She pressed the button to extend the telescopic staff and moved forward to engage the assassin.

Other humans and aliens passing by stayed out of the way while Phina and Todd worked together to fight the Qendrok. It was different fighting someone with four arms instead of two since there were two sets of arms to watch and only the top set had any physical tell as to his movements.

Phina tried to read the alien's mind, but she met the same resistance that she had the first time she met them. She still tried as she could occasionally get an intention or focused thought.

With that small advantage, she renewed her determination and speed, recalling and enacting moves she had seen Braeden do when fighting. She didn't think she had the moves quite right, but they were still effective enough combined with her speed and flexibility. Todd had drawn another knife after giving her the rod and fought with both hands.

Between the two of them, and with occasional ankle swipes from Sundancer, they were gaining ground, inflicting more damage on the Qendrok than they were receiving from him. His body had several slices and growing bruises, while Phina hadn't yet gotten any cuts from the assassin's knives. Todd had one on his arm that he had gotten when he threw the staff to her, and that was almost healed.

The expression on the alien's face gradually changed from fierce and determined to dawning desperation.

Just as Phina saw an opening and thrust the butt of her staff at his throat, the Qendrok stepped back with panicked eyes and grasped one of his wrists with another hand. He disappeared before her eyes, much the way the

Empress did. However, unlike when Bethany Anne stepped into the Etheric, Phina felt a disturbance around her that quickly moved away.

The corridor was still and quiet until a growing buzz of excited conversation and clapping came from the bystanders.

Phina shook her head and turned to Todd, who was still catching his breath. "So, I guess that was one of the assassins I needed to worry about."

He flashed her a grin and wiped his knives on a cloth before sheathing them. I guess so." He pulled out a wipe from a pocket and used it to clean up the blood residue from the healed wound on his arm. He shrugged at her raised eyebrows and merely said, "Always be prepared."

"Hmm." Phina glanced down and was surprised to notice that her dress was perfectly intact. Something to ask Alina about later. She hefted the staff once then pressed the button to withdraw the telescopic ends. "Pretty handy that you had this with you."

Todd nodded and took the rod as she handed it back to him, sliding it in a pocket in his pants. "I got a second one so I could spar with you and learn how to use it better. Looks like you weren't doing too badly for a beginner." He gave her a questioning smile.

Phina dusted herself off and looked around to make sure there was no other trouble, though she shrugged in answer to his question. "I just did what I've seen Braeden do."

"Ah." He looked around, then gestured to ask if she wanted to continue walking. "The Gleek representative? Is that the person you know who uses a staff?"

She nodded to both questions, and they began walking back to her apartment suite with Sundancer trailing behind. The Previdian was both visible and uncharacteristically quiet. "Yes. He has used one for over a century, so he's pretty good with it."

Todd nodded, and after a brief moment asked a little too casually, "Are you two close?"

Phina almost tripped when she realized that Alina was right and he *was* interested in her romantically. Something to think about later. She gave him a small smile. "Like brother and sister. He's been a big help with working through the mental changes."

She could practically feel Sundancer's ire directed at her from behind, so she added, "Sundancer too, of course. He's taught me some useful techniques since he got here."

Todd returned her smile with a touch of amusement as she got a ping from ADAM through her implant.

>>**Phina, you are okay?**<<

"Yes, ADAM. I'm fine." She spoke out loud so Todd would know, but she continued the rest of the conversation privately. He nodded his understanding as they turned to head to the nearby tram. There were several seconds of delay before ADAM responded.

>>**Meredith informed me that there was an assassination attempt. You appear to not have any wounds from the visuals she is feeding me.**<<

Yes, it was an assassination attempt by the Qendrok, and yes, I'm fine. No wounds to speak of. Your wording makes it sound like you aren't on the station.

>>**Keep it to yourself, but no. I am not.**<<

Phina had a couple of seconds to process that if ADAM

was not on the station, then neither was Bethany Anne since his computer processor currently resided in her head. No wonder he didn't want her to share that news. People might start panicking if they knew the Empress had gone walkabout.

>>**Bethany Anne, and TOM, and I, are relieved that you are all right, but she is far from happy that the Qendrok attacked the station, and particularly that they are targeting you. She said to tell you that the gloves have to come off.**<<

Phina felt a surprising warmth. *Thank you all for being concerned about me. Should the response be more of a slap or a punch in the face?*

>>**The latter.**<<

I think I understand. I'll let Link know. Should we still wait until after the wedding, or prepare to leave immediately?

They exited the tram and began walking to her apartment as she waited for the answer.

>>**Bethany Anne says that family comes first. Then they get the fist. If that's not enough, she will come personally and give them her size-seven boot.**<<

Phina's eyes widened. *Is that really what she said?*

>>**No, that's a heavily edited version of what she said, without all the creative cursing, name-calling, and body parts mentioned. Would you like me to repeat her full response?**<<

Phina laughed and shook her head. *No, thank you, ADAM. I got it.*

>>**Be safe, Phina. We would be upset if something happened to you.**<<

Thank you, ADAM. Please thank TOM and the Empress, too.

>>You're welcome, Phina. Bethany Anne told me to remind you to call her by her name and stop Empressing her to death.<<

Phina smiled as they turned into her corridor. *"Thank you. I'll try to remember in private. In public, I'm still going to be very respectful."*

>>Understood.<<

They said goodbye, and Phina looked up as they approached her door. She took out her keycard and turned to smile at Todd. "Thank you for walking me home."

He nodded and stood nearby as she opened the door.

Phina waited for him to walk away, but he stayed there. "Goodnight, Todd."

He crossed his arms and squared his shoulders as if he expected a rebuke. "I took the liberty of contacting Greyson Wells, Maxim, and Braeden while you were speaking with ADAM. With this attempt, the assassin popped out of nowhere and disappeared just as quickly. We don't know how he did that yet. You need guards. We are going to take a rotation where one of us will be with you at all times. That way, you have a backup in case another one pops up without warning."

Eyebrows raised to their fullest extent, Phina closed her eyes briefly as she tried to keep her temper, then gestured as she stepped into the apartment suite. Sundancer followed, grumbling about milk and fish before disappearing into the shadows of the room. "Come in. I'm not having this conversation where other people can hear."

Todd glanced at her warily but with concern as he passed by to enter. It was the latter that allowed Phina's anger to cool. She was bothered at their high-handedness and making decisions for her, but she had to remember that they cared about her, and she couldn't keep them out of things entirely.

She gestured to the couch for Todd to take a seat, then stepped out of her heels and stalked around the room as she mentally went through the argument that would ensue should she decide to go that route. She shook her head, making angry noises and gestures as she fumed. But, her mental argument ended with her seeing his point. She realized that they only had her safety in mind and that agreeing to be guarded, at least for now, was the sensible option. She decided to go through it again but speaking calmly and talking logically. It ended in the same result, just much faster.

She sighed and waved a hand as she fell into her favorite chair. "Fine. How's this going to work with sleeping arrangements?"

Todd frowned as he sat half sprawled from where he had watched her pacing. "Not that I'm complaining, but I expected you to be upset or argue."

Phina pulled her legs up to tuck under her skirt as she tapped her head. "I had that argument already and decided that you all have a point. So, how are the logistics going to work?"

The corner of his mouth pulled into a smile. "Well, I guess I'm glad Braeden decided not to bet, or I would have been out twenty credits."

Phina narrowed her eyes. "You bet on my response, huh?"

"Yes." He said it confidently, yet he looked at her questioningly.

"What did you bet?"

He put his hands behind his head and leaned back as he thought. "Let's see. Greyson said fifteen minutes and that you would be in my face. Maxim said ten minutes. I said five or less, and Braeden said he wouldn't bet but that you wouldn't argue at all. So he would have won."

He shrugged and leaned forward in time to see the pillow Phina had pulled from behind her flying at his face. He caught it before it hit, grinned, and threw it back at her. "Don't like to be bet on, huh?"

She caught it in plenty of time and lobbed it back with more force. "Don't like to be bet on that I would be arguing."

He caught it and grinned. "Know what we didn't bet on?"

Phina couldn't help the smile at how pleased he looked. "What?"

"How well you handled that assassination attempt." She blinked in surprise as he continued, "You didn't hesitate and immediately responded to the attack. You didn't worry about not having any weapons and used what you had, then backed up to reassess when it didn't work. You adapted to working with a new weapon and working in tandem with someone else so we didn't get in each other's way. You didn't break down, get upset, or any number of other responses you could have had. You handled it like a pro."

Phina sat there processing and responded with, "Huh, you're right." She was mentally reviewing the fight for the second time when Todd chuckled. She looked up to see him shaking his head, his eyes shining in amusement. "I can see why Maxim said that you don't make a big deal about your accomplishments."

She frowned. "Is that a problem?"

Todd tucked the pillow behind his head and flashed her a smile. "No, but it reinforces my point from before that you can handle more than you realize. Also, if you are treating this as a passing everyday occurrence, you are ready to step up your training."

Phina thought about that, then nodded. "Sounds like fun."

He chuckled again and shook his head. "So, do you have a spare blanket? I'll bunk down here on the couch. You can call out if one of them shows up."

She sighed at the reminder that she would be having babysitters for the foreseeable future and nodded. "Alina isn't using the other room much anymore. You can sleep there."

Phina's heart beat faster as she stood up and began walking down the hall to make sure he would have what he needed.

She wondered what it said about her that she handled assassination attempts like they were no big deal, but having Todd sleep in the other room made her extremely nervous.

CHAPTER NINETEEN

Etheric Empire, QBBS *Meredith Reynolds*, Phinalina Residence

"So, what do we know?" Greyson asked as he settled down on the second chair in the living room area.

Maxim passed out the doughnuts and coffee he had picked up on the way since they were meeting pretty early in the morning and he wanted food in his belly to wake him up more—and coffee, of course.

"Would it not be wise to wait for the ones who were present?" Braeden asked, looking up from his study of the sugary treat.

Scowling, Greyson leaned forward to grab a coffee and doughnut. "I suppose the eyewitness account would help, but we all know what happened."

"Not really." Maxim settled on the end of the couch with his chocolate-frosted doughnuts and sugared coffee. "Just the broad strokes. The details are what I'm interested in."

Greyson sighed, then took a quick sip of his black

coffee, wincing at the heat. "I am, too. I just want to get on with figuring out how to respond and prevent it from happening again."

Maxim nodded his agreement as he started in on his doughnuts. He had been worried when he'd heard of the assassination attack until receiving the news that both Todd and Phina were all right. Before he could continue his thought to Greyson, the pad of paws from Sundancer coming into the room from the bedroom area preceded a yawning Todd, who still wore his clothes from the day before. He nodded to them then stepped forward to grab coffee and doughnuts of his own with an appreciative smile.

Curious on both Alina's and his behalf, Maxim pinged Todd on their implants. *Did you...*

His friend looked at him with sleepy confusion until Maxim's eyes darted toward the bedrooms. Todd raised his eyebrows in disbelief and responded over the implant. *What, you think I talked her into bed after an attempt on her life? Things between us aren't there...yet. No, she took the news we were going to be guarding her well. I slept in Alina's bed.*

Maxim gritted his teeth and stopped himself from going wolf. He glanced down and realized he had almost spilled coffee over himself from his tightening grip. He couldn't stop from shooting a glare at Todd, who appeared confused before dawning realization passed over his face.

Do us both a favor, Maxim growled. *Don't mention those words in the same sentence again.*

Todd appeared apologetic. *Sorry, man. I wasn't thinking. You know I would never...*

Maxim mentally waved him off as he calmed down. *I*

know that. But my wolf side doesn't like hearing about another man in Alina's bed. He muscled past the reaction again before shaking his head. *I think it would be fine except I've been anxious about the wedding.*

Todd frowned before biting into his glazed doughnut. *Is there something wrong? I thought things were great between you two.*

Shaking his head, Maxim settled into finishing his breakfast. *No, things* are *great between the two of us. I've been waiting so long to find someone I fit with that it seems surreal. Like something will happen before then to prevent it, or I'll wake up and it's all been a dream.*

Todd soberly glanced toward the bedrooms. *Yeah, I know what you mean.*

You haven't talked to her? Maxim felt surprised. Todd usually faced things head-on and straight forward.

No. Todd hesitated before shrugging. *Just doesn't feel like the right time. We are still getting to know each other.*

Well, if you hadn't tried to give her away to me out of your nobleness to save her from your gun-shy-around-women self, you would be a lot further along. Maxim finished his doughnut then drained the rest of his coffee.

Todd glanced at him ruefully. *Figured it out, huh?*

Took me a while. Maxim settled back to think it over as they waited for Phina and caught sight of Sundancer slinking in the shadows. Seeing those blue cat eyes training squarely on himself made him feel like he was being thoroughly examined. He lost his train of thought for a moment before finally continuing. *Giving the training assignment to me didn't make sense after I realized what she was being trained for. You were the better person for that all along since you've learned to compensate against much stronger opponents, and you have more diverse and intuitive fighting styles. Still, I can't complain since it would have taken a lot longer to meet Alina.*

Todd nodded and set aside his empty cup. *I can't deny it. I thought I was helping you both. I knew Phina was amazing from the first time we met, and you and Pete are the two best men I know. You know he's been hung up on Tabitha even if he won't admit it. So, I figured why not see if you can find happiness?"* He shrugged.

Maxim knew him well enough to see that the other man was uncomfortable. Maxim shook his head at the other man's thoughts. Todd wouldn't see how much he deserved happiness too. *Your self-sacrificial attitude is going to get you killed someday, man.*

Todd had a faint grin. *Well, if it does, it will probably be to save one of you chuckleheads, so it would probably be worth it.*

Maxim winced. *Don't even joke about it. That's not something I want on my conscience.*

Todd looked like he was going to respond, but he was distracted when they heard Phina's footsteps coming from her bedroom.

Maxim sighed when he saw how his friend's face changed at the sight of her. Todd was *so* gone, and the man didn't even acknowledge to himself how serious it was. He hoped Todd did finally talk to Phina. Soon.

"If you two are done gossiping, maybe we can begin now?"

Phina pulled back her freshly washed hair and braided it before she stepped into her boots. She lightly stomped to settle her feet then reached for her black jacket before remembering that Alina was making her a new one. Sighing and shaking her head she strapped on her knives and slid her tablet into her pocket before heading out of her bedroom.

She had been woken up by a grumpy Link half an hour ago when he'd arrived far too early to have this confab. It wasn't until she started waking up in her shower that she realized he meant to dissect the assassination attempt and see what they could learn about it.

Phina quietly exited the room and heard Link say caustically, "If you two are done gossiping, maybe we can begin now?"

She walked in to see Link, Braeden, Maxim, and Todd waiting for her, along with two doughnuts and a cup. Todd gave her a small smile which she returned as she walked over to the table.

Seeing as the rest appeared to have eaten, she gathered what was left and settled in her chair to eat. She opened her mouth for the first bite then looked around the room. She knew Sundancer was nearby, although she couldn't see him. She was concerned about how quiet he had been lately and decided to ask him about it later. However, she did notice an absence.

"Where's Will?"

There were mixed reactions to her question, all of which she found interesting, but Link frowned impatiently. "Why would he be here?"

She lifted an eyebrow. "He's been assigned to our delegation, which means he should be involved in any discussion about the Qendrok."

"This is a security and planning meeting, which is not his area." Link said impatiently. "He won't be able to contribute much to the conversation."

Phina's eyebrows rose at the dismissal. "He's learning, and it's related, so he should be here."

He gave a long-suffering sigh. "Fine. Meredith, could you ask Will Jameson to join us?"

"I have already asked him at Phina's request. He said he will be here within a few minutes." Meredith spoke with her usual calm and untroubled tone.

Link frowned and turned to Phina. "When did you do that?"

"When you were being your cheerfully delightful self earlier." She smiled then stuffed a bite of doughnut in her mouth.

He sighed and shook his head, "Just once, it would be nice if you would follow what I say without argument."

Maxim and Todd snickered as Phina shrugged and waved the rest of her doughnut in the air. "I do follow what you say...when it makes sense."

Link stared at her in disbelief, then chuckled. "You are so like your parents. Fine. I'll try to make more sense and not just react to my panic over almost losing you, okay?"

She smiled, happy she had something in common with her parents, and nodded as Will buzzed the door. Meredith opened the door to let him in. He gave them a quick grin and shook his head at the proffered doughnut. "Thank you, but Mom made omelets."

Phina nodded, happy she could eat a second one, as she

waved him over to the rapidly reduced seating available. Will settled in with greetings all around before Link gave a long-suffering sigh and waved at Todd and Phina.

"Now, can we finally hear what happened?"

Since Phina was eating, she gestured for Todd to go first. He explained the sequence of events that happened, along with a glowing review of her response, much like what he had shared the night before. She found herself squirming as she didn't feel she deserved the praise.

You do, Sundancer quietly spoke into her mind. *Everything Todd said is correct. You handled yourself well and didn't panic, which isn't how most newer fighters respond.*

Compliments instead of caustic comments? *What's going on Sundancer? You've been quiet lately.*

Todd finished up before the Previdian replied. *I'll talk to you about it later. Now isn't the time.*

Link turned to her as she mentally spoke firmly. *There will be a later, Sundancer.*

"Anything to add?"

Phina nodded and raised a finger before she stuffed the rest of her second doughnut in her mouth, then swiped her hands together to dust off the sugar. Finally, she settled back with her cup that she had happily found contained tea instead of coffee. She lined up her observations, bringing the incident to the forefront of her mind.

"First, Sundancer and I both noticed that something was happening before it did. I think they are using the Etheric to move invisibly. I felt fluctuations in what I've begun to recognize as the Etheric and realized that the disturbance was going to converge behind me."

Todd nodded, his focus on her when she looked up at

his words. "That matches what I observed. Phina reacted before I noticed the assassin was there. When he disappeared, I wondered if he had used the Etheric since it looked exactly like Bethany Anne when she does it." He frowned in thought. "One difference. She just *steps*. This guy did not. He grabbed his arm first."

Nodding, Phina took a sip. "The Qendrok have not been known to work with the Etheric. Xoruk said that most of the Qendrok can see connections or influence from the Etheric, which he categorized as power levels, but few could use it. I believe this assassin was given a piece of tech that wrapped around his wrist. From what Xoruk told me about their religious faction, they likely got it from this goddess they worship who has promised them power. Perhaps this tech, perhaps something else."

Phina didn't like the extrapolations she made from that, but since it wasn't a concern for the moment, she set it aside for another time. She realized that her head felt clearer than it had been since before Aunt Faith had given her the serum. Stars, it felt great to get back to analysis and extrapolation after the morass of emotional mess that she had been dealing with since her body adapted to process the serum and the subsequent changes. More so, whatever changes had been made, by the serum and by ADAM and TOM, had increased her mental processes. She tried to control her elation at that knowledge since the topic at hand was so serious, remembering that Xoruk and Jokin had possibly been captured or killed. That killed the mood.

Link took that news badly, frowning and drumming his fingers on the arm of his chair. "That is troubling. We have nothing to counter or detect that tech."

She shrugged. "Except Sundancer and me. We aren't exactly inconsequential." At least, that was what they had been telling her.

He turned to look at her impatiently. "Yes, but I mean our tech. They could pop out anywhere. It sounded like you only had a few seconds warning."

Sundancer stepped out of the shadows, his small body hesitant but his face serious as he spoke. "That was with little time to react. Phina and I can extend that warning with practice."

"How long?" Maxim leaned forward intently.

Sundancer lowered his hind legs to sit catlike. "It's difficult to say, but with extensive practice over the next several days, it should be longer than that. Perhaps ten seconds, maybe longer. It depends on how far away they are traveling from as well, which may be of note to discover."

Todd nodded. "I'll contact Dan and General Reynolds to see what we can find out with Reynolds' and ADAM's help."

Link nodded then turned to Phina. "Anything else?"

She frowned as she thought it through. "The assassin was quiet except for saying 'death to the abomination.' What surprised me more is that while he was a decent fighter, he didn't seem *extraordinarily* good. I thought their assassins were supposed to be this dark force of amazing fighters?"

Phina glanced at Todd. "What do you think?"

He considered it briefly, then nodded. "I would agree with that. It seemed more like he was rusty than that he wasn't good. His skills were decent, but his execution was lacking."

Link squinted in concentration. "The incident that happened two years ago gave me an up-close view of their fighting. I didn't see this device when I was fighting them then."

Braeden spoke up quietly. "Perhaps this device is new and has caused them to be lazy in their skills."

Link nodded at the same time as Phina. "That would fit. They've probably been drinking their goddess' Kool-Aid and figured their new tech and this so-called goddess would give them an edge. If they've gotten away with assassinations without being caught this way, perhaps they *have* gotten rusty. Still. We can't count on that."

Phina nodded and shared her earlier thought. "This sounds like a similar version to what the Kurtherians are doing with the Leath, right? The Empress said that a clan of Kurtherians was setting themselves up to be gods. Maybe they are branching out?"

The men blanched, giving her a concentrated flash of mental denial.

Link shook his head with a pained grimace. "I hope not. Fighting a war on two fronts is not conducive to our health. I suppose we can't discount the idea. You are right; there are similarities."

Will looked around. "So, what's the plan?"

Link took a deep breath before he spoke. "The Empress is sending a delegation to them since they've turned tail and run. Perhaps to give themselves plausible deniability from this assassination attempt, perhaps not. But, she wants to send a large contingent to give them the option of revolutionizing their political and religious system."

Maxim asked in disbelief, "Give them the option? After an assassination attempt?"

Phina cleared her throat. "That was before the attempt. ADAM told me afterward that Bethany Anne says the gloves are off."

Link chuckled. "Which means that we will strongly support and encourage revolution in every possible way. Bethany Anne won't stand for a status quo after that."

Etheric Empire, QBS *Emissary*

"You're useless!" Qartan bellowed in rage and disbelief. "You're supposed to be one of the best we have! How could you fail?"

He stood in front of his throne-like chair and glared at the assassin lying prostrate in front of him. Two of his most loyal assassins stood behind the male in their postures of respectful obedience. The failure had one job, and not only did he botch that job, but he'd jeopardized any future attempts. "Now they know for sure we are targeting that abomination and will be more prepared later! Do you know what happens to those who attack Etherian citizens? Now, instead of a nice and tidy anonymous death, we have a live abomination still running around causing trouble!"

Qartan raged until he ran out of steam, then plopped into his chair and eyed the silent assassin with displeasure. "Well? Anything to say?"

The assassin—Qartan hadn't bothered to learn his name—looked up with disillusioned anger in his eyes. Alarmed, as the assassin opened his mouth Qartan jumped up, cutting off the thoughts he had allowed to misfire.

"I *believe* what you were about to say was thank you for magnanimously allowing you to remain alive?"

The assassin got to his knees, allowing his anger to overtake self-preservation. "No. You are a tyrant! The target you sent me to kill was a young human girl. You said the goddess required this threat to be taken out, but how can a girl be a threat to a powerful goddess? Either you are lying or she is lying!"

"That's sacrilege! This girl is an abomination and will always be one!" Qartan gave a curt gesture, and the first loyal assassin standing behind the failed one cut the kneeling Qendrok's throat.

Thank the goddess Qartan had had the foreknowledge to have this confrontation in private! There could be no questions from his fellow acolytes about his right to rule or his goddess' power. She would lead them on the right path. She would grant them ascension. They would have unimaginable power! Qartan had thrown in everything he had to align with her, and he would do all she asked.

Qartan dispassionately watched the assassins carrying the body of their former comrade out of the room. His mind spun with plans.

This abomination had fought off one of his best assassins? Let's see what she could do with what he threw at her next.

CHAPTER TWENTY

QBBS *Meredith Reynolds*, **Phinalina Residence**

"There's so much to do, Phina, and the wedding is happening so soon!" Alina lay on Phina's bed, tears streaming down the sides of her cheeks.

Phina wasn't sure how to respond as she cautiously sat down next to her best friend. Alina had blown into the apartment as the guys were leaving, saying that she hadn't seen Phina in forever and they should "do something."

She had followed Phina into her room and continued to cry while Phina was picking up things to put away that she hadn't gotten to earlier.

Not sure what Alina needed, Phina's mind grabbed onto her first thought. "Is there something wrong between you and Maxim? Are you guys okay?"

"Stars, yes." Alina wiped her face with the backs of her hands. It didn't help much. Phina grabbed tissues for her while Alina continued. "Maxim has been the best. A total rock. You know he could have been deployed while you were in your coma, but he requested to be stationed here so he could help and support me."

She wiped her face with the tissues then grabbed Phina's hand. "I know it wasn't your fault, Phina, but I felt so alone at first with you not here. Plus, with being concerned about you, I was a mess." She shook her head, tears still leaking. "It got better after a *long* while, and Maxim is the reason it did."

Phina got teary-eyed herself while she tried to comfort Alina. "I'm sorry. I would have been here for you if I could have been. I'm happy you have Maxim, and I'm one hundred percent behind you both." She gave Alina a long hug then continued, "So, if it isn't Maxim, are you overwhelmed with finishing things for the wedding?"

Alina gave a watery laugh. "Yeah. I don't know what is left to do. I feel like I'm going crazy."

"You aren't going crazy, but I think I can help." Phina thought through the list Alina had shown her a couple of weeks before. "You have the location, right?"

Alina grabbed another tissue but she seemed to be calming down. "Yeah, it's this awesome restaurant called Horizons that Maxim took me to for our first anniversary of when we started dating." She smiled, and her eyes showed more excitement. "I can't wait for you to see it, Phina. It's amazing!"

Phina smiled, relieved Alina was responding and seeming to feel better. She moved to the next thing on the mental list. "Officiant?"

"Mal suggested her dad. We asked him, and he said yes." Alina got up to throw away the tissues and wash her face and hands. Her voice echoed from the other room.

"Which was a relief because I wasn't sure who to ask if he said no."

"Mister Prez? Nice!" Phina thought he would do a great job. His voice sounded good, too, which was part of what had kept her attention in her Ethics class.

Phina continued down the list. Dresses by Mal and Alina, of course. Food would be handled by the restaurant. "What about the flowers?"

"We could only get them for bouquets, but they look beautiful. They already showed them to me." Alina smiled dreamily as she sat on the bed again. "The petals are so soft."

Phina nodded, smiling in amusement. Knowing Alina, she was trying to think of how to get that texture into her clothes. "So, what colors are we in for?"

Alina blinked, then turned to Phina with a knowing look. "You mean, what will you have to suffer through? Don't worry, it's nothing terrible. The colors are a nice deep red, light pink, and white. Since I'm wearing white, you've got the red, and the bridesmaids are pink."

Feeling relieved, Phina smiled at her friend. "Thanks, Alina."

Her best friend grinned. "And to make you feel better, it's the same design you asked me to make for the event that happened just after you went into your coma. So, no matter what, you should have things covered."

Phina's eyes widened. That event, the same one Anna Elizabeth had talked about to celebrate the diplomats, seemed so distant now. The dress had been one of the things she had looked forward to, and dresses and heels weren't her thing. "Wow." She hugged Alina tightly. "And here I thought I was trying to make *you* feel better. Thank you for thinking of me when it's a day that's all about you."

Alina hugged her, tears threatening again. "Of course! You're my best friend. If you aren't happy, I'm not happy."

After another gentle squeeze, Phina let go, and they quickly went through the rest of the list. Alina widened her eyes in amazement. "We do have everything done! I can't believe it!"

Phina smiled at Alina's response, then frowned as she realized two things were missing from the list that had featured in many of the rom-com movies Alina enjoyed. "What about the bachelor party and your honeymoon?"

Alina deflated and sighed. "I don't know. I should have asked Maxim what he was thinking about them, but I felt terrible about asking him to take more time for a honeymoon when he had arranged to be here so much for the past year. Besides, you guys are going somewhere right after the wedding and he's going to need to be there for that."

Phina frowned and pulled out her tablet to send a message asking Maxim what he was thinking for the honeymoon. While she waited for the answer, she asked Alina. "And the bachelor parties? Isn't that something I'm supposed to help take care of?"

Alina nodded with a small frown of concern on her face and a huge sigh as she flopped onto the bed. "You and the best man. The problem is that Maxim doesn't have one. He's got five groomsmen and can't decide who should be his best man. The wedding is in a few days!" She threw her hands up in exasperation. "It's been driving me crazy!"

Phina's tablet pinged with a message from Maxim

saying he wasn't sure what to do about the honeymoon with the delegation happening.

After taking a deep breath, Phina nodded, more to remind herself she could do it than to reassure Alina. "All right. Leave both of them to me. I'll take care of it."

Alina's relieved smile was worth any effort.

QBBS *Meredith Reynolds*, Diplomatic Institute

Phina breathed a sigh of relief that everything was coming together. After Alina had calmed down and left, she had messaged the groomsmen—Drk-vaen, Ryan Wagner, Todd Jenkins, Peter Silvers, and Craig Miller— and suggested that since there wasn't an official best man and nothing had been figured out yet, they should reserve space for it in All Guns Blazing two nights before the wedding and combine the parties.

They could hang out for a while, and if they wanted to separate later, they could. It hadn't taken long to get responses.

Sounds good. —Todd

Roger that. I'm considering adding a little something to the schedule afterward. —Ry

Phina had narrowed her eyes at that when she received a couple more.

I have reservations about anything Ryan has in mind. Otherwise, it sounds fine. —Drk

We should do something that Maxim would hate us for. Give him a night he'll always remember. —P

Phina had rolled her eyes and raised a hand to reply when another message popped up.

That's what I'm talkin' about, man! Total embarrassment! —Ry

She thought about banging her head against the wall for having the idea. Alina was going to kill her if this got out of hand and it affected the wedding. She had only met the man briefly, but she had begun to hope Craig would be a voice of reason. Sadly her hopes had been dashed.

Wahoo! An evening with beer and the ladies, then guys' night out with exotic dancers and whiskey sounds good to me! —Craig

Add a lap dance for Maxim and we can call it a night. —Ry

Phina hadn't known what to think about strippers and lap dances as she stared at her tablet. She barely felt curious about sex, let alone watching other people with minimal clothes on. She had shaken her head and decided to ignore it.

So, we'll meet you guys at six at AGB and hang out for a while. I'm going to reserve it now. Then you guys can go do whatever while we do our own thing. I think

we'll come back to our place for pizza, Cokes, and ice cream and watch romantic action movies that have a splash of funny while we chat. See you all then! —Phina

She had figured she would use her full name so they didn't confuse her for Peter. Putting it from her mind, she moved on to the next thing.

"Meredith, who do I talk to for reservations at All Guns Blazing?"

The EI's voice came from the speakers in her room. "That would be Cheryl Lynn. Would you like me to connect you to her now?"

"That would be great, thanks, Meredith."

She talked to Cheryl Lynn and made sure there would be enough space for the right timespan.

"Absolutely! Bethany Anne wondered if you would celebrate here and approved the areas needed for you whenever you need them. I'll make sure we are ready for you." The woman's light voice sounded competent and professional but friendly.

"Wow! Thank you so much, Cheryl Lynn!" Phina had felt almost comfortable talking to the Empress now that the woman had put her on the floor so many times, but that Bethany Anne had thought to go out of her way to help make Maxim and Alina's wedding special made Phina appreciate her more.

They disconnected and Phina saw she had several more messages.

That sounds good. Can I hang out with the females instead? —Drk

Come on, man! You're killing me here. —Ry

I can't help it if your mating rituals that aren't mating rituals because you aren't intending to mate are confusing. You humans have strange ideas. —Drk

You know, I'm in the same room with you... you could have told me this in person. —Ry

Phina had snickered at that.

Pizza and Cokes after a bunch of beers does sound good. —Todd

It does. I still think we need to do something embarrassing for him, though. —P

All right. Booze with the ladies, strippers and a lap dance for M, then we crash the ladies again for pizza and Cokes. Solid? —Craig

As Phina had finished reading this with eyebrows raised, responses from the rest of the guys came in with agreement and confirmations. Well, okay. She rolled her eyes at the guys' nerve. Apparently, they were all right with inviting themselves over.

Here's the list of all the guys who were on the guest list. You can decide who to invite. I don't know how big a group you guys are thinking, but we will probably have about a dozen, maybe as many as fifteen if they all come. —Phina

She had gotten acknowledgments, and the group chat had gone quiet after that.

She wondered if they hadn't realized she was still on the message thread. She chuckled about that as she entered the mostly empty classroom that had an open doorway.

After her meeting with the Empress, Phina had looked at the classes she still needed to pass and the upcoming trip and decided to message every teacher of the classes she still needed, asking them to allow her to test out. She invited them to make the tests as difficult as they liked but informed them that she needed to take them before she left the station. She'd requested that all the tests be administered over the next two days, and Anna Elizabeth had approved. So, five days before the wedding, she was about to take the first of several exams.

Her mind felt clear, her emotions weren't all over the place, and her body felt fine. A far cry from when she had struggled before going to the Aurians' planet.

She sat and nodded at the teacher overseeing her testing and accepted the first test. She looked it over briefly through to the end before looking up and smiling at Professor Emerson. He returned it thinly and with obvious disdain.

Oh well. It was a good thing there wasn't a grade passed on how good her relationship was with the teacher, or she would have failed. As it was, she was confident she knew the material cold despite her suspicion that he had made it as difficult as possible.

The smile remained on her face as the teacher told her to begin.

QBBS *Meredith Reynolds*, All Guns Blazing

Phina entered All Guns Blazing the night of the party and looked around for someone in charge. She threaded her way to the bar through the friendly raucous crowd and asked for Cheryl Lynn. The bartender, whose name tag read Dave, looked up with a smile.

"Hi! Yes, she's on her way out."

She gave him a smile of thanks then waited until a woman walked toward her. She was dressed in what some people called business casual with a tablet in one hand and held her other hand out to Phina with a friendly smile. "Hi, I'm Cheryl Lynn. Come on through to the back where we have everything set up."

The noise level dropped considerably when Phina followed Cheryl Lynn into the back room. She glanced around, then realized. "Noise dampener?"

"Yes. We didn't want the sounds of the bar to get too loud for conversation." Cheryl Lynn flashed an approving smile at Phina as she stopped at a grouping of booths with a wave. "What do you think? Is this enough space for your group?"

Phina looked around, counting seat space and comparing it to her mental list of everyone who had responded over the past few days. She had been sending a lot of messages in between her exams—which she had passed with flying colors, planning out Maxim and Alina's honeymoon, and helping with preparations for the delegation. Fortunately, almost everyone could come even though it was last minute.

Sundancer had told her he would make himself scarce, but he would be paying attention in case the assassin came back.

She gave the other woman a small smile and nodded. "Yes, it looks great. Thank you."

"Do you have any decorations or anything we can help you set up?" Cheryl Lynn looked at her expectantly, but Phina couldn't help looking surprised and confused.

"Umm... Am I supposed to decorate? I haven't done this before. I knew I should have looked it up." Phina grimaced and took out her tablet.

A reassuring hand touched her shoulder, and she looked up to see Cheryl Lynn shaking her head with a small smile. "It's all right. I asked because I want to help. If you don't mind adding to the tab, I can put something together?"

Phina sagged in relief. "Thank you, that would be great. If you could also set up a tab for any drinks people get while we are here? Food, too, as long as it's snacks."

"Of course." Cheryl Lynn nodded then they chatted about specifics before she left with a reassuring smile.

After slumping into a nearby seat, Phina sighed and made herself sit quietly. It was a good thing she had come an hour early. She took a moment to adjust her mental shield so it would block out the large number of people whose minds were currently a lot less controlled than normal. Phina had to be careful to keep the shields strong enough to block the mental clutter, but permeable enough to still intake enough Etheric energy. She let out a breath slowly when she was finished. Tonight would definitely test her mental shields and filters.

She shook her head then grabbed her tablet to move on, confirming the pizza and Coke order and time of delivery, then decided to add decorations to the apartment and made some contacts for that.

She received a message with the last approval for the honeymoon plans just as she was about to put her tablet away. A small knot inside that she hadn't been aware of loosened. Now Phina needed to make reservations for Maxim and Alina. Thankfully, someone had decided that even though she was in a coma, she would still receive the same stipend, so she had a bunch of backlogged credits saved up. Hopefully, everything would come together and Maxim and Alina would love everything.

Phina looked around the soon-to-be-filled reserved section of the bar and reminded herself that everything would be fine. As long as Alina and Maxim had fun, that was all that mattered. None of those invited were assholes, so everyone should get along, and they were all adults, so there shouldn't be any problems. Right?

The knot in her belly tightened up again.

CHAPTER TWENTY-ONE

QBBS *Meredith Reynolds*, All Guns Blazing

"So there we were, racing into the room chasing the rabbits." Craig chuckled as he relayed the story, his arm around Hallie. Maxim rolled his eyes to the ceiling and sighed. He knew what was coming, and it didn't paint them in a great light. "Full speed, of course. Suddenly, we were asses to the ceiling, hanging by the nets that the girls had laid to catch the rabbits. Maxim gave me this look like it had been my fault, but by that time, I was following him! Of course, we were in wolf form, so I couldn't tell him that."

Scattered chuckles sounded from the group situated in the booths that Phina had reserved for them. Maxim tuned his friend out as he continued sharing a story. Maxim had experienced the infamous rabbit hunt, and he had also heard Craig's version of it several times over. He couldn't complain since he hadn't seen Craig as often after he had moved out when he finally had made it official with Hallie several years ago.

He looked over the people who had come. Drk-vaen and Sis'tael sat together on their special seats for four-legged Yollins. They'd had their mating ceremony last year after her father had acknowledged that it was a good match. Not that they wouldn't have done it without the male's go-ahead, but the approval had made it easier.

Ryan sat with Celeste near Todd Jenkins, who had fina-gled a reason to sit with Phina, much to Maxim's approval and amusement. Todd Grimes, who had come with girl-friend number...five, Cassy, maybe...sat near his sister, Tina who had come from her secret research base. She had her head together with Yana and Mischa, of course, both diplomats who had been out on assignment but were able to come for the wedding.

A very pregnant Mal and the girls from the clothing shop sat together, listening to Craig's story with amuse-ment and whispered giggles. Tim Kinley, Rickie Escobar, Joel Holt, and Joseph Greggs were sitting together, a couple of them eying the single women. Masha and Ron were speaking to each other seriously in low tones that Maxim couldn't grasp over the other voices and noises, even with his advanced hearing.

"Are you all right, Maxim?"

He looked at Alina with a smile and tried to relax. This was a fun night out with friends. He suspected the guys were planning something later, but for now he was happy to be here with his friends and the woman who meant the universe to him. He had owned a purpose, to protect his team and follow his Empress to the end, but he had still felt incomplete before meeting Alina. He thought back to his conversation with Todd and Peter more than two years ago when he'd lamented that no one cared to see who he was beneath the surface. Alina didn't just see beneath the surface but valued who he was and protected him in her own way as much as he protected her.

"I'm good, sweetheart. Just thinking about our friends and how lucky I am to have you."

Alina started out giving him an understanding smile that turned to amusement. "You *are* pretty lucky to have me, aren't you?"

He scooted her closer with the arm he had wrapped around her and bent down to whisper in her ear. "I absolutely am."

"Maxim!" she protested in a whisper. "You can't do that now. You know what it does to me."

He grinned, happiness making it a tad wider than normal as he spoke quietly. "Just want you to be thinking about me later when you women go off on your own."

"Holy shit!" Craig stopped in the middle of another story to gape at Maxim in disbelief. "Look at you; you're grinning! You all see this, right? Mister Serious is showing teeth!" As the others made noises of surprise as well, Craig turned to Alina and made bowing motions with his head and hands that caused her to giggle. He stopped and grinned, chuckling with amazement.

Alina waved him off, protesting. "Oh, stop. Maxim smiles all the time."

Craig scratched his head as his eyebrows rose. "Maybe since you've come in the picture. Before that, it was super rare."

Hallie nodded, agreeing. "He's right. Maxim always has

our backs, but I wouldn't say he smiled all that much before you came into his life."

Amid choruses of agreement, Maxim leaned in and whispered, "See, I told you I'm lucky to have you."

Alina's beaming face looking up at him with happiness lit up his world.

Masha leaned closer to Ron and spoke quietly, ignoring the ruckus that usually surrounded Craig when he got going.

"Ron, I need to know if you've got something I can use. I've come across too many aliens who are bigger than I am in this form. I need an edge, and preferably something quieter and less bloody than a set of Jean Dukes Specials. I don't always have the luxury of time to clean myself up after a shift."

The R&D man frowned in concentration as he considered the problem. "Hmm... Less messy than a projectile, but still lethal?" He focused on her until she nodded, then returned to his mental calculations. "Well, barring projectiles and explosives, the best lethal force would be an electric current. That would be quiet and get the job done. The problem is the applicator and mechanism."

Masha glanced at the others and suppressed a smile at the competition happening between Craig and Ryan as to who could tell a taller tale about Maxim. Those two were trouble. She internally sighed as she thought about their Academy days. It was a lifetime ago. It almost felt like another life. She turned back to Ron and leaned in again. "What about an Etheric solution?" At his look of surprise, she raised an eyebrow. "Come on, Ron. I know you've been working with it. Only Anne has done more at this point."

"How did you..." Ron stopped himself and rolled his eyes in exasperation. "Spies. Of course." He shook his head at her surprise and pointed at his face. "Genius here. I've been supplying you guys with creative weapons and tools. It wasn't hard to figure out."

She pressed her lips together but nodded. "So, can you do it?"

"Well, I can't create something out of thin air. I need an applicator that's conducive to... Hold on." He blinked in thought, then turned and called across the aisle to the other group of seats. "Seraphina! Hey, could you come over here for a minute?"

The young woman in question leaned around Todd Jenkins at his call to look, who didn't appear pleased at the interruption. Phina nodded at Ron's question, then instead of asking Todd to move, she put her hands on the table to push herself up, used the seat to jump up on top of the back of the booth, then flipped to the floor.

Masha's eyebrows rose despite the long-standing and hard-won control she had used for most of her life. As a Wechselbalg, that control had been taught alongside reading, math, and manners. Masha studied Phina, speculating who would win between the two of them.

Phina ignored everyone's surprised and excited cries at the move—although Maxim, Alina, Todd, and the Yollins appeared amused—and walked over to Masha's side of the booth. She sat on the edge of the seat and faced Ron.

Phina's green eyes were startling in the middle of her dark hair and olive skin tone, but there was no mistaking who she was. Phina's features would have given it away if Masha hadn't already known. She looked exactly like her parents.

"You can call me Phina. What's going on?"

Ron leaned forward toward her and appeared interested, which caused Masha's eyebrows to twitch in surprise. "What do you think of your telescopic staff?"

Ah, of course. She should have known better. Ron was only interested in his work. The other woman's eyes sparkled with intrigue. "You made it?"

"Yes, Todd said it was for you. Is it working well? Any issues?" Ron pressed.

Phina shook her head. "Not that I've come across so far, and I've used both Todd's and mine. Just need to get my new pants from Alina when she's done with them so I have somewhere to keep it."

"What do you think about adding an Etheric current to it?" he asked.

Masha's eyebrows slowly rose at the conversation that ensued, one she understood very little of aside from that there needed to be a thing that pulled the Etheric, another thing that converted it to electricity, and a third that pushed the output. That was enough for her. It surprised Masha that Phina could follow Ron's technical explanation with the help of a few clarifying questions. It seemed that Ron was surprised as well and was currently looking at Phina with new eyes.

"Question." The two looked at her, surprise on Ron's face. He probably had forgotten she was here. "How are you going to keep the current from electrocuting me?

Remember, this started with me needing a weapon. I need to be able to hold onto this thing while I use it."

"What about gloves?" Phina offered, looking introspective. "It would be cooler if you could also use them to have better grip when climbing and holding onto the staff."

"Beats using my claws," Masha agreed, glancing at Peter and Maxim. "We weren't all blessed with the ability to turn Pricolici."

Ron looked intrigued by the idea. "Jean finally gave me my own office, so I have more space for projects. I'll play around with it and see what I can do."

Tina leaned over the back of the seat behind Ron and banged her hand on the table, startling him. "Hey, no work talk! This is supposed to be a party, so let's party it up!"

As the three of them joined the rest of the group, who were getting louder due to the number of beers that had been passed around, Masha eyed Phina with speculation. She had been Greyson's first recruit. It appeared that Phina was his latest. She found it odd that he hadn't brought Phina to Spy Corps headquarters yet to train.

Masha decided that she would have a talk with him soon and see if he would change his mind.

After speaking to Masha and Ron, Phina drifted around the group for a while, talking to the other bridesmaids about their dresses, Mal about her baby, some of the guys about fighting technique, and several people about the upcoming wedding, and Maxim and Alina in general.

She felt relieved that everything was coming together and everyone seemed to be having a good time. Also that Alina hadn't broken out into songs about princesses finding love yet, as she tended to do when she was tired or tipsy.

The group was getting ready to separate when Maxim pulled her aside and asked about the tab. "Let me know the total and I'll pay you back."

Phina shook her head, grinning. "Not a chance. I've got it. You don't need to worry about it."

Maxim frowned as he looked down from his taller height. "The tab is going to be a lot for one person, and you are getting pizza and Cokes, too."

She patted his arm as she smiled. "It's all right. Alina is my family. You guys have the wedding covered, so this is where I can contribute. Besides, the credits are sitting there since I wasn't spending anything for a couple of years, and I don't need much."

He still looked concerned but finally nodded. "If you are sure."

Todd Jenkins turned from watching Ryan, Craig, and Rickie see who could chug a beer bottle the fastest. "I'll split the tab with her, Maxim, so it's not on one person." He looked at Phina and added, "If that's okay with you?"

Phina shrugged, not sure what she should say. "If you want."

He smiled wryly. "Well, I haven't been in a coma, but I have plenty of credits sitting around, too. Also, this helps distribute the check more evenly between the guys and girls."

She nodded her agreement with the plan, then waited uncomfortably as goodbye kisses from the guys who had come with girls turned into a contest to see who could kiss the longest before coming up for air.

The single girls were all clapping and whistling. Most of the single guys hooted and hollered. Ron sighed and took out his tablet. Todd side-eyed her as he watched the scene with amusement. "Not a fan of kissing?"

Phina frowned as she considered it but shook her head. "I've never done it, so I wouldn't know. But, it seems private, so I have a hard time watching. It's the same with movies. It feels voyeuristic to me."

Todd gave her a small smile. "I'll be interested to see if you change your mind after you've experienced it."

It wasn't until all of the women were back at their apartment passing out pizza that she wondered if his comment was made because he wanted to be the one kissing her.

"You can't deny the power of a well-placed uppercut," Joel argued.

Maxim shook his head. "That works if you can get in close. Roundhouse, then a long knee to the gut."

"No way," Craig cut in. "Knife hand to the throat then a hard knee to the nose when they double over."

"You need to have both hands for that to work," Maxim pointed out wryly.

Craig waved both hands. "What do you call these, you ass?"

Todd tuned out the conversation and looked around the bar that doubled as a strip club and sighed, wishing he was with Phina eating pizza and drinking Coke. He would much rather see what he could do to move his relationship along with that one particular woman than watch a random one gyrate and contort her body. He turned to observe the other guys and could immediately see who was comfortable and who was not with their current location.

Craig, Ryan, Rickie, and Peter were the only ones paying attention to the stage. Maxim, Drk-vaen, Tim, Joel, and Joseph were talking about their fighting styles, arguing about which was better, and some of the incursions they'd been part of. Ron's neck seemed to be perpetually flushed as he studiously read, tapped, and swiped on his tablet.

Maxim's face was also still red from the lap dance he had been given. He hadn't known what to do with his hands so he had held them behind him and braced himself, letting it happen because it was expected but not engaging or appearing to enjoy it. His face and neck had grown more and more red as time passed, while most of the guys heckled or gave encouragement. Peter and Ryan had taken pictures, which would probably be fodder for giving Maxim a hard time later.

The dancer had finally finished with an amused expression. Rickie had paid for another dance for himself and had displayed far more enjoyment. She'd gone off happy with a large tip while the men settled themselves around a couple of tables.

Maxim had gotten ribbed by the guys for his stiffness until he finally shrugged and said, "Alina said I could look but not touch. I didn't want to accidentally touch by mistake."

Todd, Drk-vaen, and Ryan, who had seen Alina on a

rampage before, had winced and nodded and said some variation of "Good call."

When the four who were engaged in the show turned back to the table and were debating the merits of a pitcher versus bottles of beer, Todd checked the time, saw they still had an hour and a half before Phina had said they could meet up with the girls again and decided that something had to be done.

He stood up and waved a server over to pay the bill, then turned to the other guys, half of whom were still involved in their discussions. The rest were giving him questioning glances.

"Come on, guys. Let's go see which one of you can put your money where your mouth is."

They looked at him with varying interest. "Where we going?" Peter asked as he got up and walked over.

Todd grinned and beckoned them to follow. "This way, boys. Let me show you some real fun."

Forty minutes later, they joined the crowd at the fight club, yelling and hollering as Ron fought Ryan. Even though it was clear that Ryan would win, the men were surprised that Ron had some moves in him and was putting up a decent fight. He finally tapped out and Joel replaced him, eventually winning against Ryan with a quick takedown that had the Marine's back on the mat.

Peter joined Todd on the sidelines and clapped him on the back. "Good idea." As they watched Joseph swap with Ryan, the bigger man leaned over and nudged him. "So, when are you finally going to ask her out?"

"Who?" Todd asked as he kept his eyes on the two

Guardians in the ring. The referee started them and quickly backed off.

Peter half-rolled his eyes at Todd. "Come on, man. Don't play that game with me."

Todd returned the look. "Like you get when a certain Ranger is mentioned?"

The other man grunted in acknowledgment. They were quiet for a minute watching before Peter finally wondered, "What's it say about us that we're both highly skilled, battle-hardened warriors, and we're scared to talk to the women we're interested in about a little thing like starting a relationship or even going out on a date?"

Todd shook his head and grinned, thinking about Phina. "Probably that the women we're interested in are highly skilled badasses who can be hella scary when they want to be?"

"Just the way we like them." Peter grinned as Joel got slammed into the side of the ring and fell. He lay there stunned long enough to get called out. "Your turn." Peter gestured to the ring, then gave Todd a half-pat, half-push.

As Todd entered the ring and prepared to fight Joseph, he decided that he would talk to Phina about it after the wedding and try to keep close to her as much as their duties allowed. Being scared, as much as he could joke about it with Pete, wasn't something he could allow himself to dwell on.

People fight for what they want, and every day he was more certain that Phina was worth fighting for.

CHAPTER TWENTY-TWO

QBBS *Meredith Reynolds,* **Phinalina Residence**

"I love this part!"

The women had polished off the pizzas, a chocolate fudge cake Cheryl Lynn had arranged, and were working on popcorn as they drank Cokes and watched a movie about married secret spies who had found out that the other person was also a spy.

Phina watched it in amazement from her seat on the floor, wondering how someone could keep a secret from a person they loved for so long. As much as secrets were part of her business, Phina couldn't help thinking that she needed to trust the other person completely for a relationship to work. Secrets implied a lack of trust. Her thoughts spun until she heard laughs about the husband's best friend.

"That guy is always funny in his movies," Yana commented before popping some more kernels in her mouth.

"Yeah," Hallie snickered. "He can be a buffoon at times."

Phina agreed, then commented with her eyes on the screen. "He reminds me of Ryan, Craig, and Rickie."

There were murmurs of agreement, but she felt a stare off to her right and heard an outraged protective voice. "Are you calling Craig a buffoon?" She turned to see Hallie's narrowed eyes glowing yellow as she dived over Mischa with her hand raised.

Phina dropped the popcorn and grabbed Hallie's wrist before her hand connected. Her body strained as a large part of the force and momentum hit her, but she held on and stared at Hallie's surprised face.

Gasps sounded from Mal, who sat in Phina's comfortable chair for the occasion since she was pregnant, and the girls from the boutique as they hadn't seen many fights before. The others displayed varying levels of surprise.

"No." Phina spoke evenly, wanting to explain and not further upset the other woman. She could see how Hallie had made that connection. "I meant that I see the three of them joke around and often try to cover how they feel with comedy or use humor to try to release the pressure and tension. I think all of them hide how smart they are, and sometimes that can make it difficult to let someone in."

There was silence in the room as they stared at each other before giggles burst out around the room. Tina nudged Hallie and said, "Come on, Hallie, you know she's right about that. You're being overprotective again."

Phina let go as the other woman sagged and sighed. "I know. God, Phina, you are so right about that! It took me forever to get Craig to admit he wanted more than just a good time when it was clear that he did."

Celeste agreed from her seat on the couch, waving a handful of popcorn. "Ryan is the same way. The man is so confusing! I'm never sure if I should bring up where our relationship is going or not."

Alina offered Hallie another Coke after she moved back to her seat then gave the two of them a sympathetic smile. "Guys are confusing because they are confused about how they feel. It's easier for them to act than talk about their feelings."

Groans and choruses of "So true," sounded around the room, even from Sis'tael, before the sound of crunching popcorn was heard.

"Sorry for squishing you, Mish."

The diplomat waved a hand with a smile. "That's all right. I've gotten used to it."

"Oh!" Tina grinned. "That sounds like a story."

Yana chuckled and nodded. "It is. You've got to hear this."

The women moved closer as they leaned in to listen. Phina looked around the room and realized that aside from her nights getting together with Alina and Sis'tael, this had been the first time interacting and getting along with a large group of women. A misunderstanding, sure, but it worked out. It felt...good.

Really, really good.

"*Quiet.*"

Phina hissed at the loud and jovial men piling in the door far later than she had expected them. She got a better look at them and gaped in surprise and concern. "What happened to you? You look like you all got drunk or in a fight. Or both," she added after seeing the staggers and healing wounds.

"That'sh cuz we did," Ryan slurred as he staggered past Maxim and Ron, using them as crutches as he headed over to the couch. "Got the good stuff, too." Meaning the alcohol that worked on those with nanocytes, Phina assumed, since half the group were Wechselbalg.

Ryan collapsed on the couch face first and lay there unmoving. Some of the other guys found places in the living room area to crash too. Craig stumbled off, and Phina later found him tangled with Hallie. The same with Maxim and Alina. Rickie was snoring in a pile on the floor near the bedrooms. Todd and Peter grabbed space on either side of the door. Ron sat in one of the chairs, thankfully not hers, and promptly fell asleep. The others grabbed anywhere they found room.

After staring at them dropping one by one, Phina sighed and went to get more blankets. The women had given up on the men joining them after a few hours of waiting, chatting, and movie watching and finally gone to sleep in one of the two bedrooms. After passing the blankets out, some of which she placed on top of the guys since they were already asleep, and turning the lights low, she kept one blanket for herself and settled down in her chair. She figured a room full of warrior men would be better able to help against assassins than women who weren't trained for it, should there be an attempt during the night.

She had just closed her eyes when she realized that

someone was trying to get her attention. She looked around and saw Todd looking at her intently from his spot by the door. Hoping he had a good reason to do so, Phina used one of the filters Sundancer showed her to send and receive mental messages and not read much more into other people's minds.

Did you need anything?

Todd blinked, but that was the only outward sign he had heard her. *Yes.*

Phina gave him the "get on with it" look she had picked up from Link. He finally asked, *What can I go out and get for breakfast in the morning?*

Why did she feel like he wasn't saying what he originally wanted? She waited a few seconds, but he didn't elaborate. *Well, it's morning already, but I'm going to make pancakes when I wake up. It's a family tradition for celebrations.*

That sounds nice. What can I do to make that easier for you?

You can sleep, for starters. I'm not going to be in the mood to wrangle sleep-deprived guys with fight and booze hangovers. That can be your job. She gave him a small smile that he returned with a small salute.

Phina resumed her sleeping position and finally drifted off.

She woke when she heard loud whispers indicating Todd was doing his appointed job. Sighing, she checked the time and saw that several hours had passed and it was an hour most would be up anyway, although perhaps not after having such a late night. She left her blanket on the chair and went into the kitchen to make the pancakes for everyone.

After some time, during which she heard the buzzing of conversation and the water running in the showers, Phina slipped past Rickie and Ryan, who were discussing the different sounds that could be made with varying body parts, and deposited the mountain of pancakes, syrup, plates, and utensils on the table where everyone could get some. She called everyone in to eat and went to get a quick shower and change.

She came out to see everyone sprawled out around the apartment, some still eating and others finished. She moved to enter the kitchen when Alina asked, "Phina, are you planning on working out? You've got your exercise gear on."

Phina turned to see Alina snuggled next to Maxim holding a mostly empty plate, while his had been polished off. She gave her best friend a shrug and attempted to act like it was no big deal with being the center of attention, particularly with her tight but stretchy exercise clothes on.

"I was hoping to get a workout in. At least an hour or so. I need to do something physical to release some tension before we get caught up in wedding things." She attempted a smile, but it didn't get very far. She wondered if that was what had partly driven the guys to fight last night, but maybe they just liked using their bodies to move as much as she did. Muscle didn't like to sit still, and most of them had a *lot*.

Todd spoke up from the wall he had been leaning against while he ate since there weren't enough seats. "I'll go with you. There's something I want to try." He looked around. "If any of you want to come, I need Phina to get used to multiple assailants."

Phina straightened in surprise, but her eyes brightened. She wondered if that would give her more of a challenge. "Sounds good."

Hallie nodded, sounding eager. "I want to watch. You guys should have seen it. I threw a punch at her last night, and she just grabbed my hand and stopped it without any effort."

"You threw a punch?" Craig asked, looking at Hallie in surprise.

"What happened?" Ron frowned in confusion, his manner studious, though his clothes displayed he'd had just as interesting a night as the others. "I thought we were the ones at a fight club, not you guys."

Hallie blinked and spoke almost hesitantly. "Oh, it was…"

"A misunderstanding," Phina finished firmly.

Yeah." Hallie gave her a small grateful smile. "A misunderstanding. It's all good now."

Phina smiled then turned to the kitchen. "Give me a few minutes and I'll be ready."

She entered and moved over to the table to see an empty platter. Correction, a mostly empty platter with one lone pancake.

"You guys couldn't have left more for me?" she called.

"What are you talking about? There were at least three there." Yana stepped in as she spoke, then stopped in confusion at the single pancake. She put her hands on her hips and walked out with an attitude as she continued, an edge in her voice, "All right, who took the rest of those pancakes?"

Phina shook her head at the ensuing discussion and

spread syrup on the pancake before rolling it up and walking out. She waved it as she walked through the group to emphasize her point.

"It's fine. One is enough for now. I think less is better before a workout anyway." She turned at the door and smiled at everyone in the room. "Thank you all for coming to celebrate Maxim and Alina's upcoming wedding. I hope you had fun." She looked around until she found Maxim and Alina with their arms around each other's waists. Tears sparked at their happy smiles and seeing how close they were. She gave Alina their hand sign for "I love you," then decided that leaving before the tears fell was a good idea.

"See you all later if you aren't coming with me."

She flashed another smile then hurried out, hoping to use the walk to calm down.

And eat her rolled-up pancake.

QBBS *Meredith Reynolds*, Training Room

"So, they are going to get straight into the fighting?" Hallie asked as they sat down by the door to watch.

Alina nodded as she settled herself and flipped her hair back. "Phina usually learns quickly. Maxim said she's one of the fastest people he's trained. She often doesn't need to see something done more than once and then she does it herself, so they can move through techniques more quickly that way. Then she practices it on her own in between training sessions."

Masha frowned as she looked at the group on the training area of the floor discussing how they would approach fighting Phina. "But they aren't demonstrating anything. And this is her first time fighting multiple people? They have five guys over there. That's too many."

Alina shrugged, then smiled at her best friend, who stood at the far wall covering her ears to help her not hear the guys' conversation. She had grown resigned to seeing her best friend fight when Phina had first started, and now that she saw how much the girl enjoyed it, Alina couldn't help cheering her on.

"I've seen Phina fight before, and that was when she was trying not to die from overload. I've been watching her since she woke up, and the foggy confusion that was in her eyes over those last couple of months before the coma is gone."

Phina had told the short version about what had happened to the women last night since most of them knew the wedding had been delayed because of her coma. "I don't know if you've noticed how she moves, but that's changed, too. I don't think you need to worry about her, but if there's a problem, Todd is watching instead of fighting, so he will stop it."

Peter had left for work, but he told them he would be watching the feeds to see how it went. Everyone else had followed them to the training room, both to spend more time together since it had been so long since Maxim had gotten together with his friends from the Etheric Academy at the same time and because they were all curious about what Phina could do after her flip off the bench in the bar last night, as well as when she had stopped Hallie. Alina had been surprised about that, too, and she had seen Phina training before.

Todd nodded at the guys in front of them then turned to call to Phina. "We're ready."

Phina nodded as she dropped the towel she had held over her ears and walked to the middle of the room. Glided over. She moved like a dancer, as if always ready to move.

Alina had a little daydream, wondering what it would have been like if Phina's parents hadn't died. Would she have continued with gymnastics? Phina had quit after they died because her aunt had said it was a frivolous waste of time and money, something that Alina had gotten upset over and one of the few things Phina had argued about with her aunt before recently.

Maybe Phina would have branched into dancing. The times Phina had done gymnastics or danced with her eyes closed, when Alina had been able to convince her to have a dance party, had been some of the few times Alina had seen Phina set aside the weight that always seemed to be on her shoulders.

Phina wouldn't talk about it much, even to her, but from what she did say, Alina knew Phina felt like the people in the Empire needed her. Not like they did with the Empress. No one could do what Bethany Anne did or replace who she was to the Etherian people. Phina needed to be ready to help and protect them from the shadows while the Empress led from the front. Like a failsafe was what Phina had described, although she hadn't used those exact words.

Alina wanted to make sure her best friend was taken care of now that she was getting married. Phina should never feel alone.

She watched intently as Todd spoke to Phina, giving

her a smile and a quick touch on the upper arm before moving to take a spot on the side to watch as the guys circled Phina. She moved into her ready stance and briefly closed her eyes before opening them with a different focus.

Oh, yeah. Todd definitely had the hots for her best friend, and Phina liked him back, which was as rare as a sale in Alina's favorite shoe store. Rarer, since Alina couldn't remember there being another time Phina had expressed interest in anyone even obliquely. Alina grinned and began scheming while the guys sparred.

And so did Phina.

"Oooohhh." Celeste breathed in surprise as Phina ducked under Tim's punch, then slid under Joel's guard to kick out his knee before knifing her body into a handspring that shot her feet into Joseph, causing him to stagger. Phina was already moving, launching herself off Joseph and into a forward handspring. She landed straight and launched into a flying roundhouse that caught Craig in the head. Hallie sucked in a quick breath but let it out when she saw Craig was dazed. The guys paused in surprise at how quickly she had moved, then quickly resumed the bout.

"Wow." Scattered mutters of surprise came from the women around Alina, as well as Ron, who had sat out with Alina and the other women. Ron had said that last night's escapades had been enough for him for a while.

Phina had landed on the floor and immediately was caught from behind by Ryan, who held his arms around her. Instead of getting out of the hold, she grabbed his arms and used them to hold herself up as she brought her feet up to kick Tim as he moved in. The force caused him to jerk at the impact, but being such a big guy, her kick didn't do as much damage as it would have to one of the others. Ryan released Phina at the sudden weight on his arms and she dropped into a crouch and rolled under Tim's legs.

Alina moved from side to side, trying to see around Joel and Joseph, who had moved in front of the group observing from the side. It looked like Tim had bent down to grab Phina's hair, but Phina had grabbed his wrist and pulled as she continued to roll, causing him to topple over.

The next that Alina saw, Phina ran a step before jumping onto Joel and locking her legs around his neck. As he reached up to grab her legs, Phina used his head to give her leverage to pull herself up and around and sat on his shoulders.

Phina clapped the poor guy open-handed on his ears as Maxim came up behind the two of them. Since Maxim was the taller of the two guys, Phina reached back and used his head to pull herself into an aerial somersault as Joel fell to his knees with his hands over his ears.

Alina knew Phina's core muscles were strong from the gymnastics and pole exercises she did. Part of Alina wished that she could have muscles that strong, but she consoled herself with the knowledge that her more feminine curves made her damn sexy. Since Maxim didn't seem unhappy about her lack of physicality, Alina decided to put away that wish and be happy for Phina that she could do these amazing things.

She winced at seeing Phina kick Maxim's knee out and shook her head. Alina still had a hard time watching two people she cared about so much fighting, even when it was practice or playing.

Tim had recovered and moved in to grab Phina's arm and do a move Alina missed when Ron leaned over to whisper in an awkward but feigned casualness, "So.., Phina. Has she...or is she... Well, seeing anyone?"

Eying Todd, Alina leaned closer and spoke quietly. "I know she is interested in someone who is interested in her, but they haven't talked about it yet."

"Oh." Ron sat back in puzzled concentration, perhaps deciding whether that meant Phina was seeing someone or not.

She initiated a comm call on her implant.

"Yes?" Todd answered absently.

Alina could see him focusing on the fight. One of the guys had flung her off him. Phina twisted in mid-air and landed hard in a crouch, then sprang forward to kick Joel into Craig before turning to block a hit from Maxim.

Alina subvocalized, *Hey, Todd. Are you planning on telling my girl Phina you are interested in her?*

Todd gave her a startled glance then turned back to the fight. After another moment, he responded. *How did you know?*

Alina pursed her lips in thought then continued their private conversation. *Maybe because it's obvious? Well...* She glanced at her best friend, who was currently climbing Tim's back to put him in a chokehold which caused his face to turn purple. *Obvious to everyone but Phina, anyway.*

She turned to Todd in time to see his shoulders slump. *Then she's not interested. All right. Thanks for telling me.*

Alina's eyes widened. That was not what she had

intended for him to get out of that comment. She barely kept herself from physically responding as well as verbally. *Whoa, cool your jets, space cadet. That's not what I'm trying to tell you.*

He glanced at her with interest sparking in his eyes before he turned back to the fight. *It isn't?*

No, I'm trying to say that if you are interested, you need to do something to make it clear to Phina. Such as saying the words, or kissing her, or something. She is observant about everything except interpersonal relationships. Haven't you noticed that when people compliment her physical appearance, she doesn't believe them?

He made a noise that she interpreted as a thoughtful grunt of acknowledgment, so she continued, *Part of it is that she doesn't care about appearance. Clothes are just a means to an end for her, no matter how hard I've tried to convince her otherwise over the years, I might add.* Alina mentally rolled her eyes at her best friend's quirky refusal to admit that clothes were important.

At the risk of breaking the Best Friends Code, I'm going to tell you something I think you should know. A large part of it is that she is afraid to care about someone and get invested with them and then have them decide that her quirky passions and interests make her too much trouble to have a relationship with.

Alina sobered, trying to make sure Todd understood this important thing. *Phina is afraid of loss after losing her parents, but she has still been willing to open her heart to people and let them in—and we are better for it because she is loyal and commits to the relationship. Not to mention she will protect the people she cares about to the best of her ability. You need to make sure that she is who you want, with all her quirks and every-*

thing, because if you don't and she commits to you...and then you decide later that she isn't what you want?

Alina swallowed the tears that were welling. *Then I think it will destroy an important part of her that she might not get back.*

CHAPTER TWENTY-THREE

QBBS *Meredith Reynolds*, Training Room

It will destroy an important part of her that she might not get back.

Alina's words rang in Todd's head as he watched Phina launch off Craig's chest to flip in the air and land on Joseph, knocking him down.

His mind focused on the woman he had come to know over the last couple of years, and particularly over the last several weeks. He understood Alina's warning far too well. Rejection from someone you loved could deter you from experiencing it with anyone else. Wasn't that why Todd hesitated now, even though he normally wouldn't categorize himself as someone who would shrink from something important?

Todd was afraid of getting burned again.

But, as he watched Phina's singular focus while she assessed and moved quickly from one person to the next, he realized that Alina was right. Once Phina decided on a course, she took it and didn't look back. If Phina did have feelings for him, once they'd made that commitment to each other, he could count on it to remain. She wouldn't betray him like his first wife had. Phina wouldn't consider it.

He sighed in relief and glanced at Alina again. The blonde woman met his gaze, waiting for him to respond over his implant. He finally nodded and gave her a small smile.

Thank you, Alina. I appreciate your advice.

You're welcome. She flashed him a grin and subtly nodded at Ron. *He's asking about her, so you may not want to wait too long.*

Todd glanced at Ron and internally sighed when he saw the younger man watching Phina intently. Would it be better for Phina if he stepped aside for him?

Todd took a deep breath and turned back to Phina just as she was grabbed from behind again, this time by Joseph. She grabbed the back of his head and dropped her weight as she pulled forward, rolling him over her. She darted away from his grasping fingers, then jumped up over Maxim's kick, launching off of him and beginning to flip toward Craig.

At the last second, Maxim's fingers grasped Phina's ankle, causing her to swing down to the floor. She kicked out of the man's hold in time to do a partial handspring as she hit the floor, crouching and looking around warily at the men's positions to decide her next move.

Todd shook his head and clenched his jaw. He didn't think it was an accident that he was drawn to Phina, and he wasn't going to step aside. Not until he knew for sure what Phina's feelings were on the matter.

In this, at least, Todd was done with being self-sacrificing. It was time to actively pursue the woman he'd been admiring for over two years.

Todd let himself into the holding area, though they may as well call it what it was—a prison. It was smaller and far nicer than any prison he had seen on Earth.

The guard on duty signed him in as per procedure, not questioning why Todd had come since he was authorized to visit those being held when he wished to do so. After finishing, the guard waved him over to the door that accessed the visiting rooms.

All too soon, he entered the room to see a thin woman about Phina's height sitting at a table. He nodded to the guard standing nearby. At the swish of the door opening, the woman looked up eagerly, but her face fell as soon as she laid eyes on him.

"Expecting someone else?" Todd asked.

"Hoping, more like," Faith Rochelle mumbled as she played with the hem of her shirt.

Todd watched her for a moment before moving over to sit in the visitor's chair. He had accessed records earlier and had seen the note added by ADAM that Faith Rochelle was slowly dying from the serum she had made. Judging by the woman's gaunt frame, that wouldn't be far off.

"Are you here to have a conversation or gawk at me?" Faith glanced at him with a glower.

"Examine or observe more than gawk," Todd replied evenly.

The woman sniffed. "Makes no difference from my end."

After crossing his arms and ankles he watched her fiddle with her shirt until he spoke with a measure of compassion in his voice. "You have been told that you are dying?"

She froze then looked up to meet his eyes. "Yes," she whispered, and dropped her head again, but not before he saw anguish cross her face.

He frowned, wondering what was going through the woman's head. He felt protective of Phina, but he was also objective since he hadn't been familiar with the woman before.

After a time he asked the foremost question in his mind. "What made you decide to give your niece a serum when there was any number of things you could have done to protect her?"

Faith froze again then shook her head as she straightened, her face frowning in confusion. "I...don't know. It made sense at the time. 'Alter the nanocytes' kept ringing in my head like it was the most important thing I could ever do. I was so afraid for Phina that I knew I had to do something to take care of her. She was in danger, I knew it." She paused then shook her head again. "That's all I can remember thinking. I had to do it."

Todd took in everything he was seeing and hearing, growing still at her word choices. If he didn't know any better... He stopped himself and shook his head. That didn't make sense, either.

"Do you want to commit harm to Phina or any member of the Etheric Empire?" he asked.

Faith's eyes widened. "No, I never intended to harm Phina, or anyone." Her face crumpled and she threw her hands up. "It's all wrong! Everything is wrong. Chris and Simon should never have left me alone like this."

Todd couldn't help feeling compassion. Something wasn't right with the woman, whether it was psychological or something else. It didn't negate her treatment of Phina, but he couldn't deny that Faith needed help. Still, he had a job to do, self-imposed though it was.

"So, you didn't know that Phina has assassins after her?"

Faith looked up in alarm, splotches of tears on her worn face. "What! Is she okay?"

He unfolded his arms and raised a hand to calm her. "She's fine. She handled herself very well."

The woman blinked in confusion. "Handled herself?" Dawning comprehension turned to horror. "You don't mean she had to fight one off herself?"

Todd's eyebrows rose as he watched her. She was not responding as he had expected based on reports of past behavior. "Yes. Over the past couple of years, minus the time in her coma, Phina has become very adept at fighting. She successfully held off five guys in training earlier today, four of them were Wechselbalg. The assassin wasn't a concern for her, although we are expecting a larger response soon since he failed."

Faith's expression showed satisfaction with Phina's accomplishment, but as her face turned to alarm near the end she reached forward though her hands couldn't grasp his with the distance. "Please, please make sure she stays safe."

Todd nodded firmly. "I intend to do so."

The woman straightened at the reassurance but hesitated, chewing on her lip, which seemed to have become a common occurrence judging by the state of it. Finally, she met his eyes, her gaze imploring. "I know I don't have a right to ask this, being in here, but could you let me know when they attack again?"

He watched her carefully but couldn't sense anything other than a genuine concern for Phina. The incongruity between her past actions and current attitude bothered him, but he finally nodded and spoke up. "Meredith?"

The EI's voice emitted from the speakers in the room. "Yes, Commander Jenkins?"

"Please inform Faith Rochelle any time Phina is attacked by anyone who is not training with her."

"Understood."

As Todd stood up, Faith gave him a small smile of relief. "Thank you. I appreciate your kindness."

"Of course." He nodded, then turned to the door and exited the room. As he headed for the entrance he initiated a message over his implant. "ADAM, when you have time, there's something I would like you to do."

───────

Phina let herself into the apartment, took a shower and changed, then cleaned up from the party the night before.

She was thinking about dinner when she realized that she had hardly seen Sundancer in days.

She frowned and closed her eyes in concentration, focusing on the connection between her and Sundancer. He was.. close, but not in the same room with her. She followed that inner locator into her room and froze when she found him sitting on her dresser next to the box of important things, with the lid open and her parent's envelope in plain sight.

He looked up at her approach, his pink wrinkled face solemnly. *It's time, Phina.*

After swallowing her protest, Phina slowly moved over to stand in front of the bed. She looked at the letter nestled with her mother's pendant and sighed. "I know. I've been afraid to find out what it says. Right now it could say anything, but once I read it I'll know."

Sundancer nodded as if her half-formed thought made perfect sense. Or maybe he could read her mind to know what she meant. *You savor potential and fear absolute outcomes.*

Phina shrugged as her forehead creased in concern. *Absolute outcomes that are negative, certainly.*

He pawed it and pushed it toward her. *Just read it.*

She swallowed then nodded and gingerly lifted the letter, giving the envelope one last perusal. Her name was written on the front. Or rather, her parent's nicknames—

Phina, our angel.

Phina took a deep breath, then carefully opened the envelope and slipped out the several sheets of folded paper enclosed. A separate card fell out onto the dresser, surprising her. She shifted the other papers into one hand and curiously picked up the card that had "Our angel—11th birthday" written on it. She turned it over and almost dropped it when she saw a printed picture of herself with her parents surrounding her, about to blow out the candles on her birthday cake. They were all smiling, her more excitedly, and her parents looked proud...and loving.

Her vision grew blurry and she backed up to sit on her bed, tucking her feet up underneath her. She didn't know how long she sat there staring at the faces of the two people she loved most as tears fell. She had seen pictures of them before, occasionally, since her aunt hadn't liked to see them. However, counting back she realized that this must have been one of the last pictures they had taken before leaving for that last mission.

She felt a nose nudging her hand and looked over to see Sundancer next to her, giving a kitty-cat look of sympathy which quickly turned to a glare when he read her thoughts. She shrugged and wiped away her tears with the back of her hand before wiping it on her pants. "Sorry, you look like a cat so it's indelibly linked in my brain."

Rather than giving her more grief he sighed and pointedly looked at her letter. *Read it.*

Phina's mouth pulled into a twitch that might have become a smirk if she had put more effort into it. Her thoughts sobered quickly when she turned to her task. She set the picture to the side and slowly opened up the nine-year-old letter.

Our dear Phina,

We hope you will never have to see this letter, just as

you've never seen the previous letters we wrote for this purpose. But, just in case we don't make it back to you we have some important things that you need to know, and I have so much to tell you, our fiery, sweet angel.

First, we love you with all our hearts. Totally and completely. Our lives were not whole without you in them and we have never regretted having you or the way you came to be in this world for a single second. We hope you have felt our love for you and this is merely a reminder of something you already know. Just remember, that never, ever will change, no matter how long we live.

Phina's vision grew blurry with tears again, so much that she had to move the letter before it got wet. She did remember her parents and their love for her, but it had become more like a distant memory. Reading this brought on a rush of emotion and it was overwhelming. The love they'd shared with her, the loss of them all over again. Finally, she was able to see long enough to get tissues and wipe her face so she could continue.

Second, we need to tell you something important that may be difficult for you to understand if you are reading this at a younger age.

She read through an explanation of everything that Link, TOM, and ADAM had shared regarding her birth, with more private details about her mother's desperation to have a child and knowing there had to be some way out in the universe for it to happen.

This was our way, my angel. We wouldn't have had you any other way, and I believe that this was the path we had to take or you wouldn't have been the amazing person you are. I have watched you grow from a tiny baby to a bright and curious toddler who got into everything because you wanted to know why, to a gangly little girl who was more comfortable with learning things than playing dolls with Alina, to the big, bright girl you are now, having so many interests, but particularly hearing your father's spy stories. I have no doubt you will be just as unique and amazing when you become a teen and later a woman in your own right.

Phina pushed back the tears that threatened to flood at the memories that popped in her head as she read the words. How could she have forgotten so many of them? She frowned and shook her head. She made herself take deep breaths to compose herself enough to continue. Sundancer's warm body leaning against her was a comfort, as well as his warm presence in her mind.

Third, I hesitate to share this, but think you should know, those stories your father told? They are not just stories. They are real, or mostly. Your father does like to embellish to tell a good tale. But it's true that we are spies and we take our job seriously. That is what we are leaving to do. If we don't make it back, it's what we died for. I'm sorry we lied to you. It was to protect you and everyone we know. I hope you have remained our sweet girl and haven't grown bitter or angry since we've been gone. If you have, please find a way to release it as it will hurt you.

That was the Mom she remembered. The wise, kind, and patient person she had always been, trying to make sure she, Phina, and her dad lived in harmony together. She turned the page and continued, feeling comforted.

Fourth, baby girl, you need to know that our family is special, and you are the most precious. My family has always had girls, and those girls grow up to be strong, determined women who thrive through adversity. Each of us has certain gifts that some call psychic abilities. Your great-grandmother could sense intent, such as if someone wanted to harm another. She became one of the first female detectives. Your grandmother could persuade others to her point of view and became a politician, though more diplomatic than legislative. She didn't make anyone do anything against their will, just pushed them to have little shifts of thought. I always knew when someone was lying to me, which became very useful in my career as a spy, and with my cover as a negotiator before we joined the Empire.

I don't know what gift you may have or how the genetic changes TOM and ADAM made may have affected you. You are a brilliant and wonderful girl, no matter what, my angel. To protect you as a baby they minimized your abilities so you could grow strong and healthy. However, they assure me that it isn't permanent, and if you choose to, they can adjust the nanocytes to allow you your heritage and any other advantages that haven't come out yet from the nanocytes. Just ask Meredith to get in contact with them and what it's about.

Phina rose and slowly began pacing as she thought this out. Her family had psychic gifts and she had them, too. She frowned as she remembered how easy it had seemed to learn telepathic communication with Braeden, and how sensitive Sundancer said she was to the Etheric. Could this also be a factor for those?

It was certainly something to consider. She wasn't sure she could parse out which of the abilities she had were from this heritage and which had come through the changes since, but did it matter? She had what abilities she had, and had it on good authority that there was no going back now. Aunt Faith's serum had taken that choice away from her. She grimaced and shook her head not wanting to dwell on that anymore.

She settled herself down on the bed again and continued, Sundancer leaning into her for comfort. Phina petted and scratched him with one hand as she read.

That brings me to something else, my angel. There's another family who I met when I was pregnant with you—the Jamesons. Specifically, Fiona and her son Will. They both have small gifts like our family, and their family has been good friends to us. Fiona was like a sister to me and I appreciated her advice and encouragement when I struggled after a job. Yes, baby girl, your mother admits that she needs help sometimes. Your father says it's about time, but, with his stubbornness, he has no room to argue.

So, the Jamesons. You may wonder why you don't remember them? Sadly, we had to decide not to see them anymore when you were three since our work as spies had grown more dangerous. There were groups we were after who had a reputation like the mafia back on Earth. If you crossed them they would not only kill you but everyone in your family and your friends, too. We

didn't want to put them in danger. We wanted them safe on the MR.

We didn't want you in danger either, but selfishly we wanted to see you, my darling girl. You may remember that for several years we were often gone and only came home for a few days at a time. This is why. We tried to protect you as much as possible. We hope that we continued to do that no matter what happened with our death. Just as we hope that you will seek out the Jamesons at some point so you can have people who care about you in your life. I know Fiona well, and she would welcome you with open arms and feed you while she listened. Please do that, my angel. You need people in your life who care about you since you get lost in your head so much. Hush, now, that's not a criticism, just me knowing you as your mom who loves you and wants you safe and happy.

Phina slowly nodded and realized that was why Fiona hadn't wanted to bring it up. The reason was related to her parents spying and she would have felt it wasn't her business to talk about it. She smiled at her mom's comment in the latter part. Phina knew she did get stuck in her head a lot. She had forgotten how her mom had gently encouraged her to join the rest of the world.

She shook her head in bewilderment. "Sundancer, why have I forgotten so many memories about my parents? No one did anything to me, did they? Can you tell?"

Sundancer stood and stepped his front paws up on her leg looking into her eyes. She felt warmth in her head that she recognized as Sundancer's mental presence. Finally, he sat down and met her gaze with his bright blue eyes. *I sense only your presence in your thoughts. I suspect that your habit of suppressing emotions is at fault. Since memories are tied to emotions, suppressing one likely suppressed the other.*

Phina sighed and shook her head in frustration. "I need to do what Todd said and let the emotions out and feel them."

Sundancer nodded and placed his chin on her lap, half closing his eyes. *Yes. I did mention that he's a wise and discerning individual? You are keeping him, are you not?*

She snorted then chuckled and petted the Previdian. "That's not up to me."

He opened his eyes to look up at her skeptically and she amended her statement. "It's not solely up to me. He gets a say, you know."

Hmph. That is not how we do it on Previdia. His little triangle nose crinkled adorably, the thought earning her a reproving stare.

"Oh?" Phina was surprised to hear something more personal from Sundancer since he'd been relatively quiet on the subject so far. "How is it different?"

The males preen and show their talents to be admired and the females choose their male. If there is more than one interest, the females commence battle to decide who will win.

Phina's eyebrows rose higher the more she heard. "And you think this is better than how we do it?"

Well, it has the benefit of knowing where things stand rather than this muddled version where you don't know if the other is interested.

"Hmm..." She thought that over but couldn't help commenting further. "True, but doing battle makes the male too much of a thing to be won for my tastes. I would rather be wanted in return. How do those females know they are cared about?"

Sundancer nudged her arm to elicit pets and once she acquiesced he settled to answer, though his tone sounded a tad wistful. *Previdian males are drawn to strong females. The female who won would be admired, certainly. We do not have marriages such as humans appear to have, with lifelong commitments.*

"Why not?" Phina gave him long strokes from his head to his tail. His wrinkled pink skin felt surprisingly soft. "Is it a difference in desire, or of culture?"

Both. Sundancer lifted his chin for scratches. *Since a Previdian could hear the call at any time, permanency is not a cultural value. Besides, we live for over three hundred years. I can't imagine living with a female for that long. That you humans can do it is strange to me.*

Phina paused the scratches and raised an eyebrow. "Because we like having love and companionship throughout our life?"

He gave her an aggrieved pout, likely both at the topic and that she had stopped the scratches. *Because females are bossy.*

"Ah, that one was nowhere in my mind." She resumed the ministrations then had a thought. "Does that mean that you've had a partnership with a female before?"

Of course. He responded with his eyes mostly shut and his chin on her knee. *I have had three partnerships, fifteen children, and fifty-seven grandchildren.*

Phina's mouth dropped open to gape at the pink creature. "What? Why aren't you with them?"

Because I am here with you.

Emotions flooded her, mostly gratitude and sadness. "Does that mean you won't go back later?"

Sundancer remained silent for several long moments. *It is unlikely. Paired Previdians usually stay with their pair until their deaths. My older cousin I mentioned—the one that had gone to Earth before—he is the only one I know of that survived. He had gained greater attention because it is mostly unheard of for a Previdian to return since the pairing connection is so close. However, his pair died before that closer connection could be established. He was...altered, but mostly unharmed by the experience.*

"I'm sorry," Phina whispered, briefly closing her eyes. "I didn't know you had left everything knowing you couldn't go back. Is that why you were so cranky when we met?"

He opened his eyes a slit and gave her a reproving glare. *Magnificent and magnanimous beings do* not *get cranky.* He paused then sighed, closing his eyes again. *Perhaps I was, a little. It is an honor to be chosen since few are now. It is what our vow is for—to hear the call, leave our people and find our pair, helping them with their Etheric abilities. However, I did not anticipate how difficult I would find it to leave knowing I wouldn't return.*

Phina continued to pet him, but being more attentive now that she knew how much he had sacrificed to be here. "Thank you, Sundancer. I'm sorry you had to leave your home. I hope that eventually, you will be happy to be with me, woefully inadequate though I am in my understanding." Her mouth pulled into a smile as she attempted to tease him.

He bobbed his head though he leaned into her hand. *You have several failings and you were not the type of person I had visualized myself with.* Phina rolled her eyes but didn't get a chance to say anything before he continued. *But I know you now. You are admirable in your desire to help others and give so much to see people safe. I believe that the ancestors put us together for a reason.*

"High praise indeed, Sundancer. Thank you." She smiled and stroked his ears. He shook his head as if shaking off something that rubbed him the wrong way and gave her a long-suffering look before curling up next to her with his nose tucked in.

Finish your letter.

Phina sighed and nodded, turning to the pages in her hand to continue. There wasn't much left.

Next, my angel, you have an uncle, of sorts, who you should have at least met since we are entrusting this letter into his care. His name is Lincoln but we call him Greyson in deference to his cover. He is one of our oldest and dearest friends, as well as our boss. However, we adopted him into our family since he is so alone. We won't share his secrets, and he wouldn't wish us to. Just understand that he lives most of his life hiding who he is from others, and he needs people in his life to remind him that there's a man with a need for love and friendship under that persona. Please be his family for us, sweetheart. He needs you.

Link hadn't changed much in the years since her parents wrote the letter. She would be Link's family, of course. Glancing at Sundancer's napping form, Phina decided she would be his family, too. Neither of them should feel alone.

She glanced down and saw that the next paragraph

wasn't in her mother's neat handwriting but a larger scrawl. Her father's. She swallowed and continued reading.

Lastly, my baby girl, we chose your name for a reason. Seraphina, which means "fiery one". Seraphim are agents of light and purity, burning away the darkness. We chose Grace as your middle name because light and purity should also be tempered with love and kindness.

We have always worked in the shadows, as you may now realize. Your mother is amazing, you know. You get your smart mind from her as well as the fiddling ADAM and TOM did before you were born. She has been seeing a pattern taking shape in the universe over the past couple of decades that causes her concern. It's nothing she can pinpoint, but she describes it as a shadow that is slowly taking hold. We have been working to find and identify this shadow. Perhaps it is the Kurtherians, and perhaps it is something else. It's not clear enough to tell. However, we both believe that the Empire and its people are going to be in danger at some point. Not just from the Leath and their Kurtherian gods. This is something else.

I hate to ask this of you, Phina, but we need you to keep your eyes open to this threat. It's not been solid enough to share our belief yet with others, though we've noted every concern and discrepancy in our reports. We need you to be the amazing woman I know you will be and protect the Empire from the shadows. Universe willing, we will have more time with you and we can do this together, but if not, you will need to continue our

search. **I know you can do it, baby girl. I have faith in you.**

The letter switched back to her mother's handwriting.

Of course, your father didn't mention that he was the one to find a lot of those troubling spots that fit the pattern and realized their significance. You know how he is- and neither of us would change a thing about him.

Time grows short and we need to leave. We love you ever so much Phina, my angel. Be safe, be happy, and be the amazing person you are. You carry all our love and hope within you.

Phina finished reading, mixed emotions filling her and tears rolling down her face. She laid the letter and picture back on top of her box on the dresser and curled up around Sundancer, hugging him to her. He nuzzled his nose into the space near her throat and purred to comfort her and let her know he was here for her. But mostly, he kept quiet while she let the stuffed back tears and emotions flood through her. She had suspected she would respond this way when it all came out, which is why she had put off reading the letter.

As she lay there, she thought about that last paragraph by her dad. What shadow had her parents meant? Of course she would do her best to protect the Empire, but she was only one person. She thought about dumping the problem in Link's lap since he was head of Spy Corps, but she couldn't help shying away at the thought. It was her parents' last request. She wouldn't shirk her duty to the Empress and the Empire, even if it wasn't an official mission. She couldn't do it.

She kissed Sundancer on the head in thanks before

getting up to wash her face, her thoughts buzzing about an analysis program she could make to sort through the data the Empire received. It would take time, certainly, but she thought it might be doable.

But first, training with Braeden early, and then, she told herself as she opened the closet to retrieve a towel and found her maid of honor dress hanging right in front of her, *I have a wedding to attend tomorrow.*

CHAPTER TWENTY-FOUR

QBBS *Meredith Reynolds*, Phina's Training Room

Braeden shuffled his feet as he wheeled his staff around
to strike, then block. Phina met his staff easily but with the
small hesitations that came from inexperience. He focused
on gradually increasing both the pace and the strength of
the blows.

Phina adjusted and continued to follow his pace, her
small frown the only indication that she wasn't comfortable with the movements yet. He turned his staff, but
instead of the blows he had been using, Braeden stabbed it
forward. Only her quick reflexes as she flexed her spine
allowed her to avoid the tip.

Good.

After a few more minutes, Braeden brought the exercise to a halt and nodded, his eyes warm with affection.
*You will do well. Just remember what I told you about using the
staff.*

Phina recited, *Stab like a knife, block like you mean it,
strike with the fulcrum. Always move forward, never move back-*

ward, dance to the side but avoid rotating to show your back. Defense is the best offense.

Braeden gave her a rare grin. *Exactly right. Now you need to practice both with a partner and separately. It's the best way to learn.*

Seeing the troubled look come into her eyes, he let his staff drop and opened his arms. Phina dropped hers and rushed forward to give him a big hug.

When she drew back, Phina looked up in concern. *You are certain you need to go?*

Nodding, Braeden put a hand on her shoulder. *Yes, I'm certain. I've been away for quite a while, Phina.*

I know. I feel like I have hardly seen you since I woke up. Her eyes got bigger and sadder.

Braeden remained silent since he knew he would miss her too. Yet, he knew his time was done here, his purpose complete. A Gleek always knew. *I came here to help the Empire understand us Gleeks and to help mentor you in your abilities. I have accomplished those goals. Now that Sundancer is here to help you work on your mental abilities, you don't need me to teach you.*

Phina sighed. *I know, but I still need you as a friend and as my family.*

I will always be here for you when you need me. His mental voice was soft. *We still have some time before I leave.*

And in the meantime, we can test our mental abilities, Phina responded gleefully now that she remembered they could speak mentally whenever they wanted.

That too, Braeden agreed. Her enthusiasm was almost enough for him to wish he would be in the congregation for the wedding.

Almost.

QBBS *Meredith Reynolds*, Horizons Restaurant

"Here are the bouquets!" Mal said with relief as she waddled over to Alina and Phina, who knelt carefully arranging the short train behind Alina before moving to check her veil. Mal handed a larger bouquet of deep red, light pink, and creamy white flowers to Alina and a smaller one to Phina while she kept a smaller one for herself.

She beamed when she took in Alina. "Girl, you are so beautiful! Just look at you. Maxim won't be able to take his eyes off you!"

Alina smiled nervously at her boss and friend through her veil. "Thanks, Mal. You look amazing too! Pregnancy agrees with you."

Celeste, Nadine, and Sis'tael moved more sedately, holding their bouquets. Their dresses were the same style as Phina's—minus her special modifications that weren't visible from the outside—but in a light pink that closely matched the flowers. Sis'tael's dress had been designed to fit her Yollin physique, but she looked both pleased and amazed as she occasionally glanced down and stroked the fabric. She had told Phina at the last fitting that it was rare for Yollins to wear dresses, thinking more about what would be practical.

Mal smiled and smoothed the light pink fabric over her round belly. It was her first pregnancy and part of the reason she had given Alina a promotion, so she could take care of the boutique while Mal took care of her son. "He's ready to come out, that's for sure. I can't wait!"

Alina reflexively smoothed her dress, nervously straightening and primping to make sure she looked her best. Her wedding dress was relatively simple but elegant. The front plunged to her waist, coming to a point, and wide, long triangles of creamy white synthetic satin rose to cover her chest and reached up into a halter. The skirt was fitted around her hips and flared out mid-thigh into a short train in the back. Several thin decorative fabric strings laced from the halter on the back of her neck and fanned to the sides over her bare back before crossing her waist. Alina and Mal had collaborated on the design, and it fit Alina beautifully.

Phina finished fiddling with the veil and reached down with her free hand to hold Alina's. Her friend focused on her with a wobbly smile. Phina squeezed her hand gently. "You have nothing to be nervous about. You are beautiful. Your dress is amazing. You know Maxim loves you and is crazy about you. Your life together is just beginning."

The other women surrounded them with encouraging smiles and murmurs of agreement. They ignored the occasional person passing by through the corridor. The manager of Horizons hovered nearby, waiting anxiously for the signal to start the procession.

Alina made an effort to smile, but her face crinkled as she grew emotional. "Oh, stars! Don't make me cry, Phina!"

Phina swallowed her own emotions and nodded with a small smirk. "Well, all you have to do is follow us until you get to Maxim and not fall on your face."

Alina gasped and gripped Phina's hand, her face tight with worry. "What if I do fall? I'm so nervous."

Carefully giving Alina a gentle hug, she whispered.

"Then Maxim and I will race to see who can catch you first, and we will laugh about it later when I let him win."

Alina gave a small snort of laughter, which was what Phina had been going for. Phina pulled back and gave Alina an encouraging smile. "Even if something does happen, the important thing is that at the end of the day, you will be married to the man you love."

The other women reached over and held or patted Alina's shoulder as they agreed before Phina continued, her eyes focused on her best friend.

"You have been waiting for this moment your whole life, Leena. You're the star of the show, and you are going to shine. You can do this."

Alina straightened her shoulders and nodded, giving Phina a beaming smile. "Thank you, Phina. Let's go knock their socks off!"

Confident that Alina's mind wasn't on her nerves anymore, Phina gave the manager a nod to start the music as the girls arranged themselves before Alina in the order they were walking into the room. The bride had decided she would walk in alone, telling her parents firmly that if they came to the wedding, it would be as guests. She didn't want her day dragged down by depressed and regretful feelings about the past.

The manager spoke to someone over his implant. The music began as he opened the doors to the restaurant, revealing the decorated and populated tables on either side of an aisle that led to Mister Prez, with Maxim and the groomsmen standing to one side.

Behind them and to the sides of the room were decorative arches with a gothic feel that extended the length of the wall and up to the center of the angled ceiling. In between stood artfully shaped panels inlaid with screen displays that gave the effect of looking out of an old cathedral onto a vista that changed depending on the setting. This effect had been the inspiration for the name of the restaurant. The display currently showed a setting sun that gave the room a soft glow.

The women slowly walked in one at a time holding their bouquets, beginning with Sis'tael, then Celeste, Nadine, Mal, and Phina. As she entered, Phina felt self-conscious in her deep red dress. Two wide strips of silky fabric rose from the wide ruched waistband to cover her chest, then crossed before they wrapped around her neck and tied in the back with a bow. Her back was bare down to the band. The long, billowing skirt with its slit in the front that bared her full leg with every other step made her feel more feminine, something that rarely happened, and the way it draped where the skirt overlapped the slit kept everything nicely covered, which was a relief.

Alina would call her dress sexy and stylish. Phina was just happy that the special modifications gave her security in knowing that she wouldn't have a wardrobe malfunction. Phina wasn't used to wearing something so blatantly feminine with a color that made her stand out.

Still, it was better than pink.

She tried to hide her uneasiness by keeping her posture straight and wearing a smile. While she walked to the front, her eyes darted around the room, taking everything in, seeing different species scattered among the tables where everyone was seated and many Guardians and Marines here to support Maxim.

As her gaze passed over the groomsmen, something snagged her attention. Todd stood in the row of groomsmen staring at her so intently that her cheeks flushed. She thought back and realized that this was only the second time he had seen her wearing a dress, and this one was what Alina would call sexier with the slit.

Phina drew her eyes away so she could finally step into her spot and turn to watch Alina walk down the aisle.

She had to stop herself from tearing up. Alina glided down the aisle with a blinding smile, her eyes only for Maxim. So much love and caring and hope for the future shone on both their faces.

Others in the room seemed to react similarly, causing Phina a need to focus on her intermediate-level mental shields and stabilize them from the influx of emotions and thoughts flying around.

She regained her focus as Maxim reached out to Alina and held her hand as they turned to Mister Prez to start the ceremony.

"Welcome, everyone, and thank you for being here to celebrate the joining of two amazing people in the unity of marriage, an important and sacred partnership."

Phina listened with half an ear, processing everything Mister Prez said as he spoke on love and how a lasting partnership in marriage worked when commitment, communication, compromise, and collaboration were utilized. The other half of her attention was on making sure that no one was going to cause trouble. She wanted nothing to mess up Maxim and Alina's wedding day.

She frowned as she used her filters, sensing a few who weren't happy with the marriage. However, as she focused on them, she realized they were women who thought they should have had a shot with Maxim and that Alina was too young for him.

Hmm... Nothing actionable. Just grumpy envy.

Phina tuned in during the vows, almost tearing up as she heard them say their own to each other. The couple exchanged beautiful rings and turned back to hear the rest of the ceremony.

She caught stray thoughts from Todd that were about her and she glanced over to meet his eyes again. She smiled briefly and turned her mind and eyes away, trying to respect his wishes for mental privacy.

Phina turned her full attention to Mister Prez as he declared, "It is with great pleasure that I now pronounce you husband and wife."

She grinned and clapped with everyone as much as was possible while holding two bouquets. Everyone stood, the Guardians and Marines whistling and cheering. After a few moments, it simmered down so Mister Prez could continue.

Just as he started giving Maxim permission to kiss the bride, Phina turned in alarm as she felt vibrations in the Etheric. Not a ripple like the last time. This felt more like a storm or a stampede.

And it was headed this way.

Todd had been watching Phina throughout the ceremony.

He couldn't take his eyes off of her as she walked into the room wearing one of the sexiest and most elegant dresses he had ever seen. She had met his eyes and glanced away after a long moment with a flush in her cheeks that made her more beautiful.

Yeah... He had it bad.

However, her reaction also gave him hope that Phina might reciprocate his feelings. He had to talk to her soon and see if he wasn't just making it up because he wanted to see it.

He watched her hold back tears at certain times and keep an eye out around the room as if searching out trouble at others.

Todd was too focused on Phina to pay much attention to the ceremony, although he did appreciate Alina promising to help Maxim laugh in her vows. That man needed happiness in his life.

Phina had completed another perusal of the room when their eyes met again. Damned if he didn't see the steel in her eyes underneath her happiness for Alina. Phina had an unconscious generosity of spirit that not many people did. She had her own goals, yes, but they were all a method for helping others. She seemed to think herself more closed off and out of touch with her feelings, and he wouldn't completely disagree, but it didn't take someone with telepathy to sense that her capacity for compassion and caring ran deep.

She smiled at him and turned her focus toward the officiant who was wrapping up the ceremony. Todd did as well, but his eyes moved to Phina.

She was looking away and frowning, then her eyes

widened in alarm. Todd stiffened, knowing that something was wrong.

"You may kiss your—"

Sundancer's yowl cut off Mister Prez's words as Phina yelled, "Assassins incoming!"

Some guests shrieked in alarm, but they had planned for this possibility. Maxim pulled Alina and Mister Prez to the side while the groomsmen drew the short swords that had been harnessed upside-down under their jackets.

While the Guardians and Marines in the audience pulled their weapons or grew claws to protect the non-combatants, Todd took out Phina's telescopic staff and turned toward her in time to freeze with shock.

Phina had tossed her and Alina's bouquets aside and taken her heels off. What astonished him was seeing her take hold of her skirt and give it a hard tug. The long skirt pulled off, and she tossed it to the side, revealing what could have generously been called a minidress but more resembled a tunic with slits in the side. The leg that had been hidden by the skirt bore a thigh leg sheath holding one of her knives.

Todd shook his head and recovered from his shock, but at the same time tall, green, four-armed assassins began popping in around the room. He had reached an estimate of two dozen before he stopped counting and more were still appearing in random spots.

He ran toward her and yelled, "Phina, catch," as one assassin popped in between them.

She looked at him at the same time as the assassins converging on her with fierce shouts of, "Abomination!"

"Oh, shit," Todd muttered and hiked the rod over to her like a football.

He fought off an assassin who came close but couldn't help watching as Phina arrowed in on the staff...and an assassin.

She leapt and continued her run, using the shocked assassin's arms as step stools. She jumped off his head and grabbed the staff. Her face was set in determination and anger, likely because they had upset the wedding she had been hoping would go well. If he hadn't been watching, he would have missed the whole thing since Phina's movements were so fast.

Todd beat back the assassin he had in front of him, who had apparently decided to give up on personal hygiene. When he glanced back, she had pushed the button to telescope the weapon while she flipped in the air and was using the lengthened staff to hit the assassin beneath her in the head while his hands were scrambling to grab her. The force of Phina's strength with the staff combined with the momentum of gravity caused the assassin to stagger, which made Phina's landing difficult.

She got her legs underneath her so she would land on her feet, but she had to take a step to balance before pirouetting and slamming the staff into the assassin's neck. He had begun to turn, but she was able to make the hit by changing the angle.

Todd breathed a sigh of relief as the assassin dropped and quickly turned away to meet the Qendrok assassin attacking him.

As he fought, he had three thoughts.

He was glad they had trained yesterday with multiple assailants since several assassins kept trying to slip by everyone else to get to Phina.

Her dress must have been specially made to detach the skirt like it did and have a method to stay on without riding up. Trust Phina and Alina to plan for something like this.

And last, Phina looked mighty fine in her shortened dress. Beautiful, sexy, and like a fiery angel of justice.

Maxim had been centimeters away from kissing his bride when Phina yelled, "Assassins incoming!"

Damn it!

Why couldn't the assassins have waited one more minute? He had his beautiful bride in his arms, and he wished they could have finished the wedding.

He hurriedly ushered Alina and Mister Prez to the side so they wouldn't be in harm's way. When they had realized the assassins were gunning for Phina, they had talked about contingency plans for if the Qendrok crashed the wedding. He was playing his part.

Once they were both by the wall, he turned to Alina's anxious yet beautiful face while she gripped his arm tightly.

"Stay here, *malyshka*."

She nodded, her eyes wide but not nearly as afraid as he was expecting. There appeared to be anger simmering in there. "Be careful."

"Always," he vowed.

She gasped and let go of his arm. "Behind you!"

He turned as he pulled his short sword out from behind his back, eliciting another gasp from Alina since she hadn't known about that particular wardrobe addition. It was a good thing he and all the groomsmen had wide shoulders, which allowed their jackets a little extra room for the sheaths to remain unnoticed.

He took a step forward to meet the assassin. They fought for a minute as chaos reigned. He feared they would have difficulty continuing the reception without cleanup. He could have changed to his Pricolici form, but that would mean tearing the suit Alina had made for him. That would be a last resort.

He registered another assassin moving in on his left as he evaded another strike from the irritated assassin in front of him.

"No!"

He barely registered Alina's angry shout as he blocked the newcomer's knife then quickly did a back strike at the first assassin, giving him a deep gash in his chest that would be fatal if they didn't have any Pod-doc technology.

The assassin turned pale as he saw the long line of blood seeping out next to his amulet with the black band. He fell to his knees while one hand scrambled for his wrist.

Maxim turned away, ignoring the assassin disappearing, toward the new assassin and froze in shock with what he saw and heard.

"Don't you hurt my husband!" Alina had taken her five-inch heels off and was furiously swinging them at the bewildered larger assassin who winced and tried to fend the angry woman off.

"You." She swung her left heel at his head, causing him to duck to avoid her. "Are ruining. My. *Wedding*!" Each of Alina's words was punctuated by a swing of a shoe as she inexpertly but effectively distracted the alien from attacking Maxim.

Maxim winced as the sharp heels punctured the alien's body and shook his head, though he beamed with pride as he stepped forward and put a calming arm around Alina while he held his short sword between them and the assassin who grimaced and backed up, his astonished and discomfited eyes still on Alina. He moved away, deciding to stagger off and find a less volatile victim.

Maxim's eyes tracked him heading in the wrong direction for victims, however, since Phina was currently in the middle of whacking two more of the four-armed assassins and seemed happy to add another, based on her smirk.

Deciding the assassin was taken care of and no others were within striking distance, he turned to Alina as he curved his arm to pull her closer and grinned. "I like hearing you call me your husband."

She beamed up at him and dropped her shoes to clutch his arms. "I like saying it."

"You know what I like more?"

She leaned closer with eyes sparkling with warmth, protectiveness, and magic—Alina's magic.

"You wanting to protect me."

Tears shimmered as she vowed, "I'll always do my best to protect you like you protect me."

Maxim nodded but nudged her as he dryly added, "If

you're going to make a habit of doing it physically, I'm going to insist on you learning how to do it properly."

She glanced at her heels on the floor then peered at him. "I thought I was doing pretty good. My heels aren't called stilettos for nothing, you know."

He winced, then saw motion from the corner of his eye and sliced across the jugular of an assassin who had run up to them with his knives raised. He pushed the assassin back to fall on the floor and escorted Alina over to the wall, nudging the footwear weaponry on the floor with his foot. "*Malyshka*, it's undignified to be bested by a high heel."

"Yes, I was *so* concerned with the assassin's dignity when I was trying to keep him from killing you." Alina rolled her eyes as she turned to stand with Mister Prez.

He grinned and gave her a quick kiss. "I know."

He bent down and picked up the beleaguered heels and handed them to her, eliciting a happy grin. "Just in case." He held her briefly and added, "But *malyshka*? Let me protect you now, okay?"

He released her without waiting for an answer and began stalking another of the dozens of assassins that had attacked. It looked like the numbers were down by at least half now. Some assassins were on the floor, and some had disappeared like that earlier one.

As he strode away, he heard Mister Prez asking Alina why she looked so pleased with Maxim going off to fight more of the Qendrok.

She laughed, sounding amused, and yes, pleased. "No, no. I'm pleased because Maxim gets me. Only Phina understood me before."

"Oh? I don't doubt it, but how could you tell?"

Maxim glanced back to see Alina, still gorgeous even with blood spatters, her veil halfway pulled out and her hair untamed now that it was partially freed from its confines. She hugged her heels to her chest and gave Maxim a blinding smile when she saw him watching before responding to the older gentleman.

"He gave me back my heels."

Mister Prez appeared perplexed, but Maxim winked at his beaming bride before turning to deal out more pain to the guys who thought they would crash his wedding and get away with it.

QBBS *Meredith Reynolds*, Holding Area

Faith rocked on her bunk, trying to occupy her mind with anything other than her current preoccupation. It didn't work.

The question that Todd Jenkins had asked rang through her head. What *had* made her think that her serum was the answer? Part of her mind told her that it didn't make sense. That there were numerous ways, as he had pointed out, that she could have used instead. She began listing them out in her head and came up with twenty-seven before the ideas began petering out.

Yet another part of her brain said that changing the serum was the answer. That her problems would be solved if she changed the nanocytes.

How could both be right?

If there was one thing Faith knew for sure, it was that Phina was in danger and had to be protected.

Her brain began hurting as she started thinking harder

about why it was right to change the serum. An agonizing pain shot through her brain, causing her to clutch her head and collapse on the bed.

A cool, impersonal voice spoke from above. "Faith Rochelle."

She stopped trying to think more and lay there for a moment. Her brain ached, but it wasn't the sharp pain of a moment ago.

"Yes?" She finally asked.

"You requested to be made aware when there was another attempt on Seraphina Waters' life. Fifty-two assassins have attacked the wedding where Phina is in attendance."

Faith jolted upward in shock. "What! That's so many!"

"Plans have been made and defenses are in place. Phina has proven herself capable. There are others there to help."

Shaking her head, Faith stood up and staggered but felt fine after a moment. She clutched her drab clothes in worry and fear. "Meredith, please! I know I harmed Phina, but I didn't mean to. I feel like I've been in a fog and nothing makes sense. I need Phina to be okay! Please, let me go help? I need to do something to help make up for hurting her!"

Faith almost forgot to breathe. Would Phina even be alive? She couldn't be dead. She *couldn't* die. It wasn't right. Nothing about this was right.

Faith almost gave up hope until she heard, "Request approved. Your implant has been reactivated. I will open the doors for you, notify the guards, and give you directions through the implant."

She exhaled in relief, then ran the few steps to the door and saw it open.

"Thank you! Oh, thank you, Meredith!"

Faith raced down the hall as fast as she was able, seeing the guards frowning but letting her through. As she reached the front door, Faith almost staggered in shock when she heard Meredith's response over the implant.

"Thank the Empress. She gave the permission."

CHAPTER TWENTY-FIVE

QBBS *Meredith Reynolds,* **Horizons**

Phina threw her dagger into an assassin in front of her, then gripped her staff with two hands and thrust it behind her into the chest of a second assassin. A crunch that hopefully meant broken bones reached her ears while she twirled the staff in one hand into the head of the third assassin on her right.

She leaned forward to grab her dagger as the first assassin fell, slicing to the side as she pulled it out and extended her left arm to stab the assassin on her left.

She ignored the number of cuts that marked her body, both partially and mostly healed, trying to move faster and to think smarter so she had economy of movement with a hit in every strike. She had been training with Braeden every day since she had received her staff, and that had helped her figure out the best moves to use with her height and strength.

However, Phina needed to focus on learning how to manage her Etheric energy flow while she was fighting.

She had a feeling being able to use the influx of Etheric more effectively would make fighting easier, if not less bloody and painful, if she could heal faster or read their minds at the same time as she fought them or something else equally miraculous-seeming at the moment.

Right now, she focused on the next five steps and added more as she went along.

Todd, Maxim, Pete, Craig, Drk-vaen, and Sis'tael were fighting around her, pulling off the assassins when they surrounded her two deep. Others were spread out, fighting beyond them. They'd discovered in their sparring the day before that since Phina hadn't learned how to fight in tandem with others against multiple opponents. It would be easier for her to fight as she could, and everyone else would help keep them from overwhelming her should there be more than one assassin.

They had thought maybe five or ten would show up if they decided to take advantage of her being in a public place. They hadn't counted on over fifty.

Whoops and shouts sounded around the room as they whittled the assassins down. There were sixty-three guests, and non-combatants comprised almost half of those, so the combatants were outnumbered. Since some were guarding those who weren't fighting, including Ron, the ratio was more than two to one.

In their planning meeting after the sparring session, the Wechselbalg had decided that they would stay in human form if possible to minimize damages to the restaurant, so that limited their effectiveness as well. However, since the tricky thing about these opponents was the extra arms with accompanying weapons, that wasn't too bad.

"Die, abomination!" an assassin growled as he thrust his knife toward Phina's belly. She dodged it and swiped his legs with her staff, causing him to fall.

"The goddess demands your death!" another green assassin snarled, swinging four knives at once. Eyes widening, she quickly slid underneath and thrust her knife into his gut, then rolled away as she saw another Qendrok come in close, rising to sweep his knees.

Peter chuckled as he blocked a stroke of a knife from an assassin, then feinted in before striking. "Hell, Phina. You've got them all riled up with their melodrama."

"It's my effusive and charming personality, no doubt," she replied with no inflection before lifting a leg to launch off one assassin over to attack another, wincing as she received another slice on her arm.

Todd shook his head in amusement as he prevented the assassin that she had gut-stabbed from swiping at her side before stabbing him in the heart. "And they clean up after themselves too."

Phina glanced over and watched his assassin disappear before using her staff to stabilize her in an aerial over a downed assassin, who groped for his wrist, to meet another attack. She wished there was a way to tell the assassins apart, but except for slight facial differences they looked and dressed the same, from their black banded amulets to their clothing wraps and bare feet.

She glanced around the room and realized that they were down to around a dozen of the assassins left, and those were spread out. Alina still stood by the wall with Mister Prez. The other non-combatants were huddled on the edges of the room or under tables, and the guys were beginning to ratchet the tension down with jokes and banter since the odds were now in their favor. Phina breathed a sigh of relief that they would get through this with no casualties when she heard a loud voice right behind her.

"For the goddess!" She whirled to see an assassin charging toward her while the remaining assassins returned the yell, "For the goddess!" as they left those they were fighting to run straight for her again.

The guys stopped in surprise as the assassins began converging on her, then chased after them.

Lifting her weapons, she pulled on her determination and her Etheric connection to increase her speed and strength.

Phina heard an anguished wail that she didn't have time to worry about since she couldn't see anything but green skin, red wraps, and the glint of knives, causing her to feel enclosed. The assassins were bigger than her, taller than her, and had more arms and weapons than her. But she'd be damned before she would let them intimidate her or give up before she had tried everything.

So, she gave it everything as she channeled her fear and anger, whirling, kicking, stabbing, leaping, and twirling her staff to gain momentum to strike.

Just when she thought it wouldn't be enough, she realized that there weren't as many assassins around her as there had been. The guys appeared in her vision wearing grim expressions as they flung the assassins away and applied appropriate measures to show their displeasure.

She kicked the last assassin away with a sigh of relief,

causing him to trip over a couple of bodies and land on the floor.

He looked around and seemed to realize everyone else had either done their disappearing act or lay dead on the floor. He turned to Phina, who staggered due to her freshly inflicted and healing wounds.

She raised her knife-wielding hand again in case he attacked and gave him her fiercest glare, sending the mental message. *Go. Tell Qartan we are coming to finish what he started, and not even his goddess will be able to save him.*

Phina was relieved to see that instead of attacking, he grabbed his wrist and did a disappearing act of his own.

It wasn't until she couldn't see him anymore that she looked around, her eyes snagging on one of the bodies the assassin had tripped over. It wasn't a large green body, but a smaller one with dark hair, lying crumpled on the floor. Instead of the formal wear of the wedding, the clothes this person wore were plain white...like those she had last seen Aunt Faith wearing.

But that couldn't be. Aunt Faith should have been in the holding area.

Her heart thudding, Phina dashed over and knelt beside the body, dropping her weapons before turning the body over to see who it was.

It *was* Aunt Faith.

Phina gasped, suddenly finding it hard to breathe. Was her aunt gone, or just badly injured? Could they save her?

"Aunt Faith?" Phina whispered.

Seeing her eyelashes flutter, Phina quickly and unwisely let her shields down to focus on her aunt's thoughts. The influx of information from everyone around her, extending far beyond the restaurant, caused her brain to throb and overwhelm her.

What are you doing? Has everything I have taught you been in vain? Get your shields up, you foolish female!

Sundancer's words cut through the confusion, reminding her that she shouldn't just be reacting. She closed her shields and did it right this time, using the filter she needed.

Sorry, Sundancer. Thank you.

Thankfully, it didn't take long and she mentally reached her aunt.

Aunt Faith? What happened?

She searched for a wound. What had happened? Blood pooled around her aunt and the body of an assassin next to her, causing Phina no small amount of worry.

She continued patting her aunt's body, registering but not paying attention to the others that crowded around to see what was happening, when she heard a weak response to her mental inquiry.

Phina? Did I save you?

Phina frowned at the nature of the question before her fingers found a wound from a knife in her aunt's back. Other hands also probed, but she ignored them to gently scan her aunt's mind to see what had happened.

Her aunt had entered the restaurant as the assassins converged on Phina. She had emitted the cry of anguish Phina had heard earlier and ran after them using the abilities she had gained from the serum to move faster. Aunt Faith had reached them in time to slip between Phina as she faced another assassin and the assassin whose body she lay beside. This assassin's knife had stabbed her. She had pulled the knife out and plunged it into the surprised assassins' chest before her strength gave out, and she fell before the assassin did.

Tears shimmered in Phina's eyes when she realized that Aunt Faith hadn't cared if she died. She'd only been thinking about protecting Phina.

Yeah, Aunt Faith, she answered softly with her mind as she reached for one of her aunt's hands, squeezing gently and holding it carefully. *You saved me. Just hold on, and we'll get you into a Pod-doc.*

Phina sensed someone putting a bandage on the wound, trying to keep the compression on it so that could happen. She felt a slight squeeze of her aunt's hand as she tried to open her eyes. *No... It's too late. I'm so tired. You're safe. It's all that matters. Sorry... I'm so sorry. Things are... wrong. I wanted...to help make...it...right.*

No, we can help you! You took the serum. It should help save you.

Even though her aunt wasn't moving, Phina got the sense she was shaking her head, though her mental voice was weaker. *My choice. Simon. Chris. Miss them. Proud...of...you.*

Phina's tears overflowed as she heard the one phrase she hadn't heard from her aunt since her parents had died. *I love you too, Aunt Faith.*

Silence answered.

Aunt Faith?

A quiet voice spoke next to her. "She's gone, Phina." Todd. He had been the one to put the bandage on and feel her heartbeat.

Phina's shoulders slumped as her tears streamed down

her face. She shook her head as two sets of arms reached around her to give her hugs. Alina and Todd.

"How was she here?" Phina looked up to see Todd looking at her aunt regretfully from where he knelt beside her. She felt very aware of both Alina and Todd's arms around her.

He sighed, then turned to Phina as he spoke. "When I talked to her, she asked to be notified when you were in danger. I thought there was no harm in approving the request since she is your family and expressed concern for you. Meredith told me that when she informed your aunt earlier, she asked to be let out so she could help."

He glanced at Aunt Faith's body with a mixture of regret and approval, adding, "She told Meredith she wanted to do something to make up for hurting you. Meredith sent the request to ADAM, who got approval from the Empress. They let her out so she could come." He hesitated then continued while gently squeezing her hand and looking apologetic. "There's more I should talk to you about later, but I'm sorry that I played a role that ended with her death."

Phina shook her head, not able to stop the tears, and squeezed his hand before turning to her aunt's body. "It was her choice, and she told me that. Aunt Faith said she missed my dad and Uncle Simon and wanted to see them."

She sagged as she realized that she had no other living family now. She was alone. Closing her eyes in sorrow, she felt herself withdrawing inside until a warm mental touch nudged her with a small sniff.

Hardly alone. Have you forgotten that you chose these people as your family? They are strange ones, but they care about you.

Phina took a deep breath then nodded. *Thank you, Sundancer. I did forget for a moment.*

Alina squeezed Phina, reminding her that it was Alina's wedding day. Her head and eyes popped as she turned to Alina in concern.

"Oh, no! I'm sorry, Alina. I was hoping they wouldn't attack during your wedding, and if they did that, no one would die, so you only have happy memories."

Alina shook her head with a small wobbly smile and tear tracks down her cheeks. "I was hoping no one would die too, and I'm sorry it was your aunt, Phina. She could be a witch, but I know you still cared about her."

She hugged Phina tightly. Todd's and Maxim's arms went around them, and the hands of others offered comfort.

Phina felt warm inside. Part of her was sad that her family of origin was gone. However, she was happy her chosen family cared about her and was sad with her. That they were here to give comfort.

She leaned her head against Alina's with a sigh as she patted Maxim's shoulder then reached down to squeeze Todd's hand again, giving him a small smile. "I'm happy I have all of you."

Alina mused from her position on her shoulder as murmured conversation rose around them. "It's part of life. You know Mrs. Jameson always talked about the circle of life being births, weddings, and deaths or funerals. They are the markers of being alive and living life."

Phina made a small noise of interest at the memory she had forgotten of Will's mom. She gestured as she spoke. "We had your wedding, and Aunt Faith's dead. That just leaves a birth, but the only one I know of who is pregnant is…"

She turned her head to look for Mal and found her standing on the edge of the gathered group, holding her belly and looking down with an intent gaze. Her eyes widened in panic and excitement. "Uh, James? Mom? Dad? I think…I think the baby is coming."

Mal spoke loud enough to cut through the conversations in the room before Mister Prez and a man Phina hadn't met before, but she presumed was Mal's husband, rushed up to fuss over her and direct Mal to the nearest medical facility. An elegant black woman followed at a more sedate pace, putting her arm around Mal and leading her to the door.

Phina turned to Alina, who had been watching with a mixture of amusement and resignation, and turned to Phina just a beat behind and shrugged. "Well, you did say that the day was a success no matter what happened as long as we were married by the end of the day. And we got married."

She flipped her hand up to show off her two rings as she gave Maxim a full smile of love leaning toward adoration.

Phina looked around the room, which had taken some knocks during the fighting. The decorations and place settings were in shambles, and chairs had been knocked over. Thankfully, the fighting had been contained to the center of the room. She didn't want to know how much it would have cost to replace one of the special screens. The guests had begun to congregate in small groups, discussing the wedding, the fight, and…other things, she realized as she saw couples speaking quietly and standing close to each other.

She shook her head, glancing at Aunt Faith before lifting her eyes to Mal, who was waddling out of the door with plenty of help.

"Essentially, yes, but this wasn't what I had in mind."

Maxim looked around the room and sighed. "It's going to take time to clean things up. I guess we won't be having the reception now."

"Oh?" Phina raised an eyebrow. "I thought the reception was kickass."

They laughed, and Alina nudged her with a grin before accepting Maxim's help to get up. "Come on, Phina. You know we couldn't do anything normal and boring."

Phina looked up at her best friend with faint amusement. "Well, we could try. It might eventually happen."

"Normal is overrated," Alina declared with a sassy pose, totally ignoring her crazy hair and that her raised veil hung by a few strands on the back of her head.

"Hmm…" Phina glanced around, wanting to comment that normal might mean that no one would die or maybe that everyone would be safe in the first place. Perhaps things would happen expectedly rather than unexpectedly. However, she sensed that Alina was trying to cheer her up, or at least put on a positive face, and Phina couldn't stand it if she made Maxim and Alina's day any worse, so she nodded sagely and quietly agreed. "Normal is too tame for our sensibilities."

She glanced at Todd, who gazed at her intently and gave her a small smile before helping her up.

He gently squeezed her hands before releasing them.

"I'll take care of arrangements for your aunt if you would like me to?"

Phina swallowed as she glanced at her aunt before nodding and giving him a watery smile. "Thank you. I would like to have a small funeral for her tonight before we need to leave in the morning."

"Oh!" Phina turned to see Alina biting her lip as she glanced between Phina and Maxim, looking like she would cry again. "I thought we would have more time together before you left."

Alina waved her hand in Maxim's direction. He reached out and pulled her in for a hug, looking down at his new wife in concern. Todd handed Phina his jacket and briefly touched her shoulder before moving to lift her aunt's body.

Phina gave Todd a brief smile in thanks before turning to Maxim and her best friend, raising a finger with a tiny smirk playing on her lips. "Neither of you are going with us."

Alina and Maxim looked over with mixed emotions as she continued with a pleased smile. "At least not yet. I asked both of your bosses for time off for a honeymoon. I tried to get a week, thinking that would be the limit with everything happening, but they each generously gave you both three weeks since neither of you ever take your vacation time." She gave them both wry and scolding looks of admonishment when their expressions turned sheepish.

"So, that's Mal's and Peter's gifts for you and Alina. She said that counts even if the baby comes. She has backup to take care of the boutique until you come home. You two have the next three weeks to yourselves at a swanky resort

Alina told me about a while ago. Your ride leaves in the morning." She waved a hand in the direction of the docks.

Alina clutched Maxim tightly in excitement and shock. "*What?* Phina! You can't be talking about the Majestic Sands Resort on H'lageh!"

Phina looked around for her tablet to confirm the details, but since her clothing was currently not serving its purpose—and was a lot more revealing than she'd realized since there were numerous gashes in the modified dress from the knives she had been fending off—she shrugged and nodded. She had the details memorized anyway.

"Of course. You told me you wanted to go. In excruciating detail," she added as she crossed her arms to cover any visible private bits, then realized that was probably why Todd had left his jacket. She put it on and rolled up the sleeves as she listened to Alina.

"That was three years ago. I didn't think you were paying attention." Alina appeared stunned. "But, how? It takes forever to get in there!"

"I always listen to what you say, Leena." Phina wanted to hug her, but she was still working on the sleeves. She settled for a smile. "Well, that's an interesting story, but the short of it is that they were happy to find an opening for personal friends of the Empress, so the reservation is her gift to you through ADAM, who took care of that. You have the added sweetheart package that gives you various treats and luxuries, like a couples massage once a week, which is a gift from your bridesmaids. You have the upgraded dining and drinks package, which lets you dine in or order whatever you want from any of the restaurants there whenever you like, which is your gift from the groomsmen. And I took care of everything else, including the adventure package so you can explore both the island and under the water." She shrugged and smiled at her stunned friends, who looked like they were in shock.

"Unless you would rather not go? I can always cancel it." She grinned when they uttered a loud, "No!" in unison.

Alina and Maxim hugged her tightly before releasing her and giving her big smiles.

"Thank you, Phina. Thank you so much!"

Alina's eyes were tearful again as she gave Phina another hug. Phina wrapped her arms around Alina and closed her eyes.

Her aunt was gone, but Alina had always been her family, and she was still here.

CHAPTER TWENTY-SIX

Etheric Empire, QBS *Emissary*

Zultav landed with a heavy jolt that caused him to again fall on his backside. He grimaced as he recalled the kick from the abomination that caused him to trip over the bodies behind him.

Yet, having watched the abomination during the attack, he had a difficult time understanding why she had been labeled such. She had a strange composition of Etheric energy facilitation, certainly, and a large capacity to access it to his inexpert eye, judging by the glow emanating from her head.

Yet, she had done nothing that the Qendrok's strongest fighters couldn't have done. She had just done it better and faster, he admitted with a wince as he rubbed a large bruise on his torso.

The others in the room who had faced them were also capable fighters, especially those bigger guys who hit like sledgehammers. He pulled his clothing away from a wound on his back that had been caused by a man's fist, wincing in pain, though he covered it.

He pulled his thoughts from their wanderings. The female had fought hard to defend herself and those around her. She hadn't followed up and slaughtered those who had escaped her, letting them go when she could have intercepted them.

She had even let him go to give Qartan a message. He recalled how startled he had been to hear a voice not his own in his mind. That did not fit the actions of one deserving the moniker "abomination."

Yet, as Qartan was fond of pointing out, the assassins were not encouraged to foster independent thought.

He looked around the room where they had started the jump from perhaps an hour earlier. He and fifty-one of his fellow assassins had been ready, if not eager, to follow Qartan's directive to kill the abomination. Their leader had somehow received information as to the location where she would be.

Forty-six bodies filled the room, only fifteen of them still alive from his quick perusal. His heart skipped a beat when he realized what that meant for the assassins. The losses were devastating. Yet, he found he could not blame the abomination—no, the *target*—for their losses. She had been defending herself.

Qartan entered the room with a scowl as he observed the bodies lying still and so few looking up in attention. "What in the goddess' name happened? You are supposed to be the best!"

A quick scan showed Zultav that he was the least

wounded of his brethren. He stood and straightened into the posture of obedience and apology.

"We did as asked and attacked the abomination, Dev Qartan."

"Well?" Qartan's eyes grew triumphant as he stepped forward, ignoring the bodies of Zultav's fallen comrades. "Where is the body?"

Zultav remained stoic as he responded though inwardly his emotions roiled. "There is no body, Dev Qartan. We were unsuccessful. Or rather, they successfully withstood our attack."

"The abomination still lives?" Qartan roared in anger and displeasure.

"Yes, Dev Qartan. I was the last to return after she defeated me. She gave me a message to pass on to you." He tapped his head with two fingers, trying to convey the mental nature of the message. Or warning.

The remaining assassins stirred uneasily as they collected themselves into a semblance of attention.

Qartan scowled at the news and snarled at them. "What use is an elite group of assassins if you are defeated at every opposition?"

Zultav refrained from commenting that it was only against those in the Empire that they seemed to have trouble in being victorious. No other population had the same level of training and defenses.

At Zultav's silence, Qartan impatiently gestured to him. "The message?"

Zultav stood in the posture of importance and communication, which used only in the gravest circumstances. Qartan merely glowered, not using the posture of openness and reception. The lack was rude and counter to their culture. "'Go. Tell Qartan we are coming to finish what he started, and not even his goddess will be able to save him.'"

Qartan's face twitched between outrage and fear. He whirled toward the exit, calling out as he left, "We are returning to Xaldaq. Clean up the mess before we get there." He flicked fingers at the bodies of Zultav's fallen comrades.

The blatant disrespect and casual disregard of his brethren's sacrifice incensed Zultav. He clenched his teeth lest unwise words escape him.

The few assassins who remained were struggling almost as much as he was. There were no leaders among the assassins since they were supposed to obey the religious leaders.

He closed his eyes and recalled his conversation with Jokin, realizing that Qartan was evil and evil could only lead if those who were good did nothing to stop it.

Zultav hung his head with a small shake. He didn't know if he could be considered good. But he was becoming more convinced that Qartan was evil.

And evil must be stopped.

QBBS *Meredith Reynolds*, Funeral Hall

Todd watched Phina say one last goodbye to her aunt. It was a small group since Phina hadn't wanted to advertise the funeral given everything that had happened.

Link, Braeden, Maxim, and Todd stood back. Phina and Alina had an arm around each other as they stood near

Aunt Faith's body. Aunt Faith had been cleaned up. They had cleaned up and changed clothes after they were able to leave and do so.

Todd had taken care of the arrangements for Phina, interfacing with those who ran the Funeral Hall and the researchers who had taken samples of Faith's nanocytes, fluids, and tissue to study. Perhaps they could learn from what had happened so others could be helped at some point. He wasn't sure what would be done, but perhaps Faith Rochelle would be happy that her body could further the study of nanocytes.

He stood quietly, listening to Phina and Alina talk about the good things they remembered about Faith.

"She was such a witch to you at times, Phina, and I'll never forgive her for that, but she made the best baked goods I ever had. Her muffins were my favorite."

Todd stirred as that brought to mind the information he had inquired about from ADAM. He stepped forward and cleared his throat. "That's part of what I wanted to talk to you about, Phina."

The two women both turned, and though she didn't use her mental speech, Phina's expression clearly said, "Here and now?"

He nodded and gestured toward her aunt. "It has to do with why she behaved the way she had been."

Phina released Alina to turn more completely and held her hand, eyes noticeably tightened. It appeared she was steeling herself for more bad news.

Todd shook his head and did a mental rewind to start at the right spot to explain. "When I spoke to your aunt, she seemed scattered, lost, and confused. She did not appear to be the same woman you had spoken of. I wondered if she was mentally ill and asked ADAM to check that. If it wasn't physical, then perhaps it was something that could be diagnosed through her behavior."

He straightened his posture and stood with his hands behind his back, trying to ignore how close Phina stood and focus on the task at hand.

"And there was something to find?" She appeared somewhat anxious but more closed down, afraid of more bad news. Todd wasn't certain whether his news qualified or not.

He nodded and stood at parade rest as he often had when reporting to his superiors. "Yes. Meredith's and ADAM's memory extends back far longer than any previous computer, so they were able to access camera footage from years ago up to now. What they found was that Faith's demeanor and focus changed in general, and specifically toward you, almost a month after your parents died. I don't know if you recall that change?"

Todd was curious as to whether her memories would corroborate ADAM's findings, but she shook her head. "I was lost in my own world for weeks afterward. I noticed a difference, but I wasn't aware enough to add anything to what you are talking about."

He inclined his head and continued. "He noticed a pattern. She would be more negative toward you and only you; her co-workers did not receive the same treatment for a time. Gradually she would grow more caring and less negative before a larger surge of negativity. This pattern continued for years afterward, each year getting worse, the surge taking place roughly around your birthday. This last year is the first that she didn't have the same behavior, possibly due to you being in your coma."

Phina frowned as Alina's eyes widened. "She did mess up birthdays a lot. What are you saying? That she was mentally ill?"

Todd hesitated and lifted a shoulder. "I do not have definitive answers, but two possibilities fit these facts. ADAM ran the numbers for possible reasons. Two emerged at the top. One is more believable but doesn't fit quite so well. The other potential reason sounds farfetched but fits the facts more completely."

Phina took a deep breath and nodded, speaking quietly. "Please, tell me." She glanced at her aunt's body. "Her words and actions still pain me. If there is anything that would allow me to think of her more kindly, I would like to hear it."

Her words gave him a pang as he realized how much grief her aunt had caused her. She must have downplayed it when they spoke before. Todd's eyes darted to Faith, and he wondered if he would have taken the steps he had if he had realized how hard it had been. Possibly not. But if he hadn't, they would not know this information now.

"The first and more believable reason is a disorder or a combination of a couple of them, such as borderline personality disorder and paranoid personality disorder. A lot of the symptoms she exhibited indicate that could be the case. However, the regularity with which her behavior grew worse led ADAM to a different conclusion, a farfetched one." He hesitated, wondering if Phina would dismiss it out of hand.

"Which is?" Phina had drawn herself up, her shoulders and back completely straight.

Todd met her eyes, giving her a small nod of approval. "Mind control."

Etheric Empire, QBS *Stark*

Phina padded down the ship's hallway heading for the bridge. She couldn't sleep and kept thinking about everything that had happened over the last day.

Todd's information had floored her. Both that he had noticed something in her aunt's behavior and had asked ADAM to look into it, and that their conclusion was something so out there as mind control. That shouldn't be possible.

Yet Phina herself could speak mentally and use her mind to do other things that would otherwise seem farfetched. Perhaps there was someone who could control minds as well.

She shook her head sadly at the realization that her aunt could have been a victim of such a thing. It didn't make Phina feel much better about how her aunt had treated her, but it gave her a greater understanding as to why Aunt Faith had been so different after her parents had died.

Her thoughts turned to the conversation she'd had with Braeden after the funeral. He had taken her aside to say goodbye.

"Phina, I will be returning to my home planet before you return from this next mission."

"I'll miss you." She had hugged him, squeezing him

tightly. His long arms had wrapped around her and squeezed her in return.

"I will miss you too, Phina, but I can't deny the urge to move on. We need more Gleeks focusing their attention on fulfilling our mission."

"Will you ever tell me your people's mission?"

Braeden had released her and looked down to give her a small smile. "Yes. You are a sister of the heart, so it is only fair."

Phina had smiled and waited, but it wasn't what she had expected to hear.

"We are searching for our females."

Phina's jaw dropped in surprise. "What? I thought there were only male Gleeks. Isn't that why you have the Mother?"

He shook his head sadly. "That is how things are now. That is not how they always have been. Generations ago, we were all together and lived on a different planet. We were peaceful, not even practicing our fighting style yet, and kept to ourselves. One day the peace was broken when invaders came. They took a few of the males and all of the females they could fit on their ships. We did not know who they were or why they came, aside from wanting to take our people. Perhaps that was all they wanted. When they left, they destroyed our planet. Around three hundred of us males survived, most having gone to the ships to try to take our females back. By the time the males had escaped and the planet destroyed, the invaders and the females were gone."

Phina's tears had slid down her cheeks as she shook her head. No wonder the Gleek males had seemed reserved and full of anger and sorrow over their losses. "I'm sorry. That's so sad. You haven't figured out where they were taken?"

"No." Braeden squeezed her hands before releasing them to look at the screens on the wall of the Funeral Hall, showing a distant nebula and a gaseous planet that was both beautiful and deadly. "But we search the universe in the hopes that we may one day find them."

"Thank you for sharing with me, Braeden."

He smiled fondly, a strange but welcome expression on his hairless elongated face. "You are my sister of the heart."

Phina realized how much he had given up to help her and the Empire over the last couple of years. He had assured her that he would see her again and that they could always speak telepathically when needed. Still, it wasn't the same as having his reassuring presence with her.

I can help as much as that tall galumph.

She continued down the hall, glancing down at Sundancer, who padded next to her. "What's a galumph?"

An ungainly antisocial creature that wanders our world. Much smaller, though.

"Ah. I suppose that's descriptive enough of the Gleeks, though lacking in some respects."

Of course. They are not as magnificent as a Previdian such as I.

Phina eyed her constant shadow. "I have a feeling no one is."

Correct. I am heartened to hear your acknowledgment. He nuzzled her leg in passing and must have felt her tiredness. *Someone needs to sit on you so you can sleep. You need optimal mental function to process the Etheric.*

"I am not having anyone sit on me."

They walked onto the bridge as she replied, not noticing that it was occupied.

Todd turned from viewing screens of the space they flew through to give her a welcoming smile. "You need someone to sit on you?"

"Yes," replied Sundancer at the same time as Phina said, "No," with an indignant glare for the pink cat.

"Hmm. I'm unsure whether to be amused or disappointed."

Phina turned to Todd in surprise. "What?"

He gave her a small smile. "I decided I should talk to you about this the first chance I could, and this is the first time we are alone." He glanced down at Sundancer and shrugged. "Relatively, anyway."

"All right." She studied Todd as he stepped closer until they stood an arm's length apart. Todd looked into her eyes so intently she got goosebumps as she wondered what he would say.

"Phina, I think you are amazing. I have been watching you since we had that first sparring session, and what I've seen has impressed me a lot. You are brave and determined, you help your friends even when it would be easier to do something different, and you are loyal to those you care about."

He focused on Phina as she blinked and tried to decide what to say. Finally, she gave him a large smile and said, "Thank you."

Todd frowned, then ventured, "Phina, I'm trying to tell you I care about you."

Caring was good. Phina tried not to imitate a bobblehead as she nodded and reached out to squeeze his hand with an encouraging smile. "I care about you too, Todd."

He searched her eyes but didn't see something that he was looking for and closed his, looking disappointed.

Phina frowned and ran his words through her head. Was it possible he was trying to imply something more?

She spoke hesitantly, hoping he would understand. She realized she didn't like seeing him disappointed. "If you are trying to say something in particular, could you just say it or show me plainly what you mean? I don't always do well at hints or subtleties because I think of the different ways something could be intended to mean. I don't like to assume something that may not be true."

Todd looked up at her words, his eyes growing more intent as he listened. He cut off the rest of her sentence by stepping forward, putting his arms around her to hold her close, and giving her goosebumps and a whole flock of butterflies when he kissed her.

Looks like you found someone to sit on you. I'll be in the room.

Shock held Phina still. She barely registered Sundancer's words. She had just decided to respond when Todd pulled his head back and looked at her searchingly, making sure she was okay. She knew that for sure since her shields had begun to drop and she briefly caught his surface thoughts before she snapped them closed.

"Was that all right?"

She focused on Todd in time to see the fear that she might reject him in his eyes. Phina gave him a bright smile. "Well, I think I see what all the fuss is about kissing."

He chuckled and slid his arms around her a little more. "Kissing is enjoyable—with the right person."

Phina thought about that and nodded with a small smile. "I'm definitely open to more kissing."

Todd flashed her a small grin. "With me, or will anyone do?"

She quickly shook her head. "Oh, no. You're the only one I've had even a passing thought about."

His eyes crinkled in concern. "Should I worry about being a passing thought?"

Phina shrugged, blushing. "Well, it was a passing thought every time I saw you. Sometimes several passing thoughts. Especially when we're sparring. Then it's a lot more passing thoughts."

Todd grinned, then his gaze turned intent again. "So, just to be crystal clear, do you want to be in a relationship with me that includes kissing, handholding, and more when you're ready?"

She raised an eyebrow. "According to Alina's definitions, you are skipping past asking me on a date and going straight to asking me to be your girlfriend?"

He nodded. "If you want that." He spoke quietly, adding, "If you want me."

Phina's eyes shimmered with tears that she held back at the tension and uncertainty she felt from him. She wished she could go back in time and punch his ex-wife in the face. She held onto him, hoping he understood she wasn't rejecting him.

"I do, Todd." She raised a hand and put it on his chest to stop him when she felt his muscles bunching to pull her closer. Phina didn't want to hurt him, but she had to explain what she had concluded over the last week, holding his gaze and willing him to understand.

"I don't know how long we could be in a relationship without me breaking your trust and reading your mind. My shields are better with Braeden and Sundancer's help, and accidents don't happen all the time. However, when we were kissing, my shields flickered, and I heard some of your surface thoughts. I don't want to break your trust since it's something I value, but I don't think I will be able to help it sometimes."

She waited anxiously for his response but didn't expect the wide smile and warm glance he gave her.

"You're confirming that I'm right to put my trust in you, Phina. I had wondered about that same thing and talked to ADAM and Bethany Anne about it before they left. They both confirmed that you are a trustworthy person, and there wasn't a concern about you knowing any secrets I hold since you likely knew the ones pertaining to the Empire ." His expression was full of amusement and pride —in *her*. "I just ask that anything you discover that others have told me in confidence, you keep to yourself. I would also like you to talk to me if you have a question about anything you pick up, even if you think I won't want to talk about it."

"I can do that." Phina smiled in relief and gave Todd a hug, which he returned.

After a few moments, he asked, "So, that's a yes, right?"

She laughed and pulled back, nodding. "Yes, I'll be your girlfriend or whatever else you want to call it."

He grinned and pulled her closer, lifting her as he bent his head down to kiss her again.

Phina kissed Todd back and decided that she *really* liked it. In private, anyway. She still wasn't sure about kissing in public.

She wished she was a couple of inches taller so she wouldn't need to stand on her tiptoes to reach. She thought about a possible solution and decided it had merit, requiring skill that she thankfully possessed. She held on tighter to Todd's shoulders as she kissed him, then jumped up to wrap her legs around his waist and lock her ankles. Ah, much better.

Todd chuckled as he wrapped his arms around her back. "I can see that you're going to drive me crazy, but I won't be bored." His eyes changed as he gave her a look she hoped he would only use on her since it made her want to kiss him again. "And, most importantly, you'll have my back."

Her heart was lighter than it had been in a long time as she folded her arms around his neck to bring them closer. She gave him a warm smile before kissing him. "Sounds about right to me."

CHAPTER TWENTY-SEVEN

Nearby Star System, QBS *Stark*

The planet Xaldaq loomed in front of the ship as they approached. Phina stood on the bridge watching with Link, Todd, Will, Peter, and a handful of other Guardian and Marine leaders.

Todd stood next to Phina, close enough that there were raised eyebrows but not enough to be inappropriate for a professional setting. She wished they were holding hands.

I am distraught that your most pressing concern is holding hands with your new male friend.

I like his hands. They're strong and nicely calloused.

Sundancer gave her the mental equivalent of a hacking hairball. *This is not what I imagined our conversations would be like.*

No, you had someone stuffy and boring in mind.

Dignified and eloquent.

As I said.

The *Stark* approached the atmosphere and descended

near the main city where the compound of the religious leaders and assassins was located.

They had been traveling for almost a week now. During that week, Phina had experienced an amazing and treasured time in getting to know Todd better since they had spent much of their time together talking, sparring, and, yes, kissing.

I am leaving if you are merely going to be mentally blathering on about your male, superior to other humans though he may be.

You just like the way he gives scratches and ear rubs.

Of course.

"Approaching the city now," Stark announced, with less snark than usual. Perhaps Link's lower amount of travel during the year and a half she was in a coma had a sobering effect on the newer AI. She resolved to have a conversation with him soon. No one should feel lonely and alone.

As they approached the city, she saw a ship taking off in the distance. Phina frowned at the image as something twinged in the Etheric, but before she could reach out, she was distracted by Link's words.

"Stark, keep us above the city for now, and help Phina if she needs it."

Phina pulled out her tablet per the plan they had decided on over the last week and searched for a way to connect to the electronic systems below. Thankfully, her tablet had been upgraded to handle all the tasks she would be asking of it.

After a few moments of searching, she frowned. "Stark, are you seeing what I'm seeing?"

"Yes, their level of technology is surprisingly low."

Link glanced at her in concern. "Will the plan still work?"

"Just a minute." Phina searched for every bit of technology and access she could find. Finally, she had an answer.

"They have one main system in each city or town aside from the extra system in the religious leader's facility in the main city. I can access the system network and broadcast from here, but there is no guarantee that the people will be in front of the screen at the time."

"Hmm..." Link frowned in thought as he viewed the screen depicting the city, small dots showing the Qendrok coming out of their homes to see the foreign ship hovering above them.

Phina had continued to search the capabilities of the system in place and added her findings. "It appears that they typically send out a loud signal when there is a message from their religious leaders that calls them to the temple. I can initiate that protocol from here."

The Guardians and Marines who were unknown to her gave her surprised and skeptical looks, although they remained quiet as they observed the small distance between her and Todd, who gave her a smile of happiness and pride.

Link merely grunted and flicked his fingers, which she took as approval. She set off the signal and monitored the system, fingers tapping quickly as she closed off access to anyone except her.

Phina glanced up at the screen to see the tiny dots moving toward the temple in the center of the city. She kept track of the system and saw someone attempting to access it from the religious leader's compound. They were not successful, likely only having the rudimentary skills to keep the system functional.

Since that required little of her mental space or effort, she did a search for Xoruk and Jokin, hoping to find out what had happened to them. She accessed all available systems, including their ships. The result caused her to cry out, drawing everyone's gaze. Phina shook her head as anger filled her, but set aside her findings for later.

On one side of her screen, she viewed the camera feed in the chamber where they must have typically recorded the message from their leader who would broadcast to the temples around the world. Chaos seemed to be the order of the day. She directed the audio feed into her implant and heard someone shouting in the distance through the buzz of conversation.

"I don't care if the Empress herself is on one of those ships! We need to man our defenses. Get those sheep into their homes now, and fire on those ships!"

She recognized Qartan's voice and turned to give Link a nod. She checked the screens and saw that the majority of the people were within the temples. She gave it another minute for the stragglers, then gave Link the signal, having warned everyone to stay silent when he spoke. She piped the audio into the speakers within the temples and the leadership chamber.

"Greetings to the Qendrok from the Etheric Empire. If you are in your capital city, you may have noticed our ships overhead. There is a reason our ships are here, and you have your leader Qartan to blame for it."

Phina heard shouts in the chamber, and since those

milling around had found seats or stood against the wall in the outside of the room, she could see Qartan gesturing to a Qendrok to do something to cut the feed off. *Not on my watch.* She doubled the security and gestured to Link, who nodded and continued in his gravest tone.

"We have commandeered your communications system to deliver a message from our Empress. Don't bother trying to shut it off. We have ensured that our message will be heard by everyone so that all may see and hear what your leader has done in your name for his own sake."

Phina ran the clips in sequence. First, the one in the reception hall where Qartan had called her an abomination and refused to work with her. Next, she inserted a clip she had found of him raging unreasonably about the abomination and another where he bragged that their goddess had promised to raise up a select few as gods. This moved into slices of their conversations with Xoruk, when he'd warned her about the goddess Qartan followed and that he ordered the assassination of anyone who held higher power than him, including those who might have been *vaddrakken* like her.

Next, she showed a view of Xoruk and Jokin asking for the Empire's help with overthrowing the faction that had been oppressing their people. She added a clip from the ship they had used where Qartan flogged Xoruk and Jokin —which had elicited her anger earlier— before ordering an assassin to attack Phina and the subsequent attack where she and Todd fought him off.

The others on the bridge stirred at these scenes, she saw in satisfaction. She wasn't the only one appalled and angry at Qartan's actions. Though as she used the lightest filter she had, Phina found their buzzing was also for her fighting them off. They didn't know much about who she was, which was good. It wasn't supposed to be widely known.

Finally, she showed the entire attack on the wedding and the scene she had found of the assassins in the ship when they returned, with Qartan's casual disregard of their lives and blatant disrespect.

As soon as it finished, she played one last recording, that of the Empress which she had sent from her ship.

A red-eyed Bethany Anne stood alone on the bridge, pissed off, with her hair flying around her as she pulled from the Etheric.

"I am Bethany Anne, the Empress of the Etheric Empire. Your leader came to *my* home and disrespected *my* representatives. I stayed my hand for the sake of peace, although it greatly displeased me to do so. However, your leader sent an assassin after one of my trusted people..."

Phina straightened, pleased the Empress thought to say so despite her youth.

"...I have decided to grant the request of representatives Xoruk and Jokin to assist in the removal of your leader since he has abused his position."

The Empress' eyes blazed red. "However, Qartan is too fucking stupid to live. He has squandered over fifty of his people against mine in another assassination attempt *in my own fucking house*. I give you one choice. One chance. Choose now. Revolution or death. For those who have committed the greatest wrongs, there will be no choice. The sentence is death. For you to stand aside while

Quartan ruins your people is a dereliction of your duty to yourselves and your people."

She leaned into the camera, her beautiful face becoming something they would see in their nightmares. "You have participated in gross injustice. Help us make it right, and ensure that this will *never* happen again."

Her face winked out, leaving an empty screen. Link waited three seconds to let the message sink in, then added, "You have a very short time to decide. For your sakes, make the right decision."

Phina turned off the audio feed and turned to the view on her tablet showing the chamber inside the religious compound. She squinted at the small screen, then brought the feed up on the big screen in front of them.

Shouts of protest and arguments could be heard, along with quieter voices. Phina decided to share the scene with those watching in the temples as well. Better to see the results for themselves rather than after the fact. They couldn't see much yet since those in the chamber had gathered around the area where Qartan had stood and blocked the view.

Nearby Star System, Planet Xaldaq, Religious Compound

Zultav heard the Empress' message with nervous dread and resolve. He had watched Qartan seethe with indignation but no remorse as he heard Xoruk and Jokin's role in bringing the Empire here. He sent two guards to bring them.

After seeing Qartan's face, Zultav had no doubt they

were about to see an execution. The Empress finished her warning, which almost made him piss himself since she was the scariest being he had ever seen, then that first voice spoke up, telling them they had little time.

Qartan and his allies, who had made the deal with their goddess, began speaking over each other. The rest of the religious order looked on with varying expressions of alarm and anger. The other assassins stood in their positions.

"We must do something!"

"The goddess will help us!"

"How will we deal with the Empire?"

"The goddess left when she saw them coming."

"What can we do?"

"Is she still going to let us ascend?"

"All is not lost." Qartan broke in, causing them to stop and listen. "All we have to do is give the Empire sufficient inducement to leave us alone. We can take those ships. We will bring the females and younglings here. They won't fire on us knowing they might kill them."

Zultav turned his gaze toward Kuvaq, one of the older assassins who remained after so many of their brethren died in the attack. Kuvaq gave him a nod of agreement. Qartan blathered on about plans to use others as fodder while the assassins were sent to take out the leaders in the Empire. As if the assassins hadn't tried with one young female and lost too many to count.

There were more religious males than assassins now, but those assassins had heard enough. At Zultav's nod, all of the assassins stepped forward.

Qartan turned at the movement with a frown, watching

Zultav and Kuvaq walk toward him. "What are you doing? I didn't order you to do anything. Go back to your posts!"

Zultav met Qartan's beady gaze with resolve and anger. No more. The suffering Qartan had brought to them was too much.

Their intentions must have made themselves clear to the putative leader. He stiffened, then stepped back, pulling others in front of him. "You are under my orders! You Dak will stay in your rightful place! I command you to stop!"

Zultav bared his teeth as he stepped between those who were in his path while the rest of his brethren closed in on Qartan's cronies. "We would have followed you if you hadn't squandered us exactly as the Empress spoke of. She seems to value her people. You do not. You would throw away our people for your own ends. You are not worthy of being a leader or of being followed. Our brotherhood is no longer yours to do with as you please."

He heard the thud of bodies hitting the floor and saw the alarm in Qartan's face. His brothers had taken care of the others as they had planned.

After Qartan had left the room with his brothers lying dead on the floor after their failed assassination attempt, Zultav had spoken with the others. They had concluded that their time of following the leadership blindly was finished and that Qartan and his faction needed to be stopped. They had just been waiting for the right moment to act.

He quickened his pace after the backpedaling panic-ridden worthless excuse for a Qendrok. Zultav drew his knife in his lower left hand and grabbed Qartan's neck in his upper right, lifting him with enough force to choke him.

Qartan squawked out of clenched vocal cords. "It is against the law to kill your leader."

Zultav grinned harshly as he leaned toward Qartan's face. "Didn't you hear? It's a revolution."

He stabbed Qartan in the heart, twisting the knife to make sure he would suffer and have no chance of surviving.

Lowering the dying leader, he dragged the mostly dead body through the surrounding group of wary, horrified, and tentatively relieved Qendrok. He approached the camera, stopping close enough to be seen and far enough away that they could see him throwing Qartan's body on the floor.

"The brotherhood gives you Qartan and his co-conspirators. They would have used us all for fodder, including the females and younglings."

"Dak Zultav?"

He turned at hearing the weak voice behind him to see Xoruk and Jokin entering the room, supported by the guards who had been sent for them. Xoruk looked down at the body by Zultav's feet with a bewildered frown.

"What have you done?"

Zultav straightened. "What had to be done, Dev Xoruk. The Empire is here after a large-scale assassination attempt on the female Qartan named an abomination. They gave us the ultimatum of revolution or death."

Jokin gave Zultav a sharp glance. "He was still your leader, Dak Zultav."

Zultav met his eyes evenly. "He was not deserving of the honor, Dev Jokin."

Jokin and Xoruk exchanged glances before sighing. "No, he was not," Jokin replied with a glance at the body before turning to the cameras.

"I assume the Empire is watching. You can come down, Delegates. We will make certain you are not attacked."

The previous voice spoke again. "Heartening, Jokin, thank you. We will be there shortly."

Phina sagged against the wall, hoping it would help keep her upright. They had been up for over thirty hours at this point, and there was yet more to do. Qartan and his faction had done a lot to keep their people repressed and ignorant of the changes happening in the universe. Much of that was predicated on the lack of technology available on the planet.

She shook her head and turned to listen to Link's conversation with Zultav. The assassins had told them they would not lead the people, nor would they serve the leadership as they had in the past.

"Perhaps that is for the best." Link patted the conflicted but determined assassin's arm. "Too much power is easily abused, as you have found out."

Zultav changed his arm position and nodded. "Yes, we have found this to be true. Hopefully, Xoruk and Jokin can work with you to decide what the leadership will become and what alliance our people will have with the Empire."

Phina nodded tiredly as she glanced at the larger group

where Todd, Will, and Peter stood with others of the Empire, as well as Xoruk and Jokin. A medic was doing what they could to heal the Qendrok leaders without placing them in a Pod-doc. "That is part of what we are here for."

Link appeared preoccupied as he watched Zultav's arms move. She nudged him. "Is something wrong?"

He hesitated, then looked at the assassin. "Zuktav, do you know anything about a plot within the Empire?"

Zultav frowned, puzzled. She saw a thought occur to him and he froze, appearing cautious as he asked, "What is your position in the Empire?"

"I'm known in both the diplomatic and spy circles."

"Hmm." He called another assassin over, having a short conversation that she had a hard time following even with the translation program in her implant. It appeared that Kuvaq was cautious about something and Zultav wanted to speak, gesturing at them occasionally. They turned to the diplomat spies, cautious but resolved.

Zultav gestured at his friend. "This is Kuvaq. He is the oldest of us." After exchanging greetings, he continued, "One of Qartan's cronies boasted in the presence of us both that soon they would have full access to the spy arm of the Empire. The rest was vague hints, but it sounded like there was someone on the inside of your spy organization who would be allowing them access."

Link and Phina exchanged glances. Link's eyes were tight and anxious. This was the first major indication they'd had that Link's gut feeling was right. He reeled and steadied himself with a hand on the wall.

Phina thanked the assassins. "Let me know if there is anything we can do to help your people."

Zultav and Kuvaq bowed. The older Qendrok's voice sounded rough from disuse. "We will tell you. You have allowed us to help ourselves with the space to act, which was what we needed."

She smiled as they walked away and turned in concern to Link. "Are you all right?"

Link startled, forgetting his situational awareness. She was too concerned to tease him about it. He shook his head, with his face revealing little though his eyes were akin to dread and anguish. "Phina, maybe I'm too old for this. What have I missed with my role being so divided between the diplomats and the spies? My people deserve better."

"Hey." She stepped forward and placed her hand on his shoulder. "That's why you are training me, remember? You already knew you were spread too thin."

"Yes," he answered but shook his head remorsefully. "I wanted to start training you before you turned eighteen, but I wanted you to also have more time without the weight of everything on your shoulders the way it has been on mine."

She stepped forward to hug him and patted his back. "Thank you for giving me that time. I'm here now, and I'm going to help as much as I can." She stepped back and gave him an encouraging smile. "We will take care of everything together. You aren't alone." She thought back to meeting Masha and patted his shoulder before backing up. "I don't think you are as alone as you think you are. You just like taking care of things on your own and don't always recognize the help."

Link frowned in protest. "That's..." He stopped and thought before finishing. "Yeah, that's probably true."

Phina grinned as Todd walked over from the larger group with a smile just for her. She turned to him with a welcoming smile as Link groaned. She glanced at him in surprise.

"Just great. I was hoping I had more time before this happened." He gestured between Phina and Todd with a disgruntled frown.

It didn't fool her for a minute. She could see the twinkle of warmth in his eyes as he tried to push back the unwelcome news they had heard. She shook her head ruefully. "How long have you known?"

"Probably longer than either of you did since you both seemed determined to stick your heads in the sand. Glad you got it sorted out." He smiled at them, pleased as pie as if he was the one to make it happen.

Phina shook her head as she turned to Todd. "I need to sleep. I've been up too long."

Todd nodded but didn't get a chance to respond before Link waved them both away. "Go. This mess will still be here in the morning."

They nodded and excused themselves, holding hands once they were alone as they returned to the ship where they would be sleeping. Phina's heart was lighter as they shared a companionable silence. The night felt peaceful but also alive as various sounds from people in the city and creatures in the woods reached her ears. The religious compound lay right between the city and the natural elements of the planet. Their ships had landed to the side of the walled compound.

Phina's tablet beeped, letting her know she had a message once they entered the ship. She pulled it up as they walked to her room. Fiona had responded to the message Phina had sent on the way to Xaldaq, letting the woman know she had opened the letter and knew why her mom had kept them apart, as well as the knowledge of their shared psychic gifts. The conversation with Fiona seemed so long ago, even though it had only been a few weeks.

Phina,

Thank you for your message! I'm so happy you reached out to let me know. I hope you don't mind, and I could never come close to your mom, but I've thought of you as one of mine ever since you were a tiny girl.

Sometimes it's hard to believe you are so grown up even though you are the same age as Will. I hope you are looking out for each other? I worry sometimes, but knowing you have each other's backs relieves that anxiety for me. Yes, for both of you, baby girl. That's how family works.

At the risk of sounding smothering, I insist you come to dinner when you get home. Will tells me you have a gentleman friend now, and he is

welcome too. Your friends and loved ones will always be welcome.

Your mom was amazing, and you are just like her, Phina. Be the fantastic woman you are, save the universe (I always teased your mom about that), and then come home so I can give you a big hug and know you are safe.

With love.

— Fiona

Tears crept down Phina's face as she finished reading.

"Hey." Todd put an arm around her and looked down in concern. "Are you all right?"

Phina nodded as she handed Todd the tablet to read while she wiped her tears. Sundancer sat watching them from the bunk on the top and passed her warm, comforting feelings.

Todd finished reading and set the tablet down to hug her. "You sure you are all right?"

She nodded and tried not to cry anymore as she hugged him. It felt nice to stand enfolded in his strong arms. She felt safe with him, and that was something she hadn't felt since her parents had died. She tried to explain the jumble of emotions in her head and heart while Todd listened patiently, stroking her back every so often.

When she finished, he told her quietly, "I think your parents tried to love you by giving you as much family as possible. I understand feeling alone for a long time. It's easy sometimes to feel alone even among a lot of people. It's being known that is important, and feeling known by people you care about."

"Hmm." Phina thought about that and slowly nodded against his chest. "I think I see what you mean."

"Do you feel like you don't deserve other people caring about you for some reason?"

Phina froze and didn't answer, but Todd gently nudged her chin up so she could meet his kind eyes. She exhaled heavily and mumbled, "Maybe."

He smiled and ran his hand down her hair in a soothing gesture. "You have such confidence in your skills that it surprises me sometimes when you don't have that same confidence in yourself. I understand. When people have been hurt, it's hard to believe sometimes that you are worth being loved and cared about by others."

"Listen to him, Phina. He is a wise and discerning individual."

Phina glanced at Sundancer. "You just want to be petted, too."

"This is true. All should bask in my magnificence and give me pets and scratches. And fish."

Todd and Phina laughed, but Phina had a thought and turned to Todd, her gaze sharpening on his. "Do you feel that way too? That it's sometimes hard to believe you are worth being loved and cared about?"

Todd swallowed and nodded. Phina scowled and hugged him harder. "I want to punch that ex-wife of yours. You are amazing. It's her fault if she couldn't see it."

He grinned, the shadows that haunted his eyes disappearing. "You are too, Phina. I guess we need to keep reminding each other until we believe it."

Phina gave him a beaming smile. "That sounds fine with me." She hesitated then added, "Are you all right if I consider you part of my family too?"

Todd quirked an eyebrow, but she could see the question pleased him. She remembered he didn't have any family of his own since they had left Earth and resolved to make sure he knew he didn't need to feel alone anymore. "As long as it's the kissing kind of family. I don't think I could go back to keeping my hands off you."

She responded by reaching up and kissing him, which he returned enthusiastically.

Sundancer grumbled about wise and discerning individuals being demoted to enamored and randy as he jumped off the bed and disappeared out the door that shut behind him.

Phina couldn't help feeling regretful about Aunt Faith and whatever had happened there. Phina hoped she was at peace now. She resolved to see what she could find about the possibility of mind control, so the questions she had would be answered.

She focused on Todd, wanting him to know she cared about him and that he wasn't alone anymore. She would get rest tonight and help put together a plan for the Qendroks' future so they would be safe and protected, never being used again for someone else's self-aggrandizing agenda.

Then, she would work with Link to discover this potential traitor in Spy Corps. If the pattern Phina saw emerging was what she thought it to be, then soon she would be able to expose the growing darkness working against the Empire. Perhaps it was the same darkness her parents had seen.

One thing Phina had learned: light always breaks the darkness.

She was determined to be that light.

The End

Seraphina's story continues with *Diplomatic Agent,* available at Amazon and through Kindle Unlimited.

Claim your copy today!

Hello again! I can't thank you enough for choosing to read the first three books of our series, and now our author notes here. :)

I've been part of the KGU fan community since I picked up *Death Becomes Her*, Michael's first book, about four years ago. However, I have been more on the periphery since it's difficult sometimes to extrovert, even through social media. Perhaps it's my insecurities that cause me to be so surprised at how amazing and supportive you all have been since the first book has come out. I like to think though that it's mostly just that you all are awesome! 😄

Thank, you, thank you, thank you! As I write this there are 207 ratings for *Diplomatic Recruit* and just under 180 for *Diplomatic Crisis*. And most of them are five stars! Seriously, you all fantabulously awesome! Even if there were no fans, I would still have a compulsion to write, but you all just make the effort worth it by 1000%. *hugs* Okay, I'm moving on before I start crying! 😄

Writer's Block

So, one of the things I've had to learn how to deal with as a new author is writer's block and what to do to move past it. I had a few issues with the first two books, but I got a few chapters into *Resurgence* and had a major one. Like, I couldn't write for two weeks because nothing was coming, no matter what I did. Anyone else cope with this? Seriously, so frustrating!

I finally began reading a book about finding your own writing process which included what to do with writer's block. One of the major reasons listed was that my subconscious was telling me there could be a plot issue that needs fixing. Another was a relationship issue between characters that I needed to resolve. That got me thinking...and I finally realized I had a major problem I needed to fix, not just in this one, but in the previous two books as well. 😬

Relationship Problems

If you've read *Last Adventure First*, the short story prequel, or the prologue in *Recruit*, you might remember a passage where Phina states there is no one she's particularly interested in, and if there ever was, that person would have to be extraordinary.

Well, of course that meant at some point she had to find someone she's interested in! 😄 It's like a bull with a red flag waving to a storyteller! So, what to do...who could this mystery man be?

Did you know that I originally I had it in my head that Link and Phina would get together? Don't look at me like that! 😄 It made sense at the time. Both spies, pushing each other's buttons, and a whole lot of snark, right? I'm telling you, it made sense! I even had a scene where they realized how they felt about each other. It was super-touching.

But it didn't matter what I thought. Obviously they disagreed, and I wasn't listening until I got this major case of writer's block.

I finally came to terms with that when I got to the scene where Todd comes to find Phina after she ran from the medical center. I was still kind of slogging and getting very little written till then. Then Todd enters, and he's talking to her and listening and...it suddenly hits me that he's exactly the kind of person she needs in her life.

They fit in a way Link and Phina did not, and as I looked back on all the scenes that gave me trouble in the first two books, it was for exactly this reason. They kept telling me they were family, and I just wasn't listening.

So, now you know one of my secrets—I have voices in my head. 😄 All characters in current or future stories and boy, it is sometimes loud in here!

Spoilers

Long-time KGU fans, you have foreknowledge about the future of some of the characters in this series that new fans might not have. Please, please be careful about mentioning that knowledge in the reviews or on FB. You know why after you've read this book, so I think it's important. Thank you so much! 😊

Sundancer

What do you think about Sundancer? 😄 I honestly wasn't going to have any sort of companion for Phina. There were no puppies around to steal...*ahem* **borrow** for Phina, so I resigned myself to nothing being there.

Well, Sundancer changed that in a big way by popping in my head with the speech he's yowling when Phina walks onto the docks. I don't even remember what I was doing, but I know I froze until I could wrap my head around who this new person was.

As soon as I could drop what I was doing, I raced to my phone and feverishly began typing whatever came out. It ended up being most of that whole first scene with him, though I added things later.

I was still writing chapter five or so at this point and there was no plan for a companion at all! Thankfully, my co-conspirators (aka Michael and Nat) thought it would work out, so here we are! :)

Sundancer Scene

I've been in the midst of editing (which makes me acutely aware that our editors are amazing and worth their weight in gold, diamonds, and everything valuable!) and got a writing itch. I have to write something every so often or it drives me crazy! Since we had already finished book four and didn't have anything planned beyond that yet, I started wondering what Sundancer would be like if he was a cat on earth. You know you would have wondered eventually! 😄

———-

Sundancer sat staring out the window, watching all the people hurrying around the station. His tail twitched as they scurried like ants scattering after a leaf was dropped on their hill—a little panicked for no reason, and scuttling to all corners, hoping not to be too late.

His eyes began to close sleepily when he noticed a man dashing to the train he currently watched from. Though in a rush, the man adroitly maneuvered through the crowd. He even stopped to help a woman with a small child who'd lost his toy.

Yes, Sundancer thought. *He will do nicely.*

He waited until the man settled into his seat, lulled into complacency. The conductor called for last passengers just as the man pulled out an old-fashioned timepiece from his pocket. After glancing at it, the man placed it on the tray in front of him as he rummaged in a pocket.

Gotcha.

Sundancer skillfully jumped from overhead compartment to backrest. With a wave to his dignity, the cat leaped into the man's lap, grabbed the timepiece carefully in his mouth, then lunged to the floor.

Loud, sharp tones came from behind him as he trotted forward. Skillfully hurdling legs, luggage, and other items, he never let the man lose sight of him as he was chased down the now-moving train compartment. He finally leaped into the lap of his human, dropped his prey, and meowed loudly.

"Sundancer! What on earth? Oh."

The cat looked up and saw that the man had arrived, puffing. The two humans stared at each other in dazed wonder. Sundancer mewed in satisfaction, then began to wash the dust off his paw.

Humans...so much work.

Website

I have a new website, including a newsletter! :) Feel free to check it out! If you haven't read *Last Adventure First* yet, you can download it for free after you sign up. http://seweir.com

What's Next

Have you been wondering about the mysterious Spy Corps over the last few books? In *Diplomatic Agent*, Phina,

Link, and Sundancer chase the rumors of the traitor back to the base of Spy Corps, where she encounters new friends, new enemies, and a whole lot of trouble!

I can't wait for you to read it!

Until next time!

AUTHOR NOTES - MICHAEL ANDERLE
JULY 13, 2021

Thank you for both reading this story and these author notes in the back!

Sarah brought up an interesting comment regarding writer's block.

Writer's block is a subject that not all authors agree happens or the cause if and when it does. Some believe they are stuck in a multi-month or multi-year burnout instead of writers' block. Others believe it isn't real at all.

How can one stop creativity?

For writer's block, I fall in the camp that it's a normal feeling for an author that the (perhaps nascent) author doesn't realize is caused by THEM. Just as Sarah mentioned, it is usually a subconscious awareness that YOU ARE @#%)*@ UP YOUR STORY!

Now figure out where the problem is, and (normally) the block goes away, creativity comes rushing back, and the words drop to the keyboard like rain on a spring day.

Or… you know…Nothing Happens.

An author might have additional problems. Health is a

major component, along with stress. For me, family stress is a major challenge to write through. My family issues consume the front of my mind, and I can't focus on the story.

Unlike other authors who write to forget their troubles, getting lost in the land of the story, I can only focus on the here and now. So, I try to keep my family troubles to a minimum.

I mentioned stopping creativity up above. The great horror writer Stephen King said in his book 'On Writing' that you need to constantly fill your creative well.

How? He suggests always reading. I've found when you are writing at beyond 'King Speed' (2,000 words a day every day but Christmas) that you might need to turn to other entertainment or information that you can consume that is faster than a book.

I was once so depleted in the creativity department that I thought about what fired my creative juices. Upon consideration, I realized that sometimes it was just an image that could bring an idea to mind.

Taking that bit of realization to mind, I jumped into the car and went to a comic book shop. Actually, I think I went to three that day.

I was really dry.

Purchasing $200-$300 worth of comics and pop-culture items that day, I took them back to my Condo in the Sky™ (my name for our condo on Las Vegas Blvd when we lived there) and started reading.

It worked. I created something like two or three series ideas from that effort, and I have duplicated that effort a couple of more times since. It hasn't worked every time, but just sitting back and enjoying stories is a benefit I continue to practice.

Before I sign off, I'd like to say thank you to those who have added their own reviews to Sarah's work. It helps her personally (as she has mentioned) and professionally. I understand some may not wish to do a review, and I understand.

Just reading and wishing her continued good health into the universe is more than we can ask.

May you have a wonderful week or weekend ahead of you and more stories that make you feel in your future.

Ad Aeternitatem,

Michael Anderle

The Empress' Spy
Diplomatic Recruit (Book 1)
Diplomatic Crisis (Book 2)
Diplomatic Resurgence (Book 3)
Diplomatic Agent (Book 4)

Printed in Great Britain
by Amazon

82540646R00226